Piers Anthony was born in Oxford in 1934, moved with his family to Spain in 1939 and then to the USA in 1940, after his father was expelled from Spain by the Franco regime. He became a citizen of the US in 1958 and, before devoting himself to full-time writing, worked as a technical writer for a communications company and taught English. He started publishing short stories with *Possible to Rue* for *Fantastic* in 1963, and published in SF magazines for the next decade. He has, however, concentrated more and more on writing novels.

Author of the brilliant, widely acclaimed *Cluster* series, and the superb *Split Infinity* trilogy, he has made a name for himself as a writer of original, inventive stories whose imaginative, mind-twisting style is full of extraordinary, often poetic images and flights of cosmic fancy.

D0488863

By the same author

PIERS ANTHONY

Anthonology

GRAFTON BOOKS
A Division of the Collins Publishing Group

LONDON GLASGOW
TORONTO SYDNEY AUCKLAND

Grafton Books
A Division of the Collins Publishing Group
8 Grafton Street, London W1X 3LA

A Grafton UK Paperback Original 1986

Copyright © Piers Anthony 1985

ISBN 0-586-06973-9

Printed and bound in Great Britain by
Collins, Glasgow

Set in Times

All rights reserved. No part of this publication may
be reproduced, stored in a retrieval system, or
transmitted, in any form, or by any means, electronic,
mechanical, photocopying, recording or otherwise,
without the prior permission of the publishers.

This book is sold subject to the condition that it
shall not, by way of trade or otherwise, be lent,
re-sold, hired out or otherwise circulated
without the publisher's prior consent in any
form of binding or cover other than that in
which it is published and without a similar
condition including this condition being imposed
on the subsequent purchaser.

Contents

Acknowledgments

'Possible to Rue' © 1963 by Ziff-Davis Pub. Co.

'The Toaster' © 1985 by Piers Anthony

'Quinquepedalian' © 1963 by Ziff-Davis Pub. Co.

'Encounter' © 1964 by Ziff-Davis Pub. Co.

'Phog' © 1965 by Ziff-Davis Pub. Co.

'The Ghost Galaxies' © 1966 by Galaxy Pub. Corp.

'Within the Cloud' © 1967 by Galaxy Pub. Corp.

'The Life of the Stripe © 1969 by Sol Cohen

'In the Jaws of Danger' © 1967 by Galaxy Pub. Corp.

'Beak by Beak' © 1967 by The Condé Nast Pubs.

'Getting Through University' © 1968 by Galaxy Pub. Corp.

'In the Barn' © 1972 By Harlan Ellison

'Up Schist Crick' © 1972 by David Gerrold

'The Whole Truth' © 1970 by Harry Harrison

'The Bridge' © 1970 by Galaxy Pub. Corp.

'On the Uses of Torture' © 1981 by Piers Anthony

'Small Mouth, Bad Taste' © 1970 by Avon Books

'Wood You?' © 1970 by Mercury Press

'Hard Sell' © 1972 by Universal Pub. and Dist.

'Hurdle' © 1972 by Universal Pub. and Dist.

'Gone to the Dogs' © 1985 by Piers Anthony

Possible to Rue

I started writing fiction seriously on the way to my BA in Creative Writing. My thesis for graduation was a 95,000 word novel, *The Unstilled World*, that kept the College President up much of the night. No, he wasn't a science fiction fan; he just had to read all the papers, and hadn't anticipated one that was 300 pages long. That novel was never published, though later I revamped a portion of it that is now part of the *Battle Circle* volume.

The first story I wrote, 'Evening', I submitted to the first *Galaxy Magazine* amateur story contest in 1954. In 1955 I received notice that my story was among the top ten entries, but that they had decided to have no winner. Sigh – my literary career had been launched in typical fashion. Meanwhile, my later friend andy offut (that's the way he capitalized it) entered a similar contest sponsored by *If Magazine* and won it. Fate has generally treated me that way; I seem to have a propensity for just barely missing the cut.

But I have always been ornery. I refused to comprehend the message that I wasn't wanted in Parnassus. This is my advice to other hopeful writers: be ornery, keep trying, don't get the message, so that you, too, can suffer years of frustration, irony and humiliation. Once every decade or so the worm does turn.

I tried other stories on other markets, receiving rejection slips and a curt note from H. L. Gold not to try to compete with the big boys. (And where are you now, H. L.? Suppose I had followed your arrogant advice?) In

1958 my story 'The Demisee' was accepted by Damon
Knight at *If Magazine* – which then ceased publication
just long enough to unsell my story. I had missed the cut
again. But I kept trying, while earning my living in such
mundane pursuits as delivery driver, the US Army, elec-
tronics technical writer and state social worker.

But still I longed to be a writer; the dream would not let
go. Finally my wife went to work, so that I could try
writing full-time for one year. This is my second major
item of advice to other hopefuls: have a working spouse
to earn your living while you grasp for the impossible.
We agreed that if I did not succeed, I would recognize
the nature of my delusion, give it up, retire to productive
mundane work and be at literary peace. One of my fifth
cousins did exactly that, ending his writing attempts to
become an executive at Sears.

It was now late in 1962. I wrote a fantasy story and
sent it off to the *Magazine of Fantasy and Science Fiction*
– let's just call it F&SF – and a science fiction story that I
sent to *Playboy*. They both bounced. I wrote another
fantasy and tried F&SF again, while trying the first two at
other markets. They all bounced. I thought I might try a
British magazine – I was after all born in England, and
was a subject of the King/Queen for twenty-four years –
but I didn't have the address. So while I was trying to get
it, I sent my second fantasy story to *Fantastic*, just to
keep it in circulation. And suddenly it sold.

After eight years, nineteen stories, and thirty rejections,
I had a $20.00 sale. I was a success!

That story, of course, was 'Possible to Rue.' It was
published in the April 1963 issue of *Fantastic*, and
thereafter sank without a trace, until this moment. I make
no special claims for its merit; it just happened to be the
chip thrown up by the wave. I include it simply because it

was the point at which my worm turned, my first success as a commercial fiction writer, of interest for historical consideration. Perhaps scholars more intelligent than I am will be able to trace in this story the genesis of my later career as a writer of light-fantasy novels. The rest of you can take satisfaction in the fact that at least it isn't very long.

'I want a pegasus, Daddy,' Junior greeted him at the door, his curly blond head bobbling with excitement. 'A small one, with white fluttery wings and an aerodynamic tail and – '

'You shall have it, son,' Daddy said warmly, absent-mindedly stripping off jacket and tie. Next week was Bradley Newton Jr's sixth birthday, and Bradley, Senior had promised a copy of *Now We Are Six* and a pet for his very own. Newton was a man of means, so that this was no empty pledge. He felt he owed it to the boy, to make up in some token the sorrow of Mrs N's untimely departure.

He eased himself into the upholstered chair, vaguely pleased that his son showed such imagination. Another child would have demanded something commonplace, like a mongrel or a Shetland pony. But a pegasus now –

'Do you mean the winged horse, son?' Newton inquired, a thin needle of doubt poking into his complacency.

'That's right, Daddy,' Junior said brightly. 'But it will have to be a very small one, because I want a pegasus that can really fly. A full grown animal's wings are non-functional because the proportionate wing span is insufficient to get it off the ground.'

'I understand, son,' Newton said quickly. 'A small one.' People had laughed when he had insisted that

Junior's nurse have a graduate degree in general science. Fortunately he had been able to obtain one inexpensively by hiring her away from the school board. At this moment he regretted that it was her day off; Junior could be very single-minded.

'Look, son,' he temporized. 'I'm not sure I know where to buy a horse like that. And you'll have to know how to feed it and care for it, otherwise it would get sick and die. You wouldn't want that to happen, would you?'

The boy pondered. 'You're right, Daddy,' he said at last. 'We would be well advised to look it up.'

'Look it up?'

'In the encyclopedia, Daddy. Haven't you always told me that it was an authoritative factual reference?'

The light dawned. Junior believed in the encyclopaedia. 'My very words, Son. Let's look it up and see what it says about . . . let's see . . . here's *Opinion to Possibility* . . . should be in this volume. Yes.' He found the place and read aloud: '"Pegasus – Horse with wings which sprang from the blood of the Gorgon Medusa after Perseus cut off her head."'

Junior's little mouth dropped open. 'That has got to be figurative,' he pronounced. 'Horses are not created from – '

'". . . a creature of Greek mythology,"' Newton finished victoriously.

Junior digested that. 'You mean, it doesn't exist,' he said dispiritedly. Then he brightened. 'Daddy, if I ask for something that does exist, then can I have it for a pet?'

'Certainly, Son. We'll just look it up here, and if the book says it's real, we'll go out and get one. I think that's a fair bargain.'

'A unicorn,' Junior said.

Newton restrained a smile. He reached for the volume marked *Trust to Wary* and flipped the pages. '"Unicorn – A mythological creature resembling a horse – "' he began.

Junior looked at him suspiciously. 'Next year I'm going to school and learn to read for myself,' he muttered. 'You are alleging that there is no such animal?'

'That's what the book says, Son – honest.'

The boy looked dubious, but decided not to make an issue of it. 'All right – let's try a zebra.' He watched while Newton pulled out *Watchful to Indices*. 'It's only fair to warn you, Daddy,' he said ominously, 'that there is a picture of one on the last page of my alphabet book.'

'I'll read you just exactly what it says, Son,' Newton said defensively. 'Here it is: "Zebra – A striped horselike animal reputed to have lived in Africa. Common in European and American legend, although entirely mythical – '

'Now you're making that up,' Junior accused angrily. 'I've got a picture.'

'But Son – I thought it was real myself. I've never seen a zebra, but I thought – look. You have a picture of a ghost too, don't you? But you know that's not real.'

There was a hard set to Junior's jaw. 'The examples are not analogous. Spirits are preternatural – '

'Why don't we try another animal?' Newton cut in. 'We can come back to the zebra later.'

'Mule,' Junior said sullenly.

Newton reddened, then realized that the boy was not being personal. He withdrew the volume covering *Morphine to Opiate* silently. He was somewhat shaken up by the turn events had taken. Imagine spending all his life believing in an animal that didn't exist. Yet of course it was stupid to swear by a horse with prison stripes . . .

'"Mule,"' he read. '"The offspring of the mare and the

male ass. A very large, strong hybrid, sure footed with remarkable sagacity. A creature of folklore, although, like the unicorn and zebra, widely accepted by the credulous . . ."'

His son looked at him. 'Horse,' he said.

Newton somewhat warily opened *Hoax to Imaginary*. He was glad he wasn't credulous himself. 'Right you are, Son. "Horse – a fabled hoofed creature prevalent in mythology. A very fleet four-footed animal complete with flowing mane, hairy tail and benevolent disposition. Metallic shoes supposedly worn by the animal are valued as good luck charms, in much the same manner as the unicorn's horn – "'

Junior clouded up dangerously. 'Now wait a minute, Son,' Newton spluttered. 'I know that's wrong. I've seen horses myself. Why, they use them in TV westerns – '

'The reasoning is specious,' Junior muttered but his heart wasn't in it.

'Look, Son – I'll prove it. I'll call the race track. I used to place – I mean, I used to go there to see the horses. Maybe they'll let us visit the stables.' Newton dialled with a quivering finger; spoke into the phone. A brief frustrated interchange later he slammed the receiver down again. 'They race dogs now,' he said.

He fumbled through the yellow pages, refusing to let himself think. The book skipped rebelliously from *Homes* to *Hospital*. He rattled the bar for the operator to demand the number of the nearest horse farm, then angrily dialled 'O'; after some confusion he ended up talking to 'Horsepower, Inc.', a tractor dealer.

Junior surveyed the proceedings with profound disgust. 'Methinks the queen protests too much,' he quoted sweetly.

In desperation, Newton called a neighbour. 'Listen,

Sam – do you know anybody around here who owns a horse? I promised my boy I'd show him one today . . .'

Sam's laughter echoed back over the wire. 'You're a card, Brad. Horses, yet. Do you teach him to believe in fairies too?'

Newton reluctantly accepted defeat. 'I guess I was wrong about the horse, Son,' he said awkwardly. 'I could have sworn – but never mind. Just proves a man is never too old to make a mistake. Why don't you pick something else for your pet? Tell you – whatever you choose, I'll give you a matched pair.'

Junior cheered up somewhat. He was quick to recognize a net gain. 'How about a bird?'

Newton smiled in heartfelt relief. 'That would be fine, Son, just fine. What kind did you have in mind?'

'Well,' Junior said thoughtfully. 'I think I'd like a big bird. A real big bird, like a roc, or maybe a harpy – '

Newton reached for *Possible to Rue*.

The Toaster

Buoyed by my first sale, I kept writing. I submitted a long science fiction poem, 'Strange is the Measure', to four markets and retired it. Then I wrote 'The Toaster' and tried it on the leading SF magazine, *Analog*. That magazine, in its prior guise as *Astounding*, had been the light of my life in the late 1940s when I discovered the genre; how nice it would be to have one of my own stories represented on its hallowed pages! Alas, three and a half months later my story came back, rejected. I have always wondered how a magazine that publishes every month can take several months to consider a story; surely the editor should run out of stories at that rate! (The answer, of course, is the slush pile: that towering stack of unsolicited manuscripts from hopeful writers like me that the editor postpones reading as long as humanly possible. Editors don't take three months to look at my fiction *today*.) I tried it on *Galaxy*, and then on *Fantastic*, and finally on *Cosmopolitan*. All bounces, so I retired it, as I had run out of markets and postage adds up. Hopeful writers have to pay the postage both ways, you know, if they want to get their stories back. This, then, is a failed story; it has never before appeared in print. Is it worse than 'Possible to Rue'? Only about one in four of my stories ever sold, which is one reason I had to graduate to novels. It was economics, not natural inclination, that forced the move – but once I had done it, I discovered that I liked being a novelist better than being a storyist.

Some of my fans today don't realize that I ever did write stories.

The announcer bonged respectfully. 'Speak your piece,' the cheerful white-haired woman said briskly.

'Miss Porter to see Miss Porter,' it said.

The woman frowned, but with a twinkle. 'You make about as much sense as a cheese factory on the moon,' she commented. 'Now let's try it again, and this time use *names*.'

The announcer paused in confusion, then got its circuits adjusted. 'Miss Ophelia Porter is present at the subterranean access and has expressed the desire to pay a personal call on resident Miss Adelaine Porter.'

'Why that's fine, just fine.' Miss Porter busily smoothed her old-fashioned apron. 'Why didn't you say so in the first place?'

'I'm already in, Auntie,' a voice tinkled behind her. 'I snuck into the 'vator while you were dickering with the blurt-box.'

Miss Porter smiled without surprise and turned to face the girl. Ophelia stood in front of the freight receptacle, resplendent in purple pantaloons and a conical hat. Her dark hair was gathered into a single enormous braid, and her eyes were artfully shadowed. 'Why do you think I stalled the contraption, dear? What on earth are you wearing?'

'Playsuit, Auntie. See?' Ophelia pirouetted into the centre of the room, the sides of her garment parting to reveal her thighs.

Miss Porter snorted. 'Seems to me you're still a little young for that sort of play. Nine years old – '

'Ten, Auntie. And I – '

The announcer rang urgently. 'Miss Porter can not

be – ' It hesitated. 'Miss Ophelia Porter can not be located,' it said with mixed triumph and chagrin.

'Well, find her, Blurtbox,' Ophelia exclaimed with impish glee. She knew that the announcer was too primitive to discern the difference between voices.

'It's a pleasure to serve you, madame,' the machine said dubiously.

The old woman clapped her hands together sharply. 'Don't call me "madam", you clamourous contraption. Get back to your business.'

'Yes, Miss Porter,' it said, cutting off quickly.

Ophelia had already made herself comfortable in the archaic couch. 'When's it coming, Auntie?' she demanded. 'The Toaster, I mean.'

Miss Porter favoured her with a mock frown. 'I should have known you didn't come calling all by yourself out of love for your old maiden great-great aunt.' She settled into a chair herself. 'It's due at ten o'clock. That will be in a quarter of an hour. Why don't you run out and play for a little while, dear, while you're waiting?'

Ophelia looked baffled. 'Outside?'

'Why certainly, dear. When I was a girl a century ago I used to delight in running through the forest paths, feeling the wind take my dress. When I was your age – '

'But Auntie – what about the radiation?'

Miss Porter looked up, surprised. 'Dear me! I had forgotten about that. I suppose you can't go out these days.'

'Why do you still use those old-fashioned toasters, Auntie? Is it because you're eccentric?'

Miss Porter raised an eyebrow. 'Your father's been putting strange notions into your head, dear. Toasters and I have an ancient affinity.'

She leaned back and closed her eyes. 'I was just ten

years old when I used my first toaster – if you could call it that.' She smiled reminiscently. 'That was in the year 1930. My mother let me put slices of homemade bread on a clean section of the old wood stove. Sometimes the pieces burned – but oh, my, it was delicious.'

Ophelia was pleased. 'We learned about bread in Cultural History class.'

Miss Porter didn't seem to hear. 'Of course, when I became a young woman I bought my own toaster. That was in 1940; it was one of those simple side-door affairs. I had to plug it in to start, and unplug to turn it off. When I opened the doors the toast was supposed to slide down and flip itself over, so that I could do the other side without burning my fingers. But it didn't always work.'

'How come you didn't have any children of your own?' Ophelia inquired directly. 'Back when you were a luscious young piece?'

Miss Porter opened her eyes, tolerant of the child's language; times had changed. 'Why you see, dear, I never married – '

'But you don't need to be married to have children. Down at the free love clinic – '

'Some people feel that marriage has its advantages nevertheless, dear,' Miss Porter said gently. 'And a woman must wait until she's asked.'

'Daddy says he heard lots of men asked you. He says they were howling after you like hounds after a bitch in he – '

'Your father's long overdue for a spanking, I'm sure,' Miss Porter said severely.

'Oh, they don't spank people anymore, Auntie.'

'Really?' she inquired with interest. 'And what do they do these modern days?'

'You were telling me about your toasters,' Ophelia said uncomfortably. 'What did you get in 1950?'

Miss Porter leaned back again and let her old eyes close. 'I was thirty then, and thrilled by the advances they had made in toasting. Two slots in the top for the bread, and when you pressed down the handle it ticked away for three minutes – or was that the egg timer? – and then up popped the toast.'

'What's an egg?' Ophelia asked.

The old woman sighed. 'Ask me that on another day. Today is Toaster Day. In 1960 there were no levers at all – you just dropped in the bread, and the toaster lowered it and popped it back at you in less than a minute. Sometimes I would eat a few berries, too – '

'Berries?' Ophelia put in, shocked. 'You *ate* them?' Her eyes were big and round.

'Why of course, dear. High bush blueberries fresh from the wilderness, though of course there wasn't much of *that* left even then. And sometimes strawberries – '

'Oh, *Earth* berries,' Ophelia said, sighing with relief. 'I thought you meant Betelgeuse Berries.'

Miss Porter wondered briefly what kind of fruit that could be, but decided not to inquire. Her great-great niece could be disconcertingly graphic. 'Let me see – in 1990 my toaster took the bread out of the package by itself, and buttered it hot and served it up on a little plate. I didn't have to do anything except order the bread and sweep up the crumbs. And in 2000 I didn't even have to do that.'

'It's here!' Ophelia squealed. Miss Porter opened her eyes once more and saw that a machine had materialized in the freight receptacle. It was larger than the old model and looked exceedingly complicated. She was not as enthusiastic about its arrival as Ophelia evidently was;

the old one had served her well for ten years, also fixing meals, answering the viz, washing dishes and making the bed. The new one might be more ambitious, and that was not necessarily good.

'Are you going to show me a toast now, Auntie?' Ophelia exclaimed, dancing in front of the machine.

'Gracious, dear – do you mean to tell me that your family never fixed toast? We'll attend to that right away.' She eased herself to her feet and faced the machine. 'Toaster: front and centre!'

The machine rolled forward a few inches and hesitated. 'Is Mistress addressing me?' it rumbled sonorously.

'Don't call me "mistress", you overstuffed tin can. At least, not in that masculine voice. Yes, I mean you. Come here.'

The machine moved into the centre of the room and cleared its speaker. 'I am your new Automated Service Tribune,' it said in a feminine pitch. 'I am a utility deluxe robotic housekeeper, model T-Zero. May I be of service?'

'You certainly may,' Miss Porter said crisply. 'I am Miss Adelaine Porter, your new mis – your new owner. I want you to prepare me two pieces of your finest buttered toast, with jelly on the side.'

'Beg pardon?' Tribune said. 'Did the Mistress ask for toads?'

'I said toast, you box of bolts. Two pieces.'

Tribune retreated in confusion. 'Perhaps if the Mistress would describe what she wants – '

'I want two slices of bread heated until they char on the outside, with churned bovine extract spread on the upper surface. Does that make it quite clear, hardwarebrain?'

'Mistress must be aware that no bread has been manu-factured for a number of years,' Tribune protested. 'And the zoo would hardly allow any of its valuable endanger-ed-species bovines to be molested – '

Miss Porter tapped her foot menacingly. 'I want you to know that I'm a hundred and ten years old and set in my ways and I WILL HAVE MY TOAST. I'm going to give you just one more chance to perform, you – what did you say your name was?'

The machine drew itself up on its rollers. 'I am your Automated Service Tribune. You may call me AST for convenience. Model number T-Zero.'

'Well, give me some T-zero-A-S-T. T O A S T! Do you understand me, you silly Ast?'

The machine retreated and clicked to itself. Finally it rumbled to a decision. 'If Mistress persists in making an illogical or nonsensical request, it will be necessary to escort her to a clinic for a psychiatric examination.'

Ophelia came up to her nervously. 'It can do it, Auntie,' she warned. 'Those T-Zero models have special – '

Miss Porter patted the girl's hand. 'A foolish consist-ency is the hobgoblin of little minds,' she quoted. 'I'm consistent, but I'm not foolish. I've had experience with wilful machines.' She opened her purse and extracted a small object.

'Auntie – that's a megawatt disruptor!' Ophelia cried.

'It certainly is, dear.' She activated it and slapped it against the braincase of the machine.

'But that will burn out the computer circuits of the AST!'

'It certainly will, dear.'

'But then it won't be able to answer the viz or do your shopping or supervise your entertainment,' Ophelia said. 'It won't be able to do *anything*.'

Miss Porter laughed as she nonchalantly discarded the

spent disruptor. 'You are mistaken, dear. Stripped of its modernistic, male-inspired notions, it will have to revert to the limited functions of its ancestry. In short, it will MAKE TOAST.'

'Yess Misstresss,' the machine slurred dutifully. It retreated into itself for a few minutes of internal clicks and gurgles. Evidently something quite complicated was going on inside. At length, a slot opened and a plate emerged containing two pieces of hotly buttered toast.

'That's very good, Tribune,' Miss Porter said, patting the machine on its lobotomized dome.

'Thank you, Misstresss,' it replied slavishly.

Miss Porter took the plate and handed one of the pieces to her niece. 'This, my dear, is toast. Eat it.'

Ophelia took it and bit in dutifully.

Suddenly her face lighted. 'Auntie!' she exclaimed incredulously. 'It's GOOD!'

Quinquepedalian

By early 1963 our situation was getting desperate. My wife had been unable to find regular work – she got turned down for being 'overqualified' – and we were afraid I would have to terminate my year's writing at six months despite my one sale. Writers and their families don't exist on air, you know. But then she landed a job at the *St. Petersburg Times* newspaper and we were okay for the nonce. Still, I had some trouble turning out fiction steadily; the creative genius doesn't necessarily function on a set schedule. This was, in fact, my first and only siege of the dreadest malady of the trade: Writer's Block. I indulged in a lot of correspondence – about 40,000 words a month – and compiled a massive Index of Book Reviews – later virtually pirated by another outfit – and struggled to keep at least one story in the mail at all times. And in the course of that year I did learn how to conquer Writer's Block, and have never suffered from it since. Then in June 1963, seven months after my first sale, I had my second. This was a science fiction story, seven thousand words long, for which I was paid $140 – two cents a word. It was a good rate, and I was thrilled. It was published in the November 1963 *Amazing Stories* and reprinted six years later. I do feel that this story represents the kind of innovative imagination and logic that characterize my science fiction novels, and I remain pleased with it. I can't think why *Galaxy* bounced it before *Amazing* took it; the fact is, all my first ten sales were

rejected somewhere before being accepted elsewhere.
Maybe I was overqualified.

A note on the original editing: The magazine editors
have a habit of inserting meaningless spaces in the
author's text. Maybe blank lines make them feel more at
home. So when you see these in the remainder of this
volume, don't blame me; there are no blanks in *my*
narrative, or pointless untitled chapters.

It lay there, an identation in the soil, two inches deep
and nine feet in diameter. It was flat, it was smooth, and
the sand and the dirt were twined with rotted leaves and
stems in a marbled pattern. The edge, cut sharp and
clean, exposed a miniature stratum leading up to the
unpressed forest floor, and spoke of the weight that had
stood on that spot, moulding the earth into the shape of
its fundament.

It was the mark of a foot, or a hoof, or whatever it is
that touches the ground when an animal ambulates. One
print –

Charles Tinnerman shook his head sombrely. A single
print could have been a freak of nature. This was one of
many: a definite trail. They were spaced twenty or thirty
feet apart, huge and level; ridges of spadiceous earth
narrowed towards the centre of each, rounded and
smooth, as though squirted liquidly up between half-yard
toes. Some were broken, toppled worms lying skew,
scuffed when the hoof moved on.

Around the spoor rose the forest, in Gargantuan splendour; each trunk ascending gauntly into a mass of foliage
so high and solid that the ground was cast into an almost
nocturnal shadow.

At dusk the three men halted. 'We could set up an
arc,' Tinnerman said, reaching behind to pat his harness.

Don Abel grunted negatively. 'Use a light, and everything on the planet will know where we are. We don't want the thing that made that,' he gestured towards the trail, 'to start hunting *us*.'

The third man spoke impatiently. 'It rains at night, remember? If we don't get close pretty soon, the water'll wash out the prints.'

Tinnerman looked up. 'Too late,' he said. There was no thunder, but abruptly it was raining solidly, as it must to support a forest of this type. They could hear the steady deluge flaying the dense leaves far above. Not a drop reached the ground.

'The trees won't hold it back forever,' Abel remarked. 'We'd better break out the pup tent in a hurry – '

'Hey!' Fritz Slaker's voice sang out ahead. 'There's a banyan or something up here. Shelter!'

Columns of water hissed into the ground as the great leaves far above overflowed at last. The men galloped for cover, packs thumping as they dodged the sudden waterfalls.

They stripped their packs and broke out rations silently. The dry leaves and spongy loam made a comfortable seat, and after a day of hiking the relaxation was bliss. Tinnerman leaned back against the base of the nearest trunk, chewing and gazing up into the bole of the tree. It was dark; but he could make out a giant spherical opacity from which multiple stems projected downward, bending and swelling for a hundred feet until they touched the ground as trunks twelve feet in diameter.

Don Abel's voice came out of the shadow. 'The monster passed right under here. I'm sitting on the edge of a print. What if it comes back?'

Slaker laughed, but not loudly. 'Mebbe we're in its

nest? We'd hear it. A critter like that – just the shaking of the ground would knock us all a foot into the air.'
There was a sustained rustle.

'What are you doing?' Abel asked querulously.

'Making a bed,' Slaker snapped.

'Do you think it's safe?' Abel asked, though his tone indicated that he suspected one place was as unsafe as another. After a moment, the rustle signified that he too was making a bed.

Tinnerman smiled in the dark, amused. He really did not know the other men well; the three had organized an AWOL party on the spur of the moment, knowing that the survey ship would be planetbound for several days.

The bark of the tree was thick and rubbery, and Tinnerman found it oddly comfortable. He put his ear against it, hearing a faint melodic humming that seemed to emanate from the interior. It was as though he was auditing the actual life-processes of the alien vegetation – although on this world, *he* was the alien – and this fascinated him.

The other two were soon asleep. Sitting there in silence, the absolute blackness of a strange world's umbra pressing against his eyeballs, Tinnerman realized that this outing, dangerous as it was, offered him a satisfaction he had seldom known. Slaker and Abel had accepted him for what he was not: one of the fellows.

Those footprints. Obviously animal – yet so large. Would a pressure of a hundred pounds per square inch depress the earth that much? How much would the total creature weigh?

Tinnerman found his pack in the dark and rummaged for his miniature slide rule. The tiny numbers fluoresced as he set up his problem: 144 times the square of 4.5 times pi divided by 20. It came to about 460 tons per print. And how many feet did it have, and how much weight did each carry when at rest?

He had heard that creatures substantially larger than the dinosaurs of ancient Earth could not exist on land. On an Earth type planet, which this one was with regard to gravity, atmosphere and climate, the limits were not so much biological as physical. A diminutive insect required many legs, not to support its weight, but to preserve balance. Brontosaurus, with legs many times as sturdy as those of an insect, even in proportion to its size, had to seek the swamp to ease the overbearing weight. A larger animal, in order to walk at all, would have to have disproportionately larger legs and feet. Mass cubed with increasing size while the cross section of the legs squared; to maintain a feasible ratio, most of the mass above a certain point would have to go to the feet.

Four hundred and sixty tons? The weight on each foot exceeded that of a family of whales. Bones should shatter and flesh tear free with every step.

The rain had ceased and the forest was quiet now. Tinnerman scraped up a belated bed of his own and lay down. But his mind refused to be pacified. Bright and clear and ominous the thoughts paraded, posing questions for which he had no answer. What thing had they blundered across?

A jumping animal! Tinnerman sat up, too excited to sleep. Like an overgrown showshoe rabbit, he thought – bounding high, hundreds of feet to nip the lofty greenery, then landing with terrific impact. It could be quite small – less than a ton, perhaps, with one grossly splayed balancing foot. At night it might sail into a selected roost . . . or *onto* . . .

He turned his eyes up to the impenetrable canopy

above. In the flattened upper reaches of the banyan . . .
a nest?

Tinnerman stood, moving silently away from the bodies
of his companions. Locating his pack a second time he
dug out cleats and hand spikes, fitting them to his body
by feel. He found his trunk, shaping its firm curvature
with both hands; then he began the ascent.

He climbed, digging the spikes into the heavy bark and
gaining altitude in the blackness. The surface gradually
became softer, more even, but remained firm; if it were
to pull away from the inner wood the fall would kill him.
He felt the curvature increase and knew that the diameter
of the trunk was shrinking: but still there was no light at
all.

His muscles tensed as his body seemed to become
heavier, more precariously exposed. Something was pulling him away from the trunk, weakening his purchase;
but he could not yet circle any major portion of the
column with his arms. Something was wrong; he would
have to descend before being torn loose.

Relief washed over him as he realized the nature of the
problem. He was near the top; the stem was bending in
to join the main body of the tree, and he was on the
underside. He worked his way to the outside and the
strain eased; now gravity was pulling him into the trunk,
helping him instead of leaving him hanging. Quickly he
completed the ascent and stood at last against the massive
nexus where limp melded into bole.

Here there was light, a dim glow from overhead. He
mounted the vast gnarled bulk, a globular shape thirty
feet in diameter covered with swellings and scars. It was
difficult to picture it as it was, a hundred feet above the
ground, for nothing at all could be seen beyond its damp

mound. Although it was part of a living or once-living thing, there was no evidence of foliage. There was no nest.

The centre of the crude sphere rose onto another trunk or stalk, a column about ten feet in diameter, pointing straight up as far as he could see. He was not at the top at all. The bark was smooth and not very thick; it would be difficult to scale, even with the cleats.

Tinnerman rested for about ten minutes, lying down and putting his ear to the wood. Again the melody of the interior came to him, gentle yet deep. It brought a vision of many layers, pulsing and interweaving; of tumescence and flow, rich sap in the fibres. There was life of a sort going on within, either of the tree or in it.

He stood and mounted the central stalk. Quickly he climbed, spikes penetrating at fingers, knees and toes, bearing him antlike up the sheer column without hesitation. The light above became brighter, though it was only the lesser gloom of a starless night on a moonless planet. Ahead the straight trunk went on and on, narrowing but never branching. Huge limbs from neighbouring trees crossed nearby, bare and eerie, residual moisture shining dully; but his climb ignored them. Fifty feet; seventy-five; and now he was as high above the bole as it was above the ground. The stem to which he clung had diminished to a bare five foot diameter, but rose on towards the green upper forest.

Tinnerman's muscles bunched once more with strain. A wind came up; or perhaps he had come up to it. At this height, even the slightest tug and sway was alarming. He reached his arms around the shaft and hung on. Below, the spokes of other trees were a forest of their own, a fairyland of brush and blackness, crossing and recrossing, concealing everything except the slender reed he held. Above, the first leaves appeared, flat and heavy in the night. He climbed.

Suddenly it ended. The trunk, barely three feet through, expanded into a second bole shaped like an upsidedown pear with a five foot thickness, and stopped. Tinnerman clambered on to the top and stood there, letting his weary arms relax, balancing against the sway. There was nothing else – just a vegetable knob two hundred feet above the ground. All around, the dark verdure rustled in the breeze, and the gloom below was a quiet sea.

No branches approached within twenty feet of the knob, though the leaves closed in above, diffusing the glow of the sky. Tinnerman studied the hollow around him, wondering what kept the growth away. Was this a takeoff point for the hidden quarry?

Then it came to him, unnerving him completely. Fear hammered inside him like a bottled demon; he dared not let it out. Shaking, he began the descent.

Morning came, dim and unwilling; but it was not the wan light filtering down like sediment that woke the explorers. Nor was it the warmth of day, soaking into the tops and running down the trunks in the fashion of the night water.

They woke to sound: a distant din, as of a large animal tearing branches and crunching leaves. It was the first purposeful noise they had heard since entering the forest; as such, it was unnatural, and brought all three to their feet in alarm.

The evening deluge had eradicated all trace of the prints leading up to the giant structure under which they had taken shelter. Beneath it the spoor remained, as deep and fresh as before; one print near the edge was half gone.

Slaker sized up the situation immediately. 'Guarantees the trail was fresh,' he said. 'We don't know whether it was coming or going, but it was made between rains. Let's get over and spot that noise.' He suited action to word and set off, pack dangling from one hand, half eaten space-ration in the other.

Abel was not so confident. 'Fresh, yes – but we still don't know where the thing went. You don't look as though you got much sleep, Tinny.'

Tinnerman didn't answer. They picked up their packs and followed Slaker, who was already almost out of sight.

They came up to him as he stood at the edge of an open space in the forest. Several mighty trees had fallen, and around their massive corpses myriad little shoots were reaching up. The sunlight streamed down here, intolerably bright after the obscurity underneath. The noise had stopped.

There was a motion in the bush ahead. A large body was moving through the thicket, just out of sight, coming towards them. A serpentine neck poked out of the copse, bearing a cactuslike head a foot in diameter. The head swung towards them, circularly machairodont, a ring of six-inch eye-stalks extended.

The men froze, watching the creature. The head moved away, apparently losing its orientation in the silence. The neck was smooth and flexible, about ten feet in length; the body remained out of sight.

'Look at those teeth!' Slaker whispered fiercely. 'That's our monster.'

Immediately the head reacted, demonstrating acute hearing. It came forward rapidly, twenty feet above the ground; and in a moment the rest of the creature came into sight. The body was a globular mass about four feet across, mounted on a number of spindly legs. The creature walked with a peculiar caterpillar ripple, one ten-foot leg swinging around the body in a clockwise direction while the others were stationary, reminding Tinnerman of the problems of a wounded daddy-long-legs. The body spun, rotating with the legs; but the feet managed to make a kind of precessional progress. The spin did not appear to interfere with balance or orientation; the ring of eye-stalks kept all horizons covered.

Slaker whipped out his sidearm. 'No!' Tinnerman cried, too late. Slaker's shot smacked into the central body, making a small but visible puncture.

The creature halted as if nonplussed, legs rising and falling rhythmically in place. It did not fall. Slaker's second bullet tore into it, and his third, before Tinnerman wrested away the gun. 'It wasn't attacking,' he said, not knowing how to explain what he knew.

They watched while the monster's motion gradually slowed, huge drops of ichor welling from its wounds. It shuddered; then the legs began pounding the ground in short, violent steps, several at a time. Coordination was gone; slowly the body overbalanced and toppled. The great mouth opened like a flower, like a horn, and emitted an earshattering blast of sound, a tormented cry of pain and confusion; then the body fell heavily on its side.

For a moment the three men stood in silence, watching the death throes. The creature's legs writhed as though independently alive, and the head twisted savagely on the ground, knocking off the oddly brittle eye-stalks. Tinnerman's heart sank, for the killing had been pointless. If he had told the others his nighttime revelation –

From the forest came a blast of incredible volume.

Tinnerman clapped both hands over his ears as the siren stridence deafened them with a power of twelve to fifteen bels.

It ended, leaving a wake of silence. It had been a call, similar to that of the creature just shot, but deeper and much louder. There was a larger monster in the forest, answering the call for help.

'Its mate?' Abel wondered out loud, his voice sounding thin.

'Its mother!' Tinnerman said succinctly. 'And I think we'd better hide.'

Slaker shrugged. 'Bullets will stop it,' he said.

Tinnerman and Abel forged into the brush without comment. Slaker stood his ground confidently, aiming his weapon in the general direction of the approaching footfalls.

Once more the fog-horn voice sounded, impossibly loud, forcing all three to cover their ears before drums shattered and brains turned to jelly. Slaker could be seen ahead, one arm wrapped around his head to protect both ears, the other waving the gun.

The ground shook. High foliage burst open and large trees swayed aside, their branches crashing to the ground. A shape vast beyond imagination thundered into the clearing.

For a moment it paused, a four-legged monster a hundred feet high. Its low head was twelve feet thick, with a flat shiny snout. A broad eye opened, several feet across, casting about myopically. A ring of fibres sprouted, each pencil-thick, flexing slightly as the head moved.

Slaker fired.

The head shot forward, thudding into the ground thirty feet in front of him. The body moved, rotating grandly, as another member lifted and swung forward. They were not heads, but feet! Five feet with eyes. The monster was a hugely sophisticated adult of the quinquepedalian species Slaker had killed.

The man finally saw the futility of his stand, and ran. The towering giant followed, feet jarring the ground with rhythmic impacts, hoofs leaving nine-foot indents. It spun majestically, a dance of terrible gravity, pounding the brush and trees and dirt beneath it into nothingness. As each foot lifted, the heavy skin rolled back, uncovering the eye, and the sensory fibrils shot out. As each foot fell, the hide wrinkled closed, protecting the organs from the shock of impact.

The creature was slow, but its feet were fast. The fifth fall came down on the running figure, and Slaker was gone.

The quinquepedalian hesitated, one foot raised, searching. It was aware of them; it would not allow the killers of its child to escape. The eye roved, socketless, its glassy stare directed by a slow twisting of the foot. The circle of filaments combed the air, feeling for a sound or smell, or whatever trace of the fugitives they were adapted to detect.

After a few minutes the eye closed and the fibrils withdrew. The foot went high; plummeted. The earth rocked with the force of the blow. It lifted again, to smash down a few feet over, leaving a tangent print.

After a dozen such stomps the creature reversed course and came back, making a second row ahead of the first. This, Tinnerman realized, was carpet-bombing; and the two men were directly in the swath.

If they ran, the five-footed nemesis would cut them down easily. If they stayed, it would get them anyway, unless one or both of them happened to be fortunate enough to fit into the diamond between four prints. The odds were negative. And quite possibly it would sense a near miss, and rectify the error with a small extra tap.

They waited, motionless, while it laid down another barrage, and another. Now it was within fifty feet, mechanically covering the area. Behind it a flat highway was developing.

Saturation stomping, Tinnerman thought, and found the concept insanely funny. Man discovers a unique five-footed monster – the Quink – and it steps on him. Would the history books record the irony?

He saw the answer. He gave a cry and lurched to his feet, flinging his pack aside and plunging directly at the monster.

The foot halted, quite fast on the uptake, and rotated its eye to cover him. It gathered itself, crashed down, an irresistible juggernaut. The earth jumped with its fury; but Tinnerman, running in an unexpected direction, had passed its arc.

He halted directly under the main body of the quinque-pedalian. If his guess were correct, it would be unable to reach him there. It would have to move – and he would move with it.

Far above, the main body hovered, a black boulder suspended on toothpicks. Above that, he knew, the neck and head extended on into the sky. A head shaped like a pear – when its mouth was closed. The first foot turned inward, its eye bearing on him. It hung there, several feet above the ground, studying him with disquieting intelligence. It did not try to pin him. Balance, Tinnerman judged, was after all of paramount importance to a creature two hundred feet tall. If it lost its footing, the fall of its body would destroy it. So long as it kept three or four feet correctly positioned and firmly planted, it could not fall; but if it were to pull its members into too small a circle it could get into serious trouble. Several hundred tons are not lightly tossed about.

The quinquepedalian moved. The feet swung clockwise, one at a time, striking the ground with a elephantine touch. The bars of Tinnerman's cage lifted and fell, crushing the terrain with an almost musical beat; the body turned, gaining momentum. The feet on one side seemed to retreat; on the other they advanced, forcing him to walk rapidly to keep himself centred.

The pace increased. Now the feet landed just seconds apart, spinning the vast body forward. Tinnerman had to break into a run.

Small trees impeded his progress; every time he dodged around an obstruction, the hind feet gained. On an open plain he might have been able to outrun the monster; but now it had manoeuvered him on to rough ground. If it didn't tire soon, it would have him. In time it could force him over a cliff that its own legs could straddle, or into a bog. Or it might forget him and go after Abel – and he would have to stay under it, not daring to place himself outside its circle. His respect for it mounted; he was in the eye of a hurricane, and would soon have to find some other place of safety.

Tinnerman studied the pattern of motion. At this velocity, the individual feet did not have time for more than peremptory adjustments; the maintenance of forward motion dictated an involved but predictable pattern. One foot had to vacate the spot for the next; he was not sure whether two feet ever left the ground at the same time, but could see sharp limitations. If he were to cross a print just vacated –

He timed his approach and took off to the side, almost touching the ascending foot. It twisted in flight, its eye spotting him quickly; but it was unable to act immediately. It struck the ground far ahead, casting up debris with the force of its braking action, and the following member lifted in pursuit.

Tinnerman ran straight out at breakneck speed. He had underestimated Quink's versatility; the second foot went after him much more alertly than an ordinary nervous system should have permitted. In a creature of this size, many seconds should have elapsed before the brain assimilated the new information and decided upon a course of action; yet the feet seemed to react promptly with individual intelligence. This thing was far too large and far-flung for the operation of any effective nervous system – yet it operated most effectively.

The shadow of a leg passed over him, and Tinnerman thought for a detached moment that he had been caught. But the impact was twenty feet to his rear. The next one would get him, unless –

He cut sharply towards a medium large tree at the edge of the clearing. He dared not look; but he was sure the creature behind was milling in temporary confusion. It could not dodge as fast as he – he hoped.

He reached the tree and ducked behind its fifteen foot diameter, feeling safe for the moment.

Quink brought up before the tree. One foot quested around the side, searching for him. He could see its enormously thick hoof, completely flat on the underside: polished steel, with a reddish tinge in the centre. Probably natural colouration; but he thought of Slaker, and shuddered.

The wooden skin drew back, uncovering the eye. The

ankle above the hoof widened, the skin bunching in a great roll. He knew now that it settled when the foot rested, coming down to make contact with the ground. He had rested against that swelling last night; he had climbed that leg . . .

As though satisfied that it could not reach him so long as he hid behind the tree, the quinquepedalian paused for an odd shuffle. Tinnerman peeked around the trunk and saw the legs bunch together in a fashion that destroyed some previous theories, then spread out in a trapezoidal formation. One foot hung near the tree, supporting no weight, and seemingly over-balancing the body somewhat. Then the near foot hefted itself high, swinging like a pendulum, and threw itself against the tree with resounding force.

The entire trunk reberberated with the blow, and a shower of twigs and leaves fluttered down from the upper reaches. The foot struck again higher; again the tree quaked and loosed a larger fall of detritus. Tinnerman kept a cautious eye on it; he could be laid low by a comparatively small branch.

The single foot continued its attack, striking the tree regularly about fifty feet above the ground. At that height the foot was about the same diameter as the tree, and the weight behind it was formidable. Yet such action seemed pointless, because damage to the tree would not affect the man behind it.

Or was he underestimating Quink again?

The pounding ceased, and he poked his head cautiously around once more. Was the thing retreating? Somehow he did not expect it to give up easily; it had demonstrated too much savvy and determination for that. It was a remarkable animal, not only for its size.

Three legs stood in a tripod, while two came up

simultaneously. Tinnerman's brow wrinkled; it did not seem possible for it to maintain its balance that way. But it was acting with assurance; it had something in mind.

The two feet rose, together, one held just above the other. In awe, Tinnerman watched the lofty body topple forward, unable to stand upright in such a position. Suddenly the two feet thrust forward with staggering power; the entire body rocked backward as they smashed into the tree. And this time the timber felt it. A gunshot explosion rent the air as the fibres of the trunk split and severed, wood splaying; and the large roots broke the ground like sea monsters as the entire tree hinged on its roots.

Now Tinnerman could see how the clearing had been formed. The parent opened a hole in the forest, so that the baby could feed on the little saplings. As the vegetation grew, so did the child, until tall enough to reach the foliage of full-sized trees.

A few more blows would fell this one. Tinnerman waited for the next impact, then fled, hidden from view, he hoped, by the tilting trunk. The creature continued its attack, unaware that the real quarry had gone.

Tinnerman picked up the trail, human prints this time. Abel should have escaped during the distraction, and would be heading for the ship.

The mighty forest was quiet now, except for a slight rustle ahead. That would be Abel. Tinnerman moved without noise instinctively, disinclined to interrupt the medication of the great trees' eternal beauty. And knew that he was a fool, for the forest hardly cared, and the quinquepedalian, with all its decibels, would not worry about the distant patter of human feet.

'Don,' he called, not loudly. Abel turned at once, a smile on his face.

'Tinny! I'm glad you got away.' He too was careful of his volume, probably the monster could not hear, but it was pointless to ask for trouble. 'You seemed to know what you were doing. But I was afraid you had not made it. I would have waited for you if – '

'I know, Don.' Abel was no coward; if there had been any way to help, he would have done so. When dealing with the quinquepedalian, loitering was futile and dangerous; the person involved either got away or he did not. The most practical recourse was to trek immediately for the ship, so that at least one person would live to tell the story.

'Ship takes off in twelve hours,' Abel said, shaking his pack into greater comfort. 'If we move right along, we can make it in six hours. Can't be more than twenty miles.'

'Going to make a full report, Don?' Tinnerman was uneasy, without being certain why.

'Fritz was killed,' Abel said simply.

Tinnerman put out a hand and brought him to a stop. 'We can't do it, Don.'

Abel studied him with concern. 'I'll give you a hand, if you got clipped. I thought you were OK.'

'I'm all right. Don, we killed that thing's baby. It did what any parent would do. If we report it, the captain will lift ship and fry it with the main jet.'

'Code of space, Tinny. Anything that attacks a man – '

'It didn't attack. It came to the defence of its child. We don't have the right to sentence it.'

Abel's eyes grew cold. 'Fritz was my friend. I thought he was yours too. If I could have killed that monster myself I'd have done it. You coming along?'

'Sorry, Don. I have no quarrel with you. But I can't let you report Quink to the captain.'

Abel sized him up, then took off his pack. He didn't ask questions. 'If that's the way it has to be,' he said evenly.

Don Abel was a slow man, cautious in his language and conservative in action. But he had never been mistaken for a weakling. His fists were like lightning.

Tinnerman was knocked back by two blows to the chin and a roundhouse on the ear. He held back, parrying with his forearm; Abel landed a solid punch to the midriff, bringing down his guard, and following that with a bruising smack directly on the mouth. Tinnerman feinted with his left, but got knocked off his feet with a body check before getting a chance to connect with his right.

He rolled over, grasping for the feet, and got lifted by a blinding knee to the chin. His head reeled with a red haze; and still the blows fell, pounding his head and neck, while Abel's foot stunned the large muscle of the thigh, aiming for the groin.

Tinnerman's reticence fell aside, and he began to fight. He bulled upward, ignoring the punishment, and flung his arms around the other man's waist. Abel retaliated with a double handed judo chop to the back of the neck; but he held on, linking his forearms in a bearhug, pulling forward. Abel took a fistful of hair, jerking Tinnerman's head from side to side; but slowly the hug lifted him off his feet.

Abel was free suddenly, using a body motion Tinnerman hadn't met before, and once again fists flew.

It took about fifteen minutes. Abel finally lay panting on the ground, exhausted but conscious, while Tinnerman rummaged in the pack for first aid. 'I knew you could take me,' Abel said. 'It had to be fast, or that damn endurance of yours would figure in. You ever been tired in your life, Tinny?'

Tinnerman handed him the sponge, to clean up the blood. 'Last night I climbed the Quink,' he said. 'I stood on its head – and it never made a motion.'

'Quink? Oh, you mean the monster.' Abel sat up suddenly. 'Are you trying to tell me – ' A look of awe came over his face. 'That thing with the legs, the big one – you mean we slept under – ' He paused for more reflection. 'Those tracks – it does figure. If it hadn't been so dark, we would have seen that the monster was still standing in them! That's why there were leaves under there, and a couple of prints from the front feet. It must have been asleep . . .' His mind came belatedly to grips with the second problem. 'You *climbed* it?'

Tinnerman nodded soberly. 'It couldn't have slept through that. I used the spikes . . . I didn't catch on until I saw the way the leaves had been eaten around the head. All it had to do was open its mouth – but it let me go. Live and let live.'

Abel came to his feet. 'OK, Charlie – we'll wait six hours before heading for the ship. That'll give us time to look this thing over. Don't get me wrong – I haven't made up my mind. I may still tell the captain . . . but not right away.'

Tinnerman relaxed. 'Let's see what we can learn,' he said. He reassembled Abel's pack, then glanced up.

The foot was there, poised with Democlesian ponderosity fifteen feet above their heads. The eye was open, fibrils extended. The quinquepedalian had come upon them silently.

'Split!' Tinnerman yelled. The two men dived in opposite directions. Once more the ground bounced with concussion, as he raced for the nearest tree. He slid around it, safe for the moment.

A glance back showed the monster hauling its foot back into the air. Only half of Don Abel had made it to safety. Then the huge hoof hovered and dropped, and the grisly sight was gone. There was only another flat print in the earth.

Abel might have been fast enough, if he hadn't been weakened by the fight. Just as Slaker would have been more careful, had he been warned. The quinquepedalian was the agent; but Tinnerman knew that he was the cause of the two deaths.

Now Quink approached the tree, spinning in her stately dance, hoofs kissing the shadowed ground without a sound. She stood.

Why hadn't she crushed them both as they fought, oblivious to the danger above? She must have been there for several minutes, watching, listening. One gentle stomp, and vengeance would have been complete. Why had she waited?

Fair play?

Was this thing really intelligent? Did it have ethics of its own – her own?

The familiar foot came around the trunk, perceptors out. He stood calmly, knowing that he was safe from immediate harm. He stooped to pick up a handful of dirt, tossing it at the light-sensitive area. The eye folded shut immediately, letting the earth rattle over the bare hide. Fast reflexes.

Too fast. An animal of this size had to be handicapped by the distance between brain and appendages. It was manifestly impossible to have an instantaneous reflex at the end of a limb one hundred feet long. No neural track could provide anything like the speed he had witnessed.

Tinnerman moved to the other side of the trunk, as though getting ready for a dash to another tree. The foot swung around at once, intercepting him from the other direction. There was no doubt that it learned from experience, and could act on it immediately.

But how could that impulse travel from eye to brain and back again so quickly? Usually, an animal's eye was situated quite close to the brain, to cut down neural delay. Unless Quink had a brain in her foot –

The answer struck him stunningly. There *was* a brain in the foot. There had to be. How else could the pedal members be placed so accurately, while maintaining perfect balance? There would be a coordinating ganglion in the central body, issuing general orders concerning overall motion and order of precedence for the lifting of the feet; there could be another small brain in the head, to handle ingestion and vocalization. And each foot would make its own decisions as to exact placement and manner of descent. Seven brains in all – organized into a mighty whole.

The foot-brains could sleep when not on duty, firmly planted on the ground and covered by a thick overlap of impervious skin. They were probably not too bright as individuals – their job was specialized – but with the far more powerful central brain to back them up, any part of Quink was intelligent.

'Creature of the forest,' Tinnerman said to it in wonder. 'Quinquepedalian, septecerebrian – you are probably smarter than I.' And certainly stronger. He thought about that, discovering a weird pleasure in the contemplation of it. All his life he had remained aloof from his fellows, searching for something he could honestly look up to. Now he had found it.

Eleven hours later, on schedule, the ship took off. It would be three, four, five years before a squat colony ship came to set up frontier operations.

Quink was stalking him with ageless determination and rapidly increasing sagacity. Already she had learned to anticipate the geometric patterns he traced. He had led her through a simple square, triangle and star, giving up each figure when she solved it and set her body to intercept him ahead. Soon she would come to the conclusion that the prey was something more than a vicious rodent. Once she realized that she was dealing with intelligence, communication could begin.

Perhaps in time she would forgive him for the death of her child, and know that vengeance had been doubly extracted already. The time might come when he could walk in the open once more and not be afraid of a foot. At night, while she slept, he was safe; but by day –

Perhaps, when the colonists came, they would be greeted by a man riding the mightiest steed of all time. Or by the quinquepedalian, carrying its pet. It did not matter who was ascendant, so long as the liaison was established.

'Creature of the forest,' he said again, doubling back as he perceived her bulk in wait at an intersection of the triquetra pattern. For a moment he stood and looked at her, so vast and beautiful, spinning in the dance of his destruction. 'Creature of the forest,' he said, 'Thou art mighty.

'Thou art mightier than I.' There was an answering blast bels in magnitude, like a goddess awakening beyond the horizon.

Encounter

I had earned a total of $160 in my trial year of writing,
October 1962 to October 1963. (Twenty years later,
October 1982, my fantasy novel *Ogre, Ogre*, written with
an Ogre as the hero because someone had called me
an ogre at conventions – I had never even been to a
convention – became my first to make the *New York
Times* bestseller list. Thereafter I declared that to be the
Month of the Ogre, Oct-ogre.) I was technically a success,
but that just wasn't enough money to live on. So, reluctantly, I retired as a full time writer and went back to
school to become an English teacher. What a terrible
fate! But I continued to write and market stories part
time, and every few months another sale would develop.
'Encounter' was the fourth; the third was a collaborative
story published in *Analog* (yes, I finally made it there!),
excluded from this solo volume. I had read someone
else's story that had a wall, the story didn't go the way I
expected, so I wrote my own story with a wall – and a
message. Yes, I'll tell you the message; I'm not shy
about that sort of thing. It is that man is not made for
paradise, any more than a tiger is. My stories do tend to
have messages, which seems to infuriate some critics.
I see nothing wrong with entertainment, escape from
mundane concerns, humour – or meaning, and I don't
really understand the attitude of those who feel otherwise.

In the evening of the twentieth day, Abe Sale came
across the wall. On either hand a wide bare rift extended,

north and south: behind him Omega Avenue retreated towards the dawn, all the way to the Atlantic. Ahead the blank concrete severed the right of way; he could not pass.

In the days of automation and leisure, it was Sale's habit to walk the endless city streets, venting in this asocial manner his seething urge for expression. His body was strong with many miles of foot labour, twenty in a day, questing through a metropolitan purgatory. Because there were half-crazed animals wandering in the plains of the empty parking acreages, he was armed; because it grew cold at night, he was clothed; because no normal person would open the ground-level apertures, he was self-reliant.

This was rough territory. The dogs were small, but the packs were large, and not everything fled at sight of a weapon. Even the great rats were restrained, here, keeping to the shadows; something was holding them back, and Sale doubted that it was fear of Man.

It took a resourceful stranger to survive in the open municipality. Sale survived. Armed with his heavy steel staff, he feared nothing on the streets so far; but there were times when retreat was expedient, and he was not a fool. Now, having travelled four hundred miles west on Omega, he had encountered a phenomenon that defied credibility: the end of it.

He studied the wall, and found that it was high: a sheer cliff of stone and steel and mortar, not to be scaled by naked hands. It was as tall as a building, travelling as far as the eye could see; and the moat that the pavement formed beside it prevented access from any neighbouring roof.

Sale could not tarry here; not far behind was a pack,

lean and hungry. He had to have a place to sleep in relative safety.

He turned the corner, south, to pace the wall. A block away, another wanderer turned the corner north; thus they came upon each other by surprise. The other creature was a solitary feline of enormous size. Never as plentiful as the dogs, and always alone, these cats represented no threat to him. In fact, with their depredations upon the rodents, they were a greater friend to man than the hounds; more than once he had lent a helping blow on behalf of a cornered member. But this – surely this was the king of cats. It was tremendous.

It advanced, and so did Sale. If it was to be a challenge for the right of way, his staff would speak for him. Against a canine pack, Sale retreated; against a single animal he did not. Yet he wondered why the striped feline refused to give way. Why did it come at him in the centre of the street, instead of lying in wait, in ambush? What was driving it?

His eyes were on the cat; but he noticed that all rats had vanished. One mystery had been solved; rats were not fools either. This was no ordinary tabby.

They sparred, the cat moving sinuously, huge muscles rippling under the loose skin; he with his staff in two hands, an effective weapon. They closed; the cat made a feint, one paw batting at the pole, but Sale was on guard. Even now he was not afraid; there was exhilaration about single combat that warmed his body, fired his imagination.

Ever alert for the danger behind, Sale suddenly tightened. He knew without turning that the trailing pack had arrived; he could hear the yips and growls as it massed. It had cut off his escape; he would have to kill at once and get away, before the canines fell upon him.

Behind the cat, more dogs turned the corner. This pack was unusually large, he thought, to cover two blocks. But no – the ones in front were of a different breed. Squat and hairy, with long snouts – not dogs at all, but pigs! Wart hogs, peccaries, or something of the sort. Strange indeed.

Sale had not forgotten for a moment the immediate antagonist; he identified both dogs and pigs while cautiously circling the big cat. Now two thoughts came together: the pigs were not a North American breed, and neither was the cat. He was dealing with a literal tiger! How it came to be here he had no time to wonder; if he did not dispatch it soon, the dogs would tear them both to pieces.

'And the hogs were after you,' he said to the cat, in momentary camaraderie. 'You killed one of their number, and after that your life was forfeit. You *knew* there was no retreat!'

The clamour behind him grew. The dogs were about to charge. Simultaneously the pigs advanced, short legs and hoofs beating a staccato on the pavement. Either group was formidable; together they spelled doom. He had to escape.

His eye caught a manhole in the centre of the street. He yelled at the cat, surprising it into a fleeting pause, and jumped away while it glared nervously at the converging packs. He jammed his pike into the edge of the recess, prying up the heavy cover. Grudgingly, it came; he heaved it aside and jumped into the blackness below, hand reaching out automatically for the rungs of the ladder that had to be there. He caught it, the wrench nearly breaking his wrist, and clung tightly; it was impossible to know how deep the hole went, or what might be below. An angry cascade of hoofbeats sounded above;

the vicious beasts were all around, now fighting among themselves.

The ladder ended ten feet below the surface in a greasy platform. Sale braced his feet and looked around.

Glaring yellow eyes met his.

He froze against the ladder, waiting for his vision to adjust. He dared not make a motion, even in self-defence, until he knew what he faced.

In moments he had the answer. It was the tiger.

Somehow it had followed him down the hole, while he was too preoccupied to notice. His staff was above, even if there had been room to use it here. He would have to depend on his knife.

Yet he waited, hesitating to trigger the attack. He doubted that he was a match for it; it weighed, as nearly as he could ascertain, as much as or more than himself, and its vision in this locale would be superior. He would have to keep one hand on the ladder, for leverage, and fight with the other. He did not want to kill it if he could.

Minutes passed, and it did not attack. It watched him silently. As his eyes became fully acclimatized he saw that it was not hostile at all; it simply sat there, observing.

Of course! 'You didn't come down here to attack me – you came to get away from the common enemy!' The cat made no motion; but Sale felt, perhaps illogically, that its lack of denial constituted assent. Any port in a storm; it had as much to fear from the implacable pigs as he had from the dogs. And, he was certain, either group above would gleefully destroy the refugees singly or in concert. Better to share a nest with a single enemy than face destruction by the pack. 'Truce?' he inquired, and the tiger did not deny it.

Above, the tumult rose to a vicious level. Shadows

hurtled by the hole; bits of fur fluttered down. Then a crash, and a heavy body dropped to land between the fugitives. It was a pig, its throat already torn open.

Sale realized that he was hungry. Moving carefully, and keeping one eye on the cat, he gripped the knife and approached the carcass. The tiger opened its jaws, but did not interfere. Sale hacked away, finally severing a leg; placing his foot on the remainder, he shoved it forcefully towards his companion. They ate.

It grew dark above, and quiet; but it would be foolhardy to attempt to leave now. They would have to spend the night where they were. Sale found that he could still see, vaguely; two feet to the side, his platform slid off into an open sewer, and phosphorescence coated the walls and lit the water. The air was close, but not fetid; they would get along.

Accepting the presence of the cat but never taking it for granted, Sale talked to keep himself awake. In the morning he might climb the ladder and emerge with impunity; but not yet.

'How did you get on the streets of Mid-Atlantic?' he asked the cat. 'You're an Asian animal, Tiger. You don't mind if I call you Tiger? Good. And what about those pigs? Peccaries are South American, if I remember my Nature studies. Dogs and rats run wild; they're castoffs of one sort or another. But you – '

Tiger yawned and stretched out. 'Don't do that!' Sale protested. 'In another minute you'll have me doing it too; and while I don't mean to cast aspersions on your motives – '

Tiger ignored him, and Sale continued with some of his own history. 'You see those blank buildings, Tiger; and you think the whole country has been deserted. But do you want to know something? The population of this subcontinent alone is over one billion. People, I mean; not tigers. They live in the buildings and they have a life of ease. They could go from one building to another if they wanted to, but they're simply not interested. You see, everything anybody needs or wants is delivered to his own apartment – anything. Nobody has to work. Even the few that do travel – robot repairmen, for example – use the tubes; nobody walks the streets. The buildings all have stairs and doors – building codes, you know; obsolete, but still in force – but practically all of them are sealed shut.'

Tiger got up and faced the flowing water. 'I wouldn't drink that if I were you,' Sale cautioned. Then he saw it: the long angry snout of an alligator. It came close in the luminescence, gentle ripples hinting at its length: eight, nine feet of it. If the thing attacked –

The alligator heaved itself onto the narrow platform, heading directly for the tiger. Its jaws were huge. Sale moved over, put one boot against the exposed reptilian hide, and shoved; with a splash, it slid helplessly into the water. Acting on inspiration, Sale next kicked the sodden remnant of the pig into the sewer after it; the alligator flashed in the water, taking the morsel in its teeth, and disappeared.

Sale found himself standing beside the big cat. He retreated to his own side hurriedly. Why had he done it? A fight between Tiger and the alligator could only have been to his advantage; why should he interfere?

'It was only after food, just like the rest of us,' he explained. 'Some of the blood must have dripped into the water . . .' Tiger lay down again, seemingly unperturbed.

'And what am I doing here, fighting with rats, when I have a soft apartment at home, you'll be wanting to know,' he said, resuming his previous train of thought. Tiger managed to look singularly uncurious. 'It was *because* it was soft that I had to leave my apartment. Man isn't fitted for paradise; he grows flabby, loses self-respect. A man with any guts at all has to fight; he has to overcome. And so I chose adventure; I pried open the ground level door, and saw the savage world before me. I prepared myself; I set out to find the western end of Omega.

'Now I've found it – and I'm not satisfied. I want to know what's on the other side of that wall.'

Finally Sale slept. He woke, half surprised to find himself unharmed, to a dim light spreading from the hole above. It was morning. He gripped the ladder and hoisted himself up. Cautiously he poked his head from the manhole. Dead dogs and pigs were everywhere; but that was all. Near the wall the rats were out in strength, gnawing on the remains.

'All clear!' Sale called down to Tiger, wondering whether the animal could get up the ladder. But the tawny body emerged easily.

Now that the mutual danger was over, he eyed the cat warily, not certain whether the truce still held.

He had recovered his staff and wiped it off, now holding it ready; but Tiger ignored it. A snarl to scatter the rats; then the cat was off, loping south along the wall.

South? Yet it had been going north to flee the pigs. Sale followed.

Two miles down, the cat disappeared. Sale followed warily, to discover a rent in the wall. A stone had fallen from it, and there was a hole leading to the other side. Peering through, he could see Tiger waiting.

He climbed through himself and stopped, amazed. The

city ended with the wall; here there was only a forest wasteland; trees and brush and tall grass growing profusely. There was animal life here too, he knew; droppings littered the ground. Somewhere he could hear the sound of a river, and the air was sweet and cool.

How had this come to be? The last natural forests had died long ago, taken while the government was still debating protective legislation.

There was no Wilderness any more; not in all of North America. Yet here –

'The zoo!' Now it came to him. There was no wilderness; but there were parks, and artificial gardens for captive specimens. The tiger; the wild pigs; creatures of a zoo, now free and roaming in its neglect. And the shrubs, from all parts of the world, grown and spread. What had been an imitation of nature now was real.

Tiger brushed by him and scrambled back through the gap, into the city.

He stared after the great cat, confused.

'Surely this, for you, is paradise,' he said after it. 'Why do you want to leave?'

But as he said the words, he understood. Tigers were not made for paradise. Only in the gaunt streets, among inimical dogs and rats, was there real challenge for the creature of independent spirit.

He wondered whether Tiger also had a problem, foraging alone, finding places to sleep safely. No-man's-land could also be no-tiger's-land, at least at times. Individualism was a fine thing; but it could not deny the need for companionship.

Did Tiger also crave company in spirit?

Sale climbed out of the zoo and stood once more on the street. The cat was there, waiting.

'Come,' he said, heading north. The tiger came.

Phog

Critics have also objected to my style of writing, calling it pedestrian or clumsy. I tend to talk back to critics of my work, and in consequence I have been blacklisted in several places. Hell has no fury like that of an ignorant critic scorned! The fact is, I use whatever style I deem suitable for the piece. Usually I prefer to have an inconspicuous style, one that does not interfere with clarity, so that the reader can absorb the story painlessly. If that means I'm no stylist, then so be it. But I think a person who places style before substance is a dunce. The following story, 'Phog', is an example of a style intended to help convey a mood. Later in the volume there will be another example, for a different mood, in 'On the Uses of Torture.' Let the critics sink their fangs into that one! Meanwhile, a note on the spelling here: the notion for this story came to me while I was grading high school spelling papers. Naturally both spelling and definition of this fog are strange. I was never a good speller myself, and grading those papers was a hellish chore.

A great boiling mass of grey-brown matter, closing in on tiger's feet: Phog.

Mat's eyes widened in shock. He was young; he lacked a foot of the height of manhood; but his mind assessed the situation immediately. A moment only did the spell of the monstrous mists hold him in thrall; then he gave the alarm in the most natural and effective manner: He screamed in terror.

His sister Sal, next born, jumped up, clutching the bright stone she had been playing with. It was a strange flat fragment, diverting them both until this instant, for it showed a hand inside when she picked it up – a hand that went away when she set it down again. And sometimes it flashed blindingly, rivalling Phoebus himself. But it was forgotten now as Sal too saw the horror that was upon them both. Her scream joined his.

Nearby, a grey-whiskered man came joltingly awake, kicking up dark sand as he scrambled to his ancient feet. He was the children's grandfather, their only surviving relative. He was too old, now, to be a worthy guardian; never before had he been lulled to sleep this far within the shadow zone. Somehow the hot safe sun had pacified his fears, putting him off guard – while Phoebus quietly withdrew, shielded by closing mists above, and left the three of them prey to their own carelessness.

His rheumy eyes took in the crying children and the encroaching horror behind them. Already Phog surrounded their position on three sides, sparing only a dwindling harbour of land – an opening they could not hope to pass in time.

'The fjords,' the old man cried. 'There is no other way!' Grasping each child by the wrist, he lumbered towards the nearest rift.

Sal came willingly – an openminded innocent who would one day be a lovely woman. Mat held back, frightened by vague tribal taboos. 'The fjords are forbidden,' he whimpered.

The man had no patience with superstition. He cast loose the boy's hand. 'Then wait for Phog. Your father did.'

Mat looked behind him. The shape was within a hundred paces, silently consuming the distance between them. Its surging hunger was manifest. 'Wait for me, Progenitor!'

The fjords were deep erosion-gullies through which the hot winds gusted. Water spumed in some, in ever-shifting patterns, cutting new channels and filling in the old with rocky debris. It was a dangerous region, shunned by most people; but the hazards would also put Phog at a disadvantage. The sharp cliffs would hinder it; the winds would tug at its fringe and tear painful rifts; the turbulent waters below would wash at its tumbling substance dissolving it. Phog, mindlessly determined, would waste its impetus filling the deep chasms, building itself up to stretch into the farther clefts, bruising itself and wasting time.

Even so, escape was not certain. Their only real hope was to avoid it long enough for Phoebus to return.

Phoebus and Phog waged perpetual war, on this forgotten colony of Man. Phoebus, the shining sun, was lord of the desiccate plain, burning down in stationary splendour, driving back every living thing. Phog was guardian of the shadow, denizen of ice and glacier, cover for the dread phogRunner.

Between these powers of light and shadow was a narrow strip of habitable territory, a buffer zone, where rain might fall and green plants grow. Here the tribe foraged for wild grains and fruits and dug into the ground for tubers; here were clear springs for water, and animals for fur. Neither Phog nor Phoebus exercised total influence; and here a furtive, timid tribe could live – waiting, waiting for rediscovery.

'Stay close by me,' the old man commanded. 'Do not touch Phog!' He led the way down the first gully, sliding on the grit and sand.

Mat hesitated again, at the brink; but behind him Phog

closed in, towering, noisome. He clambered down, no longer in doubt.

Phog reached the fjord, gathering and rising up at the edge. It spilled over and rolled down the incline in horrendous blobs. It was cutting them off from the deeper, safer centre of the gully!

'Past it!' They stumbled over the loose stones.

A foaming section wrenched free and descended, silently obscuring their escape. Sal screamed and swerved, the last to pass, but in time. The dark mass settled in the bottom, filling it up as more piled on from above. There would be no return this way.

Another cloud appeared ahead. Together, front and rear, the ugly bulks expanded, isolating their section of the gully. Above them a beating wall of solid cloud loomed, a mighty wave just beginning to fall . . .

'The side!' the old man gasped, scrambling up himself.

They reached the top of the ridge between chasms, spattered by a foul shower of froth as the silent wave collapsed behind. From this height the extent of Phog's advance was evident. The solid mist was everywhere, already overflowing on either side. Only Phoebus could save them now – and Phoebus was hiding. There was nowhere to run; the gully ahead ran parallel to the front, and the farther wall was too steep to ascend in time.

Mat's bright mind was prodded to desperate inspiration. 'The water!' he shouted. 'Swim under – if we can – '

They galloped down the slope, trying to beat Phog to the deep clear water pooled at the lower end. Water extended throughout the fjords a few thousand feet farther down, eventually unifying in a passive lake. If they could reach this first inlet in time, they'd have a chance.

A narrow grey pseudopod blew across their path, cutting them off from the water. It took on the brownish tinge as it thickened. They pulled up before it, dismayed; sometimes Phog almost seemed to strike with intelligence. This, for it, was a strategic masterstroke. They were trapped.

There was no alternative. The mottled burgeonings were almost upon them, bringing inevitable doom. 'Through it,' the old man quavered. 'As quickly as you can. There may be no Runner near . . .'

Concealing his own terror from the children, he plunged into the noxious wall. There was an eddy about him; then he was out of sight, as Phog sealed itself again.

Mat drew up short, unable to make that plunge. Sal, seeing him hesitate, lost her own courage. Their fear of Phog was too great to permit voluntary contact. Behind them a dirty mass slid over the rough slope; in a moment it would settle and draw them under anyway, but they could not move.

'Where are you?' the voice came back, muffled. 'Come, come, before it is too late – '

This time Sal answered the summons, squeezing her eyes tightly shut, holding her breath, and jumping blindly for the terrible wall ahead. It seemed to pulse and quiver with hungry anticipation. Mat, thrust into action at last, grasped her fleeting hand and dived in after her.

He had taken no breath. The choking mist of Phog's substance stifled him, burning his lungs and making his eyes smart. He coughed involuntarily, inhaling more of the foul gloom. But spurred by fear he pressed on, now running ahead of his sister and drawing her with him. He had known she would get lost, on her own; she was brave enough, but not always sensible.

The run was interminable. Phog held them back, smearing cold grease on face and hands, dragging against the body with the muck of nightmare. Sal cried out, a scream of pain and fear. 'Come *on*!' Mat gritted, knowing they dared not delay for a stubbed toe. They were almost through; they had to be.

She screamed again, piercingly. Abruptly, horribly, her grip became flaccid; her hand was torn from his grasp as she fell. The Runner had come! Terrified, Mat spurted ahead.

He was out, crashing into his grandfather. They stood together, transfixed by fear.

Minutes passed. The haze above parted; the sun brightened. Phoebus returned, saving them from a difficult swim. But Sal did not emerge.

Phog reared back, pulling together, recoiling from the direct rays. It could not face the sun. A putrid stench rose from it as its outer fringe was scorched; it retreated, seeking shade. Man and boy watched with rapt revulsion as it heaved back from the gully, back from the fjords, sucking itself in like a bulbous stomach.

On the cleared and glistening ground they saw the bones of Sal, broken and twisted and almost clean of blood. Beside them was a single print: the taloned spoor of the phogRunner.

The old man muttered incoherently, the dirty tears dribbling down his face. Mat's eyes were fixed on an object half-hidden by matted hair. It was the stone – the shining stone – that she had treasured. It flashed with the light of Phoebus, a glittering eye, watching him, condemning him to unutterable grief and shame: he who had held her hand, who could have brought her to the edge, to safety, so close, so close . . . and instead had bolted in panic.

'Phog comes!' the old man exclaimed.

Mat looked up, stroking the light growth of beard on his cheek, his pulse leaping in anticipation. The confrontation was at hand, here at the spot Phog had routed them so long ago and driven them to misery in the fjords. Here at the place of the coloured and shining stones a second trial of strength was due.

His hand rested on a crude stone structure, a box fashioned from heavy blocks, open above with a fibrous mat inside, hanging between two slanted surfaces. Gently, lovingly, his supple fingers traced the rough contour of the edge, as his eyes traced the approaching menace. There was a tremble in those fingers, a doubt in those eyes; but Mat stood firm.

For a moment his gaze flicked anxiously back over the row of structures extending beyond the horizon, each bearing its facing slabs, each set just so, just exactly so. His breath came rapidly; would the strange weapon he had forged from his dead sister's delight actually defeat Phog?

The ghastly billows came, death-grey, malefic, streaked with sordid brown. Corpulent blisters pushed out, expanded, sagged ponderously and were reabsorbed. Not a sound issued from within that sinister mass; only the belching odour emerged to panic the waiting men.

One hundred feet: a mighty bulge slimed over the ground, four times the height of a man, quivering jellylike as though it sensed its prey. Progenitor's bony body echoed that movement in sympathetic vibration. Mat's gorge rose, fouling his throat as he fought for control over his emotions. He had captured Phoebus in the stone, bringing him far across the plain, winging from surface to surface; but would this tiny spark from the sun's domain daunt Phog?

Seventy-five feet: Terror lashed his mind, convulsed his muscles; muscles hard from the hauling of great slabs. 'Now! Now!' the old man shouted, his voice a high-pitched wail. Mat gulped, shaking from head to knee, but held himself from action. He yearned to yank the curtain away – the curtain that held back the fierce sunlight chained in this final relay; but for the sake of the test he dared not unveil this light too soon.

Fifty-feet: The impalpable stuff of Phog bubbled and swirled, exhaling digestive vapours. Mat's eyes smarted; his nostrils pinched together in vain attempt to filter out the alien gas. Behind him, Progenitor coughed and racked, unable to call again.

Mat's hands gripped the warm stone spasmodically – and did not act. Suppose, somehow, Phoebus had lost his strength; suppose the light only angered the monster . . .

Twenty-five feet: Phog loomed, as tall as the distance between them, curling up into a deadly hood. Phoebus was far far away, beyond help – except for the caged beam. Somewhere inside the awful shroud, uncaged, the insatiable Runner slavered. If the weapon failed –

Mat acted. Hands now fumblingly eager lifted free the fibre shield. Suddenly there was a brightness; a coruscating beam stabbed out and struck the ground ahead. It was a ray of the sun, blinding in the gloom, harnessed by tireless labour during Mat's last foot of growth.

He took hold of the balanced stone, tilting it up. The beam followed, reflecting from the polished surface and marching along the ground, up and into Phog itself. Now –

Phog sizzled and folded into itself, trying to escape that burning light. But the darting lance played over its surface, vaporizing the rank mists wherever it touched.

To one side and the other Phog continued its advance;

but before that implacable shaft it retreated, wounded, dribbling dismal white droplets. It was unable to attack.

'It works!' Progenitor cried. 'We have defeated Phog!'

Mat answered him with a smile, allowing the old man his share of pride. Victory was sweet indeed.

The light failed.

Phog rolled back, facelessly gloating. Feverishly Mat cast about, seeking the malfunction, but there was none. The reflectors were in order, yet the beam was not coming in.

He looked up to see Phog fifteen feet distant, offering a putrescent embrace. Within it – were there malevolent eyes?

The beam snapped on. Phog recoiled furiously. Had the phantom shape within been singed? He kept the light fixed on one spot, drilling a hole in the wall before him, while his mind pondered the meaning of that brief cessation. Would it happen again?

The malodorous veil crept up around the beam, leaving a harmless tunnel. Phog was accommodating itself. Quickly he switched the light to another place.

The glow died. Phog sucked together and reached for him. Fifteen feet . . .

'Someone is cutting off the relay!' Progenitor cried.

Of course! The tribesmen knew nothing of the careful mechanisms spanning the plain. They would be out searching for food, wandering carelessly between the pylons, intercepting the invisible channel of light.

Anger flushed Mat's face. He had held Phog at bay, had tasted victory over the killer of men – only to be defeated by other people's ignorance. The beam flicked on and off again, as though to flaunt his impotence, and Phog crept up to a hungry ten feet.

'We must go,' he called, forgetting the deference due

his ancestor. But at the lip of Phog there was no time to stand on ceremony. They ran.

The banks of solid mist were far beyond their position. They were at the nadir of a deep cleft, carved by the light. Phog threatened momentarily to fill in from the sides, capturing them. Even as he ran, Mat made a mental note to provide for the protection of his flank, perhaps with additional relays, if he escaped this time.

Progenitor was puffing hugely, blowing out his white whiskers as he ran. Mat saw that the oldster could not maintain the pace for long. Yet there was no effective or honourable way to assist him; he *was* the grandfather. If only the beam were reliable, they could make a stand –

Phoebus returned, overhead, and suddenly they were safe. What determined the comings and goings of the high wisps that shrouded it and let Phog come? He would have to study this –

Progenitor collapsed by a relay, exhausted. In the distance Mat observed the tribesmen returning, meandering along the line of relays. Rage blotted his sight for an instant; then he began to think.

When the people arrived there was a pile of stones beside the pylon, buttressing the path of the beam but not interfering with it. 'Cross here,' Mat told the incurious people. 'Climb up the rocks, so; then jump over to the other side and step down.'

They looked at him and at the steps transcending empty sand, uncomprehending. 'Phoebus is here,' he explained. 'We must keep it safe, to battle Phog.' But he saw that he was making no impression. They knew nothing about his beam of light, or the principles of reflection he had devised to control it. They had no interest in anything except hunger and immediate danger and occasional ancestry of infants. Not one of them would consider standing up to the awesome enemy. Docile and timid, they had abdicated the courage and intelligence of Man. Progenitor had warned him of this.

Mat picked up a ragged stone. 'If anyone fails to use the steps,' he said, 'I will smash this against his head.'

The nearest man looked at him. The man was larger than he and older. Mat's bravado deserted him. He did not want to fight; he longed to drop his weapon and flee – as he had from Phog. He was one of the Tribe; he had no courage. If the man crossed the beam . . .

A girl was watching him, one he had not noticed before. Something about her bothered him; she seemed familiar. Then it came to him; she was the age his sister would have been.

Shame overcame his dread. The ghost of Sal mocked him in this girl's eyes. Not again would his cowardice sacrifice her body to the Runner. Not again would the bloodless bones rise to haunt his memory.

Mat hefted the stone with new purpose. He pointed to the crude stile surmounting the path of the beam. Apprehensively, the man obeyed.

After that, so did the others. It was plain that they did not understand the ritual of treading over nothing; but they gave way to his greater determination. They did the easy thing; they backed down in the face of a threat, as always.

Never again would he be like them.

Last to navigate the stile was the girl. 'You're so brave,' she said, smiling at him. 'My name is Jul.'

Three relays marched across the land to converge upon the battlefield of shining stones. The plain was pocked with the marks of their excavation, for the rocky formation had tilted deep into the earth, as though to hide its splendour. Many tribesmen had laboured under Mat's direction to bring up the flat slabs and cleave them apart to reveal the brightness inside; many fingers of growth had passed while they rubbed and rubbed to accentuate that shine with fine fibres and make the surfaces ready for Phoebus.

Two mighty structures stood at the terminus, each as high as a man could reach. Each comprised two columns bearing a great stone crosspiece, and the two arches faced each other to form a two-sided cube visible for many thousands of feet. Each column was fashioned from highly glossed stones tilted this way and that, and above the crosspieces were perched more polished fragments.

High mists shrouded the sun. 'Phog will come,' Progenitor said, excited. He was feeble now, too old to forage for himself. He would have died some time ago, had Mat not made the tribesmen bring him food. But the man's advice was valuable; only he and one other really understood what Mat was trying to do.

Abruptly he lifted the protectors from the two relay boxes near him. Immediately the bright light leapt forth, illuminating the spaces between the columns and forming a glowing cage in the dust. The effect was magical; but Mat well knew that the shafts of Phoebus travelled from stone to stone in fixed pattern, and would go astray if even a single reflector were out of place. Many times had he gone hungry while he struggled with the balance, tapping the surfaces into place, only to have others jarred out of position. The final adjustment had been interminable – but the cage was ready.

'Phog!' Progenitor announced, shivering. Increasing age had not added to his courage. He watched the distant bank with familiar horror.

Mat dropped the curtain on the relay to his right, and

the four shimmering walls blinked out. He doused the left, and the fainter bars forming a roof between the crosspieces vanished. Somehow the cage did not show up well unless there was much dust, and the dust was low, usually. But the test had been successful. 'Place the bait,' he said.

His attention was distracted by an approaching figure, while the old man struggled with the carrion. Jul was running towards them, her dark hair flying back in pretty tangles as she bounced. She had matured considerably.

Mat turned away, keeping his attention on Phog. Progenitor dragged the meat to the centre of the cage area and retreated, panting. It was a task he had insisted on doing alone.

Phog approached from one side, Jul from the other. 'Are you going to fight it?' she demanded needlessly.

Mat kept his eyes clear of her beauty. 'Go away,' he said. He knew she would not.

Phog arrived. The stench of it blasted out ahead, sickeningly. It swirled around the stone pillars and smirched the bait, burying it in thick scum. It reached across the gap towards them.

'Not yet,' Mat said tightly.

Phog advanced almost to their station. The three stood, fascinated by it as always, but no longer panicked. They knew the power damned in the relays, as the tribesmen did not; this time they stayed to conquer, not to run.

The menacing bladders distended the filthy surface, no less loathsome for all their insubstantiality. The corrupt froth washed almost at their feet.

'It comes! It comes!' Progenitor shouted.

There was a whirring within; a thump from the direction of the cage. Mat yanked away the curtains.

The fierce beams leapt to the mirrors, slicing through

—

the murky shape immediately. For the first time they saw the actual progress of the light, as it sprang from corner to corner, vaporizing the reluctant mist between and climbing in a quick spiral. In a moment Phog withdrew in agony; but it left a block of its substance behind, snared by the bright enclosure. The trap had been sprung.

The isolated mass hissed and shrank as Mat unveiled the third relay and played its beam upon the interior. 'We have you now, killer of children!' he cried. Eagerly they watched for the exposure of the scabrous monster that had to lurk within.

The cube of filth sagged into amorphous lumps. The choking stink of it filled the air as it puffed into a bubbling residue. At last it was gone, revealing –

The untouched carcass.

'But it was here,' Jul said. 'We heard it.'

Mat stared in confusion. The Runner *had* been present; the spoor was there. But it had not touched the meat.

'It needs live food,' Jul said. 'A – a sacrifice.'

He should have guessed! Furious, Mat looked at the sky. The upper vapours were thinning; Phoebus would return soon, and their chance would be gone.

Too much hung on this encounter. He could not wait for another opportunity. It would be nearly impossible to bring a live animal to the enclosure at the exact moment Phog came, and keep it there untethered. Tied, the animal would jolt the stones, disturbing the delicate alignment necessary for the cage. He had to act now, while the Runner was watching.

Mat picked up the weapon he had fashioned to cow the tribesmen: a long pointed stone fragment. He doused the beams.

Jul clutched his arm as he stepped forward. 'No,' she said. 'The Runner will kill you!'

He shook her off. 'Progenitor – you must unveil the beams. Take care that you release them together, or it will take flight as it did before.'

The ancient looked at him, comprehending what he intended. Phog was already invading the vital spot, forgetful of its recent misery there. Somewhere – was there a whirring?

'No!' Jul cried again, throwing herself before him. 'You are brave, you are a leader. No one else can drive back Phog.'

He set her aside, more gently this time. 'I will kill the Runner if I can,' he said. 'Only living flesh will lure it into the cage. Then – Phoebus will not let it escape.'

Still she clung. 'Not you, not you!' She flung back her head defiantly. 'I have no strength, no courage. This only can I do –'

Phog loomed over them, casting out its wispy tentacles. But for the moment Mat forgot it, discovering almost too late what courage was.

This girl – this lovely woman the age of Sal – was asking to sacrifice herself to the Runner, that he might live. He had shunned her as the reminder of his shame, as the sister he had betrayed by his cowardice, so long ago. Now he looked full into the face he had feared, and found there not a ghost but a vital passion, an encompassing love – for him.

He realized that there would after all be other times; that with patience and intelligence he could snare the Runner without risking human life.

An anguished scream rent the air.

'Progenitor!' He bounded to the control boxes, whipping free the restrictive curtains. The dazzling light speared out once more, forming the enclosure. But there was no further sound from the old man.

As Phog retreated, leaving another cube of itself pinioned in the silvery cage, Mat saw that Progenitor's death had not been in vain. There was a frenzied whirring within the enclosure of light. The Runner had been caught at last.

Not alone had Mat borne his guilt.

The Ghost Galaxies

My original title for this story was 'Ghost'; the editor at *If* retitled it, thereby giving away the conclusion. If you want to know the third worst bane of a writer's life, after Writer's Block and Critics, it is Editors. They tend to come across as ignorant little dictators who try to mess up a piece if they can't find a pretext to reject it outright. (Of course, editors might have something similar to say about writers . . .) The various *Galaxy* Publications, over the years, have been worse than most in this regard. 'Ghost' was a phenomenal effort on my part, requiring several drafts over several years, and mind-bending calculations. Several markets rejected it before *If* took it for a piddling one cent a word and published it in 1966. Unsatisfied, I novelized it – that is, I rewrote it, expanding it into a full novel, *Ghost*, with updated science (the story version is now sadly dated) – and the book publishers bounced it. I finally got an expression of interest from *Dell*, but the editor wanted revision of the opening. He had some good points, so I wrote 17,000 words of new material – whereupon the editor moved to another company, and the novel was rejected, and remains unsold. I'm a slow learner, but episodes like this taught me cynicism. Today I won't even start to write a novel, let alone revise it, unless I have a signed contract and money in hand. And I have this minor bit of advice for editors: if you insist on kicking the writers, don't be surprised when they start kicking *you*.

I

'Eight point eight one,' the pilot's voice counted off over the intercom. Thirty seconds passed. 'Eight point eight two.'

Captain Shetland's eye passed to the hunched man seated across the cabin, then went on to the port. Already the red shift, or something analogous, was distorting the view of space.

What an anachronism, he thought. A direct-vision port on a Faster-Than-Light ship. The *Meg II* was fresh from the construction dock and theoretically designed throughout for FTL travel . . .

'Light speed,' the intercom announced, and the port was void. 'Eight point eight three.'

'Thank you, Johns,' the captain said.

His voice did not reflect the tension he felt.

Shetland had passed the speed of light many times, but never with comfort. FTL was not simply a high velocity. The restrictions of conventional physics could not be set aside with impunity. In the captain's mind were four great dreads, and as he closed his eyes a notebook appeared, with an old-fashioned wire-coil binding. On its cover was a picture of a small and shaggy pony and a single word: PRIVATE. The booklet opened, exposing a lightly ruled sheet, and from offstage appeared an animated pencil, freshly sharpened, tooth marks on the latter end. The pencil twirled and wrote:

THE FOUR DEADLY
DREADS OF CAPTAIN
SHETLAND

1. Beacon, failure of.
2. Drive, malfunction of.
3. Personality, distortion of.
4. Unknown, the.

It pleased him to note, as always, the alphabetical arrangement of the terms, and the entire mental process of itemizing them reassured him. Fears that could be outlined in a notebook lost some of their power. This was good, for their power was great. One of them had taken, after thirty hours, the *Meg I*.

Stop that! he commanded himself. Even his carelessly wandering thoughts were exceedingly dangerous in FTL.

Shetland's gaze returned to the seated man. This was Somnanda, operator of the beacon.

Somnanda sat without motion or expression. His forehead was high, the hair above it dark but sparse. His long ears seemed to be listening intently for something beyond the confines of the cabin, of the ship itself. His eyes, half closed, were a curious, faded grey, their colour suggesting a nictitating membrane. The lips and mouth were more delicate than one would expect in so large a man. Somnanda gave the impression of nobility, almost of sainthood.

On the table before him was a small box with a facsimile of a burning candle above it. Somnanda's unwavering gaze centred upon this light. His two mighty hands rested above the table, blue-ridged veins curling over the raised tendons in back. The fingers touched the surface lightly on either side of the candle.

–

Somnanda moved. His head swivelled gradually, turret-like, to cover Shetland. 'It is well, Captain,' he said, his voice so deep and strong that there almost seemed to be a staccato echo from the walls surrounding them.

Shetland relaxed at last. Behind his eyes the notebook reappeared, reopened. The pencil drew a neat line through Dread No. 1.

The beacon was functioning properly – so far.

When a ship entered FTL, the normal universe existed only tenuously. Relative to that ship, to its crew and many of its instruments, planets and even stars became ghostlike, present but insubstantial. External light and gravity registered only as an indication on a meter. Internally, the laws of physics applied as always; *Meg II* required power for illumination, temperature control, the operation of its instruments and the rapid rotation that provided artificial gravity. But physical communication with Earth – and any electronic or laser-based signal had to be regarded as such – was impossible, because the ship no longer occupied the same specific universe as Earth.

There was complex circuitry embedded in the table beneath Somnanda's tapering fingers. But it was psionic circuitry, incomprehensible to normal science. The actual mechanism of communication was largely in the operator's mind and subject to no tangible verification – aside from the fact that it worked.

The light, a flickering mock candle, was the evidence that the beacon was functioning. It lit the way to Earth. No instrument could retrace the course of the *Meg II* with sufficient accuracy to bring the ship home. Not when the distance travelled was to be measured in megaparsecs. Not when the universe itself was indistinct. Only this steady beacon, this metaphysical elastic connection, could guide them back even to the correct galactic cluster. Only Somnanda.

'Captain.'

Shetland recovered with a start. 'I'm sorry, Somnanda. Was I worrying again?'

The man smiled slowly. 'No, Captain. You were not disturbing the beacon. I wished simply to remind you that your move was due.'

Shetland had forgotten their game of chess. The lonely hours of space made some sort of diversion essential. 'Of course.' He closed his eyes, seeing the checkered board. His king was in check. 'White, 23. King to King two. No pun intended.'

Somnanda nodded. It would be another hour before he replied with his own move, for he, like the captain, was a deliberate man. There was time, and each development was to be savoured, never rushed.

'Somnanda,' he said. The sombre head rose. 'Do you know the purpose of this expedition?'

'The Milky-Way Galaxy is only thirty thousand parsecs in diameter,' Somnanda replied seriously. 'Far too small to test the beacon properly. We are travelling far.'

That should be added to the notebook, Shetland thought. The understatement of the space age. The *Meg II*'s itinerary was to take her, literally, to the edge of the universe. As had that of the first *Meg* . . .

'Captain.'

Why did their conversation lapse so readily?' 'Again, Somnanda?'

'There is an . . . imbalance . . . in the beacon.'

Shetland felt the cold clutch of fear at his stomach. Immediately the candle flickered higher, a yellowish flash.

Fear was the nemesis of the beacon – no error there!

What irony if his own alarm at news of danger to the beacon should extinguish it! He exerted control over his emotions, watched the little flame subside and become even.

This was a temporary measure. Somnanda, a man of polite conservatism, had given clear warning. Something was interfering with the function of the beacon. It was not serious at the moment – but in FTL such things seldom resolved themselves. As the *Meg*'s speed increased, so would the disturbance, until firm action became mandatory.

But what was the source? It had to be a man who either knew or suspected their true mission and was frightened by it. The great majority of the crewmen had not been informed of the special nature of this mission and had no way to learn that the *Meg* was establishing records in FTL.

A notebook reappeared. The pencil turned about, erased the first Dread, wrote it in again without the line through the words. It sketched an arrow leading from it down to No. 3: *Personality, distortion of*. Linked dangers.

The pencil hesitated, then made subheadings under No. 3, leaving a space after each: *A. Somnanda; B. Shetland; C. Johns; D. Beeton*. The captain noted the inversely alphabetized listing and frowned, but let it stand. The pencil returned to the first, paused again, wrote:

A. Somnanda – Most experienced & reliable communicator in space. Steady temper. Personal friend.

Was he allowing friendship to influence him? This could not be afforded. The pencil backtracked, crossed out the last two words.

Still, Somnanda was the least likely of suspects. If he

lost control, there would be no appeal. No one else could maintain the beacon.

B. Shetland – Captain, experienced. Knowledge of danger. Can control emotion.

How can a man judge himself? In the act of writing he had crossed out a word, made a correction: he only *suspected* the various dangers, could not claim full knowledge. Yet his position was unique. He alone had sufficient information to accomplish their mission. He had to exonerate himself or admit failure at the outset. Rationalization?

C. Johns – Pilot (drive mechanic).

The pencil stopped. The record said that Johns was competent, but Shetland had not voyaged with him before. How could he be sure of this man? Or was he allowing himself to be prejudiced because Johns had replaced another friend?

Objectivity was essential. He would have to have a talk with Johns – but not immediately. The man, his schedule informed him, was about to go off duty and would not return until the eighteenth hour. That was convenient for another reason . . . and it was also important not to upset the sleeping schedule. Lack of sleep was one of the surest routes to emotional imbalance.

D. Beeton – Cartographer, apprentice.

The pencil stalled once more. Apprentice. That meant he had never had an assignment in FTL before. Shetland had not even met him. Young, inexperienced and in a position to comprehend both mission and danger. A very likely suspect. But again, the time was not now. Special factors had relevance, and a proper interview was quite possibly essential to the success of the mission.

Shetland turned about and set course for his own cabin. He was not tired, but he intended to sleep.

II

Ship's clock said 19. Shetland entered the pilot's compartment and stood behind the man. 'Johns,' he said.

The pilot jumped to attention. 'Sir.' He was a small, somewhat stout man, whose thin blond hair made his scalp seem prematurely bald. His features were regular except for a slightly receding chin. Shetland knew from the records, which were comprehensive, that Johns was an excellent craftsman, well suited to his job. Shetland knew – and tried to suppress his irrational dislike of the man.

'I see we stand at 19,' he said, sounding inane in his own ears. 'That, of course, is our velocity, in spite of the fact that we schedule the affairs of the ship by that clock. Would you care to translate our speed into something, ah, more specific?'

Johns tried to restrain a patronizing smile. 'As you know, sir, the drive is designed to reflect speed in miles per hour, varying exponentially with the passage of time. Our velocity is indicated by the logarithmic dial of the ship's clock. Thus our present speed, relative to galactic stasis at – '

'Assume that I'm an idiot,' Shetland said.

'Yes, *sir*!' Johns tried again. 'When the clock indicates 1, it means that the ship is travelling at ten raised to the first power, or ten miles per hour. At 2, this is equivalent to ten squared, or a hundred miles per hour. 3 on the clock is a thousand mph, 4 is 10,000 mph, and so on. 9 is already beyond the speed of light.'

'Very good. Why, then, do we call it a "clock"?'

'Because that's what it is, sir. The figure on the dial also represents the time in hours since the drive was cut in. That's the way they engineered it. We have been under way for' – he glanced again at the clock – '19.12 hours, and our present velocity therefore is' – a second pause to manipulate his slide rule, while Shetland smiled inwardly at the conditioning this exposed – 'approximately twenty billion times the speed of light.'

Johns looked up, startled at his own words. 'Twenty bil – !'

'We travel fast,' Shetland said. 'Hardly surprising in view of the purpose of this voyage.'

Johns nodded, dazed. 'Yes. Testing the performance of the drive and shield at the big MPH is a tall order. Takes us right out of the galaxy. And we've just about done it already. 19.283 is one full megaparsec per hour. One MPH. Over three million light-years in a thin sixty minutes . . .'

Shetland frowned, his fingers beating little cadences on the panel below the clock. Somnanda saw the voyage as a test of the beacon; Johns saw it as a test of the drive. What would Beeton see?

The pilot, misunderstanding, launched into another explanation. 'We have to check it out before turning it over to private enterprise. We know so little about the drive and the part of it that we call the shield. Yet it would be impossible to travel in FTL without some kind of protection. Part of the energy of the drive is diverted to form the shield that isolates us from normal space. It's actually an adaptation of the available Cherenkov radiation – '

It was time for the shock. 'Were you assuming that the *Meg II* was going to stop at one MPH?'

Johns' eyes widened. 'We're *not* stopping, sir?'

The intercom came to life. It was Somnanda. 'Captain to the beacon as convenient.'

Shetland nodded to himself. The beacon had flared. Yet it was not conclusive. He himself had made the beacon react when caught offguard. Every man had his moments.

'Does speed frighten you, Johns?'

Johns licked his lips. 'How – how much?'

'Thirty.'

Johns stared at the clock. '*Thirty*? Sir, have you any idea how *fast* that is?' He took refuge in his slide rule. 'We're doing twenty billion times the speed of light now – and that will just about *square* it, Captain.' He shook his head negatively. 'To answer your question, sir – no, I can't be frightened by that. I'm used to big figures, but this doesn't mean anything to me. I can't visualize it. So how can I be frightened? Meanwhile, I know the drive can do it, and I'm game to try.'

Shetland did not agree with the pilot's reasoning: most men *did* fear what they could not visualize. But it seemed that Johns had survived his crisis and come to terms with it. He could not be considered a prime suspect.

Beeton had to be the one. He would go and pick up Somnanda's chess move, then gird himself for the most difficult interview.

'Why thirty?' Johns inquired. ' . . . Sir.'

Because that's where Death awaits us, Shetland thought. 'Orders, Pilot.'

Death orders?

III

Beeton's cabin was typical of what was expected of a young spaceman: the neat military bunk, the foot locker, the shapely pinups on the wall.

Shetland dismissed the pictures immediately. He knew that every man under thirty put them up as a matter of protocol. But after one discounted the window-dressing, a man's room was often a pretty fair indication of his personality.

Nothing. Everything was in order, allowing no personal signs. Beeton was almost too careful to conform. Only one thing showed personality: a chess set on the corner desk, with a game in progress. Even this was no giveaway. Tedium came to everyone in space.

He examined the game with a clinical interest, noting the advantageous position held by Black. This game would soon be over.

Realization struck him. This was no ordinary game. This was a replica of his match with Somnanda, complete to the last move. A game that he had thought existed only in the minds of the two of them. And Somnanda was Black.

'What can I do for you, Captain?' The cartographer had come upon him by surprise.

Beeton was a tall, blond lad. His face had that fresh-out-of-school look: sanguine and unlined, eyes startlingly blue and innocent. But the records placed his age at twenty-four.

'I was admiring your game,' Shetland said.

Beeton had the grace to flush. 'You might call that a spectator sport, sir.'

'As spectator, who would you say had the better position?'

'Well, sir, I'm sure I could win with White.'

The captain smiled faintly. 'You should know that FTL career men are noted for memory, not intelligence, and that they retain few illusions.'

'I'm sorry, sir. I must admit that your defence, while logical from a positional standpoint, is unsound in the present case. But I do admire your ability to play without a board. I could never do that.'

Shetland resisted the flattery, not entirely successfully. He was here to judge, not to be judged, and it was going to be difficult. This boy, the record said, was a virtual genius. 'Perhaps, in time, you will show me how to win with White,' he said. 'It happens that I can see the board and pieces whether or not they are physically present. Just as I can read a book by turning the pages in my memory. Just one of the qualifications of the office.'

Beeton sat on his bunk, not wishing to ask directly the purpose of the captain's visit. Shetland did not enlighten him. 'Going into research after this trip?'

Beeton expressed surprise. 'You know?' Then he smiled ruefully. 'But you've studied the records, of course. Yes. Originally those lectures on celestial mechanics and such bored me. I would sit in the front of the class, my eyes fixed on the little box of rubber bands quivering like worms on the professor's desk, while he gave out with the poop. He used to purse his lips around the word . . . but all that changed. I'm going to settle down, get married.'

'I'm sure Alice is a fine young woman. Yes, our files are thorough.' Fencing, of course – but necessary.

Beeton gave him a curious glance, then made a hint of a shrug.

'Woman,' he said. 'That's the word that comes between "wolverine" and "wombat" in the dictionary.' Shetland opened the big dictionary in his mind and skimmed the page. It was true. 'And I want to assure you, Captain, that megalocarpous specimen on the wall is not Alice.' Shetland riffled through his dictionary again, smiled when he found the word. Beeton was playing games with him, forcing him back.

'Do you know how I met her, Captain? I was sitting in a public library, studying a text on psychology, when I overheard this kind of clip-clop, clip-clop coming up behind me. For a startled moment all I could think of was a horse. You know the sound those primitive animals make when some rich showman takes them across a concrete street, the metal-shod hoofs ringing out like castanets. I couldn't resist turning around in my chair to see what could make that kind of noise in a library. Of course it turned out to be two girls in heels. But that horse was still in my mind, and you know, their feet *did* resemble hoofs in an attractive way. Their legs were clean and supple, rather like those of a thoroughbred.

'I laughed out loud. "Now I know why they call them *fillies*," I said. One of those girls heard that, and she came over to ask me just what I meant. Her tone was severe. That was the first time I had a really good look at her, aside from her ankles. She had on a knitted green dress, form-fitting over an excellent form . . . might as well admit it. I was smitten by her appearance. One thing led to another – '

'So that was Alice.'

'No. Alice was the other girl. I didn't pay any attention

to her that time. She – well, it gets a little complicated. I don't suppose your records cover that sort of thing.'

Shetland got the point. The records were illusory. They told him nothing that would enable him to understand this too clever young man. He was being gently told to mind his own business.

How he wished he could! But Beeton was still the prime suspect, and if there was fear concealed behind that voluble facade, the captain had to know it.

'You've admitted that your early scholastics were not remarkable. What caused you to change?' For here, perhaps, the record did offer a take-off point. The shift had been abrupt, and it had been from indifferent to absolute brilliance. There were personal comments by several instructors: 'Jumps to accurate conclusions.' 'An intuitive thinker; never makes a mistake in theory.' 'Even cheating is not that sharp!'

Beeton's tone was flippant. 'Maybe I was afraid, Captain. Afraid that the ghost of my past would come back to haunt me. These days a degree is not enough; there were too many decades of assembly-line doctorates that degraded the magic. They delve into your records, as well you know. If I had left behind me a reputation for careless work – '

Was the young man still taunting him, showing the flag to the bull? Or was there genuine tension now?

'. . . though that's an unfortunate way to put it,' Beeton was saying. '"Ghost," I mean. I always was afraid of the supernatural. Sometimes I suspect that my whole interest in science was spurred by a lingering fear of ghosts. As though I were trying to shine a light in the dark corners, to prove that nothing nonphysical could possibly hurt me, because there was nothing there. Seems ridiculous now.'

Childhood fears. It did not seem ridiculous to Shetland.

For the *Meg II* at this moment the entire universe had become nonphysical. They were travelling at such a rate that an entire galaxy could be traversed in less than a second, and it made no difference whether the ship passed near or through it. How easy to invoke the sense of unreality, to renew the fierce early terrors.

How easy, too, to play upon the credulity of a meddling captain . . .

'Does the Academy still teach Einstein?' Shetland inquired with a smile.

Beeton smiled too, seeming to relax. 'It still does. But of course it's a mistake to assume that FTL disproves his work. The General Theory never did limit an object to the speed of light. Though I doubt that the old gentleman anticipated – what *is* our present speed?'

Shetland did not miss the nervous throb, the slight terror showing in the tips of the fingers. Beeton knew the time, and he could do conversions. His question seemed like a plea for confirmation – or denial.

He looked at his watch. It said 22.9, drive time. 'Just over a megaparsec per second. Our mission requires high speed.'

Beeton rose to the bait, definitely nervous now. 'It certainly does. This voyage will rewrite the text on celestial cartology. My instruments are recording the placement and pattern of every galaxy and cluster within a billion parsecs of our course – though I must admit that our present velocity makes this seem tiny. It will take many years for the computers back on Earth to assimilate the information we collect in hours. But our journey will be over in ten minutes.'

Shetland could not conceal his astonishment. 'It will?'

'Certainly. It began with the vast primeval explosion

that flung matter and radiation in every direction to populate the vacant space. Then gravity slowed this impetuous expansion and brought the universe into a state of equilibrium two billion light-years in diameter. But when the galaxies formed, the forces of repulsion came into prominence, and expansion resumed. Now five billion years have passed since the beginning, and our universe has grown to a radius of three billion parsecs. In moments we stand at the culmination of it all, our mission is over: the rim.'

To every man his own justification for the voyage, Shetland thought. To every man his own disillusion.

'Not yet,' he said succinctly.

Beeton's innocent eyes focused on him. 'You have to stop, of course. There is no point going beyond the rim of the universe.'

Shetland spoke carefully. 'According to your theory, there should be a cessation of all matter at approximately 23.1 on the clock. I have asked to be alerted the moment such cessation occurs. None has. It is now 23.2 hours. There has been no "rim". We shall not stop.'

Beeton turned pale. His breath came in laboured gasps. His eyes stared unblinkingly at the captain.

The intercom blared out behind Shetland with startling volume. 'Captain to beacon immediately!'

IV

Shetland whirled, paying no more attention to Beeton. He galloped headlong down the corridor, blood pounding in his ears. The shortness of his breath, he knew, was not entirely due to the exertion.

He burst into Somnanda's cabin. And stopped, appalled. The miniature candle, symbol of Earth-contact, was a towering column of fire. Orange light flooded the room, flickering off the walls and illuminating Somnanda's twisted face with demoniac intensity.

Shetland knew instinctively what to do. Terror was destruction to the beacon. He stood there, suppressing every vestige of feeling, quelling his own throbbing pulse with hypnotic waves of peace and security. Members of the crew had fears; these were groundless, based on ignorance. Only the captain had authority to know, and he was not afraid. Not afraid.

Not afraid.

Gradually he extended the oily calm outward. Somnanda was not afraid. No one was afraid. A temporary shock, no more. To be forgotten.

The fearsome colour faded. The column dwindled reluctantly, down, down, until it returned to its normal pinpoint above the table.

Somnanda's countenance relaxed. Apparently a disturbance in the beacon represented physical pain to him. His hands remained above the table, fingers splayed, their backs an angry red. His forehead was shining, and rivulets of perspiration were draining down the side of his neck.

'My strength has been overextended,' Somnanda said, his words slurred, voice pitched too high. 'I can not protect the beacon again. From *that*.'

So formal, even after this, Shetland thought. Yet I must talk to him. As Beeton is to me, so am I to this man of the candle. The tension is within me, and it must come out. And when my brain has translated itself into nervous impulses, and these pulses become the atmospheric vibrations which are meaningful speech sounds, and those sounds have been lost in entropy, then will my problem be over?

'A farmer once lost a sum of money,' Shetland said. 'He suspected a neighbour's boy of having stolen it, but had not proof. So the farmer went and studied the boy as he went about his chores, trying to determine by observation whether he was in fact the culprit. Though the lad performed his duties in the prescribed manner, there did appear to be something surreptitious in his attitude, as though he were trying to conceal guilt. The farmer returned home convinced. Later he discovered the money where he had forgotten it, in his own home. It had never been stolen. He went again to look at the neighbour's boy, but this time the lad had no guilty look about him.'

'The young cartographer looks guilty,' Somnanda said.

'He looks guilty,' Shetland agreed. 'He seemed almost normal until I challenged his evolutionary theory of the universe. Then – this. But I can not condemn a person on such circumstantial evidence. I too, in the last analysis, am afraid.'

Somnanda's brow wrinkled. 'I am not entirely familiar with this theory. Is there something about it that affects the nature of our voyage?'

Shetland smiled inwardly. In Somnanda's view the purpose of this journey was merely to test the beacon. The validity of one theory of the universe or another would have little bearing on that, unless one theory embodied an inherent threat to the beacon. That threat was real enough – but it stemmed from internal problems, not external.

'The evolutionary theory is one of several evolved – again, no pun – to explain the observed state of the universe,' Shetland explained. 'There are numberless clusters of galaxies in view from Earth, each retreating from every other one. The situation can only be explained by postulating a general expansion of the entire cosmos. But the nature of this expansion is open to doubt. This particular theory has all matter originating in a gigantic nucleus five billion years ago. When it exploded – '

'Now I understand,' Somnanda said. 'That would make every galaxy approximately the same age. I had assumed that the more distant ones were older.'

'They may well be,' Shetland said. 'The information we are gathering now may answer that question when we return to Earth. But it is my conjecture that this theory is invalid, because we have already passed the farthest limit the evolutionary universe could have reached, and the pattern has not changed.'

'Would this be reason to frighten the cartographer?'

Shetland paced the floor. 'I don't understand why. That's what holds me back. The elimination of a single theory should be of no more consequence than the elimination of an invalid strategy in the course of a chess game. An inconvenience, certainly. But hardly frightening.'

'Unless the alternative is more dangerous.'

'The obvious alternative at this point would be the "Steady State" theory, which has galaxies continuously forming and being formed outward by the constant appearance of new matter. Since there is no "beginning" the universe is steady in space and time and does not evolve. Individual galaxies, however, *would* evolve, and we should discover old ones as well as new ones. And the universe would be somewhat larger.'

'Larger?'

'Because the evolutionary universe would be in its infancy, limited by the five-billion-year span since the explosion. But the average galaxy will survive for ten times that length of time, and if we assume the expansion to be exponential, the universe could eventually attain a radius of ten thousand teraparsecs, give or take a decimal or two.'

Somnanda digested this. 'One teraparsec is – '

'A million megs. But our drive will take us there in just thirty hours.'

'That would be the size of the steady state universe, since it is not in its . . . infancy?'

'If my conjecture is correct. The cartographer, actually, should understand such things better than I. He is attempting to map the universe.'

'Perhaps he knows something that we do not.'

Shetland paced the floor again. 'He never mentioned steady state. It was as though it didn't exist for him.'

'Possibly he has reason for his fear. This should be ascertained.'

What decision had the captain of the *Meg I* made? Had he waited until thirty hours to question his 'Beeton?' Or had some unthinkable menace consumed his ship at the rim of the steady state cosmos?

The decision of the prior captain had been wrong. How could Shetland improve upon it, in his ignorance?

V

The ship's clock stood at 25 when Beeton entered the beacon room. 'Reporting as directed, sir.'

Shetland was afraid to waste time. He watched the candle as he spoke. 'I believe you are afraid of something,

Beeton, and it is important for me to understand. Such emotion affects the beacon.'

Beeton met him with a steady gaze in which there was not a trace of fear. 'May I speak frankly, sir?'

When a crewman felt it necessary to address that question to the captain, the result was seldom pleasant. 'You are directed to do so.'

'I'd like to rephrase the question,' Beeton said, dropping the 'sir'. He was intelligent and had probably anticipated this session. 'I think I'm afraid of the same thing you are. Will you admit that much?'

'I am afraid of many things. Continue.'

'We fear a very real danger, and it has nothing to do with the beacon. You and I know that there is death waiting for us at the edge of the universe. One ship has already been taken, perhaps others.'

Somnanda looked up but held his peace.

'The important thing to realize is that this was no freak accident. We face the same demise, unless we reverse the drive.'

'No,' Shetland said simply.

Johns poked his head in the entrance. 'Am I interrupting something?' he inquired. 'My assistant took over long enough for me to inquire – '

'You should listen to this,' Beeton said with authority. Somnanda nodded.

Shetland glanced from one to the other. Was there a mute agreement between them? How many were anxious to abort the mission? The situation was uncomfortable.

Johns also seemed to be ill at ease. 'Look, if you want me to go – '

Shetland took command. 'Mr Beeton believes that our course leads to danger. He is about to explain his reason for his request that the *Meg* be reversed prematurely.'

There was silence. Was the beacon flickering more violently than before? Whose tension was responsible? 'Go on, Beeton,' Shetland said firmly.

The cartographer swallowed, a nervous young man now that it had come to the point. The flame *was* brighter. 'You are familiar with the "steady state" cosmos,' he said, jumping, as the record advised, to an accurate conclusion. 'I had expected this theory to be eliminated by our findings. I had – hoped.'

He looked at the increasing flame, then averted his gaze. 'To most people, there is small difference between one concept of the universe and another. After all, it has no discernible effect on our daily lives. But to those of us who voyage into the extraordinary reaches, it becomes a matter of life and death.'

'Say what you mean,' Shetland growled.

'At the centre, where the galaxies are young, we are safe. But at the rim they are old. Beyond the rim – ' He paused in the yellow light. 'Beyond the rim they are dead.'

He looked at each of the others in turn and met only bafflement. 'Don't you see? They have passed on. There is nothing beyond the rim but ghosts, the malignant spirits of once living galaxies.'

Shetland looked at Somnanda, who shook his head negatively. He looked at Johns, whose mouth was hanging open.

'You're crazy!' Johns said.

Beeton jumped up, and the flame leapt with him. 'No, no,' he cried. 'You have to understand. You have to stop the ship before it's too late.'

'The supernatural is no threat to us,' Shetland snapped.

'Captain!' Somnanda's voice was urgent. Shetland

whipped around. The beacon had burst into an inferno, destroying itself.

'Stop the ship!' Beeton screamed. 'The ghost is out there – '

Suddenly Shetland's sidearm was in his hand. The tableau seemed to freeze at the moment: Somnanda in the corner, half standing, agony on his face, sweat shining in the orange glow. Johns, staring at the young cartographer, confusion and incredulity distorting his own features, scalp red under the thin hair. Beeton, standing with one fist in the air, mouth insanely wide, lips pulled back from teeth.

One word from the captain would ease this threat. He had only to agree to stop the ship. To set aside his orders.

Then Beeton was falling, engulfed in a sparkling cloud. The gas from the capsule Shetland had fired was dissipating already: but Beeton would be in a deep coma for at least twelve hours. Far past the crisis point.

'Captain.' Somnanda's voice cut through his reverie, as it always did. 'There is little doubt that the young man's terror was the cause of the disturbance. But it should have abated, had you agreed to reverse the drive.'

The flame was normal. 'I could not do that.'

Johns made a sound. 'You knew how simple it was to stop the trouble – and you cooled him anyway?'

'Yes.'

Johns stared at him with the same expression he had turned on Beeton before. 'Captain – now I'm not so sure Beeton was the crazy one. Maybe he was *right*. You never let him make his point.'

Shetland looked at the unconscious form, so peaceful now. 'If I had verified his suspicion, Pilot, his terror would certainly have extinguished the beacon.'

'Verified his – ' Johns was shocked. 'You admit it! There *is* a ghost out there!'

'Not a ghost. A ship. A ship that ceased contact suddenly. My orders are to investigate. I shall investigate.'

'By heading straight into the same trap?'

'Those are my orders.'

'Orders!' the flame was rising again. 'Captain, I can't agree to that.'

Shetland studied him sourly. '*You* can't agree, Pilot?'

'No, I can't. That ghost will eat us too. We've got to turn back.'

Beside the growing flame, Somnanda's head turned to bear on Johns.

'I see it now,' the pilot said. 'Beeton was right. After the galaxies die, they are ghosts. And they hate the living.'

He looked around, saw the flame. 'Don't you understand? *We must reverse the ship!*'

The flash, the sparkle, the dissipation – and the pilot joined the cartographer.

The flame subsided. Somnanda and Shetland looked at each other.

'Your move, Captain.'

The chess game: Somnanda could think of that at this juncture! 'I only hope my personal situation is better than that of my pieces,' he said. 'I will have to consider my move.'

'Your situation is good,' Somnanda said cryptically.

Shetland hauled the two unconscious men to the side of the cabin. 'I think it best to keep these out of sight of the other crewmen, for the time being,' he said. Then, sensing Somnanda's curiosity: 'It may seem unreasonable to sacrifice two human beings in this fashion, rather than

accede to their rather simple request. But I can delegate
their functions if necessary, while I could neither humour
their fancies nor allow their emotional stress to destroy
the beacon.' Yes, he felt the need to justify himself to
Somnanda and cursed his own frailty.

'You seem unreasonable.' From this man, this was an
observation, not an insult.

'I *am* unreasonable. Sometimes that is the only course
– just as an apparently illogical sacrifice is at times
required in order to win at chess.' The chess analogy kept
running through his mind. Was it valid?

Somnanda waited.

'Extended trips into FTL have been rare, so far,'
Shetland continued. 'Evidence is therefore inconclusive.
But there appears to be a certain . . . distortion in many
personalities as velocity increased. Perhaps it is a side
effect of the drive, or simply an emotional reaction to
isolation from the normal universe. But it is one of my
dreads, and I always watch for it. That's why I'm careful
about revealing my orders prematurely. Individual judgement can not be trusted in FTL. Normal people are apt
to become aware of it. It is futile to point out such
aberrations to the victims. They are, in effect, mental
patients. I think you have seen some of this, now.'

'Yes.'

'The captain is not excluded,' Shetland said, smiling
wearily. 'I have preoccupations and I entertain doubts. I
question the wisdom of this voyage, its apparent expend-
ability, the attitude of certain crewmen, the evidence of
the supernatural. I do not believe, at this moment, in the
beacon – that is, that it represents any valid connection
with Earth. But if it is real, why not the ghost of a
galaxy? I do anticipate extinction at the thirtieth hour –
but I will not reverse the drive.'

'I understand.'

'Because my own judgement is suspect. I can rely on only one thing to be objective: my orders. These were presented to me before the voyage began and were reasonable then; they must be reasonable now. If I desire to modify them, it is because my present insight is biased, not my earlier one. I must therefore uphold what seems unreasonable to me – and I shall.'

VI

The clock read 28.8 hours. One teraparsec per second. Soon the voyage would really be over – one way or another.

Shetland found himself in Beeton's room, looking at the chess set. Why had he come? Because there was a lingering uncertainty as the thirtieth hour approached? Or simple guilt for overriding that uncertainty?

He saw a picture of Alice, smiling for a man she might never see again. Would she be widowed before her marriage, all because a certain captain's orders meant more to him than his common sense?

It was uncanny, the way in which the young man had divined the moves and kept up with a game the captain had never advertised. But this was a private game. He swept the pieces into the box, folded the board. Beneath it was a paper, previously hidden. Shetland picked it up and saw a series of notations. They seemed to represent the strategy of a game in progress. His game?

He applied the notes to the game in his mind. They checked. But the moves were not as he would have made them. They started at the present position, but the style

was radically different. Beeton had said he could win
with White – and these notes, incredibly, proved it.
Beginning with a highly questionable queen sacrifice,
White forged to a forced advantage in the game's thirtieth
move. The series violated many of the tenets of good
positional play – yet, he saw now, was quite valid.

He would not use it, of course; the genius was not
rightfully his. But he would show this interesting lesson
to Somnanda: how independent and bold foresight could
convert a certain loss into victory. Book play was not
always valid.

By the thirtieth move.

Coincidence?

Or a message that his stupidity had prevented Beeton
from delivering? Was it natural to assume that such a
brilliant mind had been mistaken, in the one case that
counted? Or had the cartographer's terrible fear been
based on fact, not fancy – while the distortion merely
prevented him from making himself sufficiently clear?

Had Johns also, finally, responded to the actual message, seen its validity?

Assume, for the sake of argument, that Beeton had
been right. That death did wait at the thirtieth hour. That
the situation was hopeless because the man in charge
refused to deviate from the book, from his orders, no
matter what.

In chess, the answer had been a total revision of
strategy. The book had to be thrown away. In life –

The chessboard image in his mind faded into a figurative map of the universe. Galaxies of the steady state
hurtled outward, born in the centre as pawns, dying of
old age at the rim as kings.

And then, as it were, the pieces came to life. The
pawns were babies, the kings old men. The board, which

was the universe, became a city without buildings. The babies were born spontaneously in the centre and crawled busily in all directions. As they made their way outward they grew into children, and some had bishops' hats and some had horses' heads. Farther out they developed into men and women, and the men were castles and the women queens.

Finally the old kings staggered to the rim to die. The size of this city was governed by the age of the inhabitants. Where they became too old to go out farther, the city ended. Most of them died at fifty moves. The rim was a desolate grave. There was no one to bury the bodies; where they fell, they lay, they rotted, and the white bones guarded the memory of what had been.

Then, incredibly, a child appeared at the rim. By some freak it had by-passed age and entered the domain of death long before its time. A child named 'Meg'.

The ancient bones quivered with rage. No living thing should be allowed to desecrate the mighty graveyard. The angry spirits gathered their forces, concentrated their ghastly energies, opened their ponderous jaws and said:

'Captain! Captain!'

It was Somnanda. Shetland shook himself awake to see the beacon room. The yellow light was rampaging again, and this time he himself was the cause.

'Reverse the drive!' he shouted into the intercom.

Now it was 16.49 – but it was speed, not time. Once more the captain of the *Meg II* stood behind the pilot, pretending that nothing had happened.

'Captain,' Johns said. 'Captain – I want to say something.'

What was there for this man to say? That he resented being gassed, then revived to learn that his assistant had reversed the drive at 29.34, on the orders of that same captain who had shot the pilot down for urging this?

'Captain, I just wanted to apologize. I don't know what came over me. I never lost my head like that before. I don't believe in ghosts. I just – somehow I couldn't – what I mean is, you did the only thing you could do, and I can see that you were right all the time. I'm sorry I forgot.'

Johns was apologizing for his own distortion, now that it had abated with the speed of the ship, and he was able to see it for what it was. A distortion that was not his own fault.

'We were all a little on edge,' Shetland said, discovering that his dislike of the pilot was gone. Was there any point in trying to explain?

16.36. Thirteen hours of deceleration, with the *Meg II* travelling at only a tenth its former speed with every hour that the clock subtracted. And still approaching a rendezvous of terror with fantastic velocity. Twenty-nine hours deceleration would bring it to a halt in space, at almost the exact spot they would have passed in the thirtieth hour of acceleration. The exponential series that was the drive was a remarkable thing.

16.34. Only when they came to a dead halt, relative to their starting point, could they release the drive and apply the chemical manoeuvring rockets, in order to turn the ship around and begin the home journey. Then back, accelerating once more to –

Hell broke loose.

The ship bucked violently, flinging Shetland to the far wall. Shooting pains went through his left shoulder as another upheaval bounced him on the floor. An agonized keening sounded in his ears, and a red fog clouded his brain, seeming to obscure all vision above the horizontal.

Dimly he saw the pilot's legs wrapped around the bolted-down stool; Johns, more alert than his captain, had held his position. There was the smell of burning insulation in the air.

'Cut the drive!' Shetland roared. He tried to stand up, but the heaving room brushed him aside. The clamour of the suit-alert began; the hull had been pierced.

'Captain,' Johns' voice drifted back from a far distance: 'We're in FTL. We can't – '

'CUT THE DRIVE!'

Johns moved his hand, and miraculously the ship was quiet. Shetland lurched to his feet, heedless of the pain.

The alarm had ceased. Someone must have repaired the damage already. That man would get a commendation. Shetland's hands, of their own volition, groped for and found the archaic regulation fire extinguisher, not obsolete after all, as smoke curled up from the panel. Suddenly the unit was blasting noxious foam all over his boots. He turned it, already feeling the biting cold; crystals of ice flew off like broken glass as he tramped towards the control panel.

'Stop, Captain!' Johns cried. 'No need, no need. The power is off.'

Shetland lowered the extinguisher. Now he had time to assess his injuries. Pain, for the moment, was masked; it was there, but the enormity of it would only be felt later. He was surprised to discover no blood. He felt along his left arm, realizing that the trouble with the extinguisher had been due to his one-handed control. The left hand was useless, though there were no breaks.

'Captain.' Why did he always drift into contemplation, even in a crisis? 'Captain – ' the pilot's voice was shocked. 'The instruments are registering!'

'That's what they're for,' Shetland said shortly.

'But we're in FTL!' Johns, so capable in the crisis, was now falling apart. 'The drive is off. The shield is down. Why aren't we dead?'

Shetland had understood the situation the moment the ship bucked. But he was not certain he could explain it to the pilot readily. Johns might have difficulty accepting the truth.

'Do you believe in ghosts?' he inquired.

Johns stiffened. He had already denied superstition. Shetland sympathized; but this was necessary.

'No, sir,' the pilot said.

'Look at your instruments,' Shetland commanded. 'Tell me what's out there.'

Johns looked. 'We're approaching an object of galactic scope at just under the speed of light. Approximate mass – ' He faltered.

'Go on, Pilot.'

'Sir, I think the instrument is broken.'

Shetland replied with deliberate cruelty. 'Do I have to teach you elementary navigation? Where are the warning lights? You know the instrument is not broken.'

'But it can't be – '

'Don't argue. What does it say?'

Johns seemed to shrink inside himself. His lips stretched to form the words his mind rejected. 'It says – it says the galaxy we're approaching has no mass.'

Shetland smiled grimly. 'I ask you again, do you believe in ghosts?'

VII

'Yes, there *is* a ghost,' Shetland said, as the *Meg II*'s hull vibrated to the impact of her chemical propulsion. She was manoeuvring for a position to begin the return voyage.

The four of them were in the beacon room again, watching the steady flame. 'All of us had some hint of the truth,' Shetland said, 'but we were blinded by our separate conceptions of the mission and by our mutual dread of the unknown. We tried to exclude the supernatural – not realizing that when the supernatural is understood, it becomes natural. Cartographer Beeton was closest to it – '

'But I wasn't able to face emotionally what my intellect showed me,' Beeton said. 'The thing is so incredible – '

'I still don't follow you,' Johns protested. 'We're alive, and there's a – a thing out there. I'll admit that much. But nothing in the universe is solid enough to rock a ship in high FTL, and we were at 16.34. That's a light-year per second! But we were battered so badly that a crate of beans broke loose and shoved itself through the hull. Or tried to.' He laughed. 'Wouldn't *that* be an epitaph for a lost ship: torpedoed by a can of beans in FTL!'

'I, too, am perplexed,' Somnanda said. 'I understood that it was certain destruction to drop the shield while in FTL. Solid matter can not exist at a light-year per second.'

'We phased in with the ghost,' Shetland said. 'Beeton, things are clearer. Finish your explanation.'

Beeton plunged in happily. 'As I was trying to say at an earlier occasion, but somehow couldn't quite put into sensible words: At the centre of things, a galaxy is young. But in the course of fifty billion years or so it ages, and like an aging man it changes. For one thing, it puts on weight, becomes sluggish. A galaxy in its late prime is an unbelievably massive thing – so dense that its surface gravity prevents its own light from escaping. Within it, nevertheless, breakdown continues, and the prisoned energies – well, we have had no experience with such a state.

'Eventually all matter is gone – but there is still no escape for that phenomenal complex of energy. We are left with a galaxy whose material portion has passed away, but which still exists as an entity. A ghost.'

'The ghost of a galaxy!' Johns said. 'But that shouldn't affect – '

'You forget that the ghost is moving,' Shetland said. 'That un-galaxy is travelling at rim-velocity: 16.04, ship's clock. Since there is no other – '

'Which means *it* determines stasis for this area of space!' Johns exclaimed. 'Velocity is meaningless in the void. It has to be relative to some mass, or – '

'Or some ghost,' Beeton put in. 'Apparently our laws of physics change, here. We've discovered a lot more than a galaxy.'

'So we decelerated to within light speed of the ghost, and the shield came down automatically, and left us in normal space. Even at the fringe, those energies were over-loading the drive – ' Johns paused. 'But what would have happened if we had landed *inside* the ghost?'

'Or even travelled through it in FTL,' Somnanda said.

Shetland considered. 'I suspect the nature of space itself is altered within the ghost. The *Meg I* did unwittingly enter it . . .'

There was silence as the implication sank in. Was this the final evidence that man was limited after all, in spite of his limitless ambition? Hemmed in by numberless and deadly ghosts . . . or was their very existence a new challenge, greater than any before? What would the first explorers find, when they parked their fleet and penetrated, carefully, the fringe of that monster?

'Captain.'

Shetland looked up. 'Your move, Captain.'

Within the Cloud

This is another retitling, showing the editor's ignorance. My title was 'Cloud', and the fantasy is about a cloud and its foggy sense of humour. It's a minor effort – so naturally this was the first of my 'unrejected' sales. That's right – it sold the first time out, for a healthy three cents a word, and represents my only appearance in *Galaxy*, supposedly a science fiction magazine. (By this time *Galaxy* Publications also owned *If*, which had become a sloppier magazine that paid lower rates.) Probably if the editor had understood the story, he would have rejected it. Who was this editor? Such ilk need not be anonymous! He was Fred Pohl, who as a writer is one of the best in the genre. I think he's a great writer and a great guy personally; I just am no particular fan of his mode of editing, about which I will have more to say in due course. It's a Jekyll/Hyde thing, I think; I doubt that Pohl-as-Writer would stand for Pohl-as-Editor on his own material; if he did, it would suffer. But perhaps the man should be allowed to speak for himself; read his fascinating memoir, *The Way the Future Was* (Del Rey: 1978).

'Believe me, this is not a joke,' the portly tourist said. He was careful to face the man as he spoke.

'We think you can help us, and my wife won't give me any peace until – Anyway, all you have to do is look at a few seconds of film. Twenty dollars for your trouble, even if you can't make anything of it.'

–

The man nodded. He led the way to an empty classroom and set up a projector and screen, while the woman waited anxiously.

The projector started and stopped. The man grunted and unscrewed the lamp, showing them that it had blown. He signalled them to remain and stepped into the hall.

'This is eerie,' the woman said. She was perhaps ten years younger than her husband, quite pretty, but temperamental. 'Who would have thought we'd wind up visiting a school for deaf-mutes on our vacation!'

'Well, you started it,' the tourist said. 'You and that hyperactive imagination.'

'*I* started it!' she exclaimed indignantly.

'Don't you remember? That afternoon on the beach. All I wanted was to get some tan on my back, but you kept chattering about clouds – '

'I like clouds,' she said. 'They're so free, and they take so many shapes. No one tells them what to do; no one grouches at them.' She nudged her husband playfully. 'If I were a Confucian, I'd reincarnate as a cloud, and – '

'Buddhist.'

'Anyway, I'd be a cloud and just float along without a care in the world, free free free free!'

'The Buddhists and Hindus believe in reincarnation,' he said, 'but I'm not sure a cloud was their idea of Nirvana.'

'Free free free free!' she repeated. 'Why are you always so serious? You have no sense of humour at all.'

'You wouldn't appreciate my humour,' he said.

'Now look at that cloud right over us. See – it's almost like a face, looking down at us.' She nudged him.

He rolled over in the warm sand, squinting up.

'See,' she repeated urgently. 'Two ears at the sides, two sorrowful dark eyes, a long thundersome nose – '

' – and a big, ugly, voluminous, gassy mouth,' he agreed irritably. 'Wide open.'

'Half open.'

'You talk more than you look. That's a perfect "O".'

She studied the cloud more carefully. 'Well it *was* half open. If you'd looked when I told you the first time.'

'Uh-huh.' He squeezed her tanned knee comfortably and closed his eyes.

'Now it's shut again.'

He rolled over, not looking. 'Why don't you make up your – '

'No, really. It opened and closed. I'm sure. Well, I think.'

'Yep.'

'Now it's opening again.'

'Is it winking, too?'

'Now you're being – '

'A kind of cosmic Peeping Tom, staring down your bikini.'

She shut up, hurt.

He reached out, but she slid out of reach. 'Aw, now, I'm sorry. I *said* you wouldn't appreciate my – I'm *sorry*. Look, I'll go get my time-delay camera and make a series for you. Then there'll be no question.'

She was magically within reach again. In a little while he lumbered up, shook off loose sand and headed for the car to fetch the camera.

The mute returned with a fresh bulb and set the film in motion. There were a few ordinary flashes of the beach and waves and the controversial bikini; then the series on the cloud. Focus and resolution were excellent; the tourist knew how to use his camera.

The sequence itself was brief. Fifteen minutes had been reduced to five seconds, but this too had been expertly handled. The cloud was revealed as an animated, expressive face, its mouth opening and closing in apparent speech. All that was missing was the sound.

'You see?' she said. 'You see, you see – that cloud was speaking to me! Maybe it's a new form of life, like the Saucers – '

'UFO's.'

' – or something. Maybe we just never knew where to look for it before.'

'A *cloud*? A common cumulus humilis!' They had obviously been over this many times.

'Maybe it's an alien observer telling us the secrets of the universe!' She could not sit still.

'In faultless English with a slight Boston accent,' the tourist growled, but his wife missed the irony. He turned to the mute. 'Here is your money. What did you make of it?'

The man looked at him steadily with an indefinable expression, then handed him the rewound film and a written note.

'This is what it said?' the tourist demanded, not looking at the paper. 'You read the lips? You're sure?'

The mute nodded once emphatically, then smiled briefly and stepped into the hall.

The girl snatched the paper and unfolded it with trembling hands. Then wrath overcame her prettiness. She crumpled the note, threw it down, and stalked out.

The tourist retrieved the paper, spread it out and read

it at a glance. His belly shook and his cheeks puffed out
with suppressed laughter.

'I *like* that alien!' he murmured. 'I suppose our dialogue
is pretty funny, from that elevation.' Then he too threw
the paper aside and followed his wife, smiling.

'Free free free free!' he mimicked and choked over his
mirth again.

The paper remained on the floor, its six printed words
revealing more about clouds than the meteorologists
would ever comprehend:

HELP! I AM BEING HELD PRISONER –

The Life of the Stripe

Only twice have I drawn on my two years military experience: here, and for my science fiction novel *Mercenary*. This fun-fantasy was rejected by *F&SF, Playboy, Saturday Evening Post, Redbook, Rogue, Cosmopolitan* and *Knight* before being published in *Amazing* in 1969. No great revelations or significance here, just a look at a phenomenon I noted along the way. I didn't like the Army; they refused to grant me my 'leave' time (an illegal refusal, I believe) because they said I was too valuable as a survey instructor and math teacher to spare – then booted me from the job when my refusal to 'volunteer' to sign up for their US Bond programme – at 2.5% interest – prevented the unit from having 100% participation in that coercive programme. Thus I was set to weed-pulling duty and the like, and limited to the rank of PFC for the duration of my two-year hitch. But this is the nature of the Army, as anyone who has served will verify. When there is trouble abroad, they call on the Marines, not the Army, to handle it. That does make sense.

Let's just say that he was a victim of circumstance. In one way, the court-martial that stripped him of his rank was merciful, but it was also easy for us to understand his anger and humiliation. One day he was M/Sgt Morton, twenty-two year veteran of the artillery; then –

You have to understand too that it was an exceedingly tight market for stripes. For six months there hadn't been a promotion in the battery, and a good thirty men were long overdue. With the Brushfire sucking up all the quota for overseas, and an administrative economy drive Stateside, such units had little opportunity to take proper care of their own.

That's why the BC – the battery commander – arranged to spread it out. He busted Morton in stages. He reduced him one grade and cut the orders for one new mastersergeant. That maintained the ratio, you see, and gave one good man his reward. You know the way it works.

On the second day he reduced Morton another stripe and passed it on, keeping it in the battery, so to speak.

In five days five men had their stripes, and Morton was down to PFC. That's when he cracked.

He stood up in the barracks at midnight and swore no one was going to have his last stripe. 'I'm putting a curse on that stripe!' he screamed. 'It's mine. It's mine!' Then he began throwing brushes and shaving cream and shoe polish from his locker, and the MPs had to haul him away.

It didn't change a thing, of course. We were all sorry for him, but it would have been a criminal waste to throw away that stripe. Morton couldn't keep it anyway, and with twenty-five men still far too long in grade –

The following day the orders came down for private Bruce Baal, henceforth PFC Baal. He was a nice guy nobody resented much, which made it a little easier for the others. The last stripe had been used up, and we expected things to settle down again.

Morton committed suicide.

Baal got nervous after that. Nothing seemed to go right for him. The guard-roster got fouled up and he had to march instead of getting the three-day pass he'd counted on; then some of his gear got misplaced and he was reprimanded for reporting for guard duty out of uniform.

Finally he drew the one post where there was trouble: some civilian broke into the warehouse and Baal didn't catch it. He was a private again, less than a week after promotion.

The stripe went to Radburn. He was a big, hearty, strong lad, not overly bright but quite dependable. He worked in the motor pool.

Somehow the brake slipped on one of the trucks, and it rolled off the grease-ramp and smacked into the motor officer's office. Radburn took the blame.

Keene didn't concern himself about the problems of the prior wearers of the stripe. He had been in six years and had been up to corporal and back twice. His attitude was *laissez-faire*; he figured either he'd be lucky and hold the stripe a few months before he showed up drunk again for duty, or he wouldn't. He lived for nothing but softball, anyway.

He slipped in the latrine and broke his leg. The battery softball team had to face the season without its best man.

It was common knowledge that Keene got drunk next time on purpose. The stripe was developing a reputation, and he didn't want it any more.

Zelig got rolled the day after he made PFC. He lost almost a month's pay and, because he happened to be offpost without a pass at the time, the stripe.

Hartmann was implicated in the loss of some precision equipment in his care. Only after he'd been busted back to private did evidence turn up to clear him.

Fisk got his 'Dear John' from his fiancée three days after taking the stripe. He walked up to the BC during inspection and cussed him out.

Drogo didn't wait. The moment he spied the order promoting him he wrote out a statement requesting an 'undesirable' discharge. He claimed he was queer. The

BC cancelled the order and nothing more was said.
(Drogo was married: four children.)

Suddenly it seemed there was no market for stripes.
Stripes had had lives of their own ever since the grade-
freeze began, but now every man in the battalion knew
this one was cursed. It had to be retired.

About this time the economy drive loosened up a bit –
somebody did a little math and discovered just how much
it cost to train new men to replace the ones resigning –
and a new stripe came down to the battery. This one was
snapped up eagerly.

In only two days it became evident that the Morton
stripe wasn't dead yet. The allocation may have been
new, but the curse remained. It was retired again.

Three more were authorized the following month.
Somewhat apprehensively, the selected men accepted
them. The top name on the order got under a falling
plank and tore his shoulder muscle. He kept the stripe –
and was scalded as soon as he came off sick call by an
exploding coffee-urn in the mess hall. He capitulated.

Suddenly the second man had problems. After the
normal course had been run, the third one got it.

It was apparent that no one was going to hold a
promotion until that stripe was dead.

But how do you kill a stripe?

So long as there were no promotions in the battery, the
stripe was dormant. Fine – but the battery itself was
dying. Requests for transfer piled the BC's desk, and
men in other outfits went to great extremes to avoid
transfer *in*. It was bad for morale; it cast its stigma upon
the entire battalion and was even beginning to embarrass
Post headquarters.

Word came down, couched in formal, almost incomprehensible army terminology, the essence of which was 'or

else!' Something had to be done, for a very important foreign dignitary from a nation something less than cordial was scheduled to tour the post, and this battery was on the itinerary. Change it? That was not the Army Way.

The BC had a bright idea.

And so it was done: the VIP was awarded a Genuine Honorary PFC stripe in token of improving relations between differing ideologies. He departed the battery with every indication of supercilious pleasure.

The accident, occurring as it did at a US Army post, made unfortunate headlines. It did not trigger WWIII, quite, but the BC found it convenient to retire in a hurry. The stripe came home.

This time the word descended upon the *battalion* commander. The essence: 'Do *not* make excuses. Clean it up.' It was not necessary to add the 'or else' this time, for I am the battalion commander, and I have just about time to make Light Colonel before retirement. I'm not stupid, as majors go.

That, gentlemen, is why you see me out here in the rain, in the military cemetery, personally supervising this posthumous and somewhat irregular ceremony. I mean to be quite certain Private Morton knows, wherever he may dwell, that he is henceforth *PFC* Morton. I'm attaching the order to his headstone.

No one else has his stripe any more.

Any other questions?

In the Jaws of Danger

And yet another retitling by that bug-eyed-monster at *If*. My title was 'The Value of a Man'. This story is the second in the series that I later assembled into a novel, *Prostho Plus*, published by Berkley and promptly allowed to go out of print. *If* rejected the first story, accepted the second, rejected the third and fourth, and accepted the fifth, sixth, seventh and eighth. The first was published by *Analog*, which bounced the fifth. I worked up three more stories, starting the *Prostho Minus* series, but no publisher was interested despite the popularity of the first series. It's a headache, trying to make sense of editors. Actually, I harbour the deep suspicion that there is something fundamentally wrong with any editor who rejects anything of mine; I am in that respect a completely typical writer. For now I'll just say that this series started when I had to have $2300 worth of prosthodontistry done on my teeth. That was a third of my annual income then, so I realized I had better make it pay. So I turned most of the work done on my mouth into fiction – and there was a lot of it, because defective cement meant that most of it had to be done a second time, to my pain and the prosthodontist's expense. 'Value' – trust an editor to call it 'Jaws'! – here, is a simple filling – on a slightly larger scale than is normally the case. For people who ask me where I get my ideas, I can honestly say: from the dentist's chair. In the end, *Prostho Plus* earned me over $5000, handily covering the cost of my treatment. It also should have proved at last to doubting editors that I could handle humour. But they went right on rejecting my humour, carefully explaining to me that it required a delicate touch that I lacked, until I got into the Xanth series and made my fortune in humour. Editors are very slow learners.

One other note about the editing: in this story I had reference to the High Muck-de-Muck of Gleep, obviously a very important personage. The editor diddled in my text as was his wont and changed it to muck-a-muck. Now I feel that it is the author's prerogative to name the characters in his fantastic fiction, and to spell those names as he deems fit. But it seems this editor knew more of Dr Dillingham's galaxy than I did, so he corrected my spelling. (Thank God he didn't edit 'Phog'!) So I stand corrected; what I thought was 'de' was 'a'. I'll keep that in mind next time I refer to those esteemed authors L. Sprague a Camp and Miriam Allen aFord, and will make sure my next piece is a real *tour-a-force*.

And a note on gold: bear in mind that this story was written and published in 1967. The price of gold was then $35 an ounce. Just move the decimal right a place or two, and it'll be current.

I

The Enen – for Dr Dillingham preferred the acronym to 'North Nebula humanoid species' – rushed in and chewed out a message-stick with machinelike dispatch. He handed it to Dillingham and stood by anxiously.

The dentist popped it into the hopper of the transcoder. 'Emergency,' the little speaker said. 'Only you can handle this, Doctor!'

'You'll have to be more specific, Holmes,' he said and watched the transcoder type this on to another stick. Since the Enens had no spoken language and he had not learned to decipher their tooth-dents, the transcoder was the vital link in communication.

The names he applied to the Enens were facetious. These galactics had no names in their own language, and they comprehended his humour in this regard no more than had his patients back on distant Earth. But at least they were industrious folk and very clever at physical science.

The Enen read the stick and put it between his teeth for a hurried footnote. It was amazing, Dillingham thought, how effectively they could flex their jaws for minute variations in depth and slant. Compared to this, the human jaw was a clumsy portcullis.

The message went back to the machine. 'It's a big toothache that no one can cure. You must come.'

'Oh, come now, Watson,' Dillingham said, deeply flattered. 'I've been training your dentists for six months now, and I must admit they're experienced and intelligent specialists. They know their maxillaries from their mandibulars. As a matter of fact, some of them are a good deal more adept than I, except in the specific area of metallic restorations. Surely – '

But the Enen grabbed the stick before any more could be imprinted by the machine's clattering jaws. 'Doctor – this is an *alien*. It's the son of the high muckamuck of Gleep.' The terms, of course, were the ones he had programmed to indicate any ruling dignitary of any other planet. He wondered whether he would be well advised to substitute more serious designations before someone caught on. Tomorrow, perhaps, he would see about it. 'You, Doctor, are our only practising exodontist.'

Ah – now it was becoming clear. He was a stranger from a far planet – and a dentist. Ergo, he must know all about off-world dentition. The Enen's faith was touching. Well, if this was a job they could not handle, he could at least take a look at it. The 'alien' could hardly have stranger dentition than the Enens themselves, and success might represent a handsome credit towards his eventual freedom. It would certainly be more challenging than drilling his afternoon class in Applications of Supercolloid.

'I'm pretty busy with that new group of trainees,' he said. This was merely a dodge to elicit more information, since the Enens tended to omit important details. They did not do so intentionally; it was just that their notions of importance differed here and there from his own.

'The muckamuck has offered fifty pounds of frumpstiggle for this one service,' the Enen replied.

Dillingham whistled, and the transcoder dutifully printed the translation. Frumpstiggle was neither money nor merchandise. He had never been able to pin down exactly what it *was*, but for convenience thought of it as worth its exact weight in gold: $35 per ounce, $560 per pound. The Enens did not employ money as such, but their avid barter for frumpstiggle seemed roughly equivalent. His commission on fifty pounds would amount to a handsome dividend and would bring his return to Earth that much closer.

'All right,' he said. 'Bring the patient in.'

The Enen became agitated. 'The high muckamuck's family can't leave the planet. You must go to Gleep.'

He had half expected something of this sort. The Enens gallivanted from planet to planet and system to system with dismaying nonchalance. Dillingham had not yet become accustomed to the several ways in which they far excelled Earth technology, or to the abrupt manner of their transactions. One of their captains (strictly speaking, they didn't have officers, but this was a minor matter) had required dental help and simply stopped off at the nearest inhabited planet, skipping the normal formalities, and visited a local practitioner. Realizing that local technique was in some respects superior to that of the home planet, the captain had brought the practitioner along.

Thus Dillingham had found himself the property of the Enens – he who had never dreamed of anything other than conventional retirement in Florida. He was no intrepid spaceman, no seeker of fortune. He had been treated well enough, and certainly the Enens respected his abilities more than had his patients on Earth; but galactic intercourse was more unsettling than exciting for a man of his maturity.

'I'll go and pack my bag,' he said.

II

Gleep turned out to be a water world. The ship splashed down beside a floating waystation, and they were transferred to a tanklike amphibious vehicle. It rolled into the ocean and paddled along somewhat below the surface.

Dillingham had read somewhere that intelligent life could not evolve in water because of the inhibiting effect of the liquid medium upon the motion of specialized appendages. Certainly the fish of Earth had never amounted to much. How could primitive swimmers hope to engage in interstellar commerce?

Evidently that particular theory was wrong, elsewhere in the galaxy. Still, he wondered just how the Gleeps had circumvented the rapid-motion barrier. Did they live in domes *under* the ocean?

He hoped the patient would not prove to be too alien. Presumably it had teeth; but that might very well be the least of the problems. At any rate, he could draw on whatever knowledge the Enens had, and he had also made sure to bring a second transcoder keyed to Gleep. It was awkward to carry two machines, but too much could be lost in retranslation if he had to get the Gleep complaints relayed through the Enens.

A monstrous whale-shape loomed in the porthole. The thing spied the sub, advanced, and opened a cavernous maw. 'Look out!' he yelled, wishing the driver had ears.

The Enen glanced indifferently at the message-stick and chomped a casual reply. 'Everything is in order, Doctor.'

'But a leviathan is about to engulf us!'

'Naturally. That's a Gleep.'

Dillingham stared out the port, stunned. No wonder the citizens couldn't leave the planet! It was a matter of physics, not convention.

The vessel was already inside the colossal mouth, and the jaws were closing. 'You mean – you mean this is the *patient*?' But he already had his answer. Damn those little details the Enens forgot to mention. A whale!

The mouth was shut now, and the headlight of the sub speared out to reveal encompassing mountains of flexing flesh. The treads touched land – probably the tongue – and took hold. A minute's climb brought them into a great domed air chamber.

They came to a halt beside what reminded him of the White Cliffs of Dover. The hatch sprang open, and the

Enens piled out. None of them seemed concerned about
the possibility that the creature might involuntarily swallow, so Dillingham put that thought as far from his mind
as he was able. His skull seemed determined to hold it in,
unfortunately.

'This is the tooth,' the Enen's message said. The driver
pointed to a solid marble boulder.

Dillingham contemplated it. The tooth stood about
twelve feet high, counting only the distance it projected
from the spongy gingival tissue. Much more would be
below, of course.

'I see,' he said. He could think of nothing more
pertinent at the moment. He looked at the bag in his
hand, which contained an assortment of needle-pointed
probes, several ounces of instant amalgam, and sundry
additional staples. In the sub was a portable drill with a
heavy-duty needle attachment that could easily excavate
a cavity a full inch deep.

Well, they *had* called it a 'big toothache'. He just
hadn't been alert.

They brought forth a light extensible ladder and leaned
it against the tooth. They set his drills and transcoders
beside it. 'Summon us when you're finished,' their parting
message said.

Dillingham felt automatically for the electronic signal
in his pocket. By the time he drew breath to protest, the
amphibian was gone.

He was alone in the mouth of a monster.

Well, he'd been in awkward situations before. He tried
once again to close his mind to the horrors that lurked
about him and ascended the ladder, holding his lantern
aloft.

The occlusive surface was about ten feet in diameter. It

was slightly concave and worn smooth. In the centre was a dark trench about two feet wide and over a yard long. This was obviously the source of the irritation.

He walked over to it and looked down. A putrid stench sent him gasping back. Yes – this was the cavity. It seemed to range from a foot in depth at the edges to four feet in the centre.

'That,' he said aloud, 'is a case of dental caries for the record book.'

Unfortunately, he had no record book. All he possessed was a useless bag of implements and a smarting nose. But there was nothing for it but to explore the magnitude of the decay. It probably extended laterally within the pulp, so that the total infected area was considerably larger than that visible from above. He would have to check this directly.

He forced himself to breathe regularly, though his stomach danced in protest. He stepped down into the cavity.

The muck was ankle-deep and the miasma overpowering. He summoned the dregs of his willpower and squatted to poke into the bottom with one finger. Under the slime, the surface was like packed earth. He was probably still inches from the material of the tooth itself; these were merely layers of crushed and spoiling food.

He remembered long-ago jokes about eating apple compote, pronouncing the word with an internal 's'. Compost. It was not a joke any more.

He located a dry area and scuffed it with one foot. Some dark flakes turned up, but no real impression had been made. He wound up and drove his toe into the wall as hard as he could.

There was a thunderous roar. He clapped his hands to

his ears as the air pressure increased explosively. His footing slipped, and he fell into the reeking centre section of the trench.

An avalanche of muck descended upon him. Overhead, hundreds of tons of flesh and bone and gristle crashed down imperiously, seeming ready to crush every particle of matter within its compass into further compost.

The jaws were closing.

Dillingham found himself face down in sickening rubbish, his ears ringing from the atmospheric compression and his body quivering from the mechanical one. The lantern, miraculously, was undamaged and bright, and his own limbs were sound. He sat up, wiped some of the sludge from face and arms and grabbed for the slippery light.

He was trapped between clenched jaws – inside the cavity.

Frantically he activated the signal. After an interminable period while he waited in mortal fear of suffocation, the ponderous upper jaw lifted. He scrambled out, dripping.

The bag of implements was now a thin layer of colour on the surface of the tooth. 'Perfect occlusion,' he murmured professionally, while shaking in violent reaction to the realization that his fall had narrowly saved him from the same fate.

The ladder was gone. Anxious to remove himself from the dangerous biting surface as quickly as possible, he prepared to jump but saw a gigantic mass of tentacles reaching for his portable drill near the base of the tooth. Each tentacle appeared to be thirty feet or more in length and as strong as a python's tail.

The biting surface no longer seemed so dangerous.

Dillingham remained where he was and watched the drill being carried into the darkness of the mouth's centre.

In a few more minutes the amphibian vehicle appeared. The Enen driver emerged, chewed a stick, presented it. Dillingham reached for the transcoder and discovered that it was the wrong one. All he had now was the useless Gleep interpreter.

Chagrined, he fiddled with it. At least he could set it to play back whatever the Gleep prince might have said. Perhaps there had been meaning in that roar . . .

There had been. 'OUCH!' the machine exclaimed.

III

The next few hours were complicated. Dillingham now had to speak to the Enens via the Gleep muckamuck (after the episode in the cavity, he regretted this nomenclature acutely), who had been summoned for a diagnostic conference. This was accomplished by setting up shop in the creature's communications department.

The compartment was actually an offshoot from the Gleep lung, deep inside the body. It was a huge, internal air space with sensitive tentacles bunching from the walls. This was the manner in which the dominant species of this landless planet had developed fast-moving appendages whose manipulation led eventually to tools and intelligence. An entire technology had developed – *inside* the great bodies.

'So you see,' he said, 'I have to have an anaesthetic that will do the job and canned air to breathe while I'm working, and a power drill that will handle up to an eighteen-inch depth of rock. Also a sledgehammer and a dozen wedges. And a derrick and the following quantities of – ' He went on to make a startling list of supplies.

The transcoder sprouted half a dozen tentacles and waved them in a dizzying semaphore. After a moment a group of the wall tentacles waved back. 'It shall be accomplished,' the muckamuck reply came.

Dillingham wondered what visual signal had projected the 'ouch!' back in the patient's mouth. Then it came to him: the tentacles that had absconded with his drill and other transcoder were extensions of the creature's tongue. Naturally they talked.

'One other thing: while you're procuring my equipment, I'd like to see a diagram of the internal structure of your molars.'

'Structure?' The tentacles were agitated.

'The pattern of enamel, dentin, and pulp, or whatever passes for it in your system. A schematic drawing would do nicely. Or a sagittal section showing both the nerves and the bony socket. That tooth is still quite sensitive, which means the nerve is still alive. I wouldn't want to damage it unnecessarily.'

'We have no diagrams.'

Dillingham was shocked. 'Don't you *know* the anatomy of your teeth? How have you repaired them before?'

'We have never had trouble with them before. We have no dentists. That is why we summoned you.'

He paced the floor of the chamber, amazed. How was it possible for such intelligent and powerful creatures to remain so ignorant of matters vital to their well-being? Never had trouble before? That cavity had obviously been festering for many years.

Yet he had faced similar ignorance daily during his Earth practice. 'I'll be working blind, in that case,' he said at last. 'You must understand that while I'll naturally do my best, I cannot guarantee to save the tooth.'

'We understand,' the Gleep muckamuck replied contritely.

Back on the tooth (after a stern warning to Junior to keep those jaws apart no matter how uncomfortable things got), equipped with a face mask, respirator, elbow-length gloves, and hip boots, Dillingham began the hardest labour of his life. It was not intellectually demanding or particularly intricate – just hard. He was vaporizing the festering walls of the cavity with a thirty-pound laser drill, and in half an hour his arms were dead tired.

There *was* lateral extension of the infection. He had to wedge himself into a rotting, diminishing cavern, wielding the beam at arm's length before him. He had to twist the generator sidewise to penetrate every branching side pocket, all the while frankly terrified lest the beam slip and accidentally touch part of his own body. He was playing with fire – a fiery beam that could slice off his arm and puff it into vapour in less than a careless second.

At least, he thought sweatily, he wasn't going to have to use the sledgehammer here. When he ordered the drill, he had expected a mechanical one similar to those pistons used to break up pavement on Earth. To the Gleep, however, a drill was a laser beam. This was indeed far superior to what he had had in mind. Deadly, yes – but real serendipity.

Backbreaking hours later it was done. Sterile walls of dentin lined the cavity on every side. Yet this was only the beginning.

Dillingham, after a short nap right there in the now aseptic cavity, roused himself to make careful measurements. He had to be certain that every alley was widest at the opening and that none were too sharply twisted. Wherever the measurements were unsatisfactory, he drilled away healthy material until the desired configuration had been achieved. He also adjusted the beam for 'polish' and wiped away the rough surfaces.

He signalled the Enen sub and indicated by gestures that it was time for the tank of supercolloid. And resolved that *next* time he went anywhere, he would bring a trunkful of spare transcoders. He had problems enough without translation difficulties. At least he had been able to make clear that they had to send a scout back to the home planet to pick up the bulk supplies.

Supercolloid was a substance developed by the ingenious Enens in response to his exorbitant specifications of several months before. He had once entertained the notion that if he were slightly unreasonable, they would ship him home. Instead they had met the specifications exactly and increased his assessed value, neatly adding years to his term of captivity. He became more careful after that – but the substance remained a prosthodontist's dream.

Supercolloid was a fluid, stored under pressure, that set rapidly when released. It held its shape indefinitely without measurable distortion, yet was as flexible as rubber. It was ideal for difficult impressions, since it could give way while being withdrawn and spring immediately back to the proper shape. This saved time and reduced error. At 1300° Fahrenheit it melted suddenly into the thin, transparent fluid from which it started. This was its most important property.

Dillingham was about to make a very large cast. To begin the complex procedure, he had to fill every crevice of the cavity with colloid. Since the volume of the cleaned cavity came to about forty cubic feet, and supercolloid weighed fifty pounds per cubic foot when set, he required a good two thousand pounds of it, at the very least.

A full ton – to fill a single cavity. 'Think big,' he told himself.

He set up the tank and hauled the long hose into the pit. Once more he crawled headfirst into the lateral expansion, no longer needing the face mask. He aimed the nozzle without fear and squirted the foamy green liquid into the farthest offshoot, making certain that no air spaces remained. He backed off a few feet and filled the other crevices, but left the main section open.

In half an hour the lateral branch had been simplified considerably. It was now a deep, flat crack without offshoots. Dillingham put away the nozzle and crawled in with selected knives and brushes. He cut away projecting colloid, leaving each filling flush with the main crevice wall, and painted purple fixative over each surface.

Satisfied at last, he trotted out the colloid hose again and started the pump. This time he opened the nozzle to full aperture and filled the main crevice, backing away as the foam threatened to engulf him. Soon all of the space was full. He smoothed the green wall facing the main cavity and painted it in the same manner as the offshoots.

Now he was ready for the big one. So far he had used up eight cubic feet of colloid, but the gaping centre pit would require over thirty feet. He removed the nozzle entirely and let the tank heave itself out. The cavity was rapidly being filled.

'Turn it off,' he yelled to the Enen by the pump as green foam bulged gently over the rim. One ton of supercolloid filled the tooth, and he was ready to carve it down and insert the special plastic loop in the centre.

The foam continued to pump. 'I said TURN IT OFF!' he cried again. Then he remembered that he had no transcoder for Enen. They could neither hear him nor comprehend him.

He flipped the hose away from the filling and aimed it over the edge of the tooth. He had no way to cut it off himself, since he had removed the nozzle. There couldn't be much left in the tank.

The rivulet of green coursed over the pink tissues, travelling towards the squidlike tongue. The tentacles reached out, grasping the foam as it solidified. They soon became festooned in green.

Dillingham laughed – but not for long. There was a steamwhistle sigh followed by a violent tremor of the entire jaw. 'I'm going to . . . sneeze,' the Gleep transcoder said, sounding fuzzy.

The colloid was interfering with the articulation of the Gleep's tongue.

A sneeze! Suddenly he realized what that would mean to him and the Enen crew.

'Get under cover!' he shouted to the Enens, again forgetting that they couldn't perceive the warning. But they had already grasped the significance of the tremors and were piling into the sub frantically.

'Hey – wait for me!' But he was too late. The air howled by with the titanic intake of breath. There was a terrible pause.

Dillingham lunged for the mound of colloid and dug his fingers into the almost-solid substance. 'Keep your jaws apart!' he yelled at the Gleep, praying it could still pick up the message. 'KEEP THEM OPEN!'

The sound of a tornado raged out of its throat. He buried his face in green as the hurricane struck, wrenching mercilessly at his body. His arms were wrenched cruelly; his fingers tore through the infirm colloid, slipping . . .

IV

The wind died, leaving him gasping at the edge of the tooth. He had survived it. The jaws had not closed.

He looked up. The upper cuspids hung only ten feet above, visible in the light from the charmed lamp hooked somehow to his foot.

He was past the point of reaction. 'Open, please,' he called in his best operative manner, hoping the transcoder was still in the vicinity, and went to peer over the edge.

There was no sign of the sub. The tank, with its discharging hose, was also gone.

He took a walk across the neighbouring teeth, looking for whatever there was to see. He was appalled at the amount of decalcification and outright decay in evidence. This Gleep child would shortly be in pain again, unless substantial restorative work was done immediately.

But in a shallow cavity – one barely a foot deep – he found the transcoder. 'It's an ill decalcification that bodes nobody good,' he murmured, retrieving it.

The sub reappeared and disgorged its somewhat shaken passengers. Dillingham marched back over the rutted highway and joined them. But the question still nagged his mind: how could the caries he had observed be reconciled with the muckamuck's undoubtedly sincere statement that there had never been dental trouble before? What had changed?

He carved the green surface into an appropriate pattern

and carefully applied his fixative. He was ready for the next step.

Now the derrick was brought up and put in play. Dillingham guided its dangling hook into the eyelet set in the colloid and signalled the Enen operator to lift. The chain went taut; the mass of solidified foam eased grandly out of its socket and hung in the air, an oddly shaped boulder.

He turned his attention to the big crevice-filling. He screwed in a corkscrew eyelet and arranged a pulley so that the derrick could act on it effectively. The purple fixative had prevented the surface of the main impression from attaching to that of the subsidiary one – just as it was also protecting the several smaller branches within.

There was no real trouble. In due course every segment of the impression was marked and laid out in the make-shift laboratory he had set up near the waterlift of the Gleep's mouth. They were ready for one more step.

The tank of prepared investment arrived. This, too, was a special composition. It remained fluid until triggered by a particular electric jolt, whereupon it solidified instantly. Once solid, it could not be affected by anything short of demolition by a sledgehammer.

Dillingham pumped a quantity into a great temporary vat. He attached a plastic handle to the smallest impression, dipped it into the vat, withdrew it entirely covered by white batter and touched the electrode to it. He handed the abruptly solid object to the nearest Enen.

Restorative procedure on Gleep differed somewhat from established Earth technique. All it took was a little human imagination and Enen technology.

The octopus-tongue approached while he worked. It reached for him. 'Get out of here or I'll cram you into

the burnout furnace!' he snapped into the transcoder.
The tongue retreated.

The major section was a problem. It barely fit into the
vat, and a solid foot of it projected over the top. He
finally had the derrick lower it until it bumped bottom,
then raise it a few inches and hold it steady. He passed
out brushes, and he and the Enen crew went to work
slopping the goo over the top and around the suspending
hook.

He touched the electrode to the white monster. The
derrick lifted the mass, letting the empty vat fall free. Yet
another stage was done.

Two ovens were employed for the burnout. Each was
big enough for a man to stand in. They placed the ends
of the plastic rods in special holders and managed to fit
all of the smaller units into one oven, fastening them into
place by means of a heat-resistant framework. The main
chunk sat in the other oven, propped upside-down.

They sealed the ovens and set their thermostats for
2000°. Dillingham lay down in the empty vat and slept.

Three hours later burnout was over. Even supercolloid
took time to melt completely when heated in a fifteen-
hundred-pound mass. But now the green liquid had been
drained into reservoirs and sealed away, while the smaller
quantities of melted plastic were allowed to collect in a
disposal vat. The white investments were hollow shells,
open only where the plastic rods had projected.

The casting was the most spectacular stage. Dillingham
had decided to use gold, though he worried that its high
specific gravity would overbalance the Gleep jaw. It was
impossible under present conditions to arrange for a gold-
plated, matching-density filling, and he was not familiar
enough with other metals to be sure they were adaptable

to his purpose. The expansion coefficient of his investment matched that of gold exactly, for example: anything else would solidify into the wrong size.

Gold, at any rate, was nothing to the muckamuck; his people refined it through their gills, extracting it from the surrounding water on order in any quantity.

The crucible arrived: a self-propelled boilerlike affair. They piled hundred-pound ingots of precise gold alloy into the hopper, while the volcanic innards of the crucible rumbled and belched and melted everything to rich bright liquid.

A line of Enens carried the smaller investments, which were shaped inside exactly like the original impressions, to the spigot and held them with tongs while the fluid fortune poured in. These were carefully deposited in the vat, now filled with cold water.

The last cast, of course, was the colossal vat-shaped one. This was simply propped up under the spigot while the tired crew kept feeding in ingots.

By the time this cast had been poured, twenty-four tons of gold had been used in all.

While the largest chunk was being hauled to the ocean inside the front of the mouth, Dillingham broke open the smaller investments and laid out the casts according to his chart of the cavity. He gave each a minimum of finishing; on so gross a scale, it could hardly make much difference.

The finished casts weighed more than twenty times as much as the original colloid impressions had, and even the smallest ones were distinctly awkward to manoeuvre into place. He marked them, checked off their positions on his chart, and had the Enens ferry them up with the derrick. At the other end, he manhandled each into its proper place, verified its fit and position and withdrew it to paint it with cement. No part of this filling would come loose in action.

Once again the branching cavern lost its projections, this time permanently, as each segment was secured and severed from its projecting sprue. He kept the sprues – the handles of gold, the shape of the original plastic handles – on until the end, because otherwise there would have been no purchase on the weighty casts. He had to have some handle to adjust them.

The derrick lowered the crevice-piece into the cavity. Two Enens pried it in with power crowbars. Dillingham stood by and squirted cement over the mass as it slid reluctantly into the hole.

It was necessary to attach a heavy weight to the derrick-hood and swing it repeatedly against the four-ton cast in order to tamp it in all the way.

At last it was time for the major assembly. Nineteen tons of gold descended slowly into the hole while they dumped quarts of liquid cement into a pool below. The cast touched bottom and settled into place, while the cement bubbled up around the edges and overflowed.

They danced a little jig on top of the filling – just to tamp it in properly, Dillingham told himself, wishing that a fraction of its value in Earth terms could be credited to his purchase-price. The job was over.

V

'A commendable performance,' the high muckamuck said. 'My son is frisking about in his pen like a regular tadpole and eating well.'

Dillingham remembered what he had seen during the walk along the occlusive surfaces. 'I'm afraid he won't be frisking long. In another year or two he'll be feeling half a dozen other caries. Decay is rampant.'

'You mean this will happen again?' The tentacles waved so violently that the transcoder stuttered.

Dillingham decided to take the fish by the tail. 'Are you still trying to tell me that no member of your species has suffered dental caries before this time?'

'Never.'

This still did not make sense. 'Does your son's diet differ in any important respect from yours, or from that of other children?'

'My son is a prince!'

'Meaning he can eat whatever he wants, whether it is good for him or not?'

The Gleep paused. 'He gets so upset if he doesn't have his way. He's only a baby – hardly three centuries old.'

Dillingham was getting used to differing standards. 'Do you feed him delicacies – refined foods?'

'Naturally. Nothing but the best.'

He sighed. 'Muckamuck, my people also had perfect teeth – until they began consuming sweets and overly refined foods. Then dental caries became the most common disease among them. You're going to have to curb your boy's appetite.'

'I couldn't.' He could almost read the agitation of the tentacles without benefit of translation. 'He'd throw a terrible tantrum.'

He had expected this reaction. He'd encountered it many times on Earth. 'In that case, you'd better begin training a crew of dentists. Your son will require constant attention.' .

'But we can't do such work ourselves. We have no suitable appendages, externally.'

'Import some dentists, then. You have no alternative.'

The creature signalled a sigh. 'You make a convincing case.' The tentacles relaxed while it thought. Suddenly they came alive again. 'Enen – it seems we need a permanent technician. Will you sell us this one?'

Dillingham gaped, horrified at the thought of all that rubbish in the patient's jaw. Surely they couldn't –

'Sell him!' the Enen chief replied angrily. Dillingham wondered how he was able to understand the words, then realized that his transcoder was picking up the Gleep signals translated by the other machine. From Enen to Gleep to English, via paired machines. Why hadn't he thought of that before?

'This is a human being,' the Enen continued indignantly. 'A member of an intelligent species dwelling far across the galaxy. He is the only exodontist in this entire sector of space, and a fine upstanding fellow at that. How dare you make such a crass suggestion!'

Bless him! Dillingham had always suspected that his hosts were basically creatures of principle.

'We're prepared to offer a full ton of superlative-grade frumpstiggle . . .' the muckamuck said enticingly.

'A full *ton*?' The enens were aghast. Then, recovering, 'True, the Earthman *has* taught us practically all he knows. We could probably get along without him now . . .'

'Now wait a minute!' Dillingham shouted; but the bargaining continued unabated.

After all – what is the value of a man, compared to frumpstiggle?

Beak by Beak

For a time we had parakeets, starting with Cinnamon, passed along to us by my wife's sister. Naturally our second was Nutmeg, and then Clove, and Ginger, Saffron and Angelica – a pretty spicy flock. We constructed a cage a yard across so they could fly, as they weren't hand-tame and we felt they should have some reasonable freedom. We liked them very well; each bird had his/her personality. Then they started dying – heart-attack, tumour, the same ailments mankind suffers. We could do nothing, and it tore us up. When the last one passed on, after several years, we didn't get any more. So I wrote this story, and my heart is in it though it is all fiction. And the editor changed my spelling of 'parakeet' to 'parrakeet.' Apparently he just assumed my spelling was wrong.

The red bird was perched fetchingly on the mailbox as Humbert ambled out in slippers and tousled iron hair to pick up the morning newspaper. A gust of wind blew the front door open behind him, and a squawk came from inside.

The red visitor perked up. It fluttered across the lawn to cling precariously to the front hedge.

Humbert stopped, the banded paper in one hand. 'Lost, little fellow?' he inquired. 'Why . . . you're no cardinal. You're a parrakeet!'

He peered at it more closely. 'A beautiful, blood-red, male parrakeet. I never saw your like before.'

There was another angry chirp inside. 'My pets don't like the draught,' Humbert explained. 'I'll have to shut this door.'

The red bird hopped to the doorstep and up to the closed screen, fluttering against it and falling back.

'You *are* a tame bird!' he said. He squatted down and held out his hand, but the bird skittered nervously away. He laughed. 'Not *that* tame, I see!'

As he opened the screen the bird hopped forward again. 'You want to come in? Where's your home?' But he held the door open and allowed it to fly into the living room.

His wife bustled in from the kitchen holding a jar of instant coffee. 'Humbert, did you forget the door again? You know Blue doesn't . . .' She froze. 'Humbert – there's a bird in here!'

'Several, Meta,' he said, gently closing the door.

'I mean a wild bird. Look at that colour!'

The red parrakeet flew up to the tall decorative lamp and perched on the shade, looking at her.

'He seemed to want to come in,' Humbert said. 'He's a remarkable specimen, and half tame.'

Her attitude changed immediately. 'What a beautiful bird! I've never seen a parrakeet that colour.'

The bird spied the large cage and flew over to it. The three parrakeets inside spooked, plastering themselves against the sides in mad retreat.

Humbert approached and put his hand to the stranger again. 'Let me have a look at you, Red. I can't put you in with our family without good references. You might have the mites.' But it jumped away from him.

'Check the newspaper,' Meta said. 'Maybe there's an ad for a lost pet. Such a distinctive bird must be valuable.' She disappeared into the bedroom with her coffee.

Humbert eased himself into the easy chair. He had made it a point, since his heart attack, to move slowly and remain unexcited. He spread the paper.

The black headline leapt at him. ALIEN SPACESHIP ORBITS EARTH.

'Meta!' he called.

'Dear, I have to hurry down to the office,' her muffled protestations came back. She was active in numerous volunteer capacities as well as holding a part-time clerical position. She preferred to keep herself occupied, now that their children were married and on their own, even though money was no problem.

Humbert shrugged and did not push the matter. Probably the headline would only upset her. He read through the article, finding the information too scant. The newspaper really knew little more than the fact: a strange ship appeared a thousand miles above Earth, and now hung in an oblique orbit. There were statistics: how many minutes it took to circle the Earth, at what times it would pass over which cities, and so on, but nothing essential. There had been no communications, no threats. Just – observation?

Meta bustled through. She always bustled, never walked. 'Is there any notice?'

He'd forgotten the bird! 'I haven't seen it,' he said.

She was already through the door, and soon he heard the car start up. She would be gone for several hours. He glanced at the red parrakeet, who was on top of the cage again, searching for some way to enter.

'Oh, all right, Red,' he said, smiling. 'I'll introduce you.' He opened the cage door and reached in to catch a bird. There was the usual panicked flutter; for the birds, tame as they were, did not really like to be handled.

He snared one and brought it out. 'Take it easy, Yellow,' he said. Yellow was the youngest and most energetic of their family: a spectacular yellow harlequin with a green underside. He set the bird on top of the cage. 'Yellow, this is our visitor from Outside. Red, this is Yellow.'

Yellow shook out his feathers, stretched one wing, and sneezed. Having suitably expressed his indignation at being handled, he eyed the other bird warily. It was always this way; parrakeets took time to become acquainted.

Humbert reached in for Blue. She was a timid, retiring bird given to nervous starts and loose droppings, but of very pretty hue. In the right light, a green overcast could be seen above the deep blue breast, as though the yellow of her head had diluted the blue. She bit his finger, not hard, and did not struggle as his hand closed over her wings. Sometimes the birds would perch on his finger, but he hadn't really tried to train them. He set Blue down beside Yellow, but she took flight immediately, afraid of the stranger, and came to rest on top of the front curtains. She settled down to preen her wingfeathers.

'Well, that was Blue,' he said apologetically.

He did not try to catch Green, but shooed her out with a wave of his hand. Green was the eldest of the brood and had had more than one owner before. She was a conventional green-bodied, dark-winged female with a neat yellow bib sporting four to six black dots – they kept changing – and she bit viciously when handled. She would come quickly to eat some treat from the hand, however.

'And that's Green,' Humbert said as she flew to displace Blue from the curtain. 'You'll get to know them all in due course.' Green was contentedly chewing the edge of the curtain.

Yellow, seldom cowed very long by anything, was already making the first overture. He strode over to Red and pecked at him. Red sidled away.

'That's the way it is, Red,' Humbert said as he reached into the cage to remove the fouled newspaper on its floor. 'Very important to establish the pecking order – not that much attention is paid to it here.' Yellow was chasing the disgruntled visitor more boldly now. 'Just give him a sharp rap on the beak,' he advised Red. 'You have to assert yourself sometime.'

He put in new paper and filled the treat-cups with oats, installing a fourth cup for the newcomer. He stepped back. 'Soup's on!'

Green, always alert, arrowed across the room, the beat of her wing washing a breeze past his face. She hopped into the cage and mounted to the row of cups. Seed scattered noisily upon the fresh newspaper as she scraped energetically.

Yellow heard the sound and scrambled across the top and down the side of the cage, using both feet and his beak to hold on. Blue, realizing what she was missing, flew in at the same time. They collided at the door, fluttering for balance, and fell inside. In a moment both were upon the feeding perch, while Green chattered angrily in an effort to protect her claim.

'This is what we call "King of the Perch", or maybe "Musical Treat-cups",' Humbert explained to Red, who peered through the wire in some alarm. 'The object is to get a cropful of seed without letting anybody else eat in peace. You'll get the hang of it soon enough.'

He returned to his chair and watched while Green and Yellow, owners of the two end cups, converged on Blue in the middle. None of the three went near the new cup. While Blue's attention was taken up by Yellow, Green pecked her neck from the other side. Blue squawked and flew across the cage.

'They don't mean anything,' he said reassuringly. 'It's just a mealtime game, and there's plenty of ordinary seed available in the main dish in case anyone does go hungry. Watch.'

Sure enough, Blue flew back immediately to the row of cups, the whir of her wings startling Green into flight. Now Yellow and Blue forgot their differences long enough to do some serious seed-scattering, picking up the hard grains and hulling them adeptly in their beaks. Green scrambled up the side of the cage, using both feet and bill as Yellow had done, and recovered her place before her end cup. All three ate contentedly.

'You'll catch on, Red,' he said. 'I'll let you be, now.' The bird didn't seem to hear him.

Humbert went into his study, turned on the radio, and settled down to work on his toothpick models. The artistic constructions he had fashioned from the simplest materials were all around the house; boats and statues and geometric shapes made from slender wooden splinters and drops of cement.

The whir of wings made him look up. 'That you, Yellow?' But it was the newcomer. 'Not ready to mix yet, huh, Red?'

The bird perched upon his toothpick sculture of Meta. 'Oh . . . you want to know what I'm doing? Well, I make things like that bust of my wife you're sitting on. Don't worry – it's strong enough to hold a hundred of your kind. Well, fifty, maybe. But don't mess on it, if you don't mind. Personal dignity, you know.'

He studied the bird more carefully. Its breast and tail feathers were lighter than the back and wings, but still red. Four dark-red dots showed up against the pink throat plumage; otherwise its colouration was nearly uniform. The cere, above the vertical parrakeet bill, was blue, the signal for the male of the species, and this was the only deviation.

'You're a strange one,' he said. 'Not just your colour, but your manner. You aren't tame enough to be handled, yet you're more interested in what I'm doing than in others of your kind. It's almost as if you – '

He stopped as he became aware of the radio news broadcast. '. . . In orbit ten hours without acknowledgement of signals or any apparent effort to communicate with us. Experts are divided on whether it should be considered friendly, indifferent, or hostile. The present assumption is that its purpose is merely observational. However – '

Humbert tuned the words out of his mind. 'It's so hard to trust each other, let alone an unknown quantity. We don't know what that ship is doing in our skies, and probably it doesn't know what to make of us. But I'll bet it isn't much different from any meeting between strangers. You and me, for instance: I've never seen a bird quite like you, and you could be a dangerous alien from some other system for all I know. And you can't afford to trust me, either, because my hand could crush you in a moment. But you see, we get along. In a little while we'll really get to know each other, and then mutual trust will come. Some things just can't be pushed.'

He spread a group of picks on the table and heated his cement. 'You know, Red, I think I'll make a ship – a spaceship like the one in the sky. There's a picture of it in the . . . no! Stay clear of that glue. It's hot, and it gets awfully hard when it *isn't* hot, and they say the fumes can make hallucinations. You dip your bill in that and I'd have to scrape it off with a file. Believe me, Red, you wouldn't like that.'

He rose to fetch the newspaper, and the bird, startled, flew ahead of him into the living room. The three local residents were still inside the cage, though its door was open. Green was braced on one of the ladders, pecking industriously at its plastic rungs, while Yellow was reaching forward surreptitiously to tweak Blue's unguarded tail.

'That's another thing you'll have to learn, Red,' he said, smiling. 'Feather-tweaking. Keep your wings and tail out of range, or you'll wind up with a bent feather. It just isn't parrakeet nature to pass up a good tweak.' He thought about that a moment. 'I hope they don't try to tweak that spaceship before they get to know it well.'

Red did not accompany him to the study this time. The radio had lapsed into popular music. The melody of 'Sipping Cider' was on.

'Hey . . . I remember that one!' Humbert said, pleased. He matched the words with his own off-key accompaniment:

> 'So cheek by cheek and jaw by jaw,
> We both sipped cider through a straw.'

For a little while the years rolled back.

Later he emerged to discover Red inside the cage with the others. Yellow was friendly, but Blue still kept her distance and Green was sleeping on an upper swing, one foot tucked up and head behind a wing. According to the handbook, a sleeping bird never raised a foot and folded back the head simultaneously, but Green evidently didn't read much.

Red cocked an eye at him. 'Right,' Humbert said. '"Stone walls do not a prison make, nor iron bars a cage." That's the way Mr Lovelace put it. Our birds have the run of the house – but a familiar cage is more comfortable than a strange world. I only lock things up at night so nobody can get hurt in the dark.'

Red had been largely accepted by the time Meta came home. Less hurried now, she admired him again. 'He's just what we needed to fill out the set. Four birds, four distinctive colours. But are you sure he doesn't belong to anybody?'

Humbert admitted he'd forgotten to check the paper. It made no difference, as it turned out; there was no notice about any missing red parrakeet, that day or in the ones following. Red was theirs, as long as he chose to stay.

Weeks passed. While Humbert's elaborate spaceship model grew, Red learned every facet of parrakeet existence as locally practised. He splashed seed industriously from both the main feeder and the treat-cups, then descended to the floor of the cage to search out the fallen morsels and swallow bits of gravel. He banged at the plastic toys and threw them about as though they were enemies. He raced up and down the ladders and took flying leaps at the dangling length of clothesline. He tweaked tail feathers, and played tug-of-war with stems of millet. When ushered from the cage during cleaning time, he flew merrily over to Meta's curtains to peck at stray threads.

There were three unusual things about him. The first was his colour; the second his almost-intelligent interest in human affairs; and he was mute. Humbert never heard him chirp or warble. But since Red seemed to be perfectly healthy otherwise, it was not a matter for concern. He was one of the family.

The spaceship remained in orbit, uncommunicative. Humbert remembered that it had appeared the same day Red came, so it was easy to keep track. After a while the matter ceased to make headlines. Humbert wasn't certain why no Earth ship was sent to link with the interstellar visitor and attempt direct contact; something about a deadlocked UN session. It was easier to do nothing, in a democracy, than to agree on any positive course of action. Yet this did not explain why the spaceship made no effort to communicate, either. Surely it had not come all this way just to orbit silently?

Red became friendly with shy Blue. They groomed each other's neck feathers and shared a treat-cup. 'Do you think they would mate, if we set up a nesting box for them?' Meta inquired. 'If that mutation bred true – '

Humbert agreed it was worth a try. He read up on parrakeet nesting procedures, for they had never bred their birds before, and bought a suitable enclosed box. 'Beak by beak, and claw by claw,' he sang to the melody of 'Sipping Cider'.

But tragedy struck before the arrangements were complete.

The birds scrambled in normal fashion for their preferred roosts on the highest swinging perches as Humbert turned out the light. They went everywhere in the day time, but always sought the heights at night.

There was a bump. Alarmed, Humbert turned on the light – and found Blue beating her wings on the floor. Something was wrong: she was unable to fly!

Red came down solicitously, but Blue was not aware of him. She got to her feet and climbed to the lowest perch and clung there, her little body quivering.

–

Meta came to watch. 'What's the matter with Blue?'

'I'm afraid it's a . . . heart attack,' he said. He knew the symptoms too well, and knew that parrakeets, along with men, were subject to such things.

Blue tried to fly back up to the swinging perch, but fell to the floor again. Humbert opened the cage and reached in to pick her up. She struggled, afraid of him, but had no strength to fight. He held her and stroked her neck with a finger, knowing he could not help her.

After a while she became quiet, and he returned her to the cage. He set her on a lower perch, afraid she might fall again, but her feet grasped it securely. He turned out the living-room light, but as an afterthought left the hall light on so that she could see enough to find the top perch, just in case. It would be better if she remained put, but –

There was a flutter. He and Meta could not resist checking – but Blue remained where she was. Red had come down to join her. 'Isn't that sweet,' Meta said.

In the morning Blue was dead. She lay on her back on the bottom of the cage, and her eyes were open and already shrunken. The two others seemed not to notice, but Red hopped about nervously.

'You don't know what to make of it, do you?' Humbert said. He felt unaccustomed tears sting his eyes as he picked up the fragile body.

He inspected Blue carefully, but there was no way to bring her back. He wrapped her tenderly in his handkerchief and took the body into the back yard for burial.

Red came with him. 'We all have to go sometime,' Humbert said as he dug a shallow grave beside a rose bush.

He laid the body in the ground and covered it over. 'I

know how you must feel,' he said to Red on the bush.
'But you did what you could to give her comfort. I'm
sure you made her life brighter, right up to the end. I
think she died knowing she was loved.'

Red flew to the fence and looked at him. Humbert
knew even before the bird took flight again that this was
the end of their acquaintance.

Meta was too upset to go to work that day. She looked
at the cage, suddenly too large for the two birds within,
and turned away, only to look again, perversely hopeful,
a moment later. Humbert turned on the radio and sat
before his toothpick spaceship, the model almost complete, but could not work.

'We interrupt this programme for a special news bulletin,' the radio said urgently. 'The alien spaceship is
gone. Just a few minutes ago – '

Humbert listened, surprised. Just like that? It had left
without ever making contact with Man. All that effort to
come, then a departure as mysterious as the arrival.

He smiled. Perhaps they had been wise to avoid contact
with Earth's officialdom, for that was representative in
name only. Still, in their place he would at least have
sent down a representative, perhaps incognito, in an
attempt to come to know the temper of the common man
of the planet. That was where the truth inevitably lay – in
the attitudes of the common individual. Once that was
known, little else was required for decision.

Yes – he would have gone down quietly, and not for
any overnight stand. He would have observed for a
reasonable length of time, and if the standards of the
world differed somewhat from his own – well, there were
still ways to judge, given sufficient time.

His hand halted before the model. A representative –
perhaps a creature very like a native animal, neither wild

nor tame. Something like a parrakeet, free to enter certain homes without being challenged or held; free to observe intimately . . .

Free also to love a native girl, who might not be as intelligent, but still was beautiful and affectionate. Free to love her – and lose her?

Free to run from grief – but never to escape it entirely, though a world be forgotten, and its other inhabitants never contacted at all.

Getting Through University

This was the lead story in the August 1968 issue of *If*, and the names on the cover were Chandler, Zelazny, Pohl, Williamson, del Rey 'and many more'. That's right – even with the lead spot, Anthony was not at that time worthy of cover notice. The author is supposed to get a free copy or two, but *If* didn't bother, so my file copy I bought at the local store myself. It was obvious that I wasn't making it to fame in the story market. And sure enough, it was another idiotic retitling. My title was simply 'University', and that makes sense. In no sense does Dr Dillingham (I have two middle names; one is Anthony, used as my literary pseudonym, and the other is Dillingham) 'get through'. The story is about the admissions procedure. I have a rule of thumb: only those editors who have no taste in titles, change the titles of the authors. Certainly *If* seemed to be unable to let a decent, relevant title stand unblemished.

But this story neither begins nor ends there. It derives from personal experience in a special way. Remember when I retired from my year of writing to go back to school, to learn to be a teacher? I went to the University of South Florida, in Tampa, for two trimesters, and did qualify, and did become an English teacher – and retired again to full time writing in mid-1966. From that time on I have stayed with it, and I never want to stop. Writing is indeed my way of life, suffusing virtually every aspect of my current existence. But then, that University – I thought I'd never even get registered for my classes. I couldn't make head or tail of their requirements, and there were endless lines everywhere, and the professors there to advise confused people like me were too swamped to bother with people like me. Understand, the college I had graduated from nine years before was a very small one; I think there were ten students in my graduating class. Here there were thousands milling about, and the scale of this human maelstrom was appalling. In addition, one of the classes I needed had been closed out the day before I was permitted to apply for it; I had to get a special variance to attend. My head spinning, I was sorely tempted just to go home and give it all up. But I'm ornery, and I hung in there, and finally did get registered. What followed is too complex and fouled up to go into here; I'll just say that contemporary American education is in serious trouble, like a giant tree that is rotting at the core. And so I wrote a story about the mood of my experience – just getting registered to attend the University.

The rest of the story about this story mostly follows its publication under its junky title. Editor Fred Pohl had considered 'University' marginal and paid only 1.5c per word for it – $200 for the 13,000 word piece. But about that time he was getting assisted by two others: Lester del Rey, who had edited one of my favourite magazines back in the 1950s and who struck me as the kind of editor I could really write for – i.e. one with common sense – and Judy-Lynn Benjamin. Lester looked at 'University' and found it good. (I told you he had common sense.) So it was published despite Fred's misgivings. Then they set up an annual *Galaxy* Publications survey: the readers were encouraged to write in and vote for their favourite pieces of the year, with the top five pieces to receive bonuses. They did not differentiate between

Galaxy and *If*, or between novels and stories. (I told you Fred had no sense about editing) so naturally four of the top five finishers were novels – one of which was Fred Pohl's own (I told you he could write). So he disqualified his own (he is a decent guy, apart from his klutzhead-edness about editing) and moved the number six item up to the fifth spot. That item was 'University', the second most popular of all the under-novel-length pieces *Galaxy* Publications had published that year, beating out all those three-cent-a-worders. The readers knew what they liked, even if the editor didn't. So I was vindicated at last, and received a bonus of $100 and a guarantee of 3c per word for my future stories there – which wasn't always honoured. The story went on to contend (and lose) for that year's Hugo Award. I reported to the prominent news fanzine LOCUS that my story had been run up the Pohl-poll-pole, but for some reason that comment was never published. Professional fans, as a class, do not consider Anthony to be a clever writer. And Fred Pohl, having finally learned what the readers really liked – lost his job as editor. No, he wasn't fired; the magazines were bought by another outfit that had its own editor, and in the spoils system of Parnassus that was that. Well, he was doubtless better off as a writer anyway; he went on to win awards.

No, the story is not yet over. Lester del Rey and Judy-Lynn, similarly boosted out of their jobs, got married and she got a new job as editor at Ballantine Books, where I was unwelcome, and she proceeded to prove that nepotism pays by installing her husband as fantasy editor where he proceeded to prove just how good an editor he was, and suddenly fantasy took off for new heights. At last there was someone in charge *who knew what he was doing*. Lester and Judy-Lynn welcomed me back to

Ballantine, and so I started writing fantasy for Del Rey Books. Today that is one of the most successful connections extant; we are all getting famous. But we had got together at 'University' – and got through.

He entered the booth when his turn came and waited somewhat apprehensively for it to perform. The panel behind shut him in and ground tight.

The interior was dark and unbearably hot, making sweat break out and stream down his body. Then the temperature dropped so precipitously that the moisture crystallized upon his skin and flaked away with the violence of his shivering. The air grew thick and bitter, then gaspingly rare. Light blazed, then faded into impenetrable black. A complete sonic spectrum of noise smote him, followed by crushing silence. His nose reacted to a gamut of irritation. He sneezed.

Abruptly it was spring on a clover hillside, waft of nectar and hum of bumblebee. The air was refreshingly brisk. The booth had zeroed in on his metabolism.

'Identify?' a deceptively feminine voice inquired from nowhere, and a sign flashed with the word printed in italics, English.

'My name is Dillingham,' he said clearly, remembering his instructions. 'I am a male mammalian biped evolved on planet Earth. I am applying for admission to the School of Prosthodontics as an initiate of the appropriate level.'

After a pause the booth replied sweetly: 'Misinformation. You are a quadruped.'

'Correction,' Dillingham said quickly. 'I am *evolved* from quadruped.' He spread his hands and touched the wall. 'Technically tetrapod, anterior limbs no longer employed for locomotion. Digits possess sensitivity, dexterity – '

'Noted.' But before he could breathe relief, it had another objection: 'Earth planet has not yet achieved galactic accreditation. Application invalid.'

'I have been sponsored by the Dental League of Electrolus,' he said. He saw already how far he would have got without that potent endorsement.

'Verified. Provisional application granted. Probability of acceptance after preliminary investigation: twenty-one per cent. Fee: Thirteen thousand, two hundred five dollars, four cents, seven mills, payable immediately.'

'Agreed,' he said, appalled at both the machine's efficiency in adapting to his language and conventions and the cost of application. He knew that the fee covered only the seventy-hour investigation of his credentials; if finally admitted as a student, he would have to pay another fee of as much as a hundred thousand dollars for the first term. If rejected, he would get no rebate.

His sponsor, Electrolus, was paying for it, finding it expedient to ship him here rather than to keep him where his presence might be an embarrassment. Electrolus did not want him on hand to give further advice that might show up the oversights of its own practitioners.

If he failed to gain admission, there would be no consequences – except that his chance to really improve himself would be gone. He could never afford training at the University on his own, even if the sponsorship requirement should be waived. He had travelled all over the galaxy since unexpectedly leaving Earth, solving alien dental problems by luck and approximation, but he was not the type of man to relish such uncertainties. He had to have advanced training.

Even so, he hoped that what the university had to offer was worth it. Over thirteen thousand dollars had already been drained from the Electrolus account here by his verbal agreement – for a twenty-one per cent probability of acceptance!

'Present your anterior limb, buccal surface forward.'

He put out his left hand again, deciding that buccal in this context equated with the back of the hand. He was nervous in spite of the assurance he had been given that this process was harmless. A mist appeared around it, puffed and vanished, leaving an iridescent band clasped around, or perhaps bonded into, the skin of his wrist.

The opposite side of the booth opened, and he stepped into a lighted corridor. He held up his hand and saw that the left of it was bright while the right was dead. This remained even when he twisted his wrist, the glow independent of his motion. He proceeded left.

At the end of the passage was a row of elevators. Other creatures of diverse proportions moved towards these, guided by glows on their appendages. His own guided him to a particular unit. Its panel was open, and he entered.

The door closed as he took hold of the supportive bars. The unit moved, not up or down as he had expected, but backwards. He clung desperately to the support as the fierce acceleration hurled him at the door.

There was something like a porthole in the side through which he would make out racing lights and darknesses. If these were stationary sources of contrast, his velocity was phenomenal. His stomach jumped as the vehicle dipped and tilted; then it was plummeting down as though dropped from a cliff.

Dillingham was reminded of an amusement park he had visited as a child on Earth; there had been a ride

through the dark something like this. He was sure that
the transport system of the university had not been
designed for thrills, however; it merely reflected the fact
that there was a long way to go and many others in line.
The lifts would not function at all for any creature not
wearing University identification. Established galactics
took such things in stride without even noticing.

Finally it decelerated and stopped. The door opened, and
he stepped dizzily into his residence for the duration,
suppressing incipient motion-sickness.

The apartment was attractive enough. The air was
sweet, the light moderate, the temperature comfortable.
Earthlike vines decorated the trellises, and couches fit for
humanoids were placed against the walls. In the centre of
the main room stood a handsome but mysterious device.

Something emerged from an alcove. It was a creature
resembling an oversized pincushion with legs, one of
which sported the ubiquitous iridescent band. It honked.

'Greetings, roommate,' a speaker from the central
artifact said. Dillingham realized that it was a mutiple-
dialect translator.

'How do you do,' he said. The translator honked, and
the pincushion came all the way into the room.

'I am from no equivalent term,' it said in tootles.

Dillingham hesitated to comment, until he realized that
the confusion was the translator's fault. There was no
name in English for Pincushion's planet, since Earth knew
little of galactic geography and nothing of interspecies
commerce. 'Substitute "Pincushion" for the missing
term,' he advised the machine, 'and make the same kind
of adjustment for any of my terms which may not be
renderable into Pincushion's dialect.' He turned to the
creature. 'I am from Earth. I presume you are also here

to make application for admittance to the School of Prosthodontics?'

The translator honked, once. Dillingham waited, but that was all.

Pincushion honked. 'Yes, of course. I'm sure all beings assigned to this dormitory are 1.0 gravity, oxygen-imbibing ambulators applying as students. The administration is very careful to group compatible species.'

Apparently a single honk could convey a paragraph. Perhaps there were frequencies he couldn't hear. Then again, it might be the inefficiency of his own tongue. 'I'm new to all this,' he admitted. 'I know very little of the ways of the galaxy, or what is expected of me here.'

'I'll be happy to show you around,' Pincushion said. 'My planet has been sending students here for, well, not a long time, but several centuries. We even have a couple of instructors here, at the lower levels.' There was a note of pride in the rendition. 'Maybe one of these millennia we'll manage to place a supervisor.'

Already Dillingham could imagine the prestige that would carry.

II

At that moment the lift-vehicle disgorged another passenger. This was a tall oaklike creature with small leaf-like tentacles fluttering at its sides. The bright University band circled the centre mark. It looked at the decorative vines of the apartment and spoke with the whistle of wind through dead branches: 'Appalling captivity.'

The sound of the translator seemed to bring its attention to the other occupants. 'May your probability of acceptance be better than mine,' it said by way of greeting. 'I am a humble modest branch from Treetrunk (the translator learned quickly) and despite my formidable knowledge of prosthodontica my percentage is a mere sixty.'

Somewhere in there had been a honk, so Dillingham knew that simultaneous translations were being performed. This device made the little dual-track transcoders he had used before seem primitive.

'You are more fortunate than I,' Pincushion replied. 'I stand at only forty-eight per cent.'

They both looked at Dillingham. Pincushion had knobby stalks that were probably eyes, and Treetrunk's apical discs vibrated like the greenery of a poplar sapling.

'Twenty-one per cent,' he said sheepishly.

There was an awkward silence. 'Well, these are only estimates based upon the past performance of your species,' Pincushion said. 'Perhaps your predecessors were not apt.'

'I don't think I *had* any predecessors,' Dillingham said. 'Earth isn't accredited yet.' He hesitated to admit that Earth hadn't even achieved true space travel. He had never been embarrassed for his planet before, though when he thought about it, he realized that he had never had occasion to consider himself a planetary citizen before, either.

'Experience and competence count more than some machine's guess, I'm sure,' Treetrunk said. 'I've been practising on my world for six years. If you're – '

'Well, I did practise for ten years on Earth.'

'You see – that will probably triple your probability when they find out,' Pincushion said encouragingly. 'They just gave you a low probability because no one from your planet has applied before.'

He hoped they were right, but his stomach didn't settle.
He doubted that as sophisticated a setup as the galactic
University would have to stoop to such crude approximation. The administration already knew quite a bit
about him from the preliminary application, and his
ignorance of galactic method was sure to count heavily
against him. 'Are there – references here?' he inquired.
'Facilities? If I could look them over – '

'Good idea!' Pincushion said. 'Come – the operatory is
this way, and there is a small museum of equipment.'

There was. The apartment had an annexe equipped
with an astonishing array of dental technology. There
was enough for him to study for years before he could be
certain of mastery. He decided to concentrate on the
racked texts first, after learning that they could be fed
into the translator for ready assimilation in animated
projection.

'Standard stuff,' Treetrunk said, making a noise like
chafing bark. 'I believe I'll take an estivation.'

As Dillingham returned to the main room with an
armful of the boxlike texts, the lift loosed another creature. This was a four-legged cylinder with a head tapered
like that of an anteater and peculiarly thin-jointed arms
terminating in a series of thorns.

It occurred to him that such physical structure would
be virtually ideal for dentistry. The thorns were probably
animate rotary burrs, and the elongated snout might
reach directly into the patient's mouth for inspection of
close work without the imposition of a mirror. After
the initial introductions, he asked Anteater how his
probability stood.

'Ninety-eight per cent,' the creature replied in an
offhand manner. 'Our kind seldom miss. We're specialized for this sort of thing.'

Specialization – there was the liability of the human form, Dillingham thought. Men were among the most generalized of Earth's denizens, except for their developed brains – and obviously these galactics had similar intellectual qualities, and had been in space so long they were able to adapt physically for something as narrow as dentistry. The outlook for him remained bleak.

A robotlike individual and a native from Electrolus completed the apartment's complement. He hadn't known that his sponsor-planet was entering one of its own in the same curriculum, though it didn't affect him particularly.

Six diverse creatures, counting himself – all dentists on their home worlds, all specializing in prosthodontics, all eager to pass the entrance examinations. All male, within reasonable definition – the University was very strict about the proprieties. This was only one apartment in a small city reserved for applicants. The University proper occupied the entire planet.

They learned all about it that evening at the indoctrination briefing, guided to the lecture-hall by a blue glow manifested on each identification band. The hall was monstrous; only the oxygen-breathers attended this session, but they numbered almost fifty thousand. Other halls catered to differing life-forms simultaneously.

The University graduated over a million highly skilled dentists every term and had a constant enrolment of twenty times that number. Dillingham didn't know how many terms it took to graduate – the programme might be variable – but the incidence of depletion seemed high. Even the total figure represented a very minor proportion of the dentistry in the galaxy. This proportion was extremely important, however, since mere admission as a freshman student required qualifications that would equip the individual as a graduate elsewhere.

There were generally only a handful of University graduates on any civilized planet. These were automatically granted life tenures as instructors at the foremost planetary colleges, or established as consultants for the most challenging cases available. Even the dropouts had healthy futures.

Instructors for the University itself were drawn from its own most gifted graduates. The top one hundred, approximately – of each class of a million – were siphoned off for special training and retained, and a greater number was recruited from the lower ranking body of graduates: individuals who demonstrated superior qualifications in subsequent galactic practice. A few instructors were even recruited from non-graduates, when their specialties were so restricted and their skills so great that such exceptions seemed warranted.

The administrators came largely from the University of Administration, dental division, situated on another planet; they wielded enormous power. The University President was the virtual dictator of the planet, and his pronouncements had the force of law in dental matters throughout the galaxy. Indeed, Dillingham thought as he absorbed the information, if there were any organization that approached galactic overlordship, it was the association of University Presidents. They had the authority – by their own declaration – and the power to quarantine any world found guilty of wilful malpractice in any of the established University fields, and since any quarantine covered *all* fields, it was devastating. An abstract was run showing the consequence of the last absolute quarantine: within a year that world had collapsed in anarchy. What followed was not at all pretty.

Dillingham saw that the level of skill engendered by University training did indeed transcend any ordinary practice. No one on Earth had any inkling of the techniques considered commonplace here. His imagination was saturated with the marvel of it all. His dream of knowledge for the sake of knowledge was a futile one; such training was far too valuable to be reserved for the satisfaction of the individual. No wonder graduates became public servants! The investment was far less monetary than cultural and technological, for the sponsoring planet.

His roommates were largely unimpressed. 'Everyone knows the universities wield galactic power,' Treetrunk said. 'This is only one school of many, and hardly the most important. Take Finance, now – '

'Or Transportation,' Pincushion added. 'Every spaceship, every stellar conveyor, designed and operated by graduates of – '

'Or Communication,' Anteater said. 'Comm U has several campuses, even, and they're not dinky little planets like this one, either. Civilization is impossible without communications. What's a few bad teeth, compared to that?'

Dillingham was shocked. 'But all of you are dentists. How can you take such tremendous knowledge and responsibility so casually?'

'Oh, come now,' Anteater said. 'The technology of dentistry hasn't changed in millennia. It's a staid, dated institution. Why get excited?'

'No point in letting ideology go to our heads,' Treetrunk agreed. 'I'm coming here because this training will set me up for life on my home world. I won't have to set up a practice at all; I'll be a consultant. It's the best training in the galaxy – we all know that – but we must try to keep it in perspective.'

The others signified agreement. Dillingham saw that he was a minority of one. All the others were interested in the training not for its own sake but for the monetary and prestigious benefits they could derive from a degree.

And all of them had much higher probabilities of admission than he. Was he wrong?

III

Next day they undertook a battery of field tests. Dillingham had to use the operatory equipment to perform specified tasks: excavation, polishing, placement of amalgam, measurement, manufacture of assorted impressions – on a number of familiar and unfamiliar jaws. He had to diagnose and prescribe. He had to demonstrate facility in all phases of laboratory work – facility he now felt woefully deficient in. The equipment was versatile, and he had no particular difficulty adjusting to it, but it was so well made and precise that he was certain his own abilities fell far short of those for whom it was intended.

The early exercises were routine, and he was able to do them easily in the time recommended. Gradually, however, they became more difficult, and he had to concentrate as never before to accomplish the assignments at all, let alone on schedule. There were several jaws so alien that he could not determine their modes of action and had to pass them by even though the treatment seemed simple enough. But he remembered his recent experiences with galactic dentition, and the unsuspected mechanisms of seemingly ordinary teeth, and so refused to perform repairs even on a dummy jaw that might be more harmful than no repair at all.

During the rest breaks he chatted with his companions, all in neighbouring operatories, and learned to his dismay that none of them were having difficulties. 'How can you be sure of the proper occlusal on number seventeen?' he asked Treetrunk. 'There was no upper mandible present for comparison.'

'That was an Oopoo jaw,' Treetrunk rustled negligently. 'Oopoos have no uppers. There's just a bony plate, perfectly regular. Didn't you know that?'

'You recognize all the types of jaw in the galaxy?' Dillingham asked him, hardly crediting it.

'Certainly. I have read at least one text on the dentures of every accredited species. We Treetrunks never forget.'

Eidetic memory! How could a mere man compete with a creature who was able to peruse a million or more texts and retain every detail of each? He understood more and more plainly why his probability of success was so low. He was beginning to wonder whether it had not been set unrealistically high, in fact.

'What was number thirty-six, the last one?' Pincushion inquired. 'I didn't recognize it, and I thought I knew them all.'

Treetrunk became slightly wilted. 'I never saw that one before,' he admitted. 'It must have been extra-galactic, or a theoretic simulacrum designed to test our extrapolation.'

'The work was obvious, however,' Anteater observed. 'I polished it off in four seconds.'

'Four seconds!' All the others were amazed.

'Well, we *are* adapted for this sort of routine,' Anteater said patronizingly. 'Our burrs are built in, and all the rest of it. My main delay is generally in diagnosis. But number thirty-six was a straightforward labial cavity requiring a plastoid substructure and metallic overlay, heated to 540 degrees Centigrade for thirty-seven microseconds.'

'Thirty-nine microseconds,' Treetrunk corrected him, a shade smugly. 'You forgot to allow for the red-shift in the overhead beam. But that's still remarkable time.'

'I employed my natural illumination, naturally,' Anteater said, just as smugly, flashing a yellow light from his snout. 'No distortion there. But I believe my alloy differs slightly from what is considered standard, which may account for the difference. Your point is good, nevertheless. I hope none of the others forgot that adjustment?'

The Electrolyte settled an inch. 'I did,' he confessed.

Dillingham was too stunned to be despondent. Had all of them disgnosed number thirty-six so readily, and were they all so perceptive as to be automatically aware of the wave-length of a particular beam of light? Or were there such readings available through the equipment, that he didn't know about, and wouldn't be competent to use if he *did* know? He had pondered that jaw for the full time allotted and finally given it up untouched. True, the cavity had appeared to be perfectly straightforward, but it was too clear to ring true. Could –

The buzzer sounded for the final session, and they dispersed to their several compartments.

Dillingham was contemplating number 41 with mounting frustration when he heard Treetrunk, via the translator extension, call to Anteater. 'I can't seem to get this S-curve excavation right,' he complained. 'Would you lend me your snout?'

A joke, of course, Dillingham thought. Discussion of cases after they were finished was one thing, but consultation during the exam – !

'Certainly,' Anteater replied. He trotted past Dillingham's unit and entered Treetrunk's compartment. There was the muted beep of his high-speed proboscis drill. 'You people confined to manufactured tools labour under such a dreadful disadvantage,' he remarked. 'It's a wonder you can qualify at all!'

'Hmph,' Treetrunk replied goodnaturedly . . . and later returned the favour by providing a spot diagnosis based on his knowledge of an obscure chapter of an ancient text, to settle a case that had Anteater in doubt. 'It isn't as though we were competing against each other,' he said. 'Every point counts!'

Dillingham ploughed away, upset. Of course there had been nothing in the posted regulations forbidding such procedure, but he had taken it as implied. Even if galactic ethics differed from his own in this respect, he couldn't see his way clear to draw on any knowledge or skill other than his own. Not in this situation.

Meanwhile, number 41 was a different kind of problem. The directive, instead of saying, 'Do what is necessary,' as it had for the number 36 they had discussed during the break, was this time specific. 'Create an appropriate mesiocclusodistal metal-alloy inlay for the afflicted fifth molar in this humanoid jaw.'

This was perfectly feasible. Despite its oddities as judged by Earthly standards, it *was* humanoid and therefore roughly familiar to him. So men did not have more than three molars in a row; he now knew that other species *did*. He had by this time mastered the sophisticated equipment well enough to do the job in a fraction of the time he had required on Earth. He could have the inlay shaped and cast within the time limit.

The only trouble was his experience, and observation indicated that the specified reconstruction was not proper in this case. It would require the removal of far more healthy dentin than was necessary, for one thing. In addition, there was evidence of persistent inflammation in the gingival tissue that could herald periodontal disease.

He finally disobeyed the instructions and placed a temporary filling. He hoped he would be given the opportunity to explain his action, though he was afraid he had already failed the exam. There was just too much to do, he knew too little, and the competition was too strong.

IV

The field examination was finished in the afternoon, and nothing was scheduled for that evening. Next day the written exam – actually a combination of written, verbal and demonstrative questions – was due, and everyone except Treetrunk was deep in the texts. Treetrunk was dictating a letter home, the translator blanked out so that his narration would not disturb the others.

Dillingham pored over the three-dimensional pictures and captions produced by the tomes while listening to the accompanying lecture. There was so much to master in such a short time! It was fascinating – but he could handle only a tiny fraction of it. He wondered what phenomenal material remained to be presented in the courses themselves, since all the knowledge of the galaxy seemed to be required just to pass the entrance exam. Tooth transplantation? Tissue regeneration? Restoration of the enamel itself, rather than crude metal fillings?

The elevator opened. A creature rather like a walking

oyster emerged. Its yard-wide shell opened to reveal eye-stalks and a comparatively dainty mouth. 'This is the – dental yard?' it inquired timorously.

'Great purple quills!' Pincushion swore quietly. 'One of those insidious panhandlers. I thought they'd cleared such obtusities out long ago.'

Treetrunk, closest to the door, looked up and switched on his section of the translator. 'The whole planet is dental, idiot,' he snapped after the query had been repeated for him. 'This is a private dormitory.'

The oyster persisted. 'But you are off-duty dentists? I have a terrible toothache – '

'We are *applicants*,' Treetrunk informed it imperiously. 'What you want is the clinic. Please leave us alone.'

'But the clinic is closed. Please – my jaw pains me so that I can not eat. I am an old clam – '

Treetrunk impatiently switched off the translator and resumed his letter. No one else said anything.

Dillingham could not let this pass. Treetrunk had disconnected himself, but the translator still functioned for the other languages. 'Isn't there some regular dentist you can see who can relieve the pain until morning? We are studying for a very important examination.'

'I have no credit – no money for private service,' Oyster wailed. 'The clinic is closed for the night, and my tooth – '

Dillingham looked at the pile of texts before him. He had so little time, and the material was so important. He had to make a good score tomorrow to mitigate today's disaster.

'Please,' Oyster whined. 'It pains me so – '

He gave up. He was not sure regulations permitted it,

but he had to do something. There was a chance he could at least relieve the pain. 'Come with me,' he said.

Pincushion waved his pins, actually sensitive cilia capable of intricate manoeuvring. 'Not in our operatory,' he protested. 'How can we concentrate with that going on?'

Dillingham restrained his unreasonable anger and took the patient to the lift. After some errors, he located a vacant testing operatory elsewhere in the application section. Fortunately the translators were everywhere, so he could converse with the creature and clarify its complaint.

'The big flat one,' it said as it propped itself awkwardly in the chair and opened its shell. 'It hurts.'

He took a look. The complaint was valid; most of the teeth had conventional plasticene fillings, but one had somehow been dislodged from the proximal surface of a molar: a Class II restoration. The gap was packed with rancid vegetable matter – seaweed? – and was undoubtedly quite uncomfortable.

'You must understand,' he cautioned the creature, 'that I am not a regular dentist here, or even a student. I have neither the authority nor the competence to do any work of a permanent nature on your teeth. All I can do is clean out the cavity and attempt to relieve the pain so that you can get along until the clinic opens in the morning. Then an authorized dentist can do the job properly. Do you understand?'

'It hurts,' Oyster repeated.

Dillingham located the creature's planet in the directory and punched out the formula for a suitable anaesthetic. The dispenser gurgled and rolled out a cylinder and swab. He opened the former and dabbed with the latter around the affected area, restraining his irritation at the patient's evident inability to sit still even for this momentary operation. While waiting for it to take effect, he requested more information from the translator, which he had discovered was also quite a versatile instrument.

'Dominant species of Planet Oyster,' the machine reported. 'Highly intelligent, non-specialized, emotionally stable life-form.' Dillingham tried to reconcile this with what he had already observed of his patient, and concluded that individuals must vary considerably from the norm. He listened to further vital information, and soon had a fair idea of Oyster's general nature and the advisable care of his dentition. There did not seem to be any factors inhibiting his treatment of this complaint.

He applied a separator, over the patient's protest, and cleaned out the impacted debris with a spoon excavator without difficulty, but Oyster shied away at the sight of the rotary diamond burr. 'Hurts!' he protested.

'I have given you adequate local anesthesia,' Dillingham explained. 'You should feel nothing except a slight vibration in your jaw, which will not be uncomfortable. This is a standard drill, the same kind I'm sure you've seen many times before.' As he spoke, he marvelled at what he now termed standard. The burr was shaped like nothing – literally – on Earth and rotated at 150,000 r.p.m. – several times the maximum employed back home. It was awesomely efficient.

Oyster shut mouth and shell firmly. 'Hurts!' his whisper emerged through clenched defences.

Dillingham thought despairingly of the time this was costing him. If he didn't return to his texts soon, he would forfeit his remaining chance to pass the written exam.

He sighed and put away the power tool. 'Perhaps I can

clean it with hand instruments,' he said. 'I'll have to use this rubber dam, though, since this will take more time.'

One look at the patient convinced him otherwise. Regretfully he put away the rubber square that would have kept the field of operation dry and clean while he worked.

He had to break through the overhanging enamel with a chisel, the patient wincing every time he lifted the mallet and doubling the necessity for the assistant he didn't have. A power mallet would have helped, but that, too, was out. It was a tedious and difficult task. He had to scrape off every portion of the ballroom cavity from an awkward angle, hardly able to see what he was doing since he needed a third hand for the dental mirror.

It *would* have to be a Class II – jammed in the side of the molar facing the adjacent molar, both sturdy teeth with very little give. A Class II was the very worse restoration to attempt in makeshift fashion. He could have accelerated the process by doing a slipshod job, but it was not in him to skimp even when he knew it was only for a night. Half an hour passed before he performed the toilet: blowing out the loose debris with a jet of warm air, swabbing the interior with alcohol, drying again.

'Now I'm going to block this with a temporary wax,' he told Oyster. 'This will not stand up to intensive chewing, but should hold you comfortably until morning.' Not that the warning was likely to make much difference. The trouble had obviously started when the original fillings came loose, but it had been weeks since that had happened. Evidently the patient had not bothered to have it fixed until the pain became unbearable – and now that the pain was gone, Oyster might well delay longer, until the work had to be done all over again. The short-sighted refuge from initial inconvenience was hardly a monopoly of Earthly sufferers.

'No,' Oyster said, jolting him back to business. 'Wax tastes bad.'

'This is guaranteed tasteless to most life-forms, and it is only for the night. As soon as you report to the clinic – '

'Tastes bad!' the patient insisted, starting to close his shell.

Dillingham wondered again just what the translator had meant by 'highly intelligent . . . emotionally stable.' He kept his peace and dialled for amalgam.

'Nasty colour,' Oyster said.

'But this is pigmented red, to show that the filling is intended as temporary. It will hardly show, in this location. I don't want the clinic to have any misunderstanding.'

The shell clamped all the way shut, nearly pinning his fingers. 'Nasty colour!'

It occurred to him that more was involved than capricious difficulty. Did this patient intend to go to the clinic at all? Oyster might be angling for a permanent filling. 'What colour does suit you?'

'Gold.'

It figured. Well, better to humour the patient, rather than try to force him into a more sensible course. Dillingham could make a report to the authorities, who could then roust out Oyster and check the work properly.

At his direction, the panel extruded a ribbon of gold foil. He placed this in the miniature annealing oven and waited for the slow heat to act.

'You're burning it up!' Oyster protested.

'By no means. It is necessary to make the gold cohesive, for better service. You see – '

'Hot,' Oyster said. So much for helpful explanations.

He could have employed noncohesive metal, but this was a lesser technique that didn't appeal to him.

V

At length he had suitable ropes of gold for the slow, delicate task of building up the restoration inside the cavity. The first layer was down; once he malleted it into place –

The elevator burst asunder. A second oyster charged into the operatory waving a translucent tube. 'Villain!' it exclaimed. 'What are you doing to my grandfather?'

Dillingham was taken aback. 'Your *grand*father? I'm trying to make him comfortable until – '

The newcomer would have none of it. 'You're torturing him! My poor, dear, long-suffering grandfather! Monster! How could you?'

'But I'm only – '

Young Oyster levelled the tube at him. Dillingham noticed irrelevantly that its end was solid. 'Get away from my grandfather. I saw you hammering spikes into his venerable teeth, you sadist! I'm taking him home!'

Dillingham did not move. He considered this a stance of necessity, not courage. 'Not until I complete this work. I can't let him go out like this, with the excavation exposed.'

'Beast! Pervert! *Humanoid*!' the youngster screamed. 'I'll volatize you!'

Searing light beamed from the solid tube. The metal mallet in Dillingham's hand melted and dripped to the floor.

He leapt for the oyster and grappled for the weapon.

The giant shell clamped shut upon his hand as they fell to the floor. He struggled to right himself, but discovered that the creature had withdrawn all its appendages and now was nothing more than a two-hundred pound clam – with Dillingham's left hand firmly pinioned.

'Assaulter of innocents!' the youngster squeaked from within the shell. 'Unprovoked attacker. Get your foul paw out of my ear!'

'Friend, I'll be glad to do that – as soon as you let go,' he gasped. What a situation for a dentist!

'Help! Butchery! Genocide!'

Dillingham finally found his footing and hauled on his arm. The shell tilted and lifted from the floor, but gradually the trapped hand slid free. He quickly sat on the shell to prevent it from opening again and surveyed the damage.

Blood trickled from multiple scratches along the wrist, and his hand smarted strenuously, but there was no serious wound.

'Let my grandson go!' the old oyster screamed now. 'You have no right to muzzle him like that! This is a free planet!'

Dillingham marvelled once more at the translator's description. These just did not seem to be reasonable creatures. He stood up quickly and picked up the fallen tube.

'Look, gentlemen – I'm very sorry if I have misunderstood your conventions, but I must insist that the young person leave.'

Young Oyster peeped out of his shell. 'Unwholesome creature! Eater of sea-life! How dare you make demands of us?'

Dillingham pointed the tube at him. He had no idea

how to fire it, but hoped the creature could be bluffed. 'Please leave at once. I will release your grandfather as soon as the work is done.'

The youngster focused on the weapon and obeyed, grumbling. Dillingham touched the lift lock as soon as he was gone.

The oldster was back in the chair. Somehow the adjustment had changed, so that this was now a basketlike receptacle, obviously more comfortable for this patient. 'You are more of a being than you appear,' Oyster remarked. '*I* was never able to handle that juvenile so efficiently.'

Dillingham contemplated the droplets of metal splattered on the floor. That heat-beam had been entirely too close – and deadly. His hands began to shake in delayed reaction. He was not a man of violence, and his own quick reaction had surprised him. The stress of recent events had certainly got to him, he thought ruefully.

'But he's a good boy, really,' Oyster continued. 'A trifle impetuous – but he inherited that from me. I hope you won't report this little misunderstanding.'

He hadn't thought of that, but of course it was his duty to make a complete report on the mêlée and the reason for it. Valuable equipment might have been damaged, not to consider the risk to his own welfare. 'I'm afraid I must,' he said.

'But they are horribly strict!' the oldster protested. 'They will throw him into a foul salty cesspool! They'll boil him in vinegar every hour! His children will be stigmatized!'

'I can't take the law into my own hands. The court – or whatever it is here – must decide. I must make an accurate report.'

'He was only looking out for his ancestor. That's very important to our culture. He's a good – '

The Oyster paused. His shell quivered, and the soft flesh within turned yellow.

Dillingham was alarmed. 'Sir – are you well?'

The translator spoke on its own initiative. 'The Oyster shows the symptoms of severe emotional shock. His health will be endangered unless immediate relief is available.'

All he needed was a dying galactic on top of everything else! 'How can I help him?' The shell was gradually sagging closed with an insidious suggestiveness.

'The negative emotional stimulus must be alleviated,' the translator said. 'At his age, such disturbances are – '

Dillingham took one more look at the visibly putrifying creature. 'All right!' he shouted desperately. 'I'll withhold my report!'

The collapse ceased. 'You won't tell anyone?' the oldster inquired from the murky depths. 'No matter what?'

'No one.' Dillingham was not at all happy, but saw no other way out. Better silence than a dead patient.

The night was well advanced when he finished with the Oyster and sent him home. He had forfeited his study period and, by the time he was able to relax, much of his sleep as well. He would have to brave the examination without preparation.

It was every bit as bad as he had anticipated. His mind was dull from lack of sleep, and his basic store of information was meagre indeed on the galactic scale. The questions would have been quite difficult even if he had been fully prepared. There were entire categories he had to skip because they concerned specialized procedures buried in his unread texts. If only he had had time to prepare!

The others were having trouble too. He could see them humped over their tables, or under them, depending on physiology, scribbling notes as they figured ratios and tolerances and indices of material properties. Even Treetrunk looked hard-pressed. If Treetrunk, with a galactic library of dental information filed in his celluloid brain, could wilt with the effort, how could a poor humanoid from a backward planet hope to succeed?

But he carried on to the discouraging end, knowing that his score would damn him but determined to do his best whatever the situation. It seemed increasingly ridiculous, but he still wanted to be admitted to the university. The thought of deserting this stupendous reservoir of information and technique was appalling.

During the afternoon break he collapsed on his bunk and slept. One day remained, one final trial – the interrogation by the Admissions Advisory Council. This, he understood, was the roughest gantlet of all; more applications were rejected on the basis of this interview than from both other tests combined.

An outcry woke him in the evening. 'The probabilities are being posted!' Pincushion honked, prodding him with a spine that was not, despite its appearance, sharp.

'Mine's twenty-one per cent, not a penny more,' Dillingham muttered sleepily. 'Low – too low.'

'The *revised* probs!' Pincushion said. 'Based on the test scores. The warning buzzer just sounded.'

Dillingham snapped awake. He remembered now; no results were posted for the field and written exams. Instead the original estimates of acceptance were modified in the light of individual data. This provided unlikely applicants with a graceful opportunity to bow out before subjecting themselves to the indignity of a negative recommendation by the AA Council. It also undoubtedly simplified the work of that council by cutting down on the number of interviewees.

They clustered in a tense semicircle around the main translator. The results would be given in descending order. Dillingham wondered why more privacy in such matters wasn't provided, but assumed that the University had its reasons. Possibly the constant comparisons encouraged better effort, or weeded out the quitters that much sooner.

'Anteater,' the speaker said. It paused. 'Ninety-six per cent.'

Anteater twitched his nose in relief. 'I must have guessed right on those stress formulations,' he said. 'I knew I was in trouble on those computations.'

'Treetrunk – eighty-five per cent.' Treetrunk almost uprooted himself with glee. 'A twenty-five per cent increase!' he exulted. 'I must have maxed the written portion after all!'

'Robot – sixty-eight per cent.' The robotoid took the news impassively.

The remaining three fidgeted, knowing their scores had to be lower.

'Pincushion – fifty per cent.' The creature congratulated himself on an even chance, though he obviously had hoped to do better.

'Electrolyte – twenty-three per cent.'

The rocklike individual rolled towards his compartment. 'I was afraid of that. I'm going home.'

The rest watched Dillingham sympathetically, anticipating the worst. It came. 'Earthman – three per cent,' the speaker said plainly.

The last reasonable hope was gone. The odds were thirty to one against him, and his faith in miracles was small. The others scattered, embarrassed for him, while Dillingham stood rigid.

He had known he was in trouble – but this! To be given, on the basis of thorough testing, practically no chance of admission . . .

He was forty-one years old. He felt like crying.

VI

The Admissions Advisory Council was alien even by the standards he had learned in the galaxy. There were only three members – but as soon as this occurred to him, he realized that this would be only the fraction of the Council assigned to his case. There were probably hundreds of interviews going on at this moment, as thousands of applicants were processed.

One member was a honeycomb of gelatinous tissue suspended on a trellislike framework. The second was a mass of purple sponge. The third was an undulating something confined within a tank – a water-breather, if that liquid were water. If it breathed.

The speaker set in the wall of the tank came to life. This was evidently the spokesman, if any were required. 'We do not interview many with so low a probability of admission as students,' Tank said. 'Why did you persist?'

Why, indeed? Well, he had nothing further to lose by forthrightness. 'I still want to enter the University. There is still a chance.'

'Your examination results are hardly conducive to admission as a student,' Tank said, and it was amazing how much scorn could be infused into the tone of the mechanical translation. 'While your field exercises were fair, your written production was incompetent. You appear to be ignorant of all but the most primitive and limited aspects of prosthodontistry. Why should you wish to undertake training for which your capacity is plainly insufficient?'

'Most of the questions of the second examination struck me as relating to basic information, rather than potential,' Dillingham said woodenly. 'If I had that information already, I would not stand in such need of the training. I came here to learn.'

'An intriguing attitude. We expect, nevertheless, a certain minimum background. Otherwise our efforts are wastefully diluted.'

For this Dillingham had no answer. Obviously the ranking specialists of the galaxy should not be used for elementary instruction. He understood the point – yet something in him would not capitulate. There had to be more to this hearing than an automatic decision on the basis of tests whose results could be distorted by participant cooperation on the one hand, and circumstantial denial of study-time on the other. Why have an advisory board at all, if that were all?

'I am concerned with certain aspects of your field work,' the honeycomb creature said. He spoke by vibrating his tissue in the air, but the voice emerged from his translator. 'Why did you neglect particular items?'

'Do you mean number seventeen? I was unfamiliar with the specimen and therefore could not repair it competently.'

'You refused to work on it merely because it was new to your experience?' Again the towering scorn.

That did make it sound bad. 'No. I would have done something if I had had more evidence of its nature. But the specimen was not complete. I felt that there was insufficient information presented to justify attempted repairs.'

'You could not have hurt an inert model very much. Surely you realized that even an incorrect repair would have brought you a better score than total failure?'

He had not known that. 'I assumed that these specimens stood in lieu of actual patients. I gave them the same consideration I would have given a living, feeling creature. Neglect of a cavity in the tooth of a live patient might lead to the eventual loss of that tooth – but an incorrect repair could have caused more serious damage. Sometimes it is better not to interfere.'

'Explain.'

'When I visited the planet Electrolus I saw that the metallic restorations in native teeth were indirectly interfering with communication, which was disastrous to the well-being of the individual. This impressed upon me how dangerous well-meaning ignorance could be, even in so simple a matter as a filling.'

'The chairman of the Dental League of planet Electrolus is a University graduate. Are you accusing him of ignorance?'

Oh-oh. 'Perhaps the problem had not come to his attention,' Dillingham said, trying to evade the trap.

'We will return to that at another time,' the purple sponge said grimly. The applicant's reasoning hardly seemed to impress this group.

'You likewise ignored item number thirty-six,' Honeycomb said. 'Was your reasoning the same?'

'Yes. The jaw was so alien to my experience that I

could not safely assume that there was anything wrong with it, let alone attempt to fix it. I suppose I was foolish not to fill the labial cavity, but that would have required an assumption I was not equipped to make.'

'How much time did you spend – deciding not to touch the cavity?' Honeycomb inquired sweetly.

'Half an hour.' Pointless to explain that he had gone over every surface of number 36 for some confirmation that its action was similar to that of any of the jaws he was familiar with. 'If I may inquire now – what *was* the correct treatment?'

'None. It was a healthy jaw.'

Dillingham's breath caught. 'You mean if I had filled that theoretic cavity – '

'You would have destroyed our extragalactic patient's health.'

'Then my decision on number thirty-six helped my examination score!'

'No. Your decision was based on uncertainty, not upon accurate diagnosis. It threw your application into serious question.'

He shut his mouth and waited.

'You did not follow instructions on number forty-one,' Honeycomb said. 'Why?'

'I felt the instructions were mistaken. The placement of an MOD inlay was unnecessary for the correction of the condition, and foolish in the face of the peril the tooth was in from gingivitis. Why perform expensive and complicated reconstruction, when untreated gum disease threatens to nullify it soon anyway?'

'Would that inlay have damaged the function of the tooth in any way?'

'Yes, in the sense that no reconstruction can be expected to perform as well as the original. But even if there were no difference, that placement was functionally unnecessary. The expense and discomfort to the patient must also be considered. The dentist owes it to his patient to advise him of – '

'You are repetitive. Do you place your judgement before that of the University?'

Trouble again. 'I must act on my own best judgement, when I am charged with the responsibility. Perhaps, with University training, I would have been able to make a more informed decision.'

'Kindly delete the pleading,' Honeycomb said.

Something was certainly wrong somewhere. All his conjectures seemed to go against the intent of this institution. Did its standards, as well as its knowledge, differ so radically from his own? Could all of his professional instincts be wrong?

'Your performance on the written examination was extremely poor,' Sponge said. 'Are you naturally stupid, or did you fail to apply yourself properly?'

'I could have done better if I had studied more.'

'You failed to prepare yourself?'

Worse and worse. 'Yes.'

'You were aware of the importance of the examination?'

'Yes.'

'You had suitable texts on hand?'

'Yes.'

'Yet you did not bother to study them.'

'I wanted to, but – ' Then he remembered his promise to the Oyster. He could not give his reason for failing to study. If this trio picked up any hint of that episode, it would not relent until everything was exposed. After suffering this much of its interrogation, he retained no illusions about the likely fate of young Oyster. No wonder the grandfather had been anxious!

'What is your pretext for such neglect?'

'I can offer none.'

The colour of the sponge darkened. 'We are compelled to view with disfavour an applicant who neither applies himself nor cares to excuse his negligence. This is not the behaviour we expect in our students.'

Dillingham said nothing. His position was hopeless – but he still couldn't give up until they made his rejection final.

VII

Tank resumed the dialogue. 'You have an interesting record. Alarming in some respects. You came originally from planet Earth – one of the aborigine cultures. Why did you desert your tribe?'

They had such unfortunate ways of putting things! 'I was contacted by a galactic voyager who required prosthodontic repair. I presume he picked my name out of the local directory.' He described his initial experience with the creatures he had dubbed, facetiously, the North Nebulites, or Enens.

'You operated on a totally unfamiliar jaw?' Tank asked abruptly.

'Yes.' Under duress, however. Should he remind them?

'Yet you refused to do similar work on a dummy jaw at this University,' Honeycomb put in.

They were sharp. 'I did what seemed necessary at the time.'

–

'Don't your standards appear inconsistent, even to you?' Sponge inquired.

Dillingham laughed, not happily. 'Sometimes they do.' How much deeper could he bury himself?

Tank's turn. 'Why did you accompany the aliens to their world?'

'I did not have very much choice.'

'So you did not come to space in search of superior prosthodontic techniques?'

'No. It is possible that I might have done so, however, had I known of their availability at the time.'

'Yes, you have repeatedly expressed your interest,' Tank said. 'Yet you did not bother to study from the most authoritative texts available on the subject in the galaxy, when you had the opportunity and the encouragement to do so.'

Once again his promise prevented him from replying. He was coming to understand why his roommates had shown so little desire to spend time helping the supplicant. It appeared, in retrospect, to be a sure passport to failure.

Could he have passed – that is, brought his probability up to a reasonable level – had he turned away that plea? Should he have sacrificed that one creature, for the sake of the hundreds he might have helped later, with proper training? He *had* been shortsighted.

He knew he would do the same thing again, in similar circumstances. He just didn't have the heart to be that practical. At the same time, he could see why the businesslike University would have little use for such sentimentality.

'On planet Gleep,' Tank said, surprising him by using his own ludicrous term for the next world he had visited, 'you filled a single cavity with twenty-four tons of gold alloy.'

'Yes.'

'Are you not aware that gold, however plentiful it may be on Gleep, remains an exceptionally valuable commodity in the galaxy? Why did you not develop a less wasteful substitute?'

Dillingham tried to explain about the awkwardness of that situation, about the pressure of working within the cavernous mouth of a three-hundred-foot sea creature, but it did seem that he had made a mistake. He could have employed a specialized cobalt-chromium-molybdenum alloy that would have been strong, hard, resilient and resistant to corrosion, and might well have been superior to gold in that particular case. He had worried, for example, about the weight of such a mass of gold, and this alternative, far lighter, would have alleviated that concern. It was also much cheaper stuff. He had not thought about these things at the time. He said so.

'Didn't you consult your Enen associates?'

'I couldn't. The English/Enen transcoder was broken.' But that was no excuse for not having had them develop the chrome-cobalt alloy earlier. He had allowed his personal preference for the more familiar gold to halt his quest for improvement.

'Yet you *did* communicate with them later, surmounting that problem.'

He was becoming uncomfortably aware that this group had done its homework. The members seemed to know everything about him. 'I discovered by accident that the English-Gleep and Gleep-Enen transcoders could be used in concert. I had not realized that at the time.'

'Because you were preoccupied with the immediate problem?'

'I think so.'

'But not too preoccupied to notice decay in the neigh-bouring teeth.'

'No.' It did look foolish now, to have been so concerned with future dental problems, while wasting many tons of valuable metal on the work in progress. How did that jibe with his more recent concern for the Oyster's problem, to the exclusion of the much larger University picture? *Was* there any coherent rationale to his actions, or was he continually rationalizing to excuse his errors?

Was the seeming unfairness of this interview merely a way of proving this to him?

But Tank wasn't finished. 'You next embarked with a passing diplomat of uncertain reputation who suggested a way to free you from your commitment to Gleep.'

'He was very kind.' Dillingham did not regret his brief association with Trach, the galactic who resembled a trachodon dinosaur.

'He resembled one of the vicious predators of your planet's past – yet you trusted your person aboard his ship?'

'I felt, in the face of galactic diversity of species, that it was foolish to judge by appearances. One has to be prepared to extend trust, if one wants to receive it.'

'You believe that?' Honeycomb demanded.

'I try to.' It was so hard to defend himself against the concentrated suspicion of the council.

'You do not seem to trust the common directives of this University, however.'

What answer could he make to that? They had him in another conflict.

'Whereupon you proceeded to investigate *another*

unfamiliar jaw,' Tank said. 'Contrary to your expressed policy. Why?'

'Trach had befriended me, and I wanted to help him.'

'So you put friendship above policy,' Sponge said. 'Convenient.'

'And did you help him?' Tank again. It was hard to remember who said what, since they were all so murderously sharp.

'Yes. I adapted a sonic instrument that enabled him to clean his teeth efficiently.'

'And what was your professional fee for this service?'

Dillingham reined his mounting temper. 'Nothing. I was not thinking in such terms.'

'A moment ago you were quite concerned about costs.'

'I was concerned about unnecessary expense to the patient. That strikes me as another matter.'

'And the dinosaur told you about the University of Dentistry?' Sponge put in.

'Yes, among other things. We conversed quite a bit.'

'And so you decided to attend, on hearsay evidence.'

'That's not fair!'

'Is the colour in your face a sign of distress?'

Dillingham realized that they were now deliberately needling him and shut up. Why should he allow himself to get excited over a minor slur, after passing over major ones? All he could do that way was prove he was unstable, and therefore unfit.

'And did you seriously believe,' Sponge persisted nastily, 'that you had any chance at all to be admitted as a student here?'

Again he had no answer.

'On planet Electrolus you provoked a war by careless advice,' Honeycomb said. 'Whereupon you conspired to be exiled – to this University. What kind of reception did you anticipate here, after such machinations?'

So that was it! They resented the circumstances of his application. What use to explain that he had *not* schemed, that Trach had cleverly found a solution of the Electrolus problem that satisfied all parties? This trio would only twist that into further condemnation.

'I made mistakes on that planet, as I did elsewhere,' he said at last. 'I hoped to learn to avoid such errors in the future by enrolling in a corrective course of instruction. It was ignorance, not devious intent, that betrayed me. I still think this University has much to offer me.'

'The question at hand,' Tank said portentously 'is what *you* have to offer the University. Have you any further statements you fancy might influence our decision?'

'I gather from your choice of expression that it has already been made. In that case I won't waste any more of your time. I am ready for it.'

'We find you unsuitable for enrolment at this University as a student,' Tank said. 'Please depart by the opposite door.'

So as not to obstruct the incoming interviewees! Very neat. Dillingham stood up wearily. 'Thank you for your consideration,' he said formally, keeping the irony out of his tone. He walked to the indicated exit.

'One moment, applicant,' Honeycomb said. 'What are your present plans?'

He wondered why the creature bothered to ask. 'I suppose I'll return to practise wherever I'm needed – or wanted,' he said. 'I may not be the finest dentist available, or even adequate by your standards – but I love my profession, and there is much I can still do.' But why was it that the thought of returning to Earth, which he was free to do now and where he *was* adequate, no longer appealed? Had the wonders he had glimpsed here spoiled him for the backwoods existence? 'I would have preferred to add the University training to my experience; but there is no reason to give up what I already have just because my dream has been denied.'

He walked away from them.

VIII

The hall did not lead to the familiar elevators. Instead, absent-mindedly following the wrist-band glow, he found himself in an elegant apartment. He turned, embarrassed to have blundered into the wrong area, but a voice stopped him.

'Please sit down, Earthman.'

It was the old Oyster he had treated two days before. He was not adept at telling aliens of identical species apart, but he could not mistake this one. 'What are you doing here?'

'We all have to dwell somewhere.' Oyster indicated a couch adaptable to a wide variety of forms. 'Make yourself comfortable. I have thoughts to exchange with you.'

Dillingham marvelled at the change in his erstwhile patient. This was no longer a suffering, unreasonable indigent. Yet –

'Surely it occurred to you, Doctor, that there are only three groups upon this planet? The applicants, the students – and the University personnel. Which of these do you suppose should lack proper dental care? Which should lack the typical University identification?'

'You – ' Dillingham stared at him, suddenly making

connections. 'You have no band – but the elevator worked for you! It was a put-up job!'

'It was part of your examination,' Oyster said.

'I failed.'

'What has given you that impression?'

'The Admissions Advisory Council found me unfit to enter this University.'

'You are mistaken.'

Dillingham faced him angrily, not appreciating this business at all. 'I don't know who you are or why you were so determined to interfere with my application, but you succeeded nicely. They rejected me.'

'Perhaps we should verify this,' Oyster said, unperturbed. He spoke into the translator. 'Summon Dr Dillimgham's advisory subgroup.'

They came – the Sponge, the Honeycomb, the Tank, riding low conveyors. 'Sir,' they said respectfully.

'What was your decision with regard to this man's application?'

Tank replied. 'We found this humanoid to be unsuitable for enrolment at this University as a student.'

Dillingham nodded. Whatever internecine politics were going on here, at least that point was clear.

'Did you discover this applicant to be deficient in integrity?' Oyster inquired softly. It was the gentle tone of complete authority.

'No, sir,' Tank said.

'Professional ethics?'

'No, sir.'

'Professional caution?'

'No, sir.'

'Humility?'

'No, sir.'

'Temper control?'

'No, sir.'

'Compassion? Courage? Equilibrium?'

'That is for you to say, sir.'

Oyster glanced at Dillingham. 'So it would seem. What, then, gentlemen, *did* you find the applicant suitable for?'

'Administration, sir.'

'Indeed. Dismissed, gentlemen.'

'Yes, Director.' The three left hastily.

Dillingham started. 'Yes, *who*?'

'There is, you see, a qualitative distinction between the potential manual trainee and the potential administrator,' Oyster said. 'Your roommates were evaluated as students – and they certainly have things to learn. Oh, technically they are proficient enough – quite skilled, in fact, though none had the opportunity to exhibit the depth of competence manifested in adversity that you did. But in attitude – well, there will be considerable improvement there, or they will hardly graduate from *this* school. I daresay you know what I mean.'

'But – '

'We are equipped to inculcate mechanical dexterity and technical comprehension. Of course the techniques tested in the Admissions Examination are primitive ones; none of them are employed in advanced restoration. Our interrogatory schedule is principally advisory, to enable us to programme for individual needs.

'Character, on the other hand, is far more difficult to train – or to assess accurately in a controlled situation. It is far more reliable if it comes naturally, which is one reason we don't always draw from graduates, or even promising students. We are quite quick to investigate applicants possessing the personality traits we require, and this has nothing to do with planet or species. A promising candidate may emerge from any culture, even the most backward, and is guaranteed from none. No statistical survey is reliable in pinpointing the individual we want. In exceptional cases, it becomes a personal matter, a nonobjective thing. Do you follow me?'

Dillingham's mind was whirling. 'It sounds almost as though you want me to – '

'To undertake training at University expense leading to the eventual assumption of my own position: Director of the School of Prosthodontics.'

Dillingham was speechless.

'I am anticipating a promotion, you see,' Oyster confided. 'The vacancy I leave is my responsibility. I would not suffer a successor to whom I would not trust the care of my own teeth.'

'But I couldn't possibly – I haven't the – '

'Have no concern. You adapted beautifully when thrust from your protected environment into galactic society, and this will be no more difficult. The University of Administration has a comprehensive programme that will guarantee your competence for the position, and of course you will serve as my assistant for several years until you get the hang of it. We are not rushed. You will not be subjected to the ordeal unprepared; that unpleasantness is over.'

Dillingham still found this hard to grasp. 'Your grandson – what if I'd – '

'I shall have to introduce you more formally to that young security officer. He is not, unfortunately, my grandson; but he *is* the finest shot with the single-charge laser on the planet. We try to make our little skits realistic.'

Dillingham remembered the metal mallet dripping to

the floor, no freak interception after all. And the way the youngster had retreated before the tube . . . which, being single-shot, was no longer functional. Realism, yes.

That reminded him. 'That tooth of yours I filled. I *know* that wasn't – '

'Wasn't fake. You are correct, I nursed that cavity along for three months, using it to check our prospects. It is a very good thing I won't need it any more, because you spoiled it utterly.'

'I – '

'You did such a professional job that I should have to have a new cavity cultured for my purpose. No experienced practitioner would mistake it now for a long-neglected case even if I yanked out the gold and re-impacted it. *That*, Doctor, is the skill that impresses me – the skill that remains after the machinery is incapacitated. But of course that's part of it; good intentions mean nothing unless backed by authoritative discretion and ability. You were very slow, but you handled that deliberately obstructive patient very well. Had it been otherwise – '

'But why me? I mean, you could have selected any-one – '

Oyster put a friendly smile into his voice. 'Hardly, Doctor. I visited eleven dormitories that evening, before I came to yours – with no success. All contained prospects whose record and fieldwork showed the potential. You selected yourself from this number and carried it through honour-ably. More correctly, you presented yourself as a candi-date for the office; we took it from there.'

'You certainly did!'

'Portions of your prior record were hard to believe, I admit. It was incredible that a person who had as little galactic background as you had should accomplish so much. But now we are satisfied that you do have the touch, the ability to do the right thing in an awkward or unfamiliar situation. That, too, is essential for the position.'

Dillingham fastened on one incongruity. 'I – I selected *myself*?'

'Yes, Doctor. When you demonstrated your priorities.'

'My priorities? I don't – '

'When you sacrificed invaluable study time to offer assistance to a creature you believed was in pain.'

In the Barn

When I returned to full-time writing in 1966, I became more active in the field. I sold my first novel, *Chthon*, and worked on others, but I was not yet out of stories. I attended the week-long 1966 Milford Writers' Conference at Damon Knight's house in Pennsylvania. There I met a number of writers and editors who were great people but who I suspect regarded me as of little consequence. One example will suffice: Harlan Ellison was there, and he was in the process of assembling a massive anthology of stories to be titled *Dangerous Visions*. The theory was that many excellent stories could not be published because they were too 'dangerous' – violating editorial taboos. I agreed completely; I have never had difficulty violating editorial taboos, and have the rejections to prove it. In fact I later wrote an erotic novel, *3.97 Erect*, that was too hot for the erotic market; *Playboy* bounced it as 'Too gross for words.' If anything more erotically outrageous has been published, apart from *Candy*, I don't know of it. I poked fun at every taboo I could get at, including those of the erotic market itself, such as VD. One pays a penalty for such an attitude: unpublishability. So if Harlan really meant it, I knew I could do a story for his volume that would indeed be banned elsewhere. I asked him – and he told me that he had already overrun his budget by 50% and had closed out the volume. I was too late. Then I stood by and watched and listened as he solicited and bought (for an IOU of $150) a story for that volume from Samuel 'Chip' Delany, 'Aye, And Gomorrah.'

Thus did I get a perspective on how Harlan Ellison regarded me. Actually, Delany can write; he has won awards for several pieces including, I believe, that story in *Dang Vis*. Still . . .

Now I don't want to put too fine a point on this, but I am capable of making an impression on people when I wish to. Harlan learned the hard way, as he is the first to admit. He claims he agreed to do the sequel volume, *Again, Dangerous Visions*, just so that I could be represented in it. That may be hyperbole; Harlan specializes in hype. But for him I wrote 'The Barn' – he has a certain Pohlean taste in retitling – and I must say I found him to be a good editor. Many of the stories in the *Dang Vis* volumes are not dangerous, but I doubt that 'Barn' could have appeared elsewhere at that time. I feel that Harlan did perform a necessary service for the genre, showing that an anthology could include truly provocative fiction and be commercially successful. Today stories of similar nature are publishable – and he helped make it so.

Actually 'Barn' is a perfectly ordinary story. It's just a day on the dairy farm – with one detail changed. I've never got around to writing the sequel, 'Stockyard'; I fear that would not be a pretty story. The same goes for 'Rodeo' and 'Matador'. I don't like to hurt animals. I think more people would watch how they treat animals, if – but that's another story. Meanwhile, if X-rated material bothers you, don't read this one.

The barn was tremendous. It was reminiscent, Hitch thought, of the red giants of classical New England (not to be confused with the blue dwarfs of contemporary farming), but subtly different. The adjacent fences were there as usual, together with the granary and corncrib and round silo and even a standard milkhouse at one end. To one side was a shed with a large tractor and cultivating machinery, and to the other were conventional mounds of hay. But the curves and planes of the main structure – a genuine farmer could probably have called out fifty major and minor aspects of distinction from anything known on Earth-Prime.

Hitch, however, was not a connoisseur of barns, EP or otherwise; he was merely a capable masculine interworld investigator briefed in farming techniques. He could milk a cow, fork manure, operate a disc-harrow or supervise the processing of corn silage – but the nuances of bucolic architecture were beyond him.

This, mundane as it might appear, was it: the site of his dangerous interearth mission. Counter-Earth Number 772, located by another fluke of the probability aperture, and for him a routine investigation into a nonroutine situation. Almost a thousand Earth-alternates had been discovered in the brief decade the aperture had operated reliably, most quite close to Earth-Prime in type. Several even had the same current US President, making for rather intriguing dialogues between heads-of-state. If, as some theorists would have it, this was a case of parallel evolution of worlds, the parallels were exceedingly close; if a case of divergence from Earth-Prime (or if EP represented a split from one of the other worlds – heretical thought!), the break or series of breaks had occurred quite recently.

But only Earth-Prime had developed the aperture; only EP could send its natives into alternate frameworks and bring them back whole, live and sane. Thus it claimed the title of stem-world, the originator, and none of the others had been able to refute it. None – yet. Hitch tried not to think too much about the time when a more

—

advanced Earth would be encountered – one that could talk back. Or fight back.

On the surface, Number 772 was similar to the other worlds he had visited during past missions, except for one thing. It was retarded. It appeared to have suffered from some planetary cataclysm that had set it back technologically thirty years or so. A giant meteor-strike, a recent ice-age – Hitch was not much on historical or geological analysis, but knew that something had severely reduced its animal life, and so set everything back while the people readjusted.

There were no bears on Number 772, no camels, no horses, sheep or dogs. No cats or pigs. Few rodents. Man, in fact, was about the only mammal that remained, and it would be centuries before he had any overpopulation problem here. Perhaps a germ from outer space had wiped the mammals out, or a bad freeze; Hitch didn't know and hardly cared. His concern was with immediacies. His job was to find out how it was that livestock was such an important enterprise, dominating the economics of this world. Barns were everywhere, and milk was a staple industry – yet there were no cows or goats or similar domesticants.

That was why he now stood before this barn. Within it must lie the secret of Number 772's sinister success.

So – a little innocuous snooping, before the official welcome to EP's commonwealth of alternates. Earth-Prime did not want to back into an alliance with a repressive dictatorship or human-sacrifice society or whatever other bizarrity might be manifested. Every alternate *was* different, in some obvious or devious manner, and some were – well, no matter what Io said, that was not his worry. She liked to lecture him on the theoretical elements of alternistic intercourse, while cleverly avoiding the more practical man-woman intercourse *he* craved. In the months he had known her he had developed a considerable frustration.

Now he had to make like a farmhand, in the name of Earth-Prime security and diplomacy. A fine sex-sublimation *that* promised to be! He could contemplate manure and dream of Iolanthe's face.

He kicked a clod of dirt and advanced on his mission. Too bad the initial surveyor had not taken the trouble to peek into a barn. But virgin-world investigators were notoriously gunshy if not outright cowards. They popped in and out again in seconds, repeating in scattered locations, then turned their automatic cameras and sensors over to the lab for processing in detail while they resumed well-paid vacations. The dirty work was left to the second-round investigators like Hitch.

Behind the barn were long corrals extending down to a meandering river. That would be where the livestock foraged during the day. But the only photograph of such an area had evidently been taken of a cleanup session, because human beings had been in the pastures instead of animals. Typically blundering surveyor!

No, he had to be fair, even to a first-rounder. The work *was* risky, because there was no way to tell in advance what menaces lurked upon an unprobed alternate. The man might land in a cloud of mustard-gas or worse, or in the jaws of a carnosaur, and pop back into EP a blistered or bloody hulk. He had to keep himself alive long enough for his equipment to function properly, and there was no time to poke into such things as barns. Robotic equipment couldn't be used because of the peril of having it fall into inimical hands. The first investigator of Number 772 probably had not even been aware of the shortage of animals, nor would he have considered it significant. Only the tedious lab analysis had showed up the incongruity of this particular world.

Still, that picture was unusual. Maybe it had been a barnyard party, because in the foreground had been a splendidly naked woman. The farmers of Number 772 evidently knew how to let off steam, once the hay was in!

Once he got home, *he* was going to let off steam – and this time sweet Io would not divert the subject until well after the ellipsis.

He was very near the barn now, but in no hurry. His mission could terminate suddenly therein, and natural caution restrained him.

Transfer to Number 772 had been no problem. A mere opening of the interworld veil, a boost through, and Hitch was in the same geographic area of another frame of reality. When he finished here, a coded touch on the stud embedded in his skull would summon the recovery aperture in seconds, and he would be hooked back through. He was in no danger so long as he kept alert enough to anticipate trouble by those few seconds. All he had to do was make his investigation and get the facts without arousing suspicion or getting into trouble with the locals. He was allowed no weapon other than a nondescript knife strapped to his ankle, per the usual policy. He agreed; imagine the trouble a lost stunner could cause . . .

So far it had been deceptively simple. He had been landed in a wooded area near a fair-sized town, so that his entry had not flabbergasted any happenstance observer. That was another fringe benefit of the initial survey: the identification of suitable places for more leisurely entry. It wouldn't do to find himself superimposed upon a tree!

He had walked into that town and filched a newspaper. The language of Number 772 matched that of EP, at least in America, and he read the classified section without difficulty. Only the occasional slang terms put him off. Under HELP WANTED were a number of ads for livestock attendants. That was what he was here for.

No bovines or caprines or equines or porcines – what *did* they use?

The gentleman farmer to whom he applied at break of day hadn't even checked his faked credentials. Hitch had counted on that; dawn was rush-hour for a farm, and an under-staffed outfit could hardly be choosy then. 'Excellent! We need an experienced man. We have some fine animals here, and we don't like to skimp on supervision. We try to take good care of our stock.'

Animals, stock. Did they milk chickens or turtles here? 'Well,' Hitch had said with the proper diffidence, 'it has been a little while since I worked a farm. I've been travelling abroad.' That was to forestall challenge of his un-Number 772 accent. 'Probably take me a day or so to recover the feel of it, to fall back into the old routine, you know. But I'll do my best.' For the hour or two he was here, anyway.

'I understand. I'll give you a schedule for my smallest unit. Fifty head, and not a surly one among them. Except perhaps for Iota – but she's in heat. They generally do get frisky about that time. No cause for alarm.' He brought out a pad and began scribbling.

'You know the names of all your animals?' Hitch hardly cared about that inconsequential, but preferred to keep the farmer talking.

The man obliged, smiling with pride as his pencil moved. 'All of them. None of that absentee ownership here – I run my farm myself. And I assure you every cow I own is champion-sired.'

Cow? Hitch suspected that the labman who had made the critical report on Number 772 had been imbibing the developer fluid. No bovines, indeed! For a damn clerical error, he had been sent out –

'And if you have any trouble. just call on me,' the farmer said, handing him the written schedule and a small book. 'I'd show you the layout myself, but I'm behind on my paperwork.'

'Trouble?'

'If an animal gets injured – sometimes they bang against the stalls or slips. Or if any equipment malfunctions – '

'Oh, of course.' Yes, he could see the man was in a hurry. Perfect timing.

It had been *too* easy. Now Hitch's experienced nose smelled more than manure: trouble. It was the quiet missions that were most apt to boomerang.

He glanced at the schedule-paper before he entered the indicated cowshed. The handwriting was surprisingly elegant: 1. FEEDING 2. MILKING 3. PASTURE 4. CLEANUP . . . and several tighter lines below. It all seemed perfectly routine. The booklet was a detailed manual of instructions for reference when the need arose. All quite in order. There were cows in that barn despite what any half-crocked report had said, and he would verify it shortly. Very shortly.

Why, then, did he have such a premonition of disaster?

Hitch shrugged and entered. There was a stifling aroma of backhouse at first, but of course this was typical. A cowbarn was the barniest kind of barn. His nose began to adapt almost immediately, though the odour was unlike that of the unit he had been briefed in. He ceased – almost – to notice it.

He paused just inside the door to let his other senses adapt to the gloom and rustle of the balmy interior. He faced a kind of hallway leading deep into the barn, lined on either side by stalls. Above the long feeding troughs twin rows of heads projected, emerging from the padded slats of the individual compartments. They turned to face him expectantly as he approached, making gentle, almost human murmurs of anticipation. This morning the herd was hungry, naturally; it was already late.

At the far end was the entrance to the 'milkshed' – an area sealed off from the stable by a pair of tight doors. Short halls opened left and right from where he stood, putting him at the head of a T configuration. The left offshoot contained bags of feed; the other –

Hitch blinked, trying to banish the remaining fogginess. For a moment, peering down that right-hand passage, he could have sworn he had seen a beautiful, black-haired woman staring at him from a stall – naked. A woman very like Iolanthe – except that he had never so much as glimpsed Io in the nude.

Ridiculous; his more determined glance showed nothing there. His subconscious was playing tricks on him, perking up a dull assignment.

He faced forward with self-conscious determination. The episode, fleeting and insubstantial as it had been, had shaken him up, and now it was almost as though he had stagefright before the audience of animals.

As his eyes adjusted completely, Hitch felt a paralysis of shock coming over him. There were not bovine or caprine snouts greeting him; there were *human* heads. The fair features and lank tresses of healthy young women. Each stood in her stall, naked, hands grasping the slats since there was room only for the head to poke through. Blondes, brunettes, redheads; tall, petite, voluptuous – all types were represented. This group, clothed, could have mixed enhancingly into any festive Earth-Prime crowd.

Except for two things. First, their bosoms. The breasts were enormous and pendulous, in some cases hanging down to waist-level, and quite ample in proportion. Hitch was sure no conventional brassiere could confine these melons. They were long beyond cosmetic control. It would require a plastic surgeon with a sadistic nature to make even a start on the job.

Second, the girls' expressions. They were the blank, amiable stares of idiocy.

Milkers . . .

For some reason he had a sudden vision of a hive of bees, the workers buzzing in and out.

He had seen enough. His hand lifted to the spot on his skull where his hair covered the signal-button – and hesitated as his eye dwelt on the nearest pair of mammaries. Certainly he had the solution to the riddle; certainly this alternate was not fit for commonwealth status. Quite likely his report would launch a planetary police action, for the brutal farming of human beings was intolerable. Yet –

The udderlike extremities quivered gently with the girl's respiration, impossibly full. He was attracted and repelled, as the intellectual element within him strove to suppress the physical. To put his hand on one of those . . .

If he left now – who would feed the hungry cows?

His report could wait half an hour. It would take longer than that for him to return to headquarters, even after the aperture had been utilized. Time was not short, yet.

Hitch opened the instruction book and read the paragraph on feeding. Water was no problem, he learned; it was piped into each cell to be sipped as desired. But the food had to be dumped into the trough by hand.

He returned to the storage area and loaded a sack of enriched biscuits on to a dolly. He wheeled this into the main hall and used the clean metal scoop to ladle out two pounds to each individual. The girls reached eagerly through to grasp the morsels, picking them up whole-handed, thumbs not opposed, and chewing on the black chunks with gusto. Hitch noticed that they all had strong white teeth, but could not determine why they failed to use their thumbs and fingers as – as thumbs and fingers. Why were they deliberately clumsy? Yes, they were healthy animals – and nothing more.

He had to return twice for new bags, keeping his eyes averted from the – empty? – right-hand hall lest his imagination taunt him again. He suspected that he was being too generous with the feed, but in due course breakfast had been served. He stood back and watched the feast.

The first ones had already finished, and a couple were squatting in the corner of their stalls, their bowels evidently stimulated to performance by the roughage. His presence did not seem to embarrass them during such intimate acts, any more than the presence of the farmer restrained a defecating cow. And these cows did seem to be contented. Had they all been lobotomized? He had observed no scars . . .

Idly, he sampled a biscuit. It was tough but not fibrous, and the flavour was surprisingly rich. According to the label, virtually every vitamin and mineral necessary for animal health and rich milk was contained herein. Only those elements copious in pasture foliage were skimped. Rolling the mass over his tongue, he could believe it. He wondered what kind of pasture was available for such as these; surely they didn't eat grass and leaves. Were there vegetables and fruits out there among the salt licks?

Now he had fed the herd. The cows would not suffer if he deserted them, since the shift would change before they became really hungry again. He had no reason to dawdle longer. He could activate the signal and –

Again his hand halted short of the button. Those bobbling teats reminded him of the second item on his schedule: milking. He knew that real cows hurt if they did not get milked on time. These – udders – looked overfull already.

Damn it, he hadn't sacrificed his humanity when he obtained his investigator's licence! The report could wait.

And, a small insidious voice taunted him, there was that vision in the T-hall stall. There *could* be a naked girl in there, obviously. One that did not resemble these pendulous cows. A – virginal type . . . that looked like Iolanthe.

That was the real reason he couldn't press the stud yet. He could not leave until he screwed up the courage to check that stall – thoroughly.

He reviewed the manual, glad for the moment to revert to routine. It seemed there were six milking machines for this wing: suction devices with vacuum-adhesive conical receptors. He opened the milking room and trundled one machine up to the first milking stand and flipped the switch. It hummed.

He hesitated before undertaking the next step, but the instructions were clear and he reminded himself that a job was a job. The prospect, he had to admit, was weird but not entirely onerous. He unbolted the first gate – the entire front of the stall swung open – and approached its occupant cautiously with the milking harness.

She was a tall brunette, generous of haunch and hair as

well as the obvious. To his surprise she stood docilely
while he attached the harness: fibre straps around neck
and midriff and the chest just below the arms, with
crosspieces down the back and between the breasts. The
last was tight because the mammaries hung against each
other like full wineskins (so it wasn't a contemporary
image; nothing more apt came to mind) but he got it into
place by sawing it through. The whole was designed to
keep the cow from jumping off the stand or fidgeting too
far from the milking machine, though Hitch doubted that
the harness would withstand a determined lunge. These
animals were well-trained, and required only gentle guidance. He hoped.

He had an unbidden vision of the cow careering about
the barn, mooing, he trying ineffectively to brake her by
clinging to one milk-slick protuberance. No!

He fastened the clasps and let her to the stand. This
was a padded ramp with a cutaway in the centre for the
bulk of the milking machine and hooks for the termini of
the harness. The girl mounted it without instruction and
placed her two hands knuckle-down on the front section
and her knees on the back, so that she straddled the
machine. Her breasts depended enormously, reaching
down just beyond her elbows. The brown nipples were
tremendous, and Hitch observed flecks of white on them,
as though the very weight of milk were forcing the first
squirts out.

He brought up one milker-cup and placed it over her
right breast. It was shaped to accommodate the expanded
nipple in the centre, with a special circular flange of
flexible rubber. The outer cone adhered by suction, its
slightly moist perimeter making the seal perfect. He
attached the left cup, turned the dial to MILK and stood
back to watch the proceedings.

The feeder-cones covered only the lowermost surface of each breast, though they would have engulfed the architecture of a normal woman. They seemed to be efficient, regardless; the machine generated bursts of shaped suction that extracted the fluid quickly and cleanly. He could see the white of it passing through the transparent tubing, and hear the squirts of it striking the bottom of the covered pail as the breasts jumped to alternating vacuum. One-two! One-two! the rhythm was compelling, the pulsing whiteness suggestive of an interminable seminal ejaculation.

It's only milk! he reminded himself. But, unbidden, his erogenous zones were responding.

The girl masticated a chunk of hard cracker she had preserved, cudlike, in her cheek and waited with a half-smile. She was used to this, and glad to be relieved of the night's accumulation.

Only forty-nine to go! He left her there and proceeded to the next with considerably enhanced confidence. Cows were cows, after all, whatever their physical form.

By the time he had the sixth stand occupied, the first cow was done. He unhooked the brunette, whose bosom was now sadly slack, led her to the door in the far side of the milk room, and removed the halter. The front centre strap came away from between dangling ribbons of flesh. How much had she been good for? Two quarts? A gallon? He had no idea of the prevailing standards, but presumed she was an adequate milker. She skipped outside with a happy twinkle of buttocks, her hair flouncing. From this viewpoint, beautiful.

Before he closed the door he observed that there were great piles of apples and carrots and what looked like unshelled peanuts in the yard. The girl was already scattering them about, not yet hungry enough to do more than play with her food. And there *were* salt-licks, down beside the stream.

The following hour was hectic. It took him, once he got the hang of it, about thirty seconds to place each cow and attach the milker, and about fifteen seconds to turn her loose again once drained. But more time was required for those farthest from the milk room, and every five cows he had to replace each machine's weighty bucket. As a result he was kept hopping, and the attention he spared for each individual became quite perfunctory. Dairy farming was hard work!

Sweat rolled down his nose as he placed the final capped bucket on the conveyor leading to the processing section of the barn and put the hoses and cups into the automatic washer/sterilizer. Milking was done, the stock pastured – last time he had looked, they were roughhousing amid peanut shells and splashing in the shallow river – and he could go home with a clear conscience. Whatever pay Hitch had earned so far in this world the owner could keep, courtesy of Earth-Prime. The man would need all his resources, when the EP police action commenced!

Whom was he fooling? He wasn't even close to making the return trip to Earth-Prime. He still had that stall to check. If there were a woman there, and if she did resemble Iolanthe – well, this *was* an alternate world. Many, perhaps most of its people could be identical or very similar to those of Earth. *There could be an Iolanthe here!*

Perhaps one more available than his own . . .

He closed his mind to the thought again, not caring to face its ramifications all at once. Anyway, there were concrete, mission-inspired reasons for him to remain here longer. For one thing, these milkers were obviously virtually mindless, rendered so by what means he could not tell. But they could not have freshened so voluminously without first having been bred. That meant calving, and not so very long ago – and what had happened to the babies?

Naturally his report would not be complete without this information. This was too blatant a situation to investigate casually. He had almost come to think of human beings as animals, during the rush of the milking, but of course they were not. This barn represented the most serious breach of human rights ever encountered in the alternate worlds, and it wasn't even in the name of war or racism. These were Caucasian animals – *girls*! he reminded himself furiously. How great was the total degradation of liberty, worldwide? Were there Negro and Mongol cows, or were other races used for brute-work or sport or . . . meat?

He had to discover much more, but he could not break loose and wander around the rest of the barn without a pretext. That would attract attention to himself all too quickly. And he did not *want* to poke into the right wing . . . yet. He would have to continue his chores in a routine manner – and keep his eyes and ears wide open until he learned it all.

Next on the schedule was cleanup. He read the manual and discovered that this was not as bad as it might have been. The girls were naturally fastidious, and deposited their intestinal refuse in sumps provided in the corner of each stall. He had merely to activate the section fertilizer pump and flush each residue down its pipe, checking to make sure that no units were clogged. The smell from the vents was not sweet, but no direct handling was required.

Theoretically, however, he was supposed to check first to make sure the manure was well-formed and of the

proper colour, consistency and effluvium, since noncon-
formity was an early signal of illness. If suspicious, he
was also to probe for worms or bloodclots before flushing
a given deposit. There was a special pan and spreader
fork for this purpose. Nevertheless he ignored this instruction and flushed each sump without looking or sniffing
closely. There were limits.

'Duty ends where my nose begins,' he muttered.

He completed the cleanup circuit and could no longer
avoid the problem of the T offshoot. Now that the main
stable was empty, he could hear sounds from this wing. It
was occupied! Anxiously he reviewed his schedule. The
facts were there, obvious the moment he chose to look.
The occupants of this section were special cases: items to
take care of after the routine chores were accomplished.

He set himself and approached the wing. *There could
be an Iolanthe here* – a stupid one.

To his relief and regret, the first stall contained a sick
cow. She lay on a pallet along the side of the stall, a
shapely blonde whose mammaries had diminished to
merely voluptuous stature. He could tell they had strunk
because there were stretch-marks on them defining the
grandeur that had been. Yet at this moment her bustline
would have strained an EP tape measure.

There was a note that she had to be milked by hand, so
as not to contaminate the equipment (even through
sterilization? fussy, fussy!), and the milk disposed of. She
would be tapered off entirely, then bred again when fully
recovered. Her temperature had to be checked to make
sure her fever remained down. Her name was Flora.

He had not paid attention to the names until now,
though they were printed on the crosspiece of each gate.
His ignorance had facilitated impersonality and blunted
the terror of this monstrous barn. Now –

Hitch peered through the slats and surveyed this new problem. Milk her by hand? Take her temperature? That meant far more intimate contact than hitherto. He delved into the manual. Yes, the procedures were there . . .

Well, one thing at a time. He entered the pen with a small open bucket. 'Up, Flora,' he said briskly.

She looked at him with a disturbing but illusory semblance of intelligence, but did not move her torso. Damn the humanization wrought by knowledge of her name! He simply could not think of her any longer as an animal.

'Flora, I have to milk you,' he explained. The anomaly of it struck him afresh, and he wondered whether he should not get out of this world right away.

No, not yet. He would never be satisfied if he left without verifying that vision of Io.

Flora continued to lie there on her side, one leg pulled up. Her hair fell across her face and curled over one outstretched arm, and he noticed how neatly it matched the hue of her pubic region.

He looked in the book again. 'Milking a supine cow by hand . . .' the instructions began. Nothing like a complete manual!

He propped the bucket under the upper nipple and took Flora's breast in both hands. The feel of it gave him an immediate erection, despite everything he had seen during the mass-milking. It seemed he had been sight-anaesthetized but not touch-anaesthetized; or perhaps it was the fact that this was a true breast by his definitions rather than a gross udder, despite the stretch-marks. Or maybe it was simply the name. Had he known any blondes called Flora?

Was there a black-haired cow named Iolanthe?

In the line of duty . . .

He centred the nipple and squeezed. Nothing happened. He tried again, more positively, and succeeded in producing a transluscent driblet. One milked a bovine-cow by squeezing the neck of the teat shut and applying more gentle pressure with the remainder of the hand so that the milk had only one exit, but the human breast was structured differently. It took him several tries to accomplish anything substantial and he was afraid it was rough on her, but Flora did not move or make any sign. Once he took hold too far back and feared he had bruised one of the internal glands, but she merely watched him with sad grey eyes.

The job was inexpert and messy, but he managed to get several ounces into the bucket and probably several more on the two of them and the floor. It didn't matter; the point was to relieve the pressure, not to extract every tantalizing drop. *Why don't I just put my mouth on it and suck it out?* he thought wickedly. *Who would know?* But he remembered that the milk was supposed to be bad.

He poured the hard-won liquid down the disposal sump, flushed it, and tackled the nether breast.

'What have they done to you?' he asked rhetorically as he worked. 'What makes you all – pardon the expression – so stupid? No woman on my planet would tolerate what I'm doing to you now.' But he wondered about that as he said it; probably there were some types who –

Flora opened her mouth and he thought for a horrifying moment she was going to reply, but it was only a yawn. There was something funny about her tongue.

Now he had to take her temperature. The book cautioned him to insert the thermometer rectally, because the normal animal was apt to bite anything placed in her mouth. As if he hadn't done enough already! He had pulled some weird stunts as an interworld investigator, but this was breaking the record.

Still, she was ill, or had been, and it would be neglectful to skip the temperature. It had been neglectful to skip the faeces inspection, too, he thought, but somehow it was different now. More – personal.

'Over, Flora,' he said. 'I can't get at you from this angle.' He opened the supply box nailed to a wooden beam and found the thermometer: a rounded plastic tube about half an inch in diameter, eight inches long, with a handle and gauge on the end. The type of rugged instrument, in short, one would use on an animal – a patient that might squirm during intromission. There was a blob of yellowish grease on the business end.

When she still did not respond, he set the thermometer carefully in the feeding trough and tried to haul her about by hand. He grasped her around the middle and hefted. Her slim midsection came up and her well-fleshed leg straightened, but that was all. She was too heavy to juggle when uncooperative. He eased her down, leaving her prone on the pallet. It would have to do. At least the target was approachable, instead of aimed at the wall.

He recovered the thermometer and squatted beside her. With the fingers of his free hand he pried apart the fleshy buttocks, searching for the anus. It didn't work very well; her hindquarters were generous, and her position squeezed the mounds together. He succeeded only in changing the configuration of the crevice. He could probaly open the spot to view by using both hands, but then would not be able to insert the thermometer. Finally he flattened one buttock with his left hand and guided the tip of the instrument along the crack with his right, leaving a slug-trail of grease. When he judged he was in the right area, he pushed, hoping the slant was correct.

There was resistance, she squirmed, and the rounded point jogged over and sank in. He was surprised at the ease with which it penetrated, after the prior difficulties. He let the stem shift until the angle was about ninety degrees and depressed it until he estimated that the tip was a couple of inches deep beyond the sphincter. He readjusted himself and settled down for the prescribed two minutes.

God, he thought while he waited. What was he doing in this stable, with a naked buxom woman stretched out, he straddling her thighs and his clammy hand on her rear and jamming a rod up her rectum? His own member was so stiff it was painful.

To have you like this, Io – your dainty, chaste, aseptic little ass –

The seconds stretched out, incredibly long. He wondered whether his watch had stopped, but heard it still ticking. What would he tell the boys, in the next postmission (post *e*mission?) bull-session? That he had been milking cows? Surely they would laugh off the truth. Truth was a fleshy buttock and a dizzy feeling.

The time, somehow, was almost up, and he began to ease out the thermometer. At that point she moved again, perhaps in response to the withdrawal, climbing to her knees with her head still down. He had to follow quickly to prevent the tube from ramming too far inside, and almost lost his balance. But the new position flung open her buttocks and revealed to him the thermometer's actual point of entry.

Not the anus. Well, it probably didn't make any difference. The temperature couldn't vary that much between adjacent apertures. Carefully he drew the length of plastic out and checked the gauge. It reached the 'normal' marker exactly.

–

'Flora, you're mending,' he announced with his best bedside manner, averting his gaze from the intriguing view presented. 'You'll be spry again in no time.'

Perhaps it was the pseudo-confident tone. She rolled over, her breasts creased from the pallet, and smiled. He retreated into the passage and ladled out a pound of the special sick-animal crackers. It had been rough, for more reasons than he cared to think about.

The next occupied pen was going to be worse. It was the one in which he had seen – the girl. The one he had avoided until this moment. The one that fastened him to this world.

There could be an Iolanthe here.

He peered at the instructions before taking the plunge. This cow was in heat, and had to be conducted to the bull for mating. The handbook had, he discovered, a sketch of the barn's floor-plan, so he knew where to take her. 'It is important that copulation be witnessed,' the book said sternly, 'and the precise time of connection noted, so that the bull can be properly paced.'

Hitch took the last step and looked in, his pulses driving. It was not Iolanthe.

Just like that the bubble burst. Of *course* it wasn't Io. He had seen a black-haired girl in poor light, and his mind had been on the black-haired girl he knew at home, and the similarity of names – his stiff member had pinned the image to the desire.

This was a yearling – if that were the proper description. In human terms, about sixteen years old and never bred before. Her breasts were slight and firm, her haunches slender but well-formed, her movements animate. She paced nervously about the pen, uttering faint squeals of impatience. Her glossy hair flung out, whipping around her torso when she turned. She was, if not Iolanthe, still a strikingly attractive specimen by his definitions, perhaps because of her fire. The others had been, comparatively – cows.

Naturally a woman in heat would have sex appeal. That was what the condition was for. Mating.

Her name, of course, was Iota. The farmer had mentioned her specifically, and Hitch had made the connection, at least subconsciously, the instant he saw her first. 'All right, Iota, time for an experience you'll never forget,' he said.

She spun to face him, black pupils seeming to flare. Then with a bound she was glued to the slats, her high young mammaries poking through conically. Her breath was rapid as she reached for him. Could she, could she be –

A younger edition of Iolanthe?

Some interworld parallels were exact, other inexact. Iolanthe, Iota – both Io, as though they were sisters or more than sisters. Iolanthe might have looked like this at sixteen.

Ridiculous! It was just a mental phenomenon, a thing anchored to his yearning. A thousand, a million girls looked like this at this age.

He had a task to do. He would do it.

'Easy, girl. Stand back so I can open the gate. You and I are going to the bull-pen.'

As if in answer, she flung herself back and watched him alertly from the far side. He unlatched the gate – strange that these girls were all so dull they could not work these simple fastenings themselves, even after seeing it done repeatedly – and stepped inside with the halter.

Immediately she was on him, her lithe body pressed against his front, her arms clasped about his chest, her pelvis jerking against his crotch in an unmistakable gesture. She was in heat, all right – and she figured him for the bull!

And he was tempted, as her motions provided a most specific physical stimulation. Recent events had heightened his awareness of his own masculinity, to phrase it euphemistically. What difference would it make, to the owner, exactly *who* bred her? All they wanted was the milk when she freshened. And this whole foul system would be thrown out when the Earth-Prime troops – correction, law & order expediters – came. The chances were she would never become a milker anyway.

He looked into her eyes and read the mindless lust. Never had he perceived such graphic yearning in a woman. She had no brain, only a hungry pudendum.

She was, after all, an animal, not a human being. Fornication with her would be tantamount to bestiality, and the concept repelled him even as his member throbbed in response to the urgent pressure of her vulva.

'Get away from me!' he cried, shoving her roughly aside. God! They had even reduced women to animal cycles, in lieu of human periodicity. To control freshening, no doubt, and forestall restlessness at inconvenient times. There would be no mooning in the absence of male company, this way, except for those few days when the repressed sexuality of a year or more was triggered.

She hunched against the wall, tears coming. He saw that her emotions were human, though her mind was not. She felt rejection as keenly as anyone, but lacked the sophistication to control or conceal her reaction.

He had been too harsh with her. 'Take it easy, Iota. I didn't mean to yell at you. I *wasn't* yelling at you!' No – he had been shouting across the world at Iolanthe, who had teased him similarly for so long. Arousing the urge, but unavailable for the gratification. The difference was that this time *he* had called it off. Taking out his suppressions on this innocent wanton who could not know what drove him.

She peered at him uncertainly, her face bearing the sheen of smeared tears. He lifted the harness and shook it. 'I have to put this on you and take you to the bull. That's all. Do you understand?'

Still she hesitated. How *could* she understand? She was an animal. The tone of his voice was all she followed.

Or was it?

The animals here were incredibly stupid, considering their human origin. Obviously they had been somehow bludgeoned into this passivity. Drugs, perhaps – the biscuits could contain a potent mix. Probably most of the subjects finally gave up thinking; it was easier just to go along. But what of a young one? Her metabolism might have greater resource, particularly when she was ready to mate. To be in heat – it was the animal way to be in potent sexual love. Powerful juices there, very powerful. Counteractants?

But more: suppose an individual succeeded for a time in throwing off the mind-suppressant? Started protesting?

What was the reply of *any* tyranny to insurrection? The smart cow would keep her mouth shut, at least in the barn. She would conform. Her life depended on it.

Iota might not be stupid at all. She might be doing exactly what was expected of her. Concealing her awareness.

She was still damned attractive in her primeval way.

She had been watching him with that preternatural alertness of hers, and now she approached him again, cautiously.

He set the harness over her shoulders and reached

around her body to fasten the straps. 'Can you talk?' he whispered into her ear, afraid of being overheard. He doubted there were hidden mikes – that would not be economically feasible for a retarded technology like this – but other farmhands could be in the area.

She lifted her arms to facilitate the tightening of the clasps. A thick strand of hair curved around her left shoulder and the inside arc of her left breast. She was not as scantily endowed as he had thought at first; he had merely become acclimatized to the monstrosities of the milkers. She was clean, too, except for the feet, and there was an alluring woman-smell about her.

'Can you talk, Iota!' he whispered more urgently. 'Maybe I can help you.'

She perked up at the sound of her name. Her breathing became rapid again. She rested her forearms against his shoulders and looked into his face. Her eyes were large, the irises black in this light. But she did not smile or speak.

'You can trust me, Iota,' he said. 'Just give me some sign. Some evidence that you're not – '

She closed her arms gently around his neck and drew him in to her. Again her breasts touched him; again her hips nudged his groin. The woman-smell became stronger.

Was she trying to show him that she comprehended, or was it merely a more careful sexual offering?

What difference did it make?

He had fastened the straps long since, but his arms were still about her. He slid his hands across her smooth back, down to the slight indentations above her buttocks. She responded, putting increasing pressure against him.

What the hell.

Hitch looked about. There was no one in the stable, apart from the cows in the special stalls. He tightened his embrace and carried her upright into her own compartment. 'You want to get bred, OK,' he muttered.

He put her down in the straw. She yielded to his directions, eager to oblige. He kneeled between her spread legs, released his belt and opened his trousers, watching her. Then, unable to restrain himself any longer, he put his left hand on her cleft to work the labia apart. The entire area was slick and hot. He transferred the hand to his own loin, supporting the weight of his body with the other hand as he descended, and guided himself down the burning crevice and in. He was reminded strikingly of the manner he had placed the thermometer not long ago. There didn't seem to be any hymen.

He spread himself upon her, embedded to the hilt. He tried to kiss her, but the position was wrong and she didn't seem to understand. What opportunity would she have had to learn about kissing?

He had expected an immediate and explosive climax, but was disappointed. Iota had a dismayingly capacious vaginal tract; he could neither plumb the well to its depth nor find purchase at its rim. He realized belatedly that cows would naturally be selected for ready breeding and birthing. Entry had been too easy; there was no internal resistance, no friction.

After all his buildup, he couldn't come. It was like dancing alone in a spacious ballroom.

She lay there passively, waiting for him to proceed.

Angry, now, he pulled back, plunged, withdrew and plunged again, his sword impaling only phantoms.

And felt his weapon growing flaccid. 'Bitch,' he said.

But it was the bovine, not the canine, image that had unmanned him. It just wasn't him to fornicate with a placid, mindless cow.

She looked up at him reproachfully as he disengaged

and covered up, but he was too disturbed to care. 'Get up, animal. You want bull, you'll *get* bull.'

She stood up and he took hold of the harness leash and jerked her forward. 'Move,' he said firmly, and she moved. There was, it seemed, a trick to handling animals, and he had mastered it out of necessity. He was becoming an experienced farmer.

They travelled down long dim corridors to the bullpen, she tugging eagerly at the leash and seeking to poke into side passages. She had forgotten the frustration of the recent episode already. Obviously she had never been in this section of the barn before, and curiosity had not been entirely suppressed along with intelligence. She *was* stupid, of course; otherwise he would not have failed with her.

He didn't know much about lobotomy, but this didn't seem like it. Yet what technique . . .?

The bull was a giant of a man, full-bearded and hirsute. His feet and hands were crusted with callouses, and there was dirt on his belly. His tremendous penis hoisted, derricklike, the moment he winded Iota, and he hurled himself around his large pen. Only the stout double harness and chained collar that bound him to the far rail inhibited his savage lunges. He stank of urine.

Hitch loosed Iota and shoved her into the pen. He was anxious to have the bull cover up any guilty traces of his own abortive gesture.

She was abruptly hesitant, standing just beyond the range of the man-monster that reared and chafed and bellowed to get at her and bucked awesomely with his tumescence. She wasn't afraid of him, though his mass was easily twice hers; she was merely uncertain how to proceed in the face of so much meat.

She made as if to step forward, then withdrew. She

was trying to flirt! Hitch found quick sympathy for the
bull, allied with his own apprehension. 'You idiotic tease,
get over there!' he cried at her.

Startled, she did.

The bull reached out and grabbed her by one shoulder,
employing the same five-fingered mitten-grip Hitch had
observed with the cows. Iota spun under the force of it,
thrown off-balance, and the bull caught at her opposite
hip and hauled her to his chest backwards. He clubbed
her so that she doubled over and rammed his spurting
organ into her narrow cleft, thrusting again and again so
fiercely that her abdomen bowed out with each lunge.

That was the treatment she had been waiting for! She
hadn't even been aware of Hitch's effort, thinking it only
the preliminary inspection.

Then Iota tumbled to the floor, stunned by the impact
of the courtship but hardly miserable. She was in heat,
after all, and now that she had found out what it was all
about, she liked it. She lay on her back in the soiled
straw, smiling, legs lifted, though Hitch was sure she
would suffer shortly from terrible bruises inside and out.
What a performance!

The beast was on her again, this time from the front,
biting at her breasts while trying to get into position for
another assault. His organ glistened moistly, still erect.

'Get that heifer out of there!' someone shouted, and
Hitch started. It was another farmhand. 'Want to sap our
best stud?'

Hitch ran out into the pen, wary of the bull, and caught
hold of one of Iota's blissfully outstretched arms. It was
obvious that she would happily absorb all the punishment
the creature chose to deliver. A festoon of white goo
stretched downward from the bull's penis as he made a
last attempt at the vanishing target. Then Hitch hauled

Iota across the floor until they were entirely out of range of the monster and stood her on her feet. She was still dazed as he reharnessed her, not even wincing as the strap chafed across the deep toothmarks on her breast.

The other farmhand glanced at him as they trooped by, but did not say anything. Just as well.

About halfway back, Hitch remembered that he had forgotten to post the time of service on the bull's chart. He decided not to risk further embarrassment by returning for that errand, The bull seemed to have sufficient pep to go around, anyway.

Iota was dreamily contented as he returned her to her stall, though there was a driblet of gluey blood on one leg. Apparently there *had* been a hymen . . . Well, she was out of heat now, she wasn't a virgin heifer any more!

There was trouble in the final stall. He had been so occupied with the prior chores on the schedule that he hadn't bothered to read ahead, and now he regretted it. He had just witnessed, per instructions, a copulation, and it was as though gestation had occurred in minutes. This next cow was delivering!

She lay on her side, legs pulled up, whimpering as her body strained. There was something funny about her tongue too, as it projected between her teeth. Was there a *physical* reason these animals never spoke? The head of the calf had already emerged, its hair brown like that of the mother. Hitch had thought all babies were bald. All *human* babies . . .

Should he summon help? He was no obstetrician!

But then he would have to explain why he hadn't notified anyone earlier, and he had no excuse apart from carelessness and personal concupiscence. Better to stick with it himself.

Odd, he thought, how one could become committed

against his intention. This labouring cow was not really his problem, and she belonged literally to another world, yet he had to do what he could for her. The activities of this brutal barn were as important to him at this moment as anything he could remember. Even its most repulsive aspects fascinated him. It represented a direct personal challenge as well as an intellectual one. Iota –

As the cow struggled to force out the massive bundle, Hitch skimmed nervously through the manual. Good – the stock was generally hardy, and seldom required more than nominal supervision during parturition. Signs of trouble? No, none of the alarm signals itemized were evident. This was a normal delivery.

But the text stressed the importance of removing the new-birthed calf immediately and taking it to the nursery for proper processing. The mother was not supposed to have any opportunity to lick it down, suckle it or develop any attachment.

And how about the father? How about *any* observer with a trace of human feeling? It was as though he *had* impregnated a cow, and now his offspring was being manifested. He had failed with Iolanthe, he had failed with Iota, but he still had something to prove. Something to salvage from this disaster of a world.

The cow heaved again, and more of the balled-up calf emerged. There was blood soaking into the pallet, but the manual assured him callously that this was normal. He wanted to *do* something, but he knew that his best bet was noninterference. He was sure now that a human woman could not have given birth so readily without anaesthetic or medication. In some ways the animals were fortunate, not that it justified any part of this. That large, loose vagina –

'What's going on here?'

Hitch jumped again. The voice behind him was that of the owner! For an experienced investigator, he had been inexcusably careless about his observations. Twice now, men had come upon him by surprise.

'She's birthing,' he said. 'Routine, so I didn't – '

'In the *nightstall*?' the man demanded angrily, his white hair seeming to stand on end. It was the way he combed it, Hitch decided irrelevantly. 'On a bare pallet?'

Oops – he must have missed a paragraph. 'I told you it's been a while since I – the other farm didn't have separate places to – '

'That farm was in violation of the law, not to mention the policies of compassionate procedure.' The owner was already inside the stall and squatting down beside the labouring cow. 'It was a mistake, Esmeralda,' he said soothingly. 'I never meant to put you through this here. I had a special delivery-booth for you, with fresh clean straw and padded walls . . .' He stroked her hair and patted her shoulder, and the animal relaxed a little. Obviously she recognized the gentle master. Probably he came by the stables periodically to encourage the beasts and grant them lumps of sugar. 'In just a moment I'll give you a shot to ease the pain, but not just yet. It will make you sleepy, and we have to finish this job first. You've been very good. You're one of my best. It's all right now, dear.'

Hitch realized with a peculiar mixture of emotions that it wasn't all acting. The farmer really did care about the comfort and welfare of his animals. Hitch had somehow assumed that brutality was the inevitable concomitant of the degradation of human beings. But actually he had seen no harshness; this entire barn was set up for the maximum creature comfort compatible with efficiency, with this backward technology. Had he misjudged the situation?

Under the owner's sure guidance the calving was quickly completed. The man lifted the infant – a female – and spanked her into awareness before cutting and tying off the umbilical cord. He wrapped her in a towel that materialized from somewhere and stood up. 'Here,' he said to Hitch, 'take it to the nursery.'

Hitch found himself with babe in arms.

'All right, Esme,' the owner said to the cow, his voice low and friendly. 'Let's take care of that afterbirth. Here – I'll give you that shot I promised. It only stings for a second. Hold still – there. You'll feel much better soon. Just relax, and in a moment you'll be asleep. In a few days you'll be back with the herd where you belong, the finest milker of them all.' He looked up and spied Hitch still standing there. 'Get moving, man! Do you want her to see it?'

Hitch got moving. He did not feel at all comfortable carrying the baby, for all his determination of a moment ago to help it in some way, but that was the least of it. Its cries, never very loud (did they breed for that, too?), had subsided almost immediately as it felt the supposed comfort of human arms, and probably that was fortunate because otherwise the mother would have been attracted to the sound. But this removal of the baby so quickly from its parent, so that it could never know a true family – how could that be tolerated? Yet he was cooperating, carrying it down the dusky passages to the nursery.

The fact that he had witnessed its arrival did not make him responsible for it, technically – but the baby had, in more than a manner of speaking, been given into his charge. His prior mood returned, intensified; he *did* feel responsible.

'I'll take care of you, little girl,' he said inanely. 'I'll keep you safe. I'll – '

He was talking like a hypocrite. There was very little he could do for this baby except put it in the nursery. He didn't know the first thing about child care. And – he was no longer entirely certain that he *should* do anything specific if he had the opportunity.

He had been ready to condemn this entire world out of hand, but in the face of this last development he wasn't sure, oddly. This breeding and milking of human beings was shocking – but was it actually evil? The preliminary report had remarked on the strange peacefulness of this alternate Earth: computer analysis suggested that there was no war here, and had not been for some time. That was another riddle of Number 772. Was it because those who ruled it were compassionate men, despite the barbarity of their regime?

Which was better: to have a society peacefully unified by a true segregation of functions – men-men vs animalmen – or to have every person born to contend so selfishly for the privileges of humanity that all succeeded only in being worse than animals? Earth-Prime remained in serious jeopardy of self-extermination; was that the preferred system to impose on all the alternate Earths too?

Number 772 did have its positive side. Economically it functioned well, and it would probably never have runaway inflation or population increase or class warfare. Could it be that with the breakup of the family system, the human rights and dignities system, the all-men-are-created-equal system – could it be that this was the true key to permanent worldwide peace?

He had not seen a single discontented cow.

By taking this baby from its mother and conveying it to

the impersonal nursery, was he in fact doing it the greatest favour of its existence?

He wondered.

The nursery caught him by surprise. It was a cool quiet area more like a laboratory than the playroom he had anticipated. A series of opaque tanks lined the hall. As he passed between them he heard a faint noise, like that of an infant crying in a confined space, and the baby in his arms heard it and came alive loudly.

Hitch felt suddenly uneasy, but he took the squalling bundle hastily up to the archaically garbed matron at a central desk. 'This is Esmeralda's offspring,' he said.

'I don't recognize you,' the woman said, glowering at him. Epitome of gradeschool disciplinarian. He almost flinched.

'I'm a new man, just hired this morning. The boss is in with the mother now. He said to – '

'Boss? What nonsense is this?'

Hitch paused, nonplussed, before he realized that he had run afoul of another slang expression. This one evidently hadn't carried over into Number 772. 'The owner, the man who – '

'Very well,' she snapped. 'Let me see it.'

She took the bundle, put it unceremoniously on the desk, and unwrapped it. She probed the genital area with a harsh finger, ignoring the baby's screams. This time Hitch did flinch. 'Female. Good. No abnormalities. Males are such a waste.'

'A waste? Why?'

She unrolled a strip of something like masking tape and tore it off. She grasped one of the baby's tiny hands. 'Haven't you worked in a barn before? You can't get milk from a bull.'

Obviously not. But a good bull did have his function,

as Iota's experience had shown. Hitch watched the woman tape the miniature thumb and fingers together, forming a bandage resembling a stiff mitten, and something unpleasant clicked. Hands so bound in infancy could not function normally in later life; certain essential muscles would atrophy and certain nerves would fail to develop. It was said by some that man owed his intelligence to the use of his opposable thumb . . .

'I haven't been involved with this end of it,' he explained somewhat lamely. 'What happens to the males?'

'We have to kill them, of course, except for the few we geld for manual labour.' She had finished taping the hands; now she had a bright scapel poised just above the little face.

Hitch assumed she was going to cut the tape away or take a sample of hair. He wasn't really thinking about it, since he was still trying to digest what he had just learned. Slaughter of almost all males born here . . .

She hooked thumb and forefinger into the baby's cheeks, forcing its mouth open uncomfortably. The knife came down, entered the mouth, probed beneath the tongue before Hitch could protest. Suddenly the screams were horrible.

Hitch watched, paralysed, as bubbling blood overflowed the tiny lip. 'What – ?'

'Wouldn't want it to grow up talking,' she said. 'Amazing how much trouble one little cut can save. Now take this calf down to tank seven.'

'I don't – ' There was too much to grapple with. They cut the tongues so that speech would be impossible? There went another bastion of intelligence, ruthlessly excised.

With the best intentions, he had delivered his charge into this enormity. He felt ill.

The matron sighed impatiently. 'That's right, you're new here. Very well. I'll show you so you'll know next time. Make sure you get it straight. I'm too busy to tell you twice.'

Too busy mutilating innocent babies? But he did not speak. It was as though his own tongue had felt the blade.

She took the baby down to tank seven, ignoring the red droplets that trailed behind, and lifted the lid. The container was about half full of liquid, and a harness dangled from one side. She pinned the baby in the crook of one elbow and fitted the little arms, legs and head into the loops and tightened the fastenings so that the head was firmly out of the fluid. Some of it splashed on Hitch when she immersed the infant, and he discovered that it was some kind of thin oil, luke-warm.

The baby screamed and thrashed, afraid of the dark interior or perhaps bruised by the crude straps, but only succeeded in frothing redly and making a few small splashes with its bound hands. The harness held it secure and helpless.

The matron lowered the lid, checking to make sure the breathing vents were clear, and the pitiful cries were muted.

Hitch fumbled numbly for words. 'You – what's that for? It – '

'It is important that the environment be controlled,' the woman explained curtly. 'No unnecessary tactile, auditory or visual stimulation for the first six months. Then they get too big for the tanks, so we put them in the dark cells. The first three years are critical; after that it's fairly safe to exercise them, though we generally wait another year to be certain. And we keep the protein down until six; then we increase the dose because we *want* them to grow.'

'I – I don't understand.' But he did, horribly. In his mind the incongruous but too-relevant picture of a bee-hive returned, the worker-bees growing in their tight hexagonal cells. His intuition, when he first saw the cows, had been sure.

'Don't you know *anything*? Protein is the chief brain food. Most of the brain develops in the first few years, so we have to watch their diet closely. Too little, and they're too stupid to follow simple commands; too much, and they're too smart. We raise good cows here; we have excellent quality control.'

Hitch looked at the rows of isolation tanks: quality control. What could he say? He knew that severe dietary deficiencies in infancy and childhood could permanently warp a person's mental, physical and emotional development. Like the bees of the hive, the members of the human society could not achieve their full potential unless they had the proper care in infancy. Those bees scheduled to be workers were raised on specially deficient honey, and became sexless, blunted insects. The few selected to be queens were given royal jelly and extra attention, and developed into completely formed insects. Bees did not specialize in high intelligence, so the restriction was physical and sexual. With human beings, it would hit the human specialization: the brain. With proper guidance, the body might recover almost completely from early protein deprivation, but never the mind.

EP had researched this in order to foster larger, brighter, healthier childen and adults. Number 772 used the same information to deliberately convert women to cows. No drugs were required, or surgical lobotomy. And there was no hope that any individual could preserve or recover full intelligence, with such a lifelong regime. No wonder he had got nowhere with Iota!

He heard the babies wailing. What price, peace?

'And,' he said as she turned away, 'and any of these calves could grow up to be as intelligent and lively as we are, if raised properly?'

'They *could*. But that's against the law, and of course such misfits wouldn't be successful as milkers. They're really quite well off here; we take good care of our own. We're very fortunate to have developed this system. Can you imagine using actual filthy *beasts* for farming?'

And he had milked those placid cows and had his round with Iota . . .

He left her, sick in body and spirit as he passed by the wailing tanks. In each was a human baby crying out its heritage in a mind-stifling environment, deprived of that stimulation and response essential to normal development, systematically malnourished. No health, no comfort, no future – because each had been born in the barn. In the barn.

He could do nothing about it, short-range. If he ran amok amid the tanks, as he was momentarily inclined to, what would he accomplish except the execution of babies? And this was only one barn of perhaps millions. No – it would take generations to undo the damage wrought here.

He paused as he passed tank number 7, hearing a cry already poignant. The baby he had carried here, in his naïvete. Esmeralda's child. The responsibility he had abrogated. The final and most terrible failure.

A newborn personality, bound and bloody in the dark, never to know true freedom, doomed to a lifelong waking nightmare . . . until the contentment of idiocy took over.

Suddenly Hitch understood what Iolanthe meant by integrity of purpose over and above the standards of any single world. There were limits beyond which personal ambition and duty became meaningless.

He stepped up to the tank and lifted the lid. The cries became loud. He clapped his free hand to his ankle, feeling for the blade concealed there. He brought it up, plunged it into the tank, and slashed away the straps.

'Hey!' the matron cried sharply.

He dropped the knife and grabbed the floundering infant, lifting it out. He hugged it to his shirtfront with both arms and barged ahead. By the time the supervisor got there, Hitch was out of the nursery, leaving a trail of oil droplets from the empty tank.

As soon as he was out of sight he balanced the baby awkwardly in one arm and reached up to touch the stud in his skull.

It was risky. He had no guarantee there would be an open space at this location on Earth-Prime. But he was committed.

Five seconds passed. Then he was wrenched into his own world by the unseen operator. Safely!

There was no welcoming party. The operator had merely aligned interworld coordinates and opened the veil by remote control. Hitch would have to make his own way back to headquarters, where he would present his devastating report. Armies would mass at his behest, but he felt no exhilaration. Those tanks . . .

He held the baby more carefully, looking for a place to put it down so that he could remove the remaining strap-fragments and wrap it protectively. He knew almost nothing about what to do for it, except to keep it warm. But the baby, blessedly, was already asleep again, trusting in him as it had before though there was blood on its cheek. The mutilated tongue . . .

He was in a barn. Not really surprisingly; the alternate framework tended to run parallel in detail, so that a structure could occupy the same location in a dozen Earths. There were many more barns in Number 772 than in EP, but it still didn't stretch coincidence to have a perfect match. The one he trekked through now was an Earth-Prime barn, though, an old-fashioned red one. It had the same layout as the other, but it contained horses or sheep or – cows.

He walked down the passage, cradling the sleeping baby – *his* baby! – and looking into the stalls. He passed the milkroom and entered the empty stable, noting how it had changed for animal accommodation. He couldn't resist entering the special wing again.

The first stall contained an ill cow who munched on alfafa hay. The second was occupied by a lively heifer who paused to look soulfully at him with large soft eyes and licked its teeth with a speech-mute tongue. Had she just been bred? The third –

Then it struck him. He had been shocked that man could so ruthlessly exploit man, there on Number 772. It was not even slavery on the other world, but such thorough subjugation of the less fortunate members of society that no reprieve was even thinkable for the – cows. When man was rendered truly into animal, revolt was literally inconceivable for the domesticants.

Yet what of the animals of *this* world, Earth-Prime? Man had, perhaps, the right to be inhumane to man – but how could he justify the subjugation of a species not his own? Had the free-roving bovines of ten thousand years ago come voluntarily to man's barns, or had they been genocidally compelled? What irredeemable crime had been perpetrated against them?

If Earth-Prime attempted to pass judgement on this counter-Earth system, what precedent would it be setting? For no one knew what the limits of the alternate-universe framework were. It was probably that somewhere within it were worlds more advanced, more powerful than EP. Worlds with the might to blast away all mammalian life including man himself from the Earth, leaving the birds and snakes and frogs to dominate instead. Had it been such intervention that set back Number 772?

Worlds that could very well judge EP as EP judged counter-Earth Number 772. Worlds that might consider *any* domestication of *any* species to be an intolerable crime against nature . . .

Iolanthe would take care of the baby; he was sure of that. She was that sort of person. Prompt remedial surgery should mitigate the injury to the tongue. But the rest of it – a world full of similar misery –

He knew that in saving this one baby he had accomplished virtually nothing. His act might even give warning to Number 772 and thus precipitate far more cruelty than before. But that futility was only part of his growing horror.

Could he be sure in his own mind that Earth-Prime had the right of it? Between it and Number 772 was a difference only in the actual species of mammal occupying the barn. The other world was, if anything, kinder to its stock than was EP.

No – he was being foolishly anthropomorphic! It was folly to attempt to attribute human feelings or rights to cows. They had no larger potential, while the human domesticants of Number 772 *did*. Yet –

Yet –

Yet what sort of a report could he afford to make?

Up Schist Crick

I have read that scatology is a more reliable guide to the real freedom of a society than is erotic material. That is, more people are willing to tolerate sex than filth. Of course, more yet are happy to tolerate extreme violence, which I think is a sad commentary. I feel that there should be complete freedom of expression, but that controversial types of things should be identified, so that readers or viewers don't have to be hit in the face with it before discovering its nature. Therefore be advised: there is a scatological element to this story.

William Zether slowed to forty, alarmed by the condition of the highway. He had driven a long way on superhighways, and this was a comedown. He had thought the surface was ageing asphalt, but now decided on oiled gravel. Low-grade gravel, watered oil. Great long cracks cleft both lanes, their patterns resembling lightning frozen in mid-jag and ironed flat.

He slowed again to negotiate a chasm the width of his tyre. It petered out near the edge of the opposite lane, becoming a delta of tributary crevices. By skidding his lefts into the dusty ditch he was able to span the narrowest offshoot with his rights. He continued at twenty.

Exactly how far into the wilderness *was* this sweet village of Violet? The road map intimated ten miles, but he was sure he had gone fifteen since filling his tank at the last cluster of houses signifying a township. The motley Schist Mountains had encroached ever closer in the interim, the terrain had degenerated into waves of desert heat, and the road . . .

He crunched the brakes. The wheels skewed, dust ascended, the vehicle rocked and heaved sickly, and he came to a tumultuous halt in the midst of the car-sized sand trap he had sought to avoid.

As the choking swirl subsided, he attempted to nudge forward; but as he had feared, the wheels merely churned themselves into functional oblivion. He should have allowed the car to bull through on inertia.

Zether turned off the motor and pondered his situation. He would have to dig his way out by hand, and naturally he had no shovel and was wearing his best suit.

The car's air-conditioning had cut off with the motor, and already he could feel the perspiration gathering. He pushed open the door, untangled seat belt and shoulder harness, and climbed out – and was struck by the blast furnace that passed for a July noon hereabouts. His thirty-five-dollar shoes sank out of sight in the desiccated quicksand that engulfed the vehicle up to the hubs.

'I,' he remarked to the burning welkin, 'have had it. In spades. And I wish I *had* a spade; or at least a derrick.'

But William Zether was not a man to rail at circumstance. Perceiving that the wheels were hopelessly mired, and mindful of the fifteen miles behind, he slung his jacket over his back, wedged the felt brim of his hat over his sweltering forehead, and waded onward in the transitory comfort of shirtsleeves. Somewhere ahead there had to be civilization.

The landscape was dehydrated, and he felt thirsty already. He sloughed out of the sand. His footwear had sustained a thirty-dollar depreciation, and he preferred not to assess the remainder of his apparel. The trail before him resembled the baked bed of a sun-crazed mud shallow attacked by amateurs with dull jackhammers.

His eyes passed over the wind-scarred rubble and focused on memory. It seemed that certain essential records had been misplaced during the transfer of management from the pioneer company. A-Plus Fabrics, Inc., to its more solvent purchaser. A great deal of time had been absorbed in running down the diverse and inefficient experimental projects of A-Plus, and the files were still overloaded with corporate trivia. Thus there had happened to be a seven-year delay in the follow-up to a certain test-marketing project. He had uncovered portions of the records by diligent and increasingly circumspect part-time research, and now was taking a week's vacation to investigate the situation more directly.

Zether was glad he was a healthy, large-boned, brown-haired, virile junior exec, because this torrid hike would mean trouble for a wealthy, fat-fleshed, white-haired, febrile senior exec. He had covered about half a mile, and the locale seemed more and more like Death Valley during a drought. Blisters were surely burgeoning grandiosely on his trodding feet.

The product being test-marketed was a fabric – a very special one. Thermal-insulating, semiporous, transparent material of extraordinary lightness, elasticity, and strength. Absolutely nontearable. Cuttable only by a specifically designed tool. Unique yet embarrassingly cheap to manufacture. Or so the scanty and almost furtive records hinted. Probably the material was no more than the wish-fulfilment dreaming of a doodling A-Plus deadwood executive – but Zether had to know for sure. It just might be a live bombshell.

He was increasingly tired and thirsty. How many more miles could this tattered ribbon of crusted sludge wend its weary way through the inferno? His hope for some reasonable termination to this trek was evaporating along with the fluids of his body.

A-Plus Fabrics had developed it, and so it had been dubbed APFI via acronym. A remote site had been selected for test-marketing of apfi swatches while A-Plus wrestled with patent and mass-production bottlenecks. A report had been contemplated within a year, had not the business foundered for unconnected reasons. Seven years ago.

He stopped, letting the dust settle around his feet, rubbing his gritty eyes to verify the mirage. There was a structure ahead. He had arrived at Violet!

'Sweet Violet, sweeter than the roses,' he sang as he staggered towards it, but the remaining words of his verses were not to be found in print.

It was an ordinary backwoods hamlet. There was one general store, one church, one school, one hotel, one gasoline station, one small bank, half a post office, and a dozen TV antennae – none of these artifacts modern except the last. One farmer-type male ambled away down the single street. Violet.

Well, this did fit the specification of 'reasonably isolated community.' It could take years for news of import to leak out of a burg this sleepy and serviced by a road this bad. No problem about any aggressive competitors tuning in on the survey and beating the originator to mass marketing. Here near the headwaters of the polluted Schist River was a township that sustained itself nicely at poverty level through farming, logging, and freelance quarrying . . .

What use would such a populace have for the modernistic apfi material, assuming the fabric existed? These people hardly seemed to have caught up to nylon. Yet, through the years of the test-marketing's inadvertent duration there had been a continued and rather healthy per-capita demand, if another thread of his researches spoke truly. The company lab had continued to produce a limited supply of something labeled 'A', and the company shipping department had continued to route it to this one town, while the executive offices were unaware that the product existed. Typical coordination! But this suggested that there *was* a practical market for something, and Zether meant to cut himself in on the take by discovering on the QT exactly what it was. He had a few shares of stock and knew a few key people; he could gain control of this one product if it turned out to be worth his while. Provided no one else caught on prematurely.

Just as soon as he had cleaned up and coddled his blisters for maybe a fortnight . . .

He trompted into the lobby of the ancient hotel, heedless of appearances. It was empty, but in a moment a young woman appeared from some dusky recess. Even in the poor light and his disgruntled state he was impressed by her attributes: high fair cheekbones, elegantly coiffed black hair, finely moulded neck, superlative breasts. 'Room – hot bath – steak dinner with aperitif, delivered – do not disturb for anything short of Ragnarok,' he said as he signed the register. Oh, to get off his flaming feet!

'Rag what rock?' she inquired, perplexed.

'Armageddon. Kaput. End of the – '

Then it hit him. Cheek, hair, neck, breasts – no wonder they had caught his glazed eyeball. All were thoroughly displayed. The girl was naked to the – he double-checked – feet. All she wore was a lumpy necklace.

It was a little late to react, so he didn't bother. In the morning, he would realize that it had been a hallucination inspired by heat prostration though the lobby was air-conditioned and of conservative decor. Hardly conducive to visions of this nature.

She put away the register and took his coat, carrying it

over one slender arm. 'This way, sir,' she said coming into full view and preceding him to the curving staircase.

And the view *was* full, and the curves not confined to the stairwell. He followed, eyes lubricated by her amply flexing buttocks. He should get fatigued more often! The effect became dazzling as she ascended the steps, her hindquarters (though in truth they were full semicircles) now at his eye level, close.

She let him into the room, then entered herself. In a moment he heard water running and realized that the nymph was drawing the hot bath he had specified. 'Uh, thank you,' he said when she emerged, offering her a dollar tip.

She declined it. 'You may settle your account when you leave, Mr Zephyr.'

'Zether,' he said automatically. '*th*, not *ph*.'

She acknowledged the correction with a smile, and departed.

He stripped and dumped his sodden clothing on the easy chair, too weary to be fastidious, and marched into the bathroom. The water was fine, and he sank into its steaming ambience gratefully. Maid, proprietress – whoever she was, she had the touch. *And* the figure! His imagination wasn't *that* facile; he had seen what he had seen, every voluptuous bulge, crease, and ripple.

He soaked for forty minutes and felt much better. His calves retained some hard-core stiffness, and there were blisters on heels and toes, but he was otherwise in physical comfort. He dried off, stretched, slung the towel aside, and reentered the room. The door swung shut behind him, its latch clicking.

His steak dinner was there, reposing beautifully on its serving cart. So was the girl.

His clothing – all of it – was on the chair beyond. The towel was in the bathroom, and somehow his frantically fumbling hand couldn't locate the doorknob. He was ludicrously stranded in the ultimate dishabille, and it hardly became him.

'Is everything satisfactory, Mr Zether?' she inquired, hefting her derriere off the edge of the cart and approaching him. Her bare breasts jiggled provocatively.

'Yes, yes . . .' he mumbled, feeling idiotic and more than politely embarrassed. Naked women tended to give him a reaction. What was he supposed to do now?

She studied him speculatively. 'It looks to me as though you have an immediate need, Mr Zether. Why don't we resolve it now, so you can proceed with your dinner without distraction?'

He felt the flush spreading over face and neck. He realized that the situation had triggered the masculine salute, and she had seen it.

She stepped up next to him, so close her torso touched his at two points, while his touched hers at one, and kissed him. Then she conducted him to the bed.

Nature took its ancient course with unprecedented fury. Her body was silky slick all over and almost seemed to glow; it was highly receptive. A certain slight but critically located impediment suggested that she was, despite her availability, a virgin. Hitherto. Only the unglamorous necklace she still wore detracted from the effect, and her inherent charms compensated generously. Never had he indulged in such savage lovemaking on such short notice.

After the swift climax, she disengaged, rolled lithely off the bed, stood up, took a tissue from the adjacent box, and held it between her spread thighs. Well satisfied and passive for the moment, he watched.

She gave a peculiar twitch – and suddenly a splatter of viscosity popped into the tissue. It was, he realized with a shock, the fruit of their immediately preceding connection.

He stared, more amazed than upset. It was as though her cleft had simply spat out the residue.

She wadded the tissue and trotted to the bathroom to dispose of it. 'Better get to your dinner before it gets cold,' she said.

That wasn't all that was growing cold!

Zether realized that only a few minutes had elapsed since his emergence from the bath. He became conscious of his own nakedness again.

'Don't use those dirty clothes,' she said reprovingly as she quitted the bathroom. He heard the toilet refilling itself behind her. 'I'll find you something better.'

His suit *was* pretty grubby. 'Thanks.'

'*After* you finish eating.'

The perfect domestic! Oh, well – what was one more crazy development? 'Will you join me? Please, I insist; I hate to eat alone.'

She did not require much persuasion. 'I suppose there is enough for two. I could use the dessert plate and the salad fork . . .'

And so they shared a naked dinner, and with little further urging she was telling him the story of her life. Her name was Ella Hopping, twenty-two years old, single, and available (he had gathered as much during their two minutes on the bed), and she managed the hotel for her aging uncle.

'My folks live downstream,' she explained. 'I was visiting Uncle Ezra up here for the summer, back when I was ten. But there was a fire at my dad's store, and no insurance, and – well, my folks just couldn't afford to bring me back right away. So there I was – up Schist Crick.'

He started, but realized that he had misheard the

phrase. 'Stranded with your uncle in Violet, you mean,' he said.

'Schist Crick. I know it says "Violet" on the map, but the map's wrong. Outsiders can't seem to pronounce the name, so – but even the roads don't show up the way they are.'

Zether had discovered that the hard way. His poor car! But while he could understand the problem of the name and the cartographic euphemism, the road was another matter. 'Why don't they resurvey the area? In one week they could – '

'We've had a petition in at the Statehouse for nigh twenty years, Uncle says, but nothing ever comes of it. Some flunky said something once about a discontinuity because of the projection – do *you* know what that means?'

'I can guess. There's always some error in maps because of the problem of making a two-dimensional image of a three-dimensional subject. You just can't map the surface of the globe accurately on flat paper. That's why they have to make Greenland look bigger than Australia, when it's really much smaller.'

'It is? I didn't know that. You're very smart.'

'You've been up Schist Crick too long, Ella.'

'I know. I need someone to take me away.'

Oh-oh. She was fishing for more than a two-minute commitment. 'Usually they take up the slack, or whatever they call it, in the ocean or wilderness areas, so it doesn't bother anybody. But it sounds as though there was a slipup, and a discontinuity showed up in this area. It really should be corrected – there's no excuse for it, with modern cartographic techniques.'

'I wish the state politicians listened to that,' she said. 'Maybe if the maps were right, they'd allocate enough money to maintain our roads properly, and we wouldn't

have so much trouble and so few visitors. We can't keep
up a twenty-mile road on funds for ten.'

'Amen. My car will never be the same.'

As they finished the excellent meal, he got up the
courage to ask a more personal question. 'That trick with
the – what did you do, after we – '

'I'm wearing my suit, of course,' she said.

'Your suit?' Her attire certainly wasn't apparent to
him. Her body still glistened with sleek health – and
nothing else.

'My apfi suit. You know.'

The word struck him solidly in the solar plexus of his
mind. Apfi! He choked over his drink. What could this
delightful innocent know about apfi?

'But I forgot. You're from downcrick. I guess they
don't have apfi there. We never see it advertised on TV,
anyway. It's a special kind of fabric, very thin. Here, I'll
show you.'

He was tempted to inform her of the relevance of his
mission, but caution prevailed. The truth is, he had never
actually seen or handled any apfi; he knew of it only
through paperwork. He hadn't dared inquire too persist-
ently at the lab, lest he give his interest away. That was
another reason for this private trip. He wanted to get his
hands on a sample without betraying his motivation.

Ella hooked her finger under her necklace and caught
it with her other hand. A faint tent appeared, above and
between her breasts; only the trace refraction of the light
passing through it betrayed its gossamer presence. She let
go, and it sank down to cleave to the dual rondures
beneath, the air trapped below it escaping under the
collar and, probably, filtering through the material to a
lesser extent. 'Apfi,' she said.

It was a revelation, despite his prior knowledge of it.
Apfi – transparent and extraordinarily stretchable. It

could therefore be employed as an invisible and skin-tight garment! Ella was not nude; she was garbed from neck to toe in a single segment of apfi that fit every delightful contour of her body perfectly.

And when they had made love – when he had so urgently penetrated her – the fabric had merely yielded before the thrust and formed an effective diaphragm. Perhaps the most unusual example of its type ever applied. In the incipience of his climax he had misinterpreted that slight resistance. Afterward, she had spread her legs and popped the indentation out again.

Very neat. Chalk one up for native ingenuity. No wonder she had been so free with her favours! His hot flesh had never touched hers, except for the first kiss. He had made love to her suit!

This was cheaper than the pill – and more convenient.

It had not occurred to him before that apfi could have profound social implications. Evidently its availability had modified social mores considerably, here in Violet/Schist Crick. At least for nubile celibate girls. What would happen if it were marketed nationwide, given high-powered, multiple-media promotions? DOES SHE OR DOESN'T SHE . . . WEAR APFI?

He continued to think about it that night, after Ella had removed the dishes, brought him informal clothing for use while his own outfit was being cleaned, and gone about whatever other business she had. She was quite an efficient damsel in her fashion, and no slouch as a cook. He had been tempted to invite her for a more leisurely evening follow-up to their two-minute introduction, but had decided not to push his luck. Uncle just might catch on . . .

Back to the social implications. Think of it: every woman walking down the street clad in apfi, the gloss of its surface enhancing firm bouncy pairs of . . .

In the morning he remembered soberly that not all women were endowed quite as fortunately as Ella, and most were not just twenty-two. One woman's bounce was another's sag. Well, it had been a pleasant vision, nevertheless. Perhaps a curfew of sorts could be set: no woman over twenty-nine permitted on the streets in apfi while light remained, unless accompanied by her daughter.

Zether's first order of business after breakfast was the car. He visited the sole gas-station/garage, a hut perched on the edge of a monstrous level field, and inquired about towing service.

'Sure,' the proprietor/mechanic said, looking up from the innards of the wreck he was tinkering with. Several similar vehicles squatted untidily along the perimeter of the field. He was a white-haired man in oily grey coveralls. 'You're lucky you made it in, though. It's almost shut season.'

'Shut season? What shuts down?'

'You know – the month the roads are closed. August, usually, but it slides about a little from year to year, depending on the weather. Nobody goes through – not by car, anyway.'

The date was July 25. Zether felt uneasy. 'I'm new here. Would you mind explaining that in a little more detail?'

'No trouble. Schist Crick is a funny town. The Schist Mountains and the Schist River close it off pretty tight, so there's only room for two highways: the winter road and the summer road. The winter road is pretty good until the spring thaw washes it out along about March. The summer road works fine until the heats get it, 'long about August. They're both out in August, you see, so it's shut season.'

Both roads out? 'Because the town is shut off from the world?'

'Uh-uh. There's still TV and telephones. We're in touch as much as we need to be.'

'Then why – '

The mechanic peered at him from behind a wobbly carburettor. 'Because that's when the gals get shut of spinsterhood, or try to. Nowhere the bachelors can go, and those suits – it's getting like a tradition. Last year one of those nudies even sashayed by here, twitching her little round butt the way they do. I squirted oil on her.'

'You did *what*?'

'Some said afterwards it wasn't exactly sporting, but it was the handiest thing. Had to show her somehow I wasn't interested.'

'Is any bachelor, er, subject to this – '

'Any bachelor without a pressure oil can,' he said meaningfully.

It occurred to Zether that a jet of viscous warm fluid from a nozzle, applied so as to inundate a virtually nude female, was not necessarily a signal of masculine uninterest. Probably the mechanic wasn't much for Freudian symbolism, though. 'Why didn't you just ignore her, or – '

The man looked at him. 'Didn't want to get one leg in,' he said. 'First one's a teaser. Second – ' He did not finish.

Ouch! 'Don't you repair the roads?'

'Sure – but we never have enough money for both at once, so we have to take on one at a time. Need about six months to do one up proper, so – '

Zether remembered Ella's remark about the problems of maintaining twenty-mile roads on ten-mile funds. She had neglected to tell him about shut season, however. Conniving female! He already had one leg in, unwittingly.

He had a feeling he'd better keep the second out. 'So the winter road is out from August through January?'

'Right. Crew generally wraps up in January, so both roads are open February, and there's a month's vacation. But August – '

'I get the picture. In August the crew is still wrapping up the winter road, so the other has to wait an extra month. How come they can do the summer road in only five months – September through January – but take six for the winter?'

'Don't rightly know,' the mechanic said. 'But that's the way it is. Maybe they hurry a little for the vacation.'

'Or maybe they delay a little for shut season?'

'Maybe.' The man smiled slowly. 'Got to admit, she looked cute in oil. I hosed her off afterwards, of course; those suits clean up easily. Wish I was younger. Now, where's your car?'

Zether described the location.

'Reckon the season's started already, then. Have to leave your car there until the crew comes; no sense miring my truck too.'

'Till the crew comes – in one to six months?'

'Yep.'

Ouch again! 'Isn't there anything you can do? It will be a rusted wreck by then.'

'I can walk out there and cover it with an apfi tarp. Keep the dust out, protect the tyres and engine – '

'Apfi does that?' The silver lining was coming into view. First the clothing market, now the protective cover market. Even shut season might not be too high a price!

'Sure does. Mighty handy fabric, apfi. Don't know how we'd get along without it.'

How much profit could be had from such a thing, nationwide? A million dollars? Ten million?

Zether's blisters were hurting despite the thick pads he

had applied, and he had to walk extremely carefully and rest often. But in the course of the day he managed to explore a fair sampling of Schist Crick. What he saw took his mind off the problem of getting home, though he knew he couldn't afford to be trapped for shut season.

He discovered farmers stretching apfi over entire silos to enhance the hothouse effect, or whatever it was that went on in silos. Loggers preserved their logs in it, and kept their home-brewed beer cool by suspending it in apfi pouches that sweated very slowly when grotesquely distended. Quarry men used it to enclose dusty compartments and keep the air clean, since only gaseous substances could pass normally. Theoretically apfi would pass liquid if stretched far enough, but the beer pouches demonstrated the impracticality of this for local use. Commercially, however, Zether foresaw monstrous profits. Stretched mechanically, apfi could serve as a variable filter, good for water desalinization, osmotic techniques – the possibilities were rife. And the extremely low coefficient of friction of the single-molecule structure would improve the performance of almost any machinery, since nearly all of it had moving parts. Apfi-coated pistons, perhaps?

Though Ella kept her footing and picked up objects readily enough. Perhaps her coating of apfi even conformed to the whorls of her fingers, restoring much of the friction. Probably the material was many times as slick when applied to a polished surface; he'd have to check that out. Ideal, if it eliminated virtually all machine friction while preserving the necessary human friction.

How about sports? Apfi sails would reduce the weight of racing boats and be far easier to handle. There could even be stretched-apfi hulls. It would be like sailing in an invisible craft – a real status symbol. And apfi wings on gliders – why, a man with specially designed apfi wings might be able to fly like an insect. Apfi slides for apfi-bottomed children: two apfi surfaces meeting should be phenomenally slippery. Applications for toys – he had tò stop; his head was getting dizzy.

Everywhere, apfi was already in use, in this one town, and its potential market was stupefying. Profits of a hundred million?

There were not, to his relief, women running around in the seminude, though he had no doubt that would come when shut season got well under way. He had just about decided that Ella was the only one so far when he entered the general store for phase two of his survey. The proprietor was a middle-aged man – clad only in apfi, except for swimming trunks. Zether could make out the sheen of the skin-tight material.

He had thought of it only in connection with women – yet why shouldn't men use apfi too? Probably it was considered indoor wear for everyone. Fair enough. He would have to get into someone's house and verify this. In shut season it would become the fashion for outdoor girls as well. There could be a whole social framework for the use of apfi.

Zether bought a sample. It was priced quite reasonably, and came in a loose package marked simply 'APFI: 4 sq. ft.' This was what he wanted: to handle the stuff himself, find out how it felt. He presumed there were 8 sq. ft. or 10 sq. ft. sizes and up, but the small one would readily serve his purpose. The package weighed no more than a few ounces, and he suspected most of that was in the wrapping. Apfi was only one molecule thick and weighed almost nothing. That was why it was so flexible and transparent.

He took it eagerly into his room and spread it out. It was mounted in a hoop folded into quarters that sprang into circularity when released. Open, it resembled – here the image was suggestive in more than one way – an enormous condom. The diameter was a little over two feet, or, he was sure, the correct amount to make a total area of exactly four square feet.

He contemplated its level gloss, so thin it was easy to miss the film entirely except for the defining circle, and marvelled that this represented its unstretched state. Too bad he had not been able to obtain a sample at the company; but this way was better, in spite of blisters, lost car, and shut season. No one would know what he was doing until he had what he wanted.

Zether set the hoop on the floor, stepped into it, and lifted. The material came up around his shoes and cuffs neatly, stretching to fit. It seemed soap-bubble fragile, but he knew it was stronger, weight for weight, than any stone or steel or nylon. The specifications implied that it could not be punctured even by a driven spike; it merely stretched until the thrust had been alleviated. It was thus theoretically possible to protect nails or rivets from rust by hammering them into material coated with apfi; the film would remain intact between nail and support, cutting off most moisture. Provided the lack of friction didn't make a problem. Only a semielectrical tool that acted on the atomic structure could hole it, and the tool cost a good deal more than the fabric.

He let go, and it dropped back to the floor with the hoop. How had Ella fashioned a permanent noncollapsing suit of it?

The door opened, and Ella entered in her normal habiliment. Think of the devil! Apparently the concept of personal privacy or prudery was foreign to her; or maybe such ethics were suspended during shut season. He'd really have to watch it.

'Why, Mr Zether!' she exclaimed, floucing her tresses

prettily. 'Are you trying to put it on over your *clothing*? That'll never work.'

He had only been experimenting, but didn't protest. 'How do you make it stay in place?'

'By closing the loop, of course,' she said, touching her necklace. He saw that it was made of the same material as the apfi hoop. In fact, it *was* an apfi hoop, mysteriously convoluted. 'Here, I'll show you. Take off your clothes.'

He was a trifle slow in complying, so she assisted him. The notion of this buxom and too available young woman stripping him to the buff began to have its natural effect, but then he remembered the cynical aftermath – popped into a tissue – and the impulse died. He preferred his lovers totally nude, somehow. And he was wary of that second leg. It sounded as though local custom decreed that two acts of physical love constituted grounds for marriage, and he was definitely not ready for that. First he meant to nail down his fortune; then he would worry about domestic matters.

'Now, step into it,' she directed, and he put his bare foot into the circle. Spiderwebs clasped his toes, tickled the sole; he repressed the urge to jump away. She drew the hoop up around him, jiggling it so that the apfi fit snugly around both legs, remaining taut between them. The excruciatingly gentle contact ascended. It was like standing in a bath filling with lukewarm water. He felt it enclose calves, knees, thighs – and now the sensation was definitely erotic. No accident, that, he was sure; she was doing her unsubtle best to make him react as she addressed his groin. He fastened his attention on the image of a strongbox full of hundred-dollar bills until the apfi reached his waist; that was what he was fighting for, after all.

She made him elevate his arms, and the fabric enclosed them also. The elasticity was remarkable! Finally the settling motion stopped, and he felt no more, except for the areas where body hair held it out from the skin. He'd had to shave his torso all over to have a really snug fit: a disadvantage. She did something obscure to the hoop, and it contracted around his neck in a loose necklace like her own, preventing the suit from sliding off. He was dressed.

He flexed his arms and legs a little dubiously. The principal characteristic of the suit was its *lack* of characteristics. Only occasionally could he feel points of tension, and these disappeared as the apfi shifted to compensate. It was a second layer of skin.

'And I always thought the emperor's new clothing was a fake!' he exclaimed. 'Obviously it was an early apfi suit.'

But had the emperor had the opportunity to appreciate its erotic qualities? Even a layer of only one molecule should impair sensation somewhat – but the super-smooth surface would add back much of what was lost. *Had* added back; no wonder he had exploded in that first encounter with Ella! This was sex with an intriguing difference.

A bell rang. 'Oops, someone in the lobby,' she said regretfully. 'I have to run.' And run she did, excitingly.

He still *felt* naked, so he donned his regular clothing over the apfi suit. Underwear, socks, shoes – it all fit perfectly. It was as though the suit didn't exist, except that he thought it made his blisters more comfortable by alleviating the slight abrasions of the socks. Good.

He felt distinctly warmer, and realized that the material's insulating properties were being manifested. The suit alone was comfortable, in normal interior temperature; added clothing became too hot. That explained why Ella and the others wore nothing else, inside. Probably the people who ventured outside wore apfi under their clothing, as he was doing now, when it was cool, and skipped the apfi when it was hot. Or skipped the clothing.

Fortunately its gas porosity prevented skin suffocation. Sweat would pass upon evaporation, and air could contact the skin in a limited way. Yes, apfi made an excellent all-purpose suit, particularly for an activity like swimming; he'd have to mention that in his report.

Report? What was he thinking of! He'd make no report at all until he had acquired control of the patent, if any. He could become a billionaire!

He descended the stair and left the hotel without seeing Ella again. Just as well; she was almost too helpful, as though he were already her possession.

It was cooler outside. Dusk was approaching, and in this mountain country the extremes of temperature shifted rapidly. Burning days and frigid nights – excellent for apfi. Yes, he was becoming more and more enthusiastic about the product. He had searched for some liability, something that would detract from its sales potential on either practical or aesthetic grounds, some catch that would wash out the dream, and found none. This thing would make ten billion!

In the street he passed a blonde in an enticingly tight sweater. He peered at her, trying to determine whether she did or did not wear an apfi suit underneath. Not even any webbing between the fingers showed, yet . . .

She gave him a direct glance. 'You appear to find me attractive, stranger,' she murmured. 'I am wearing my suit, and my husband's away on the road crew, so if you'd like to – '

'Uh, no thanks,' he said hastily. 'Just admiring the scenery.' And he removed himself from the vicinity, leaving her perplexed.

The enormity of it! If just eight years of apfi had

made sex a communal activity in this isolated, probably conservative village, what would it do to the nation in a similar period? First the intemperate youth groups would discover its sexual wonders and make it a symbol of the times; then it would spread to other levels of society. The beatniks, the beardniks, the radicals – how far would they go, how rapidly, granted the freedom of the suit? And after them, the great mass of 'decent, law-abiding' people the politicians claimed to cater to. It would be a revolution!

Was the world ready for apfi?

Behind the gas station, in the field, he saw something that distracted him from conjecture momentarily: a helicopter! What was it doing here?

'Mr Zephyr!' It was the old mechanic. Was there news about his car already?

He entered the lighted station. It was cluttered with the usual paraphernalia: dented oil cans, tyres, rusty carburettors, wrenches, auto manuals, and mechanical bric-a-brac. A pay telephone nestled on the wall next to a small cash register. 'You got my car out?'

The man shook his head negatively, looking at him speculatively. 'None of my business, but are you staying long?'

'No longer than I can help. But if there's no road out – '

'I saw old Ezra Hopping, the hotel man, cleaning his shotgun. His eyesight is way too poor for hunting, but he's a pretty sharp businessman. Not much goes on he don't know about. Now, I'm not offering you any advice, but – '

But old Uncle Ezra might well be anxious to protect his niece's reputation, and that of his hotel. And to acquire a capable in-law to help out. Yes. So he was cleaning his shotgun. 'Is that phone in working order?'

'Yep.' The mechanic discreetly stepped outside. 'You can make change from the cash register, it's open,' he said as he disappeared.

Zether did just that, marvelling at the man's trusting nature. He fed the orifice and dialled the number of a companion worker who could keep his mouth shut. 'Don, I'm in a bind,' he said hurriedly. 'My car is out of commission, and I can't walk far, and there's a marriage-minded female – look, I can't explain now, but can you rent a tractor and come down here in a hurry? I'll make it worth your while . . .'

'Bill, what are you up to? Where are you?'

Zether gave a brief geographical rundown.

'That's five hundred miles!' Don exclaimed. 'I'm a white-collar wage-earner; I just can't take off in the middle of the week! Why can't you hire someone local to bail you out?'

He thought about making the necessary arrangements for an escape from Schist Crick and rescue of his car, without giving away his interest in apfi. No one *in* Schist Crick would cooperate, of course, since they would figure he was running out on shut season. As he was, among other things. No one outside would understand, let alone rely on the credit of a secretive, telephoning stranger. It had to be Don.

'Say,' Don said. 'There's something else funny. The supe was poking into your desk the other day as though he was looking for something. Wanted to know what the locked file was for . . .'

Oh, no! That was the apfi research file he should have hidden. If anybody got into that before he got back, he could kiss goodbye to his plans. And the grasping supervisor would gladly use the pretext of his late return to snoop. 'Don, believe me – this is urgent. Take that file out and bring it with you. Don't let anyone at it! Take an emergency leave and get down here with some cash . . .'

'Bill, I just can't do that, I'd be fired! If only you'd explain – '

'*When* you get here, Don; when you get here! I can't talk about it over the phone. Just trust me . . .' But he knew it wouldn't work. Don was honest to a fault, but conservative; he wasn't greedy, but he had to know all the facts before he acted, and he never gambled. He would consider apfi at best a gamble, and at worst a theft from the company.

Someone was approaching the shop; he couldn't talk any more. 'I guess you're right, Don. Sorry I bothered you.'

He hung up and turned away from the phone as a man in the uniform of the forest service entered. 'I need some gas,' the ranger said.

'Sorry, I'm not the proprietor. He – ' Zether paused. 'That copter – that yours?'

The man nodded. 'I ran low on fuel, or I wouldn't have put down here at all. Must have a leak somewhere. Have to move again in a few minutes, get back to my base.'

'Got room for a passenger?' His heart was pounding.

'It's against regulations, sorry,' the ranger said. 'No passengers. Where's the gasman?'

'I'm desperate,' Zether said. 'I have some very important business, and the roads are closed.' He pulled out his wallet and removed a twenty-dollar bill and pressed it into the ranger's hand.

The man looked doubtfully at the bribe, then made his decision. 'All right. I'll be through here soon's I find the attendant. That must be him outside. Five minutes, then I'll rev up and take off. You get out of sight and come out to intercept me as I walk to the copter, as though you had a message for me. If no one notices, I'll take you aboard. But I won't wait; if you don't meet me right on time, I'll have to take off without you. Can't risk my job. Got that?'

'Got it. Five minutes on the nose or bust. Thanks.'

Zether stepped outside and spied a public rest room behind the station. He headed for it. He should be able to see the ranger from its window.

The sign hanging just inside the dirty pane said VIOLET – UP SCIST CREEK. Nothing like a geographical identifier, he thought with a smile as he entered. Visitors would know exactly where they had paused.

Inside the cramped and smelly compartment he felt a sudden call of nature. Perhaps it was the availability and suggestion of toilet facilities, or possibly the abrupt release of tension. He decided to make good use of his five minutes.

His mind remained preoccupied with the larger problem. He could become rich from apfi, supervising its national promotion and marketing. But was it ethical? How would the courts see it? Was it possible that the social consequences would offset the dollar profit? Complete sexual freedom, the act performed as readily as a handshake . . .

Two minutes remained. Yes, he was on his way home, and in time. Proper exploitation of apfi would make his fortune. The hell with social ethics; money was far more important. Let the fuddy-duds scream; they could not halt progress. There was not one single reason apfi would not conquer the commercial world! The question was now not *whether* he would be a multibillionaire, but *how* soon. Ten years? Five?

One minute. Nicely timed. Both shotgun and supervisor had been foiled. He had grabbed his only chance to preserve his basic interests: his bachelordom and his billions.

He reached for the toilet paper without getting up. All that conjecture and experimentation must certainly have shaken up his digestion, because he had just relieved himself voluminously.

Two things occurred to him in nightmare sequence as he tore off a suitable strip. First, he was still wearing the suit. Second, he did not know how to loosen the neck loop so as to let the suit down.

Extraordinarily elastic apfi might be, so that its resistance was hardly perceptible – but it remained impervious to the passage of solids. Though a square yard of it could encompass an automobile without breaking or tearing, it would not pass so much as a grain of sand through its membrane, and liquid, for practical purposes, penetrated it only in the vapour state. He had neither the time nor the resources to stretch it the enormous amount necessary to alleviate even a portion of his problem.

He heard the footfalls of the ranger returning to his copter.

William Zether remained sitting, paper in hand, afraid to move. His despairing gaze caught the reverse face of the sign hanging in the cobwebbed window. Words were printed thereon, forming a message awesome in its relevance and profundity:

WITHOUT A PADDLE

The Whole Truth

My title was 'Not That Good', which relates to the theme of the story. I have an acute consciousness of titling; I consider the title to be an important element of the story. Editors, as a class, have abysmal title sense, as I may have mentioned several times before. I wrote this one for Harry Harrison's original anthology *Nova* in 1968; he had solicited taboo-busting fiction from me but balked at 'Up Schist Crick', 'The Bridge' and 'On the Uses of Torture'. So I sent him one that was not that good, and he published it. A writer learns how to manage editors. Naturally he missed the point. Harry is a good writer; he just needs to stick to his lathe. Nevertheless, his 'Hole Truth' pun has merit, as you will see.

The story itself has a history that may be more interesting than its content. I dreamed it up, literally, woke and recorded it, filed it for future reference – and forgot I had done so. Later, coming across the note, I wondered where it had come from. So I described it to several writing acquaintances, inquiring whether they had seen any such story in print. None had, so I assumed it really was mine. Then when I decided to write it up for Harry, I couldn't find my note. So I had to re-create it from scratch. After selling it to *Nova*, I found my original note – and discovered that it was better than the story I had actually written. Sigh – it really *was* Not That Good.

Unfortunately, the impersonal military regulations said, multiple-manned stations were not feasible at this time. Numerous learned articles had been published refuting the validity of this policy, but they were under civilian bylines and therefore ignored. That was why Leo MacHenry was a lonely man.

He had been warned that his imagination might conjure company from the vacuum, just to break the monotony of fourteen months of isolation. Such cautions were unnecessary; he knew better than to yield to hallucination. One million dollars was good pay even in the face of rampant cool-war inflation, for a single tour – but it would do him little good in the psycho ward. Thus he was cautious about crediting what he saw.

Still, it did look like a man. A live one.

The figure drifted directly towards the station, brightly illuminated by this system's nameless sun. Behind it were the stars, clear even in this seeming day because of the absence of obscuring atmosphere. An intermittent jet of gas shot out from the suit, suggesting the tail of a comet as the light caught it momentarily. Braking action; weightlessness was a far cry from masslessness, and a collision at speed with the station would flatten the visitor in ugly fashion.

Leo watched it through the small scope. What he saw was a standard UN space suit of the type suitable for survival-of-wearer up to four days in deep space, conditions permitting, and somewhat longer in a semiprotected situation. That was sufficient margin for rescue in most cases – if rescue were, according to the manual, feasible at all. Evidently there had been a wreck in space, and this survivor had been close enough.

And that was suspicious. Leo's station was mounted on a planetoid that orbited a numbered star far from Sol. Human traffic was sparse here. There was potentially valuable real estate in this system and earth wanted to hold a lease on it so that other starfaring creatures would stay clear, but it would be years before proper development occurred. The odds against a human ship-wreck here at this time, let alone a single survivor – well, it was improbable.

Yet this was persistent for a hallucination. His instruments picked up the visitor, and he was not given to misreading their signals. He had been on duty two weeks; the novelty was only now beginning to wear down, and in any event it was a little soon for cross-referenced mind-warping. It was now fairly safe to assume that what he saw was real, physically.

The odds remained bad, however. He had not wanted to think about the next most likely prospect, but now he had to. What he saw could be a Dep.

The Deps were an alien species whose stellar ambition matched Man's own. Their technology lagged slightly behind Earth's, but they made up for this by other abilities. Because they were GO star-system residents of an Earthtype planet, their needs were basically parallel to Man's, and that meant specific competition for choice worlds. A state of war did not exist currently, but the peace, to put it euphemistically, was uncertain.

The UN suit fired a last burst from its centre of gravity – jokes were rife and obvious – and contacted the surface of the planetoid. It tumbled and bounced, the wearer not expert at this manoevre. Then it righted itself and attempted to walk towards the station.

Leo smiled grimly. Walking on a low-G rock was not the same as doing it on a smooth metal hull. Here the magnetic shoes had nothing to cling to, and friction with the surface was virtually nil. The figure rose slowly into the black sky rather than going forward.

Why hadn't he spotted the wreck? It should have been well within the range of his instruments, and the telltales should have Christmassed. That was another augury in favour of a Dep intruder: a deliberately landed spy.

Though it was not like them to oversight such an important detail as a fake wreck.

The Deps: vernacular for Adepts, in turn the informal term for the species that could change its physical features at will to match those of any similar animal. Man was similar. Coupled with this was a certain force of personality that, it was said, caused the viewer to overlook minor discrepancies. Thus a Dep spy could be frighteningly effective. He looked like a man, and his faked identification seemed to check out. Even machine inspection was not always proof against error. Cases were on record where an identified Dep had been passed in spite of mechanical protest. The operator had been sure the device was malfunctioning, since the subject was obviously human.

Strenuous measures had been required to root out Dep spies from Earth's environs, and some innocent humans had been liquidated in the process. But the job had been done. Computerized laboratories were capable of identifying suspects and passing sentence, and were not affected by the subjective aura. The threat of Dep infiltration, while still present, was no longer serious.

The suited figure finally got its bearings and made respectable progress towards the entry port. Leo had to make his decision soon.

Space was large, suit-range small. Human survivor of unobserved wreck: thousand-to-one odds against? Million-to-one?

On the other hand, how about a Dep infiltration attempt, here and now? Maybe only ten-to-one against.

He could blast the human-looking figure where it stood. He had more destructive power under his thumb than Man had been capable of imagining through most of his history. He could devastate men, ships and even small planets. He was the guardian of this system, equipped to make intrusion by aliens entirely too costly to be worthwhile.

But suppose the visitor were legitimate? Overwhelming as the odds against it were, it *was* possible. Should he risk murder?

The visitor was at the port. He could not ignore it. A human would soon die out there, as the suit ran down; an alien would arrange somehow to sabotage the station.

It would be safer to blast it. His duty required that he act with cognizance of the odds. Nothing should jeopardize Earth security.

Yet – he was lonely. Two weeks had impressed him forcefully what fourteen months would be like. If he blasted now, he would not know whether he had done right or wrong. Not for thirteen and a half months, when the relief ship took in the frozen toasted fragments and analysed the flesh.

Loneliness was bad, but that grisly uncertainty would be worse. And if the body *were* human . . .

He was fairly secure, physically. He could admit that visitor and make his own investigation. He would be reprimanded, of course. It was not his business to take chances.

He was lonely. His resistance to temptation was not that good. He pressed the stud that opened the lock.

The figure entered. The port swung shut, resealed. Air cycled into the chamber. Now Leo could talk to his guest without employing monitored radio.

'Identify yourself,' he said. 'You have fifteen seconds before I fry you with high voltage.'

Muffled through the helmet, the nervous reply came: 'Miss Nevada Brown, colony ship *Expo 99*. Please don't – fry me!'

A woman!

Nonplussed, he drew his hand back from the incinerator control. He had not been bluffing. Whatever language the visitor spoke, human or alien, the meaning of his challenge would have been clear. No person got into space without becoming aware of the hairtrigger reflexes of station operatives.

Those reflexes were sadly disordered now! A man he could have dealt with. A woman – how could he kill her? Even if she were a Dep – and this was distinctly possible – it was hardly in him to – to do what was necessary. Spaceships he could blast; women, no. His conditioning was not that good.

'Take off your suit and deposit any weapons on the shelf,' he said, trying to restore gruffness to his voice. Weapons? The weapons a woman wore were part of her body. 'I'm watching you.' And he remembered belatedly to turn on the screen. He really was shaken.

Obligingly she stripped the bulky segments away. The process took some time, since a UN suit was intended to be safe, not convenient. He noted with guilty disappointment that she was adequately covered underneath. Some people wore their suits nude, to facilitate circulation of air and heat.

A woman! Human or Dep? On the verdict hung months of delight or torment worse than either loneliness or guilt. If she were really from a colony ship –

Hands quivering, he punched for information from the register.

Expo 99: WORLD'S FAIR, LOCATION MADAGASCAR, 1999. ATTENDANCE, CUMULATIVE, 42,000,000 PAID. POINTS OF SIGNIFICANCE –

He cut it off and punched a correction. It was the *ship* he wanted.

In the interval the girl had emerged from her suit. She was a young brunette, slender rather than voluptuous, and not shown to best advantage by the rumpled coverall she wore. Her hair was quite short, in the fashion of most women who went to space – apart from so-called entertainers – and her ears stuck out a bit. Not the kind he would have looked at even once, back on Earth with his million-dollar retirement fund.

But this was not yet Earth. This was isolation for another thirteen and a half months, while his station orbited its numbered sun and at length returned to a favourable orientation for rendezvous. For that lean period, *any* woman would be lovely, particularly a young one.

Any human woman.

He looked at the register's message: DATA INSUFFICIENT.

Leo punched a clarification, but he already knew what it meant. There was no such ship. The girl was a phony.

Incinerate her?

She was pathetically fragile in her tousled state, and breathing rapidly from nervous energy. She was well aware of her danger.

It flashed through his mind: *even a Dep female would be company*.

He released the inner lock and admitted her to the station.

He met her in the comfortable day room. She was still unsteady in the gravity field, after her time in a free-fall. Her shoulders and breasts sagged slightly, as though they had lost their tonus in space. She had tried to straighten her outfit, to make herself presentable; but a moment of primping could hardly undo days of suit-confinement. Particularly when the natural attributes were modest. As a pinup she was not that good.

'Sit down,' he said curtly, refusing to address her by name.

'Thank you.' Grateful but not graceful, she took one of

the overstuffed chairs. The station was small, but the day room was intended to be as homey as 'feasible', to mitigate the starkness of the duty.

'I believe you are an agent of an alien power,' he said. 'Specifically, you are a Dep spy.'

Her mouth opened. She wore no lipstick or other makeup, such things not conducive to survival in space. Her eyes were shadowed by fatigue, not artifice. Her teeth were subtly uneven. He knew her for an alien creature, yet every detail was painfully human.

'Hold your comment,' he said, preventing her from speaking. He knew he had to do this rapidly or his nerve would break. He was not a military man, though for this single tour he was subject to military regulations. Discipline in the soldier-sense was more a sometime concept than gut-reality to him. 'My name is Leo MacHenry and I have no Scottish or Irish blood that I know of. I am a civilian mercenary on duty for fourteen months, most of which lie before me. I am being well paid for this service because personality tests indicate that I am more likely to survive with my wits intact than a conventional soldier would be. I mean to complete my tour honourably and retire to rich living and overindulgent amours for the ensuing fifty years.

'I am keyed in to this station in such a way that I cannot leave it even to walk the surface of the planetoid without destroying it and myself. Only the relief ship has the equipment to re-key for the next observer. My brain waves are continually monitored by the main computer. If they stop – that is, if I should die or suffer some drastic mental change, such as entering a drugged state – the computer will detonate this station immediately. The radius of total destruct is well beyond the distance any person could travel in a space suit, because of needle shrapnel and lethal radiation. There are other safeguards of more devious but effective nature. My point is that I am to all intents and purposes invulnerable here. I made you leave your weapons' – she had had a heatbeamer and a knife, both standard for a UN suit – 'only to prevent you from attempting anything foolish before I had a chance to talk to you. I may look ordinary, but any serious attack on me will bring your demise or our mutual destruction. This in turn will summon a competent Earth-fleet ready and eager for trouble.

'I run this station. No other person can do so much as open a door except at my direction, because of the electronic and neural keying. You cannot leave, you cannot obtain food, you cannot even use the sanitary facilities without my cooperation. I intend either to execute you or to hold you here until the relief ship arrives, at which point I will turn you over to the appropriate authorities for interrogation and probably liquidation.

'I will, however, give you one chance for freedom, since your presence here will be a severe blot on my record. If you wish to leave right now you may do so; I will let you take off in your suit and return to your compatriots with the news that my station is in business for the duration. I suggest that you accept it; it is an easy way out for both of us.'

He turned his back on her to hide his own nervousness. He had done it. He had made his speech, and it was all true, except that his discipline was not that good. Not the good at all. He could let her go, but if she decided to stay he – even if she were a Dep spy –

He was lonely and, suddenly, woman-hungry. He would try to keep her prisoner, but inevitably come in time to treat her less as a suspect and more as – as what she seemed. Already he was sorely tempted. Perhaps that was what the Dep command had counted on. That he would penetrate the ruse but submit to a gradual, emotional subversion. A year was plenty of time to do the job. A year of propinquity, and he would no longer care. He would have a new loyalty. After that –

She looked up at him. 'I – I don't know what to say, Mr MacHenry. Except that I'm not – what you said. I don't know why you don't believe me. But I can't go. My ship isn't there any more. I – I didn't want to say this because I'll get in trouble, but I – jumped ship, and it went on without me. I knew I was breaking the law, but it was my only chance. To get back to Earth. So I guess you'll have to lock me up, if that's what you want.'

She was going to play it out, and she was letter-perfect! He felt, oddly, relieved. Her departure would have been a confession of guilt, and he would have had to shoot down the alien ship the moment he spotted its location. This way there was at least a chance she was real. A chance he knew he was foolish to hope for. The subversion was proceeding too rapidly, but he was helpless to inhibit it because his will to do so was uncertain.

'Your ship wasn't wrecked?' he asked. 'The – *Expo 99*?'

'Did I say that?' She was prettily surprised. 'I meant the *Exton 99*. We called it Expo, but that was just slang. Yes, it couldn't hang around for a solitary deserter, and – '

Leo left her in mid-sentence and strode to the control room. He punched for the revised designation.

Exton 99: ONE OF A SERIES OF COLONY SHIPS BOUND FOR THE SO-CALLED ADEPT SPHERE PERIMETER, PERSONNEL SELECTED BY INVOLUNTARY LOT –

Ouch! That was one of the press-gang fleets that filled their complements by pseudo-random drafts on the labour force. Volunteers for adverse locations were few, so this was a legalized piracy of talent similar to the old-time military service call-ups during the frequent wars-to-end-wars. Somehow the rich or influential seldom got called: another time-honoured corruption. Graft or draft was the word. Selection for such an expedition meant a lifetime of hard service and a death on some frontier world for the unhappy recruit.

Yet politically it was sound. It eased unemployment on Earth while strengthening the planet's galactic posture. New worlds had to be tamed and developed, and this system accomplished it on a crash basis. The volume of space Leo's own station guarded would eventually be colonized this way. The majority of the voters were beyond the age or health of eligibility, so from their safety approved the draft.

Democracy, as the exported minority discovered, was not invariably fair. Leo had obtained his exemption by qualifying for his present tour, but he retained no sympathy for the system. It was merely yet another form of involuntary servitude.

No wonder Nevada Brown had jumped ship when she had a chance! Life on Earth was crowded but affluent; life elsewhere was grim. She must have watched for her opportunity and made her move when the ship slowed for a course correction. Colony ships seldom proceeded directly to their destination, since it was dangerous to pinpoint these for enemy observers. 'The 'enemy' constituted obstructive families of draftees as well as competitive alien species.

He owed an apology to his guest. She *was* human.

Oh-oh. This was the way the Dep influence worked. He had been well briefed on this. While Nevada stood in the airlock he had verified that her given identification was spurious. Now that he had talked to her directly, he had changed his mind. It was too easy to call his first assessment an error. It had been an objective one, while

what followed was more likely to be subjective. He had
wanted to believe her story, and had substituted the name
of a real ship for the one she had invented.

Though why she hadn't given him a real ship the first
time, when the Dep researchers had surely had the
information . . .

He returned to the day room, perplexed. Nevada had
not moved. She was still rumpled, legs slightly bowed,
nose a little too long, not homely so much as imperfectly
pretty. Even her youth did not become her particularly;
she had not yet mastered the studied grace of the experienced woman, the flair for accenting the desirable and
phasing out of the undesirable.

All of which argued in her favour. A Dep courtesan
would have been a beauty, since all her details would have
been under control. Nothing about her would rankle.

Yet – he was alert for the Dep perfection. So it stood
to reason his suspicions could best be allayed by token
*im*perfections. . . .

Yet again: She *could* be valid. Her story was now a
good one, that he could not disprove. He had figured the
chances for a human shipwreck here. But a deliberate
desertion in the vicinity of a manned observation station,
by a colonist with a legitimate grievance – that was far
less improbable. Perhaps only ten to one odds against.
The same as those against overt infiltration by a Dep spy,
by his crude reckoning. That evened the odds; she was as
likely to be human as Dep.

Except that a Dep would naturally present him with a
convincing story.

What was he to believe? He *wanted* to accept her as
human. That would be so much simpler and so much
more pleasant. But he stood to lose fortune, life and
mission if he made a mistake. The wrong mistake.

The right mistake, of course, would be to kill her and

discover subsequently that she had been human. He would not be held culpable in the circumstances.

She continued to sit there, watching him with brown eyes but not speaking. The odds were with the execution – murder – but he just wasn't that reasonable.

He could obtain accurate odds for all eventualities by punching for them, but he preferred to settle this his own way. The consequence of his decision would fall on his head and soul, not the computer.

'I am not sure about you,' he said at last. 'You may be human and you may be Dep.'

Again he wondered whether the mistake of accepting a Dep lover might not be worth it. There was subtle and unsubtle fascination about –

'I can tell you about myself,' she said eagerly. 'Where I was born, who my folks are – things no alien could know – '

'Forget it. *I* wouldn't know them either. You could make up anything.'

'Couldn't you look it up in your computer? Doesn't it list everything that – '

'The register is encyclopedic, not omniscient,' he said sharply. 'It has every fact I might reasonably need or want to know – but it can't list every teenage girl in the overpopulated world.'

'I'm twenty-two,' she said, offended. 'They don't draft you until you're – '

'Anyway, the name, even if listed, wouldn't prove a thing. A Dep would research it before coming here.'

'Oh.' She pondered a moment, still justifiably nervous. 'But there must be things I know that you could verify that an alien couldn't. I've spent my life on Earth, after all. Maybe we know some of the same people and – '

'No. The only things I could verify that way would be suspect because I *did* know them. I would think you had told them to me, but actually I would be picking them out of my own memory.'

She stared at him, her small chin rumpling as though she were about to cry. 'You mean – I can't use anything you don't know, because I can't prove it, and I can't use anything you *do* know because – ?'

'Yes. So I'm afraid I'm going to have to' – she stiffened – 'hold you prisoner, until the ship comes.' He was a ludicrous weakling; he should simply have shot her. In fact, he was admitting defeat, if she were a Dep. It might mean the destruction of the station, or his own betrayal of his world, but simply lacked the fortitude to do what was necessary. He was not that good a guardian.

'Oh. I thought you were going to – I guess that makes sense, though. To turn me over to the authorities, I mean, since you can't be sure.' Her relief was pitiful. She knew now that she wouldn't be killed, whichever way it went.

She stood up. 'A Dep would know – enemy secrets, or something, too. So it would be right. I guess I should go to the cell now. I hope it's clean.'

'There is no cell. You'll have to use this room.' And a Dep would have known *that*, too.

She looked around, comprehending. 'Oh.'

'I'll reprogramme the life-services equipment to provide for your needs. You'll have to ask me for any reading matter you want, and I'll have printouts made. Most of what we have here is technical, though. The station wasn't set up for – entertainment.'

'But what will you do?' she inquired with half-coy solicitude. 'I mean, you can't stay in the control room all the time, or in the storeroom, or whatever.'

He shrugged.

'But it really makes *you* more of a prisoner than – ' she cried, breaking off unfinished.

In more ways than one, sister! 'Nevada, it *would* be convenient if there were some way to determine for certain what you are,' Leo said. 'Even an inconvenient way. But there isn't, since I don't have a lab here. So we'll just have to make do – unless you want to leave now.'

'I guess I should,' she said. 'But I'd die, and my willpower is not that good. Isn't there *any* way to – ' Her eyes brightened suddenly. 'You say the ship isn't coming for over a year?'

Leo nodded. 'Barring a blowup.'

'And I'll just have to stay here until they can identify me for sure? And if I'm human it's all right, but if I'm alien, trying to sneak into Earth's defences, they'll kill me?'

'Close enough. I explained all that before. You aren't going to accomplish anything if you're a spy, so you might as well quit. If you go now, you can save your life and my reputation.' But he was bluffing.

'So it really doesn't make any difference what happens until the ship comes,' she said excitedly. 'Except that it would be a lot nicer if I could prove to you I'm human.' She was smoothing herself out now with motions more suggestive than practical.

'Yes. But if you're thinking of the classic "proof", it's no good. A Dep can make sex too. Better than a real woman, they say. That changes nothing.'

'You're wrong,' she said with new confidence. 'Give me a few days to – to get to know you. Then I – I'll prove it. Really prove it. It'll be rough, but you'll see.'

The reliefship captain was shocked. 'You admitted an intruder? Here near the Dep frontier? Do you realize what this means?'

'I realize,' Leo said. 'It was a chance, but I'll gladly

stand court-martial for what I did. But I intend to introduce in my own defence evidence that I kept good watch and even repelled an alien probe that might ordinarily have overcome the station and made this entire system hostile to Man. They were going to radiation-bomb it, you see, so we couldn't develop it for centuries. I think they're getting desperate, to try that. That should count for something.'

'Repelled a probe?' The captain seemed to have been left behind.

'A Dep fleet that meant business. Less than a month ago. They fired saturation missiles, trying to knock out this station first. Must have cost them a fortune. I would never have nullified them all if Nevada hadn't acted as an additional spotter. She called them off by coordinates, so I was able to devote my full attention to gunning them down. Quadrupled my efficiency. Good thing, too; it's tricky trying to intercept meteor-shower type shells. The Deps hadn't expected a coordinated defence to their surprise attack.'

'Of course not,' the captain said. 'That's an overt act of war – unless they managed to cover it up somehow. It changes the whole picture. But why should a Dep spy *help* you to – why, obviously she had been sent to incapacitate you in advance.'

Leo grinned. 'I could say my charm converted her to my side, but it wouldn't stick. She's *human*. I verified that. I knew I could trust her, and we had a lot to fight for.'

'Mr MacHenry, there is no way you could have been sure of that. You have no laboratory. The Deps are unexcelled at disguise and indirection.'

'On the contrary. We have the very best laboratory. The one no alien can fool. All it takes is – '

He was interrupted by the sound of a baby crying.

The captain didn't make the connection immediately. 'I tell you the Deps are too good at – ' Then he paused, mouth open.

'Not that good, Captain. They can't hide the *whole* truth,' Leo said, smiling with something more than victory. 'Which reminds me. It will be your privilege to perform the ceremony for Nevada and me, now that the job is done. I want little Nev to have a proper name, and naturally my wife will be entitled to remain with me on Earth.'

The Bridge

These stories are presented here approximately in the order I wrote them. It can be difficult to ascertain the precise dates, as the prior story illustrates: was it when I dreamed it up, or when I summarized it for others, or when I wrote it? I normally do three drafts of my fiction, and sometimes set a draft aside while I write other fiction that may be submitted to market first. What date counts? 'University' sat a full year between its first and second drafts, while I worked on novels on deadlines. 'Bridge' was sent to *Nova* a month before 'Whole Truth' was, yet I think it is a more recent story in total history, so that is its order here. If you disagree, simply tear out these pages and insert them in your copy before 'Whole Truth'. (I try to please everyone.)

You may have noticed that the stories in this volume have been getting more provocative, here in the mid-anatomy of the volume. The change was not in me but in the market; at this time, thanks perhaps to the impact of *Dang Vis*, it was loosening up. Editors were considering material they might have burned before. Still, after *Nova* this story bounced at *Playboy*, *Cavalier*, *F&SF*, *Knight* and *Evergreen Review*. I had supposed that the sexy male mags would appreciate truly fantastic sex. I was wrong.

Meanwhile, changes were occurring in the SF magazine circuit. *Galaxy* Publications had been bought out, Pohl was gone, and the new editor was Ejler Jakobsson. Judy-Lynn remained, contrary to my prior memory; don't worry, I assure you she will get to Ballantine Books in

due course, after she finished teaching Ejler the ropes.
Ejler came to a writers' conference in my area, and I
dropped in and met him on June 12, 1969. He wanted
material. I was then mostly into novels, but I did have a
couple of last year's provocative pieces still bouncing
around. One was 'Minnie's Crew'. Somewhat warily I
mentioned it. After all, new editor or not, *Galaxy* Publications was not your avant-garde publisher. Ejler wanted
to see it. Okay, he had asked for it. I sent it. Within a
week he phoned me, accepting it. A regular SF outfit
was buying the story that had scared off the horny male
mags! A special kind of history was in the making here.
He retitled it, of course, as 'The Bridge' and published it
in *Worlds of Tomorrow* as the cover story. Yes, this time
I even got my name on the cover, printed right under
Minnie's pert breasts. No, I can't really argue with the
new title, for once; my 'Miniscrew' was a bit too cute.

Reader, be advised: this just may be the wildest sex
ever to see print in a conventional genre magazine. If
you blanched at 'Barn' or shied from 'Schist', you had
better balk at 'Bridge'. If you prefer to call my bluff, then
read on. Henceforth maybe you will have more respect
for my warnings.

1 Petite Dream-Girl

'Please.' The voice was small but distinctly feminine and
seemed to emanate inches from his ear. 'Please, Mr
Fowler, please wake up.'

'Burg to my friends,' he muttered sleepily. He was
one of those bachelors the men's magazines declined to
acknowledge – the kind that works for a living and sleeps
alone. On weekends such as this he liked to sleep late in
spite of an early bedtime. This was partly to get back at

the alarm clock and partly because it made the day shorter. At the moment he was in that transitional state he sometimes achieved upon such lazy awakening – in it he could hear and to a certain extent control intriguing dream dialogue.

'Please, Mr Fowler. We only have an hour. Please look at me.'

'Sure, honey,' he murmured, eyes closed. The voice was absolutely lovely and remarkably convincing, as though a beautiful woman lay beside him. He had never before indulged in such a pleasant trance. But he knew that it would dissipate the moment he opened his eyes. All that shared his bedroom by daylight were dirty socks, clean shirts, a portable radio afflicted with intermittent static and last night's cold-slopped coffee. And, of course, the book he had read himself to sleep on. What was it? He couldn't remember.

Something soft touched his right ear.

He twitched his head aside, instantly alert. Light blinded him, forcing his eyes shut again. This had never been part of a dialogue! Had a moth got in?

He turned his head carefully and squinted.

Suddenly he remembered what he had been reading. It was a text from a night course in British poetry. He had signed up in the hope that he might meet his dream girl on the college campus, since he hadn't met her elsewhere. Unfortunately it developed that few women took night courses and those who did were mostly centenarian schoolteachers in for recency-of-credit. But he had discovered serendipitously that old-time verse was not entirely dull; indeed, it was as though the poets were men very like himself, bound by similar frustrations but with the wit to make them elegant. Andrew Marvell complained about his coy mistress (at least he *had* one); Lord Byron rhapsodized about a maid of Athens; Dante

Gabriel Rossetti (always learn the full name, the professor admonished the class) commented on a goblet supposedly moulded in the shape of the breast of Helen of Troy. That was the poem Burg had fallen asleep on: *Troy Town*.

Heavenborn Helen, Sparta's queen/(O Troy Town!)/ Had two breasts of heavenly sheen/ . . .

He couldn't remember the rest.

He had seen those two breasts, those images of man's desire. Supple yet voluptuous, firm yet perfect. Just now.

'That's not fair, Mr Fowler. You didn't really look.'

He opened his eyes fully. A doll stood on his pillow. A nine-inch high, gracefully woman-shaped figurine dressed in yellow. Its proportions were so accurately and lovingly rendered that the effect was rather like contemplating a real woman from a distance. This replica had everything. In fact, it was very like his fanciful ideal.

'I can explain,' the doll said in that same delightful voice. 'I thought you'd like to see me nude but since you shut your eyes again so quickly I decided – '

Burgess Fowler rolled off the bed and stumbled to the bathroom. He ran the sink full of cold water and dunked his face in it open-eyed. Then, absolutely awake, he performed certain other routine morning chores and returned in his pyjamas to the bedroom.

'We have only fifty minutes left,' she complained. 'You're not being very cooperative, Mr Fowler.'

He sat down on the bed. 'Troy Town!' He was not a swearing man ordinarily. 'I don't touch drugs of any kind, so it isn't that. I drink only in moderation and never alone. I am not overtired and when I am I'm not much given to hallucinations. I – '

The doll stamped her little foot on the top sheet. Her heel made a pinpoint dent.

'The committee went to a great deal of trouble to

locate you and learn your tastes and – and get me here,' she said. 'You're wasting invaluable time, Mr Fowler. Please listen to – '

Burg brought her to him with a sweep of his left hand. 'Now, my little practical joke!' he said. 'We'll see what makes you operate – '

She was not doll-like to the touch. His hand enclosed her torso and his thumb was aware of two singularly realistic breasts – the same he had seen in the first bright glimpse? – rising and falling under the dress while his palm felt the rondure of a sweet derriere. Her waist was lithe and narrow, her hips soft and broad. She was warm and she smelled of perfume – a brand he could not name, but liked.

He set her down, disgruntled.

'You can't be alive.'

She rearranged her apparel and combed the tangles out of her hair. Her tresses were the precise shade of brown he liked, curled in just-so.

'If you will only pay attention, Mr Fowler!'

'I'm trying to – but you're hard to believe at one sitting.'

'I know I'm a little small for you but it was the best they could do. There is so little time. Please help me, Mr Fowler.'

Burg would still have dismissed her as some kind of a powered toy, except for the remembered feel of her body and her present too-human animation. A doll did not breathe, and certainly did not react as directly and specifically as she was doing. 'All right, I'll help you, mini-girl whoever you are. Whatever you say your crew sent you for. What do you want?'

'I want,' she said seriously, 'to make love.'

2. Animate Senescence

The Council of Oomus foregathered in tired splendour. All of the scions of the leading lines were present: the ranking scientists, philosophers and economists of the world. Here in the temple of the ancients, within a chamber overlooking the effete surging of the Sea of Life, they harkened to momentous developments.

The chairman withdrew his perception from the demesnes of that waning Source and broadcast for attention. Once such a signal might have bathed the planet – now it was barely sufficient to alert those nearest. The minds within the great old hall yielded courteously.

Please review the discussion of our last Assembly, the chairman thought.

The Recorder now projected his summary. *At our last Assembly, three years ago, we received the report of the Committee on the State and Sadness of our World. We reluctantly accepted the verdict of our brothers: that our present misfortune is due to a condition of animate senescence. Unless rejuvenation occurs within our lifetime, the critical point will pass and our form of life, including the animation of all our world, will inexorably perish. Therefore we agreed to undertake radical measures and invest our remaining reserves in a project promising relief. This consists of negotiating and expediting an exchange with a world possessing a surplus of the animus we require.*

An Economist interjected: *Omission! We cannot permit specific communication with another realm, though extinction be the forfeit. So has our inviolable custom been; so it must remain.*

Correction incorporated, the Recorder explained. *The exchange was to be instituted in such a way that our identity is never betrayed, yet complete satisfaction rendered to the other party. Above all, it is our custom to be ethical.*

Yet satisfaction may be achieved in divers ways. Such a programme was instituted by an ad hoc Committee and the Assembly adjourned.

The Chairman thanked the Recorder. Then: *What is the report of that duly constituted Expeditionary Committee?*

3. Courtship

'Mini-girl – mind if I call you Minnie? There are things that I might do for you, and gladly,' Burg said. 'But making love is not among them. For that you need a man. A man your size, I mean.'

'Oh, no, Mr Fowler,' she protested, laying a tiny hand on his little finger. 'It must be you. They were very clear about that. You have just the right – I mean, I exist only for you. I love you.'

There was, then, an ulterior motive of some sort. The crew that had sent her to him had a price for its service. He was not, however, obliged to accept it, since this was unsolicited merchandise. She could charm him as she wished, but that would be all. He was not going to pay any exorbitant fee for this doll, or sign any dubious documents.

The strange thing was that, whatever her secret, she did conform to his ideals of femininity. Had she been full-size, her measurements would have been about 36-24-36, or perhaps a trifle more generous, with all the other physical attributes congenial. More than that, there was an intangible charm about her, a symmetry of manner and proportion that evoked pleasure in the contemplation. Her attire complemented her features perfectly, and her face had just that quality of imperfect maturity he preferred. Even her little mannerisms, such as the conservative – yet exciting – way she put her slender fingers on him and the lift of her fine chin when she spoke – all of it was the kind of thing he had been searching for and had, in his not-so-secret heart, never expected to attain. For if such a woman were ever to appear before him, he could be certain she would be snapped up by a more wealthy, muscular or articulate male. Yet here she was.

And when she claimed to love him, he felt an adolescent thrill, square as he knew this reaction to be in an adult.

But . . .

'I feel complimented,' he told her gently. 'But I have to point out that there are sharp limits – '

'No. No limits. And we have only forty minutes. Please, Mr Fowler, we have to get started.' She sat down on the coverlet and removed her shoes. One thigh showed alluringly as her leg lifted.

He chucked her under the chin with a careful finger. 'There has to be a misunderstanding, sweetheart. You're very pretty and I like you but – maybe you'd better tell me exactly what you mean by "making love".'

She stood up. She ran a hand down her side and her yellow dress fell open. She shrugged out of it, folded it meticulously (he liked that, too) and stood before him in bra and petticoat. She drew the petticoat over her head.

'I fear our definitions coincide,' Burg said quickly. It was as though a real woman were baring herself and he wasn't used to it. 'But – surely you see that it's impossible. Physically impossible. You and I – well, it's impossible.'

'No, it isn't,' she said confidently, as she reached behind to unfasten the bra. 'You're a man and I'm a woman and I love you.' The bra came free, revealing that spectacular scale-model bosom. Then she dropped her panties.

Ah, yes – complete and desirable in every respect.

And nine inches tall.

'Now it's your turn,' she said.

'Look, Minnie – this is ridiculous. I can't – '

'Please, Mr Fowler!' she urged him. 'Get undressed.'

'You don't understand – '

She dabbed her face with a handkerchief the size of a postage stamp. 'You don't love me! You won't even give me a ch-chance!'

Feeling like both fool and heel, he removed his pyjamas. Of all the ways to be spending a Saturday morning!

'Good,' she said, looking him over demurely. 'Now lie down.'

He lay on his back next to her.

She trotted up and leaned against his chin. 'You haven't shaved.'

'I'll go take care of it right now,' he said, grateful for the pretext to remove himself from this embarrassing charade.

'No – there isn't time. Kiss me,' she said, and leaned over his face to plant her full red lips against his mouth. Her breasts nudged his cheek and she had one bare foot braced in his ear, but the overall effect, oddly, was potent.

Then she climbed up a little more so that her breasts hung above his mouth. Suddenly some more of the poem popped into his mind. Queen Helen's commentary on her own physique.

Yea, for my bosom here I sue:/(O Troy Town!)/Thou must give it where 'tis due,/Give it there to the heart's desire./Whom do I give my bosom to?/(O Troy's down,/Tall Troy's on fire!)

It was given to Burg. The breasts pressed down between his lips, their miniature nipples touching his tongue. He couldn't help warming to the sensual impact of her body.

He licked the heart's desire.

'You do want me, don't you?' she inquired.

What could he say? He was drinking from Helen's goblet and Tall Troy was on fire.

4. Expedition

The Thoughtsman for the ad hoc Expeditionary Committee presented his report. *We divided our mission into two prime areas of endeavour: first, the arrangements for the emissary to solicit a suitable exchange; second, the mechanical provisions for transfer of the shipment. Both areas had unique problems. We could not send one of our own number as emissary, for reasons hitherto discussed, so we formulated a matrix of suitable configuration and cultured it remotely to serve in lieu of direct confrontation. The proteins for the multicellular entity were garnered from the substances available on that world –*

Several interjections: *Multicellular entity? Why attempt such an unwieldly construction? Surely there is a less tedious way!*

The Thoughtsman waited for the commentary to subside. *Compatriots, our need is massive and immediate. We felt that our purpose would best be served by dealing with one of the larger species, one capable of delivering the entire shipment in a matter of hours. If our present, admittedly ambitious, scheme succeeds, we should have complete delivery by the terminus of this Assembly.*

There was a complimentary aura of awe.

Then another protest: *But at what price, Thoughtsman? We shall have to mortgage our entire resources for a thousand generations even to approach a fair exchange for such immediate service!*

Not so, the Thoughtsman replied. *We need only agree*

*to mutually beneficial terms. In this case we believe our
emissary will be able to give satisfactory value. Therefore
the shipment should cost us nothing more than the effort
of obtaining it.*

*But we cannot offer in exchange any information about
ourselves or deriving from our researches! What else, apart
from physical goods, could the emissary arrange for?*

Love, the Thoughtsman replied.

5. Act of Love

Minnie trotted down Burg's chest, stomach and abdomen,
her bare feet pattering ticklishly. When she reached the
major bifurcation she kneeled in the brush, wrapped her
arms about the cannon she found there, and pressed her
resilient breasts against it.

Troy had never stood taller.

In the living room the clock chimed eight.

This abrupt reminder of the real world brought the
weirdness of the situation home to him with renewed
force. There was of course no mini-woman; he was lying
stepped in his own concupiscence and he had better get
up before he fouled the sheet. It had been a fabulous
fantasy, ridiculous but exciting – but there were limits.

'You'll have to sit up, Mr Fowler,' she said. 'The angle
is wrong, this way.'

Burg lifted his head and saw her: a lushly naked woman
straddling the canting trunk of a leaning beech tree as
though it were a seesaw.

He sat up carefully, swinging his gross feet off the side
of the bed while she clung to her support with arms and
legs. He didn't know what to do except comply with her
requests; the trust was too incredible to argue with.

'Give me your hand,' she said.

He put out a hand and she braced herself against his thumb. She climbed just high enough to sit on the apex of the now-vertical stump, her slim legs coming down on either side. He could feel her smooth muscular buttocks and the moist warmth of her cleft as she squirmed around to seat herself firmly, facing him. Her waist was no larger than the purple hassock she bestrode.

She squirmed some more and the action was almost painfully titillating. He began to comprehend how physical intercourse could take place between them: her aperture, properly positioned, might match and seal over the vent in the hydrant.

Burg closed his eyes and let her proceed as she wished. Astonishingly, this enhanced the sensation; it felt as though she were gradually enclosing him. Tip, glans, stem, stage by stage. This was utterly impossible; Minnie's entire torso was hardly four inches long.

He felt the ejaculation coming on – but that brought him to his senses again. So there was a doll-woman perched on the tower; accepting that much, the force of the incipient eruption would surely skewer her. That would not be funny at all. He remembered reading about one of the Nazi atrocities. They had taken one of the death-camp inmates, a young girl, forced the nozzle of a fire-hose into her vagina, tied it in place and turned the water on full force. That image made him recoil all over; it applied too specifically.

'Mr Fowler!' Minnie cried.

Burg opened his eyes, then his mouth. The girl was squatting in his lap – and tall Troy was into her a good three inches, yet her torso retained its original and delectable dimensions. It was as though his substance vanished once it penetrated her.

'Mr Fowler – you're shrinking.'

So he was; that torture-image and now his amazement at what he saw had taken the starch from his ardour.

'Look, Minnie – what if I should – ?'

'We only have a few minutes,' she said reproachfully. 'You can't fail me now.'

Detumescence continued, however, and her whole body tilted to one side as her support became jelly.

'But the – where will it go?' he demanded academically. What did not come, could not go. 'You'll be – hurt.'

She brought her knees together, putting pressure on the portion of him that remained within her. His flesh responded mechanically to the kneading of her well-formed limbs and began to grow again.

'Minnie, don't you know what happens when – '

'When the semen comes? Of course I know. And it has to be within five minutes or it's all wasted. Please, Mr Fowler – you have to help, you know.'

He saw his member expanding enormously under this stimulation, pushing back into the space between her thighs. She bounced her body, taking in yet more of him. Penetration was back to three inches and still she flexed her legs and slid farther down the tower.

Burg made a last effort to get through to her intellectually before the automatic process took over. 'Minnie, there's going to be a lot of – pressure. Are you sure you have – room?'

'Do you love me?' she asked.

So even dream-girls had feminine foibles. 'Yes, I – I guess I do. It's crazy and backwards – but I love you. You're my ideal, Minnie, in miniature.'

'I'm so glad,' she said, smiling. 'And I love you, Burg.' She was finally using his first name, as though his confession of love justified an intimacy of address that the prior circumstances had not. 'And will you let me keep everything that comes?'

'It's a love offering,' he said. 'The truest kind. You can keep all you can hold, now and forever.'

'Shake on it?' She proferred a doll-like hand.

He put out his right forefinger and she grasped the finger-nail and tugged it solemnly up and down. They could not shake hands properly, he thought, but they could fornicate. What next?

'Then it's all right,' she said. 'Thank you, Burg.'

And she straightened out both legs in an L-formation, scissored them wide and slid pneumatically down as though his manhood were a greased piston. Her dainty bottom landed warmly against his scrotum.

Her four-inch torso had absorbed him – yet remained as slender and virginal as ever.

6. Pipeline

The mechanical aspect is even more critical, The Thoughtsman explained. *The research required to locate a suitable and amenable subject could be done by straight observation and analysis but the physical construction of such a massive pipeline was an appalling project. Transmission has to be virtually instantaneous because of the perishability of the merchandise and the sheer volume also generates terrific problems. We have constructed a series of gateways, transfer-points to accommodate and differentiate the ingredients of the shipment. The first stage, located on the alien planet for convenience, connects directly to the input transmitter and is exceedingly large, since it must dock the alien tanker itself. Within it is a smaller transmitter to handle the cargo alone. The second stage, based on a world of our own system, is to receive and divide the mass into a number of lesser segments, each of which is retranslated individually.*

At this point the packaging material is also filtered out so that –

Not clear, a chorus of thoughts came. *Illustrate it.*

The Thoughtsman projected a diagram:

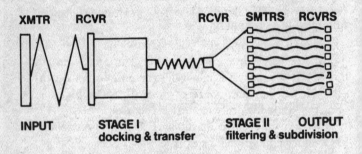

At any rate, the Thoughtsman finished, *we shall know very shortly. This Assembly chamber overlooks one of the five thousand output apertures distributed throughout our*

Now there was an aura of comprehension.

Because of the vagaries of planetary motion and interstellar transmission conditions, the Thoughtsman continued, *precise timing is essential. The other world, being of a larger order than our own, possesses a differential of duration with respect to ours that affects transmission. Our emissary has been most intricately programmed and is fully competent, but because of those time and size differentials is working under disadvantage.*

A chorus of thoughts interjected. *Are you implying that this could fail? That our tremendous effort and investment may be wasted? That you are gambling with our vital resources?*

No, No! the Thoughtsman protested. But the truth was out: the success of the entire project depended on the performance of a disadvantaged representative and they did not have sufficient resource to make a second attempt.

At any rate, the Thoughtsman finished, *we shall know very shortly. This Assembly chamber overlooks one of the five thousand output apertures distributed throughout our world. We shall witness success or failure before we disperse.*

There was nothing more to discuss. Tensely they concentrated on the aperture and waited for the verdict. Success would preserve their existence by providing the necessary hedge against continuing animate senescence; failure would bring them that much closer to extinction.

7. Climax

She sat upon him, her knees drawn up with her arms around them. 'It's almost time, Burg,' she said. 'We'd better start now. Put your hand around me.'

Start?

He curved his fingers around her body as she let go her knees to accommodate his embrace. He was amazed that she remained so delicate. He throbbed deep within her. By rights he should be projecting beyond her head, yet this was not the case.

Minnie took his fingers and pressed them against her breast and thighs. Sensitive now to the nuances of her tiny body, he reacted to the tender flesh as though it were full-size. Large or small, she *was* his dream-girl and he *did* love her. Culmination was incipient.

'Now!' she cried, flexing her entire body against him. 'Please, Burg, now!'

Stimulated by the frenzy of her flesh he let himself go. She clung to his fingers, kissing them and biting them.

Like the rumble of a live volcano it came, throbbing up from the fundament, pressuring chthonic valves, gathering into an irresistible swell. A steaming geyser distended the conduit and burst into individuality. And after it a second thrust pumped up from the depths to lay waste all hesitation. And a third, a fourth, and a fifth, spewed torrentially out in as many seconds. Then, with decreasing force, three more. And finally two others that oozed along as though squeezed from a tube of toothpaste, and apathy set in.

Troy was down.

Minnie slumped as he did, a weary but satisfied smile on her lovely face.

'We did it, Burg,' she whispered. 'We did it.'

As though, he thought, a great deal more had been at stake than an act of physical love between two people.

8. Denouement

Stage I was almost entirely filled by the tremendous turgid purple tanker from the alien world and when the first bolus avalanched from the gaping slit of its orifice the impact was such as virtually to sunder the cylinder. But the baffles held and the second transmitter channelled the viscous mass through in its entirety. The Stage II receiver, light-years distant, filtered and funnelled it into the myriad subtransmitters and it emerged at last in fractional spurts into the Sea of Life.

There was a collective sigh of minds as the Council of Oomus perceived the blast of plasma from the adjacent aperture. The shipment had come: ten thousand viable entities in this subsection alone, each living body over a foot in diameter with a flexing tail forty feet long, driving heedlessly forward as it encountered the living water.

Tall Troy's on fire! The Thoughtsman reflected for no sensible reason. What was fire? What was Troy?

And the giant, tired egg-matrices of Oomus were waiting for the amalgamation, for the vigour of new life, new notions, new chromosomes. All over the world, surrounding five thousand apertures, they were ready.

Semisentient masses capable of adapting if only granted a fresh blueprint in place of the senescent retreads of the past billion years. Now that rejuvenating strain had come – from a source whose monstrosity defied the imagination.

An hour later the second bolus arrived, as brisk and massive as the first. And an hour after that, the third.

The council remained for the full twelve hours the complete shipment took, perceiving every aspect raptly, though the last two surges were but gentle swells with little content. In all, five hundred million swimming sperm cells came, enough for every available egg. It meant salvation for Oomus. Not life as it had been, for these were alien chromosomes; but their uniformity guaranteed that every developing egg would be compatible with those of its generation. A new animation had replaced and improved the old.

And what of the emissary? the chairman inquired of the Thoughtsman as they basked in the ambient grandeur of the alien gift.

Contact has been broken, the Thoughtsman replied. *We could not maintain it longer; our mechanisms were out of power. She will have to remain there.*

Can she exist alone?

Oh yes – she is of otherworld substance but based on our own cellular design. She cannot imbibe nourishment in the alien manner but any future shipments she is able to procure will be conserved in Stage I and routed back to animate her own flesh. That segment of the equipment draws its power from the alien world and will function indefinitely. She can endure, theoretically, for a long time, many thousands of our years – if she is only able to obtain chromosome rejuvenation regularly.

I fear that is impossible, the chairman thought. *What alien would donate a cargo sufficient to reanimate an entire world just to oblige a creature like that? I deeply regret* that, in our urgency to save our form of existence, we were forced to create such an ungainly multicelled monster doomed to a brief and miserable existence.

It is hardly fair, the Thoughtsman agreed morosely. *She does have a good mind and strong feelings, since these were part of the necessary specifications for success. Had I not been preoccupied with our own concerns I would have remembered her situation and in mercy terminated her life as the mission ended. Even a monster does not deserve to suffer unnecessarily.*

But it was a minor sadness, in the face of their new joy.

On the Uses of Torture

After 'Bridge' you may be wondering what could be more provocative. The answer is the following story, 'Torture'. But this one is not sweet and sexy. I like to try my talent in new ways, and this time I set out to write the most brutal fiction the market could sustain. It turned out that I was again ahead of my time. Ejler Jakobsson bought 'Torture', but suggested revision. No, not to censor it; to make it more effective. He was really doing his job; you don't often see that. I agreed with his points, and made the suggested revision, and the story did indeed stand improved. It was scheduled for publication in the same issue of *WOT* as 'Bridge'; because magazines don't like to run two stories in an issue by the same author, this one was to appear under my alternate pen name, Tony Pedro. That is, a form of Anthony and a form of Piers. Piers is part of a huge family of names that includes Peter (English language), Pedro (Spanish), Pierre (French), Pietro (Italian), Peder (Danish), Pieter (Dutch), Petron (Greek) and perhaps others I wot not; it means 'rock'. Yes, it is the rock on which the Christian Church was built.

But when the issue was published, 'Torture' was absent. The editor had, it seemed, lost his nerve. Three years later, fellow novelist Sterling Lanier asked me if I would contribute a story to a private magazine, *Armadillo*. so I showed them 'Torture' and they bought it from *Galaxy* publications. But that issue of *Dillo* was never published either. Finally, after ten years or so, John Silbersack took it for *The Berkley Showcase*: Volume 3 –

and this time it actually did make it into print. It seemed the genre had finally loosened up enough for the hard stuff. My main frustration about the matter is the fact that Harlan Ellison wrote a story about the same time I wrote 'Torture', but his was much milder. Thus his 'A Boy and His Dog' was able to make it into print, and I believe it won an award and was made into a motion picture. People thought that was the most brutal fiction the genre had to offer; they never got to see mine. Once again I missed the cut and remained unfamous. Today I have made my name instead as a writer of funny fantasy; I can't even break in to the horror market despite having some truly horrible works in mind, because I have no credits in horror. But I can write it, and one day I will.

Gentle reader, be warned again: this story is brutal.

My fingers caress the dial. The boots stir uneasily. 'You don't know me,' I tell them. 'But you do know this box – and that is sufficient. I expect you to work well and keep your opinions to yourselves. That is all.'

They watch me, expressionless. There are twenty of them, all nonwhite humans. Some are half-caste Negroes, some Latins, a few Mongoloid, the rest mixed. The refuse of the Space Service – busted back to boot status and sentenced to hard labour here at Stockade Planetoid. Scrubbing out tankers, packing barges – that sort of thing, where human labour is cheaper than the shipping charges on heavy machinery. This barracks is listed as 'inclement', and I am expected to whip it into line.

'Roll call,' I announce. I depress a button on the box and set the dial to twenty-five. One of the boots stiffens, his breath sucking inward noisily. He is dark brown with frizzy hair and broad nostrils. I let him twitch a moment while I study him. Then, I turn and dial to zero and he subsides.

'You don't need to do that,' a Latin objects. 'We're wearing our numbers.'

So they are. This loudmouth is number 6. I depress stud number six and turn the dial to forty. He goes rigid with a cry of agony. Slowly I advance the setting to fifty, noting how his muscles strain and the sweat pops out all over his body. He is trying to scream again, but can't catch his breath. Then I drop it down to ten, so that he is only nominally in pain. 'Remember what I said about opinions?' I ask him gently.

He nods, the moisture shaking off his cropped skull. I turn to zero, and he breathes again.

After I have verified that the discipline box is properly attuned to each member of my crew, I return to number 6. 'Since you evidently like to talk, suppose you tell me why you're here.'

He hesitates. I know why: there is a kind of Geneva Convention about this prison, and technically the boots don't have to say anything to anybody about their pasts, Which is why I am inquiring. I raise my hand to the box.

'Tell him!' number 20 exclaims. I give him a token nudge at five tenths, just a reminder about talking out of turn even though he has done exactly what I want. My finger hovers over stud number 6.

'We're all here for the same reason, sergeant,' the Latin says. 'Mutiny. We were supposed to gas a continent on Severance to clear it of native life so that it could be mined efficiently, and we balked.'

'Severance,' I murmur. 'Richest lode of iridium discovered in the last decade, no intelligent or otherwise useful fauna. Why did you interfere?'

'Because it was genocide. All the animals unique to that world, all the plants – Man had no right to wipe them out. Not for the sake of a mining strike, not for any reason. To brutally gas an entire – '

'It was hardly your prerogative to impose your ludicrous sentimentality on your mission.'

'We – we're not exactly from Earth's privileged class,' he says. My hand drops towards the dial, and he continues quickly. 'I mean we feel some empathy for those who have no power of decision. Those creatures on Severance – they had a right to live, to breed, to prosper, to die in their own fashion, just as we do. They were no threat to us, only an inconvenience. We could have mined without hurting – '

'Enough. I don't care to be contaminated by your pusillanimous ravings. You betrayed your species and your world, you despicable alien-lovers. You ought to be gassed yourselves, and if I were the court-martial officer I'd see to it myself. But at least I can make you traitors earn your keep. Your rations will be reduced by a third for your first week with me, your duty hours extended commensurately. Any complaints you may entertain will be duly processed through the box.' I depress the entire bank of buttons and give them all a half-second jolt of sixty, just so they understand.

The book says the box can't kill, though it can make you wish you were dead. The book understates the case. The box stimulates the nerve endings of the skin and muscle to simulate a burn, and one hundred is the maximum the human nervous system is capable of sustaining. No torture can deliver more actual pain than that. But the real beauty of it is that no harm is done, physically, so there is no limit to the duration of the punishment. The do-gooders back on Earth are chronically campaigning against this device but the Service lobby has kept the lid on. Good thing, too; we *need* the box!

A minute has passed, and I see that they are pretty

well recovered. 'Fall out for duty,' I say. They know who is master now.

I bear down on them for the next couple of weeks. You have to when you're dealing with niggers and spics and chinks. They never had real discipline before, and they do get balky and self-righteous and sloppy. Mine have become acclimatized to pain; I have to give them fifty to make them jump.

My outfit is posting the best record in the compound, but I know there's some resistance still lurking there. I have to bring it to the surface at my convenience, not theirs. So I volunteer them for inside scrub-down on a radioactive barge. That's the worst assignment there is because, even with continuous decontamination, each hour of such duty is estimated to take a week off your life expectancy, and you're damn sick while you're exposed, too. This hulk is big; it will take them a good two weeks to GI it all.

I give them the word at lights-out, so they can dream about it. Maybe a hundred hours cumulative inside that scow . . .

Come morning by compound time, my barracks misses reveille. The company officer smirks, thinking I've lost a point. He knows I mean to have his job, in time.

I march to the barracks and slam open the lock. They are there, lying in their bunks. 'On your feet!' I holler loud enough so the whole wing can hear even without the loudspeakers. I touch them with fifty.

They twitch and groan, but don't get up.

Just as I thought. This is the tactic that retired my predecessor. They figure anyone will break if they go on a lie-down strike, refusing to work no matter how much they get boxed. And if they miss more than half a day there will be an investigation and bad publicity.

They propose to bargain with the god of the box.

They are fools, of course. I do not call them again, I do not warn them. I merely turn the dial to one hundred, depress all twenty buttons, and lock them in with the intercom disconnected. I amble down the corridor to the NCO's mess and enjoy a leisurely breakfast – coffee, eggs, bacon, one griddlecake with maple syrup, a section of fresh cantaloupe, orange juice. I'll say this for the stockade: it has excellent hydroponic facilities and a fine stable. I could not eat better on Earth.

Gloria, the civilian waitress, serves me with a smile. I chat with her and pat her shapely behind. She doesn't know my line of work, only that I'm one of the staff. Nice girl; I really enjoy seeing her.

Sated, I amble back to the barracks. The Post Commander has granted my platoon the morning off in gratitude for the men's courage in volunteering for radioactive duty. I have neglected to tell them this.

One hour has passed – the maximum any prisoner may be boxed at one hundred without specific dispensation. I drop the dial to zero and unlock. It takes a moment to clarify the situation.

Numbers 2 and 15 are in coma. Numbers 4, 9, 10, and 19 are delirious. The rest are severely shaken but will be fit to work in a few hours. I notify sick bay to fetch the two, lock the four in, and conduct the rest to boot mess for a late repast. They fall into formation without protest.

I anticipate no further trouble with them.

It has taken too much time, of course, but now I am a commissioned officer. I am in charge of a dozen barracks, and there is very little disturbance in my wing. The boots fear me and do not attempt to stand on their 'rights'.

But I am aware that with this slow progress I will never achieve the full success I crave unless I can jump several ranks. So it behooves me to volunteer for a high-risk, high-reward mission.

Gloria, my fiancée, tries to talk me out of it. She is afraid I will fail or get killed. She doesn't understand that life itself is a failure if no chances are ever taken. I must take a risk commensurate with my aspiration.

At the top of the Special Assignment roster is a planet called Waterloo; the human discoverer's half-punning rendition of the unpronounceable native designation. Waterloo is where the Earth-sphere economic advance is stalled. I know it's gauche to speak of trails through space, as though a three-dimensional volume sparsely pocked with glowing gasballs called stars and bits of debris called planets can be seriously equated with an extinct Earthside wilderness, but that's what it really amounts to. It is feasible for man to expand his sphere in this direction – the sphere isn't sphere-shaped, naturally – using Waterloo as a kind of trading post and transfer point. It is *not* feasible to bypass this particular planet. That is all, I am told, that I need to know. So I think of it as a station on a trail, and the Loos of Waterloo have set up a barricade that has to come down so the posse can get through. The assignment: bring down that barricade.

It would be easier to understand the situation if the Loos were violent, asocial monsters. But they are humanoid, at least in outline, and civilized too, though without space technology. There is evidence that they had it once, but gave it up, oddly. They are rather polite and gentle with never a harsh word, and they have hardly begun to exploit their system's natural resources. They have a lot to benefit from Earth contact and seem willing enough. All that is necessary is for an envoy to connect with their leader or governing council and arrange for an Earth/

Waterloo treaty that establishes an industrial enclave and permits free passage of commercial vessels. Ours, of course.

The kicker is that six envoys have tried it in turn. Five never came back. The sixth escaped to display the marks of his reception. He had been brutally tortured.

So there is the riddle of Waterloo. A pleasant, peaceful culture that tortures visitors. Force is out of the question, whatever the provocation. Earth could not possibly transport and land enough troops to pacify the entire planet since the men could not forage from the land. Diplomacy has to do the job if it is to be done at all. And it *must* be done, lest other spacefaring species assume control of the region and threaten Man's security.

Gloria pleads and cries and threatens and cajoles, but I volunteer. I am confident that I, as a superior individual, will succeed once more where my incompetent predecessors have failed.

I am landing now at the only suitable place on the planet. This is where a super-hard lava flow exists that can withstand the blast of chemical rockets. The ancient Loo spaceports are in shambles, quite useless today, so this natural formation has to substitute.

According to envoy number 6 (intriguing coincidence of nomenclature, that! My Latin loudmouth finally finagled a reprieve) – the Loos never kill an animate creature if they can help it. Their atrocities are calculated to induce maximum pain with minimum loss of body faculty. But their science in this respect remains crude. They do not have the discipline box.

The first two envoys (number 6 claims) died because the Loos were not sufficiently conversant with human anatomy and function to preserve them through the scheduled rigours. The next three committed suicide. The sixth made his break instead. He was a specially trained agent who was able to pull off his phenomenal escape without the use of one hand. Now he has quit the Service.

I have no such spy training. And I mean to see my mission through to the end, for marriage and considerable acclaim and fortune await me. So I will neither run nor commit suicide. The Loos will have to kill me outright – or negotiate.

Here are the Loos, coming across the plain of lava in an animal cart. They are actually rather small, only four and a half feet tall and proportionately slender. Hardly the type one would expect to find in the torture business. The gravity of this world is less than Earth-norm, but the difference isn't enough to account for such diminished stature, if that's the way it works. I don't really know or care much about exobiology. I do know their internal systems are different; they look like human mock-ups, but there are myriad distinctions. The Loos are probably the right size for what they are, though that isn't much.

'Welcome to Waterloo,' their spokesman says, using their own word for the planet but speaking English otherwise. They have evidently learned something about us and made an effort to accommodate. That should help. Maybe the earlier difficulties were the result of some linguistic confusion.

Maybe cheese is made from green moons, too. By what innocent misapprehension would they torture six envoys?

'I have come to make a treaty,' I inform the Loo. 'Between your world and mine. Mutually beneficial. You understand?'

'Yes, Envoy,' he replies. I know he is male because he has a penis. Primitives don't wear much.

He conducts me to his castle, making small talk. If he is trying to impress me with his verbal facility, he is succeeding. I doubt I could handle the Loo gabble that well, should I be moved to try. His name is something like Kule, he is to be my host for the duration, and he seems friendly enough. Innocuous, in fact. Naturally he is hiding something.

The air is balmy. I am able to breathe comfortably and to drink the local water, but that's as far as it goes.

Inside, Kule introduces me to his mate, Vibe. She is a thick individual with four teats down the front and a jelly-pudendum, and she speaks limited English. Her litter of four stands behind her: vaguely akin to bald-headed human brats.

'Do they speak my language too?' I inquire.

'To some extent,' Kule admits. 'All those who expect to deal with aliens must study the tongues. But beyond this domicile there are few you could converse with.'

We share a royal dinner. I cannot touch the Waterloo food, of course. Its chemistry differs right down to the cellular structure. A distinct and alien life-pattern. Assimilation of any of it would havoc my innards. The air and water are essentially inorganic, so I can use them, but the food – a biological antimatter, I suppose. But they have imported some Earth staples at fabulous expense (or stolen them from the prior envoys) and prepared them for me. A fattening for the Kill?

'You come politically, as did the other Earthmen?' the Loo inquires as we dine. 'To deal as between sovereign planets?'

'Yes,' I agree. He already knows this. Perhaps he is letting his family in on the secret now.

'You have courage.'

I suppose that is a way of looking at it. I find it hard to be afraid of inferiors. 'I understand that you torture envoys.'

'Certainly. We regret that your predecessors . . .

desisted prematurely. But we are now sufficiently familiar with human anatomy so that we are virtually assured you will not perish on the rack.' He took another mouthful of pudding, looking pleased.

I mouth my own dessert. 'Unless I commit suicide.'

Vibe turns green around all four nipples and the litter titters. I see immediately that I have committed a faux pas.

'Your species is prone to jest?' Kule asks uncertainly.

'Very prone.' The bad moment passes. Should I regret that I have caused this nice, homey, bloodthirsty family embarrassment? Yet if torture is one of their amenities . . .

The meal is finished. 'Shall I conduct you to the business office now,' Kule asks, 'or would you prefer to rest a little first?'

'Business before pleasure,' I reply. I doubt he has either intent or authority to sign a treaty between two worlds, however. Perhaps I am to meet someone more important.

Kule obligingly guides me to a lower chamber of the castle. It is large and set up like a theatre. Tiers of benches rise above an ample stage. I do not need the sight of several Loos suspended on boards to acquaint me with the fact that this is indeed a torture chamber.

It occurs to me to inquire why they feel the need to inflict pain on natives and aliens alike, but I realize that sadism requires no objective justification. Perhaps Kule expects me to break and run for my ship; this is his way of scaring me away from my mission.

No doubt he has never dealt with a superior man. I shall neither be bluffed nor commit a faux pas again.

Kule introduces me to my personal torturer, a legless one-eyed Loo. He cannot move; he is mounted to a pedestal before a vacant rack. I see that each client has a similarly incapacitated attendant. None of that modern mass-production indifference here!

'This is Beve, our specialist in human anatomy,' Kule says with pride. 'You can be assured that he is fully accredited. Under his direction you will suffer the most exquisite agony your system is capable of. He handled the three successful cases.'

'Successful?'

'Those who took the grail.' Kule gestures to a handsome goblet affixed to one edge of the vertical board. I perceive that it is filled with an amber fluid. A suicide cup?

It would not work for me, because of the differing metabolism, and would not have worked for the prior envoys. He is lying. No – it *would* work, but not quite in the manner intended. Not the poison, but the alien chemistry would do the human drinker in. Academic distinction.

'Who handled the unsuccessful cases?' I inquire politely.

'We do not speak the names of failures,' Kule reproves me gently. 'Incompetent practitioners are incarcerated along with their mistakes in the oubliette. If extenuating circumstances exist, they are granted a sip from the grail first.' His demeanour is grave; he does not enjoy the subject. I understand. No one likes to admit proximity to incompetence.

But it is an intriguing point, this concern about accidental death on the rack. If the client is driven to suicide, it is the tormentor's bonus, I gather. If the client dies adamant, he guarantees his torturer's demise. Very nice. But what of those who survive bloody but unbowed?

'You understand,' Kule says, hesitating delicately, 'suppressors or tranquillizers of any type are – '

' – are frowned upon,' I finish for him. 'Lest they

diminish the pain.' And I was sure they would know if I used any such, so I have no intention of cheating.

'I can stay only for the initiation,' Kule says. 'But you will be attended throughout by licenced witnesses. If you have any questions, do not hesitate to ask Beve. He can hear you, and he comprehends. If he nods towards pain, the answer is affirmative.' He retreats to one of the seats in the gallery and sets himself up expectantly.

Kule's actions and comments smack of verisimilitude: a rehearsed sequence to convince me that I am really to be tortured. Nevertheless, it is impressive.

Beve smiles, revealing his toothless and tongueless cavity, and I comprehend a trifle more. He had been tortured himself! He knows well the meaning of pain. His head is an earless globe; only poke holes penetrate the skull. Probably all his infirmities stem from similar coercion.

Beve gestures towards the rack invitingly. I play it straight: I strip down and manage to mount myself for the operation. I fit my arms and legs into the loops provided. The supports are oddly comfortable, being padded and pliable, and they brace my body in such a way that I should be able to remain suspended for a long time without bruise or loss of circulation. Though the chamber is well lighted, no direct beam affronts my eyes, and the ambient temperature is pleasant for my exposed skin. There is even a headband that takes weight off my neck without impairing freedom of motion. The rack seems to be no more than a convenient display table. Were it not for the intermittent groans associated with the adjacent projects, I could almost convince myself that this is merely a fancy sauna.

'Shall I call it quits when I'm tired?' I inquire facetiously, thinking Beve won't understand. But he nods his head to one side. Does that signify 'yes' or 'no'?

Foolish notion! What kind of torture would it be if the client could turn it off at will?

What kind? The usual kind? Torture is generally for an ulterior purpose: to obtain the subject's acquiescence to the will of the torturer. It ceases when the desired information is divulged, or the desired confession obtained, or the desired attitude embraced. Coooperation terminates it. I have applied the pain-box therapy in such manner many times.

On the other hand, torture as punishment desists only at the discretion of the torturer. This I employed when my barracks at the stockade defied me by a liedown strike. If I am to be subjected to *that* kind, no easy death by suicide should be permitted.

All of which leaves the status of Waterloo duress in question. No single explanation seems wholly reasonable. There is no information I would not freely provide, and I have no relevant confessions to make. My attitude, I should think, is good: I want only to negotiate a mutually beneficial treaty. I am not a criminal in need of punishment by any standard I know of, and I have not been treated as one here, so far. I merely happen to be an envoy scheduled for torture.

I can't claim discrimination. The other clients are natives, and the torturers themselves have been tortured.

In short, I am baffled. Well, when on Waterloo . . .

To one side is a cabinet. Beve opens it and sets up certain instruments. My view is unhampered. I can see every detail as can Kule and the witnesses in the audience. I see the light glint off the fine steel of a set of scalpels.

Could this be a kind of gladiatorial display? One measures his courage against that of other contestants, for the sadistic delight of the spectators? No – there are too few watchers, and they are as serious as jurymen. They merely wait.

Beve now reaches up to take my left hand, disengaging the arm from its supports at elbow and wrist. He sets it in a kind of elevated shelf projecting from his console and ties it firmly in place. I am reminded of the time I had to donate blood to the Service bank, back when I was a boot myself. There are even channels for each of my fingers, with straps to hold them in place. This entire unit must have been designed to human specification, from the oversized rack to the customized attachments: a telling compliment.

Beve lifts a small knife.

I have held my mind away from this reality, as though it were a bluff or something not connected to me personally. Now I can avoid it no longer: I am about to be cut.

My hand is palm-up, my fingers splayed. The knife descends on my smallest digit. I expect some delay, some offer to refrain if only I will accede to some particular demand or depart the planet promptly. But there is none. The blade stabs into my fleshy fingertip and slices shallowly down the length of the member, skipping only the portions covered by the straps.

The scalpel is sharp, and for a moment I am not aware of genuine pain. I watch the skin peel back from the wound like red opening lips. I see the rich blood well up, and I notice the little drain channels in the support shelf for such fluid. This is a sophisticated device, though primitive.

I am, I realize, in a kind of shock. I cannot believe that I am really thus casually to be tortured, though I am watching it happen.

Beve lifts a syringe and squirts a colourless jet down the gash. Suddenly there is agony: it is alcohol, or their equivalent!

'Beve!' I cry, alarmed. 'If that's organic, and it enters my system – '

He looks up at me and nods to his left, my right. Since it is my left hand that is hurting, he nods away from pain: no. He must have considered this matter and made sure I wouldn't die ludicrously. Maybe that was what happened to the first of the failures. Trust the torturer to know his business, particularly when the oubliette is gaping.

The working area is clean now. Something in that fiery liquid has stanched the bleeding. Beve is ready for the next stage. He slices across the finger at right angles to the prior cut and squirts away the new blood while I stiffen. It is as though I am holding my finger in the field of a limited-radius discipline box! Beve completes the incisions under the straps, working skilfully. He takes up a set of tongs and fastens them to –

He is tearing off the skin!

I never suspected the pain would be like this. Up to the elbow I feel it, this rending of my flesh as the dermis parts from the substructure of my finger. It is peeling back like the skin of an orange, in sections. I do not look any more. I cry out; I cannot help it. It is as though my finger is a foot in diameter and every cell is screaming with the awful hurt of that flaying.

I try to clench my fist convulsively, but the bonds are tight. I try to jerk away, but cannot budge it. My whole body tenses, but everywhere it is restrained. I can free myself by carefully extricating my limbs, but I cannot do it by involuntary reaction.

My right hand brushes against something cold. It is the grail, the chalice of death. At any time I choose to exercise physical control, I can disengage that hand, reach out, and take that cup. It has to be a conscious decision, for a careless motion would spill it. I have to *decide* to die.

Or I can disengage myself completely and bolt for the space ship, as the last envoy did. Strange that Kule never mentioned him. He must have been a sad commentary on the courage of the human species. No doubt that kind of thing is simply Not Done on Waterloo.

Not by me, anyway. I came here to unriddle this planet and arrange a treaty. I am no masochist, I do not enjoy pain – but pain will not deter me from my mission. I will not capitulate. I will show them I can withstand their worst, though I lose my entire finger.

It is a long time before it is over, subjectively. I know it is only minutes objectively. My digit has become anaesthetized. I feel only a dullness there, not unpleasant. As my eyes unscrew and clear, I look down.

Only bone and gristle remain. My finger is a skeleton. He has cut away all the flesh, leaving the gaunt joints, he has somehow tied off the conduits at the base, so no more body fluids leak out. No wonder the hurt has abated!

Kule sits impassively in the audience section, watching. *He thinks I will break now!*

'There are four others,' I tell the torturer. He nods towards pain, agreeing without humour, and suddenly my remark seems very unfunny.

Beve cleans the knives meticulously and puts them away. Evidently the cutting is over – but I am not relieved. I look at the warm bone that was my finger and I know that this is no game. I am in the care of a professional.

He brings out a device rather like a vice. It has a handle and some kind of gear chain. He mounts it on my next larger finger and cranks it tight.

I am in a way acclimatized to the cutting, but this is different. The two ribbed planes of the vice compress my flesh against the bone and do not stop. Beve puts his muscle into the chore. I am crushed in agony. I scream again, as I have to; this torment shatters my restraint.

But I refuse to plead for mercy or to touch the cup.

It is worse than the flaying, but somehow it passes. My throat is sore from exertion, and I am shaking. I imagine that a slow land tank has driven over my hand, one cleat landing squarely on that finger. I watch as he unscrews the machine.

My finger is three inches in diameter, but the thickness of cardboard. Flesh and bone have been sundered under the pressure, burst apart, and metamorphosed into red/white opacity. The pain is diminished: the thing does not belong to me any more.

Kule still watches as do the witnesses. For them very little time has passed, and this is routine. In the reprieve while the press is being cleaned and stored, I look about and see that one of my companion torturees has lost consciousness. His demon is doing something to bring him to. Does too long a period of insensibility disqualify a client? for *what*?

Beve does not hesitate. He brings out another mechanism replete with little pulleys. I am reminded of a toy train, the wheels turnings, the pistons plunging back and forth as it hugs along. But this is no toy.

This time I am able to control myself enough to watch the procedure throughout. It is a pulling gear he applies. It stretches my longest finger until the joints dislocate, until the muscles thin and part, the skin becomes transparent, the tendons snap. It is done. Only the tattered stump remains.

I feel anguish, of course, but it is as much for the irreparable damage done to my hand as for the immeditate sensation. Yes, I am becoming adapted to withstanding the pain of whatever kind. I smile at Beve, at Kule. Their worst has not broken me.

The torturer slides a narrow pan under my index finger.

He pours oil into it, bathing the member. He sets fire to the oil.

I scream while my flesh roasts, my bravery forgotten. The stench of it clogs my nostrils, brings my last meal up out of my stomach and throat and mouth . . . to be caught neatly in the bucket Beve holds up. Inferno! But I cannot relent.

At last the fire dies. It had been fiendishly persistent. A charred twig lies in the pan. Sensation is gone.

What remains for the thumb?

Beve sets a wire framework about it, the mesh fine but not at all tight. He brings a box near and places a sliding aperture next to an opening in the cage. He draws up the miniature gate.

Something like a scorpion emerges. Others follow.

Their stings are savage, but that is only part of it. The venom seems to tenderize the flesh for their mandibles without numbing it. I feel every bite.

Surely the alien injection will find its way back into my system and kill me! But the torturer must have anticipated this too. Perhaps the second 'failure' happened this way. Now they use a breed whose poison is localized, affecting only the immediate area?

After the insectoids have gorged, they stumble and fall, twitching. They are Waterloo creatures, unable to assimilate my offworld protein. Serves them right. But I know I will never use that thumb again. The portions remaining are bloated and discoloured, and the diminution of sensation that signifies loss of the member is setting in.

Kule stands. 'You have experienced the initiation,' he says. 'This token treatment only suggests what is to follow. You have made a worthy beginning, unlike your predecessors. I wish you every success.' And he turns and departs.

My right hand touches the grail. Token? *Token?*

I thought I had won, and it is only the beginning. But it is not in me to surrender, though I hardly comprehend the rationale. 'Proceed!' I cry. I am sick inside, for I know they *will* proceed. What am I proving?

Beve brings out the knives and selects one. I divine the pattern: first cutting, then crushing, then pulling, burning, and animal attack. Five distinct tortures. My left hand has stood as the demonstration model. Now these techniques will be applied in earnest.

The knife approaches my face. I dare not flinch, for that would be unseemly weakness. I have outlasted the other envoys, as I knew I would, but not the Loo subjects who are usually racked in this chamber. I must suffer what the schedule dictates, knowing that I will not die unless I choose to. I must beat them at their own game, whatever it is.

The blade hovers over my left eye . . . and my right fingers strain at the cup. Then the knife descends and the point touches my left nostril.

In the haze of pain and horror admixed with a kind of relief, my mind turns inward. There is nowhere else for it to go. I remember when a kike bashed in my nose when I was ten, and how I nearly killed him for that, though he was larger than I. No inferior ever made *me* yield. Neither will this Loo bastard. Wipe my proboscis off my face, Beve – it will not faze me! I am better than you! I defy you! I –

But *then* I was fighting. *Now* – this stripping of the flesh, of cartilage, spouting of blood, nerves cut, while I endure –

Abruptly I am starkly objective. It has stopped again, and I know that half my nose is gone, both skin and fundament. There was surely no satisfaction in the going.

How long can this continue? I remain superior, but my body is being shorn away!

Beve has already brought out the vice. I must have been distracted for a moment and did not notice. He moves the machine towards my groin.

Oh no! I fight the bonds, I grasp the cold grail, I shiver all over as I sweat. But I cannot succumb now, I am committed, I have already invested too much.

The vice closes on my left testicle and locks in place despite the obscuring folds of skin. Another truth comes clear: only my left side is being treated. I am being left with my duplicate organs. I will not be crippled completely. This encourages me tremendously, if only Beve knew!

He screws up the tool. My scrotum explodes in pain. I see the flattened remains of my crushed finger, and I know –

There is no word for what I am feeling. I am hurting terribly, oh yes – but it is more than that. There is something else . . .

I see legs. Female legs. Very firm, fleshy thighs. I see the skirts ride up along them. I see flimsy panties come down. Drawn aside by an invisible hand. I see those smooth columns part, cranking open the nether cleavage. I am precipitated at the dark gaping crevice. I thrust – and all sensation channels into my turgid conduit and fills that aperture. The quintessence of malehood is rammed into the connecting tubes, converted into potency; every turn of the handle drives another bolus through. It is a hydraulic ram, a mighty pump liquefying what had hitherto been solid. It is not pleasure so much as unmitigated urgency. All – of it – must go!

The image fades. The wine press is gone; the grape expended. My erection is collapsing in blood, and I know that despite the dream my gonad is not a super-ejaculate, but merely squashed meat.

Beve is bringing out the pulling gear. I do not look down at my torso.

This time it is my ear he attacks. I remember Gloria, my bride-to-be, with sudden overwhelming fervour: her clear lovely features, her straight delicate nose, her pierced ears stretched down by pendant earrings . . . no!

Will you love me when I am ugly with mutilation, oh my darling? Will you follow me to the torture planet, as you threatened? Will you still want to hold me?

Yes, there . . . thereis . . . thereisloveinpain . . . the purest. Love and pain must be allied. Gloria, if ever I see you again, I will never let you go. I love you. More than possible. I ache with love, I bleed with emotion, I hurt with desire, I –

The image fogs. I try to refocus it, cannot. Instead there comes the pair of fleshy thighs, now brimming with blood-red ejaculate. I recoil. Sully not the vision of Gloria with that animal passion! Make it elevated, rarefied, that pure longing man feels for angel. Up, up! I trace up past the line of the hip, seeking to cast off the revolting filth of that prior congress. Up, to the stomach, the bosom – and the four loose teats.

I know now that I have committed adultery, miscegenation, bestiality in my torment-sponsored orgasm.

My ear is gone. I see it, an elongated and tattered mass of flesh, ripped from my head. I begin to grasp the rationale of my perfidy: my ruined face could only appal Gloria. My fingerless hand could never caress her beauty. I am half-castrate. The romance is off. I know it, though she does not. There will be no feasible return to Earth for me after this. It is not a momentary challenge that I can surmount and leave behind. I will emerged changed, less than I have been. I must be satisfied with native females, if my very semen does not crucify them. This much do I give for my mission.

But I shall prevail.

Beve is heating a needle. I had thought that the oil was next, but that is only one form of fire. I know where the heat will be applied, and again my remaining fingers clutch at the grail. Yet I do not desist.

Glowing red, the spike approaches my face. I see it point-on with my left eye until it touches the pupil.

The fluids of my eyeball burst out and dribble down my cheek. Smoke and steam rise from the carnage. I smell and see clouded nausea with my right-side perceptions. Pain? The term has become meaningless. Now I do not see Gloria or the Loo sex object or even Beve. There is only the scorching dazzle of colour.

Only? No, no, no – there is more, so much much more, as that searing sword probes my optic apparatus. I see – I see – *I see the scintillating Divinity!* Nova-like, the Godhead strikes my belief. Surely this is the ultimate revelation. I bathe in the ecstasy of the sight of my Lord, the Vision Supreme . . . yes, pain is the route to the glimpse of the Eternal, and I have seen the glory, the, I see, I see.

Shattered. The agony has abated, depriving me of my soul-vision. Desolation, I, I feel, loss, gone.

Beve puts away the spent needle, turns off his flame. What can he do, more than he has done? I am invulnerable. I have withstood his mutilation. I have seen the glory. Glory, Gloria . . . in excelsis . . .

Beve brings out a slender tube. He pokes it into the hole in my face where the left nostril once stood. I feel it shoving back, abrasive but laughable as a torture, beyond the sinus cavity, down to my throat. I gag, but it continues, a snail crawling into my belly.

No, not my stomach. Beve twists, expertly, and the

tube finds the trachea and slithers towards the left lung. I cough involuntarily, but nothing stops its progress until the torturer is satisfied. Yet this is a strange, gentle procedure, after the brutality of the preceding acts.

Beve lets go the hose, now lodged in my body almost its entire length. He brings out a box, opens it. I see movement: writhing things.

There is a funnel on the end of the catheter. Beve lifts out a worm with his tweezers, and I see that the creature's front end is a disc like that of a lamprey. A myriad-toothed grinder and sucker. He places it in the funnel and angles the tubes so that the creature will slide down to the bottom. He brings out the next.

I cannot even scream as the worms consume my lung.

I see the Vision again – but this time I know it for what it is, just as I knew the pudendum the second time. The God of Fire is the nether god, I am in hell. Hell is infested by worms. The worms and maggots and vermin are the true devils here. I tour the place, entitled by my misery. I see a man, a Loo – perhaps it is Kule – I see him being subjected to the torture of the boats, an ancient Persian speciality. He is pinned face-up between two small boats that exactly fit each other, only his head and hands and feet are outside and tied there. They are feeding him the richest foods, pricking his eyes when he balks, pouring milk and honey in his mouth and over his face until he nearly chokes on it. The sun is bearing down and he cannot avoid it, though his features blister cruelly. Swarms of flies settle, completely covering his head with their noisome bodies, attracted by the honey. But the odour emanating from the interior of his prison is not sweet, for he has been many days confined and the constant enforced feasting must lead to the baser processes of nature, in quantity. And as I pass I am granted a view through a noxious peephole into the boats, and I see in the streaming shadow his naked body bathed in its own excrement and the flies breeding in that dung and urine and their massed maggots feeding on his living guts. With his extremities pinned, he can do nothing to protect himself until he expires at last and gives his carcass entirely over to the vermin.

I am minded to study the more advanced tortures of hell, but the pain that is my admission-token diminishes again and I am returned to Waterloo.

Kule is there, alas no victim of flies. 'Congratulations,' he says. 'You have now completed the first day of duress. You may step down for the night, for Beve must rest. Tomorrow, if you choose, you may undertake the second stage, but this is not necessary for a technically honourable acquittal.'

I try to talk and feel the husks of the worms rattling in the cavity that was my tender lung. After a while I succeed, raspingly: 'Will you make the treaty now?'

'No.'

'Then I will resume tomorrow.' And I faint.

I am hardly aware of time. It seems I have always been on this rack, yet I know it is only the second day. Or the third. My arm is gone, my kidney, the hair of half my head together with the skin to which it adhered, the flesh of my left side from shoulder to crotch, muscle by muscle. The stench of incineration surrounds me, dried blood and broken segments of bone decorate the floor. The Loos on the racks to either side have taken the grail and are gone in shame, but I, Christlike, persevere. The grail is the one cup I will not touch in this incarnation. Many witnesses watch me now.

Kule has now explained to me some of the history of the Loos. They did have space travel, and they colonized and made a stellar empire – but they were gentle folk, and when they were met by barbarians and tortured and driven off, they became convinced that they were not ready for space. So they retrenched and instituted a system that would bring out leaders more resistive to such hurts. Once that system was entrenched . . .

Kule is before me again, a worried worshipper. 'Step down, Envoy,' he pleads.

'Will you prepare the treaty?'

'I cannot. No one can.'

'Then I will not step down.'

'Envoy, we can not proceed further without depriving you of essential faculties. You must retain two legs for perambulation, one hand for – '

'They are of no use to me without that treaty.'

Defeated, he goes. And so Beve is beginning on my legs and right side. I am driving the Loos into a quandary.

Is it the fourth day? The fifth? How should one measure eternities? My legs are gone, my right arm, my remaining ear and nostril. I am blind. No teeth remain in my jaws. The waste products of my body drip down from a gash like that of a woman. But I can hear, for they dare not touch my inner ear lest they damage the brain and bring death.

They: I mean the interminable Beves and Kules my isolated brain conjures. I am not wholly sane at the moment. I can digest the nutrient Earth-export liquid they trickle down my blistered throat, however. I believe it is a confection of milk and honey, but I cannot taste it and my lung rattles horribly when I laugh. I can speak in a certain manner, though my tongue hangs stretched on a hook beside me: one grunt through the scorched larynx means 'yes', two 'no'.

'Will you step down, Envoy?' I recognize Kule's despairing voice.

I make three coughs, needing more information.

'We cannot continue without killing you.'

I do not answer. It is their problem.

'Step down temporarily, then, while I explain your status.'

To this much I accede. I am lifted down. I feel the comfort of warm water. I am floating, no hard surfaces attacking my vulnerability except for the strap that supports my head. I listen.

'You have surmounted the four stages of duress,' he says. Four? It could as easily have been four hundred. Nothing can benefit me now but the fulfilment of my mission.

'Very few applicants achieve this level,' Kule continues. 'Perhaps only two or three in each category, each year. Since your category is political, you are now qualified to join the governing council of Waterloo – the only alien ever to achieve this distinction. You have proved yourself by your steadfastness, and you have divested yourself of material considerations that might have biased a lesser individual. Thus you now have the potential for true objectivity, and can be a fitting ruler. Are you willing to assume this position?

At last it is falling into place! The torture gantlet is a ladder to prominence, not with respect to competitors but to the society itself. The more the subject can take, the greater his reward. And Kule is correct: of course I can no longer be bribed by any of the physical pleasures. I have no nose for perfume, no taste buds for food, no eyes for beauty, no phallus for sex. Money? What could it buy for me?

I am indeed objective.

'You can, however, continue the process into death. This is the one respectable form of self-termination, and it carries no onus for the torturer. This will earn you an honoured place in our ancestrial hierarchy, though you come from afar. Children will recite your name and deed, men will pray to your memory for courage, women will squirt their milk on your monument – '

I grunt twice. I am not intrigued by this type of deification. It sounds messy.

'On the other hand, as a member of the council you will have considerable authority. All your needs will be attended to by un-statused cowards such as myself who will also translate your directives for implementation, and – '

I grunt, suddenly interested.

'Oh yes,' Kule says deferentially. 'Approval of a treaty with Earth would be your prerogative, so long as the terms do not conflict with the interests of other members.'

Victory! No wonder Kule was unable to make the treaty. He lacked the authority. He has never undertaken the appropriate torture. Just as the torturers must earn their positions by being hoist by their own petard, so must all other officers in this society. Cowards and weaklings can't.

I grunt once, accepting the offer. I have earned it.

But Kule does not desist. 'One other matter now in your province, Councilman. There is another visitor from Earth – '

Another envoy! I am displeased. The Service should have had more faith in me.

'A female of your species,' Kule explains. 'She says you are to be wedded – '

Gloria! She *has* followed me! She must love me very much indeed.

'Shall I conduct her to your presence?'

I think about it. I realize that Gloria's action is foolish. I have no tolerance for foolishness. I am, for the first time in my life, truly objective, and I see things exactly as they are. I have no need of a companion, particularly not a wilful one. Power is sufficient for me. I grunt twice.

'She refuses to leave without seeing you,' Kule says. I am not certain whether this is an immediate reply or a resumption of dialogue at a later time. Time is a difficult and unimportant factor now. 'We do not approve of force in such situations. She must be dissuaded voluntarily if you do not wish to meet her. Would you prefer to have us offer her the token treatment?'

Token torture! An excellent suggestion.

'And if she still does not agree to leave?'

I grunt again. Let her experience the enlightenment of total amputation in that case. Should she somehow hold out until she achieves my exalted state, she may be passingly worthy company. Meanwhile, I can't be bothered.

In fact, in my supreme objectivity I wonder whether *any* of the untempered individuals of Earth are worthy of consideration. Why should I authorize a treat they haven't earned merely because their haphazardly selected government desires it? I am a Councilman of Waterloo, having at least proved my superiority absolutely. It is beneath me to deal with them. Better to make sure that *no* treaty is consummated.

It occurs to me that Earth could have been the planet where the Loos were repulsed by savages centuries ago. Full circle, poetic justice.

I turn my attention to more important concerns. We Loos are not really expert at torture, I realize. Our programme is unimaginative. When the subject knows exactly what to expect, in what order, he can prepare himself for it. The familiar is not sufficiently frightening, it does not undermine the will to resist. There are psychological aspects that could and should be utilized. I must work them out and make appropriate recommendations. And exposure: cold, thirst, hunger, sleeplessness, strong lights (prior to blinding), abrasive and continuous sound. Feed the client quantities of liquor, then tie off his privates. Rub his own excrement into his wounds. And the exotic techniques must be properly exploited, such as the Chinese Water Torture, or the Persian Boats . . .

Gloria! I shall arrange to have the boat torture demonstrated on her since it doesn't matter if she dies. How convenient! I'll convey to her that it is a test of her love for me and see how long she holds out.

Oh, there is so much to do! I have to educate this planet, now that I have the position and objectivity to do so.

I have heard it said that power tends to corrupt. I wonder whether, conversely, misery tends to ennoble?

Yes – yes it does! I can offer no finer example of that truth than myself.

Small Mouth, Bad Taste

Sphere, in England, had published some of my novels, and their editor Anthony Cheetham asked me for a story for their *Science Against Man* anthology. There was something about his first name I liked, so in 1969 I wrote 'Small Mouth' for that volume, and Dave Kyle had the bad taste to quote a paragraph from it for a volume he published. No, I don't know what paragraph; I never saw Kyle's volume, since this was a transaction called to my attention later by a reader. What got me was the audacity of it; Kyle simply informed my agent that he had all the authorization he needed, without telling him what he was using, so my agent learned of it only after I did. No, I didn't make a big fuss; I would have given permission for the use of the material had anyone bothered to ask. But editors are human, and human beings, as this story shows, are fallible.

'Man is a small-mouthed animal,' Miss Concher said as the truck stopped. 'He was less successful in the jungle than were the apes, and became carnivorous to fill his belly. Since he could no longer use those recessed teeth effectively for hunting, he had to make do with his forelimbs. Which in turn forced him to assume the bipedal stance, and he didn't even have a tail to brace against.' She nodded sagely. 'We can be sure that the first stone-thrower was not without sin; he was without food, and desperate. Tell me what you see.'

Mrs Rhodes was ready for the abrupt shift in subject. She rotated her sturdy frame a quarter turn on the seat and looked out over the landscape. 'I see an irregular network of shrubbery interspersed with dirt or gravel – what I would term a badlands. At the base of the valley is a meandering brown stream, and in the distance are grey mountains.'

Miss Concher smiled. 'Beautiful.' She was small and ancient, hair off-white and wirelike, and her eyes focused alertly though she was long blind. Personality radiated from the fine lines of her face: in crows-feet, deltas and crevasses.

'What do *you* see?' Mrs Rhodes asked. She had learned that such direct questions did not offend the old lady, who thrived on her handicaps as though they were advantages.

'I see a great verdant vale, cooler and wetter than now. Trees of many types grow on its flank, rich with fruit and nut, and the river is wide and clear despite the nearby volcano-cone. High grass waves over rolling stretches, and flowers sparkle in the gentle breeze. Birds abound, from the colourful flamingo to the huge brooding vulture. I call it a garden of Eden, for in addition to the foliage there are animals for a spectacular hunt. Baboons, pigs, gazelles, hares, rhinos, chalicothere – '

'Beg pardon?'

'Chalicothere. A large tree-cropper, now extinct. Oh yes, it was fascinating here, two million years ago.'

'Your vision is far more pleasant than mine, Miss Concher.'

'My vision is of the past, as befits me. I am closer to it than you are, by a good thirty years.' The old grey eyes pierced her again. 'Let's have the map.'

Mrs Rhodes brought out the sheet showing East Africa.

'We're in Tanganyika – Tanzania, I mean – somewhat south of Lake Victoria, and west.'

Miss Concher smiled indulgently. 'Now look at the natural features.'

Mrs Rhodes studied the map, not certain what the point was this time. 'There's Lake Victoria, of course, and only a few miles from us is Lake Tanganyika. And another long thin lake farther south, Nyasa. And mountains – to the east is Kilimanjaro, Africa's highest point, almost twenty thousand feet. And the Nile River drains to the north, and the Congo to the west.'

'Very good.' The old lady sounded disappointed, as though an apt pupil had overlooked the obvious.

'And within three hundred miles of us is Olduvai Gorge, where old Dr Leakey discovered Man's bones.'

'Bones!' But Miss Concher still wasn't satisfied. '*My* map shows the mighty continent of Africa, a vasty tropical reservoir of life. Beyond its coastlines, two thousand miles out, is the great mid-oceanic ridge, the longest continuous mountain range in all the world. And in the centre of this ridge is the rift, looping through the Indian Ocean, projecting up to slice off Arabia and parting Israel from Jordan, and a branch spiking down into Africa itself to form the Great Rift Valley wherein we now stand. And athwart that rift is a crater, as though a monstrous meteor had impacted there and smashed it into a broken circle. And the rains came, a flood like none we know today, filling the fragments of the Rift and crater – '

'Lake Victoria!' Mrs Rhodes exclaimed, suddenly seeing it come to life on the map. 'Tanganyika! Nyasa!'

'Yes. What a cataclysm! But a blessing for Man, for it was in this crazily shattered region, this verdant land protected by its new geography – it was here that he found Eden.' Miss Concher smiled once more. 'And we're here for the serpent.'

'The serpent? Surely you don't mean the one that tempted Eve – '

'Surely I *do*, my dear. Without that snake, man never

would have left Eden – and that, believe me, would have been too bad.'

'Miss Concher, I realize you're speaking metaphorically. But – *too bad*? Wasn't the Biblical exile God's punishment for – '

'Punishment can be very instructive. Look at Eden now.'

Mrs Rhodes looked around again at the bleak, baking terrain. It had changed, certainly, from the lush gardens of the past. But she felt she was missing the point.

'Trundle out the gimmick and we'll see what we can smell,' Miss Concher said briskly. The temperature hovered near a hundred degrees Fahrenheit, but it hardly seemed to diminish the old lady's energy.

'The gimmick' was hardly a device to be trundled. It was a massive electronic instrument that occupied the greater portion of their converted army truck. There was also a collapsible tower for a miniature drilling rig. Its generator was powered by the truck's motor.

'That's as good a spot as any,' Miss Concher said, indicating a declivity. Blind she might be, but she had a feel for the land.

Mrs Rhodes manoeuvred the truck and placed its tailgate neatly at the spot. This much was within her competence; it had been one of the prerequisites for the job. Not many female registered nurses could handle a three-axle vehicle with dispatch over rough ground. She could thank Mr Rhodes for that legacy.

Mr Rhodes. Her legal separation from him was hardly three months old, yet she found herself missing the crusty old engineer. Had he been too demanding, or she too independent? Now that she worked for Miss Concher she was beginning to appreciate the fact that a number of the traits she had objected to as masculine arrogance were actually natural functions of ambition. Surely her husband drove himself and others no harder than Miss Concher did.

Meanwhile she operated winch and derrick skilfully, setting up the drill-rig and anchoring it and connecting the generator. She was perspiring heavily by the time the job was done, but was glad for once that she was *not* a frail innocent beauty. The truck's motor pounded, the generator cut in, and the slender rod spun into the turf, squirting water down and spewing mud up rapidly. As the column penetrated to bedrock the rig disengaged automatically: time for the diamond bit. She made the exchange and set it working again. This would take some time.

They ate a crude picnic lunch while the drill did its job. Mrs Rhodes looked out over the worn landscape again, wondering whether anything would come of this particular project. It still surprised her when she thought of it, to be wandering in a land of natives who wore headdresses of mud and dung and who drank fresh blood with gusto. Of course their conventions made sense, and that was only part of the story –

'The small-mouthed animal,' Miss Concher repeated. 'That bunglike orifice is one of man's few distinguishing traits. That, and his voluminous buttocks, and his naked skin. Doesn't sound like equipment to conquer the world, does it?'

Mrs Rhodes was becoming used to her companion's acerbic viewpoint. 'I had always understood that man's *brain* was the – '

'Brain? Whales and elephants have larger, and porpoises have convolutions as impressive. Nothing unique there.'

'Or the specialized hands – '

'With the opposed thumb? Forget it; any tree-swinger has similar. Man's vaunted hand is one of the least specialized extremities in nature. It retains all the primitive fingers, poorly armoured, suitable neither for fighting nor digging. No, the fleshy buttocks count for more; they give him vertical control and the ability to stride, and that frees him from the forest. And his bare skin gives him a large tactile surface. But most of all, his small mouth enclosing a proportionately large air-space provides a sounding chamber, and that makes true speech possible.'

'I never looked at it quite that way – '

'But acoustical equipment is no good unless its potential for communication is realized. The incentive to speak. Find that, and you find man.'

'I see,' Mrs Rhodes said, finding herself conscious of the motions of her lips and tongue. Prior to this expedition she had never had any great interest in such researches, but the vitality and intensity of the old lady was warming her to it. Why *had* man started to speak?

'See as I do,' Miss Concher said earnestly. 'Stare down this valley and don't blink until the vision comes.'

She laughed. 'That's a child's dare.'

'Certainly. The childhood of man. Look.' Miss Concher's eyes were fixed on the distance, and half unwillingly Mrs Rhodes followed their object. 'Look – there is green everywhere, and we are in a natural pastureland on the fresh mountainside of the Great Rift Valley. There is a splendid tree with solid foliage, and we hear the rustle of a bird within it. No – it is an animal behind it – that chalicothere we saw before, browsing on leaves. The sun is beaming intermittently as small clouds nag it; the day is shaping into possible rain. Yes, it is about to rain; we shall have to seek cover under a bough – '

Mrs Rhodes kept staring, wishing there were some honest relief from the heat. Her vision began to blur, and colours appeared and disappeared. She had to blink at last, and the barren land came back into focus – but soon the distortions returned. It was easier simply to go along with Miss Concher's pleasant description, picturing the subject as well as she were able.

She closed her eyes and let the older woman dictate the entire scene. As she did so, the air seemed cooler, and she fancied the leaves fluttered on the branches of the tree, and a small bird swooped low in search of insects. Yes, rain was incipient.

A man came then – a brute of a creature with a tremendous belly. He leaned forward as he walked, his knees perpetually bent. He was naked, but the body hair was so thick that he was in fact well covered. His face was apelike: brown-leather skin stretched over massive eyebrow-ridges, a wrinkled gape-nostrilled nose, mouth bulging outward with large yellow teeth. His hair circled the face closely, beginning near the eyebrows, passing over the full cheeks well in front of the ears, and enclosing the mouth and receding chin.

This was Paranthropus: Para (akin too) + anthropus (man), of the dawning Pleistocene epoch, two million years ago.

The rainfall increased, no gentle dew, and lightning cracked nearby. From the other direction came another man-form, and with him a hairy woman clasping a cub. But these ones were smaller, their hair finer, their noses longer and straighter and the ridges over their eyes less pronounced. Still apelike in facial contour, they were closer to modern man than the one in the tree. These were Australopithecines.

'Aus-tral-o-pith-EE-cus,' Miss Concher said, establishing the accent.

Confrontation: Paranthropus smelled the intruders and roared out his resentment. The Australopithecine male hesitated as though considering standing his ground. But as the other crashed down bellowing defiance, the visiting family took fright and loped away through the downpour. Mrs Rhodes felt sorry for them.

'Paranthropus was king of the forest lowlands in this region,' Miss Concher said. 'Five feet tall and heavily built, he towered over his Australopithecine cousin by a hirsute head. He had the best foraging grounds. Small wonder Australopithecus, actually our nearer relative, was driven to scavenging in the savanna.'

'Small wonder,' Mrs Rhodes echoed, surprised by the force of the vision she had stepped into.

'Yet this ejection was his blessing. Paranthropus did not need to evolve, so he endured for a million years unchanged – and became extinct. Australopithecus, scrounging in diverse habitats, always fighting on the fringe of Eden, continued to evolve into Homo Erectus, the first true man. That is, the first bad-tasting hominid.'

'Pardon?'

'You don't like that notion? It was one of man's major adaptations for survival in the rough country. He couldn't always escape the larger carnivores, but soon he didn't have to. His meat had a foul flavour that no self-respecting predator would touch as long as there was anything else available. Thus like certain caterpillars, he survived.'

The bell sounded on the drill-rig, and both women hurried to attend to the next step.

The narrow core now penetrated deep into the layers of earth and rock, stopping at the approximate boundary between the Pleistocene deposits and those of the older Pliocene. The ground, here and anywhere, was a kind of condensed history – that earthy, earthly residue remaining after the tribulations of the moment had evanesced. The record of all events was there, lacking only the means of interpretation.

Mrs Rhodes brought up their sample: a cylinder of

rock undisturbed by unnatural forces for the better part of two million years. She inserted it entire into the hopper of the analyser and waited once more while the gimmick performed. She read the dials. 'The trace is present,' she said.

'Yes, I thought it would be. The Great Rift Valley is such a natural corridor, slicing down the eastern side of Africa. That's the beauty of it. But somewhere the trail has to diverge; then we shall find what we shall find.'

Mrs Rhodes shook her head. The analyser operated on the principle that the odour of a living creature was more durable than had been supposed until recently. Minute particles of its substance drifted in the air, impregnated nearby objects, became fixed in them. A hound could detect that smell for hours or days, but it never faded entirely. As objects became buried and finally compressed into significant strata, that tiny olfactory trace remained. An instrument of sufficient sensitivity and attunement could sniff it out many thousands and hundreds of thousands of years later, since time affected the buried layers very little.

But there were millions of traces imbedded in every fragment, many of them so similar as to be overlapping. The instrument could not categorize them all. It merely responded with a typical pattern of readings if the particular one to which it had been sensitized were present. It told nothing about the nature of the original creature, or the duration of its stay in that area; it was too crude even to identify whether the trace was mammalian, avian or reptilian, large or small. The pattern either matched or it failed to match.

How Miss Concher had isolated this particular trace she never said, but Mrs Rhodes suspected she had spent painstaking years at it. Somehow she had searched out a presence that could not be accounted for in the normal fauna of the time and region, and satisfied herself that it was significant. Now they were following the trail to its source, two million years later.

'What do you expect to find?' Mrs Rhodes inquired, not for the first or second time.

'Look – a *Dinotherium* hunt!'

She looked automatically before realizing that this was another guided vision – and another evasion. The old woman saw so clearly into the living past that it was contagious. '*Dino* – is that an animal? Or a large reptile?'

Dinotherium was mammalian. Foraging in the swampy jungle, it sought no particular conflict with other creatures, and few bothered it. Like an elephant with tusks pointing straight down, and with an abbreviated trunk, it was the largest creature of this valley, and could well afford to be peaceful. This one had strayed on to solid ground, oblivious to danger.

Behind it manlike forms approached. Dinotherium hooked another leafy branch down, unconcerned though he was aware of the intrusion. His great tusks held the branch in place while his trunk picked it over.

The men came closer, making vocal sounds rather like the barking of canines. Dinotherium, annoyed, moved along a short distance, seeking to leave them behind. But they followed clamouring more loudly, hemming him in from back and side.

Dinotherium became moderately alarmed, and ceased browsing. These gesticulating bipeds could hardly harm him, but their proximity and persistence were unnatural. He ran smoothly, desiring only to free himself of the strange situation so he could finish his browse. He bore left, away from the concentration of Australopithecines.

Suddenly he realized where he was. Ahead was a deep sharp gully, the product of seasonal flash floods, whose tumbling sides were treacherous for a creature of his size. He veered farther left – and encountered more men.

The choice was between the gully and the men, now that he was fleeing. The gully at least was a known danger. But – there was a gap in the line, an easy escape. Dinotherium charged at it.

The noise increased. Men ran to cut him off, chattering. But the nearest one stood indecisively, failing to act in time. Dinotherium plunged through the space and headed for the swamp where men would be foolish to follow.

'He got away,' Mrs Rhodes said, relieved.

'Because one man did not follow instructions,' Miss Concher said. 'The leader plainly hooted at the fool to close it up, but he didn't comprehend in time.'

'Yes, I saw that. But how does it relate to the trail we are following now? This is no Dinotherium hunt.' This time she did not intend to be put off.

The blind eyes focused on her disconcertingly. 'How much do you think that tribe lost, because of the failure of that one member?'

'I would imagine they went hungry – at least until they could set up another hunt.'

'Hunger wasn't very funny in those days, was it?'

'Of course not,' Mrs Rhodes agreed, visualizing a primitive camp, the children bawling, the women standing glumly. 'What did they do to that man who – '

'The leader banished him from the tribe, so of course he soon perished. If you're going to hunt Dinotherium, you can't afford any lapses in your organization.'

'Also, the others were mad, I'm sure. Had to take it out on someone. But how does that – '

'Communication,' Miss Concher said. 'Now Australopithecus has a compelling reason to select for that single trait. Note that – the first *artificial* selection in the history of life on Earth, and for a nonphysical trait. He can't tolerate tribesmen who can't or won't respond to spoken instructions, even if these only take the form of imperative barking. The groups with dumb members will fall on hard times, and their children will starve, while those who are selective will become fine hunting units. They will be capable of driving Dinotherium into the gully and stoning him to death there while he stumbles in the steep sand, and they will eat well and prosper. Communication is the key – the small mouth put to the uses of survival!'

'I concede that,' Mrs Rhodes said, both enlightened and annoyed. 'But what – '

'Once you're on that treadmill, you have to continue. You need the big game to feed your increasing numbers, for squirrels and sparrows won't feed an entire tribe for long, and certainly not wild fruit. You become dependent on organization, on the specialization that is the hunt. And you begin to contest with neighbouring tribes for the best hunting territory, staking it out, and so your communication is now employed man-against-man. That's a rough game, and if you quit you die. Today an army is helpless when its communications break down. Your size increases and your brain expands, as it must to handle the burgeoning linguistic concepts required to define an effective campaign. Barks meaning "run", "stop" and "kill" give way to subtler sounds meaning "run faster", "stop over there" and "kill on command only". And finally you are not just Australopithecus, you are Homo Erectus. An animal with the single specialized organ so harshly selected for: the brain.'

Mrs Rhodes refused to be diverted. 'This trail – '

'I believe,' Miss Concher said gently, 'that it was not mere coincidence or fleeting convenience that started Australopithecus along the demanding highway of verbal communication. The odds against this seem prohibitive. Some outside agency instructed him. Something forcibly directed him to speak, or somehow arranged it so that he had to communicate in order to survive at all. Something that knew where this process would lead. And *that* is what we are sniffing out now – that alien influence that shaped us into mastery.'

At last Mrs Rhodes saw the point. If somebody – *something*, for there could have been no true men then – if some agency had come to show potential man the route to success –

Man had a debt going back two million years.

And now two women, one middle-aged and the other old, were belatedly on the trail of that visitation, that phenomenally important influence. *What would they find?*

Miss Concher nodded. 'It's a little frightening, isn't it? We may not appreciate the truth one bit – but can there be any question of turning back now?'

This close to the answer to the riddle of man's progress? No, of course they could not turn back.

Down the Great Rift Valley they travelled, sniffing out the ancient trace. The natives generally ignored them. What harm could two crazy old women do, with their truckful of junk? They skirted Lake Tanganyika and traversed the length of Lake Nyasa, and the trail continued. At last they stood at the mouth of the Zambezi River, and the trace vanished.

They stood on the shore and looked eastward, Mrs Rhodes' live eyes seeing no more than Miss Concher's dead ones. Their gruelling weeks of travel and drilling had come to an unhappy halt, for the water held no scent.

'No,' Miss Concher said. 'This is merely a hurdle. It can not end here.' But for once her words lacked conviction. She had been an energumen until this moment, expending energy at a cheerful but appalling rate; now she was an old woman who could not find her knitting.

'A sea-creature?' Mr Rhodes suggested, embarrassed by her companion's weakness. She tried to envision a credible object, but without Miss Concher's guidance it manifested as a parody: an ancient octopus struggling rheumatically out of the depths, donning sunglasses and marching up the Rift to the sound of fife and drum to instruct Australopithecus. Ridiculous!

'Unlikely,' Miss Concher said. But her bulldog mind was working again, after its hesitation. 'Could have been based on the sea-floor, though. Or floating on the surface. The sea is an obvious highway for civilized species – check the map.'

Mrs Rhodes gladly did so. 'It's a long coast line. Funny that they should come to this particular place, then make a thousand mile journey overland, when they could have landed so much closer to Lake Victoria . . .' She paused. 'Unless they crossed directly from Madagascar – '

'My diagnosis exactly!' *Had* it been – or was Miss Concher trying to conceal her lapse? 'Let's rent a boat.'

What did it matter? They had a mission once more.

The crossing was not so simple as merely 'renting a boat', but two weeks later they had negotiated the physical and political hazards and were driving their truck along the west coast of Madagascar. In another two they had spotted the trace again. The trek resumed: east, into the heart of the huge island.

The palms of the shoreline gave way to rice fields and islandlike hills and occasional thatch-roofed earthern houses. Mrs Rhodes looked up one dusk to meet a pair of large eyes. 'Something's watching us,' she whispered, startled.

'Describe it,' Miss Concher said, unruffled.

She peered at the creature, beginning to make it out in

the shadow. 'Small, bushy-tailed, head rather like a fox –
but it has monkey-feet, and it's clinging to a branch.'

'Lemur,' Miss Concher said. 'Madagascar is their home-
land. The few species extant today are a poor remnant of
those that ranged the world in past times.'

'Not dangerous, then,' Mrs Rhodes said, relaxing.

'Not now. One type, *Megaladapis*, was larger than a
gorilla – in fact, was the largest primate known. And
another extinct Lemuridae, *Archaeolemur*, may have been
remarkably cunning, if we are to judge by the precocious
development of the temporal lobe during the – '

'You're leaving me behind, I'm afraid,' Mrs Rhodes
cut in gently. The old lady smiled, making no secret of
her pleasure in doing just that. It had become a kind of
game. The fact was that Mrs Rhodes, a skilled nurse, was
not confused by anatomical allusions. She merely wished
to abbreviate a developing lecture.

A modern city whose name they ignored obliterated a
segment of the trail, but they resumed operations on the
far side. Now they crossed parched savanna dotted with
palms. 'On this island, in historic times,' Miss Concher
said, 'ranged the largest bird ever known: aepyornis.'

'Now *that* sounds like a primate!'

'Its eggs weighed twenty pounds, and a mature bird up
to half a ton. Man wiped it out, of course.'

'You don't have a very high opinion of man, do you.'

'That's why I'm single.' But Miss Concher smiled again,
too enthusiastic over the progress of the search to be
properly cynical. She knew the fauna far better than Mrs
Rhodes did, identifying by description everything from a
camouflaged tree-lizard to a forest cuckoo. She also called
off a solitary baobab, the tree with the grossly swollen
trunk that seemed to have its roots in the air in place of
branches, and related an amusing myth about its origin.
She knew how to get through a thorny didierea jungle,

grown up in recent generations as though to preserve the secrets of the trail.

They moved on with growing excitement, day by day, until at last the trail debouched into a secluded valley. Repeated soundings verified it: this had been the home, two million years ago, of the mysterious traveller. Today it was wilderness, with only the shy lemurs and curious birds present. Where had man's ancient tutor gone?

'If I make out the lay of the land correctly,' Miss Concher said, 'there should be buried caves. They may have been occupied, then.'

Mrs Rhodes shook her head, marvelling anew at the spinster's talents. If she conjectured buried caves, there would be buried caves.

They drilled and drilled again, searching. On the third day the bit broke through the wall of a subterranean discontinuity. Its age fell in the correct range and the trace inside was very strong.

'Now,' Miss Concher said briskly, 'we dig.'

It had to be by hand, since the rig was not geared for wholesale tunnelling and in any event the bulldozer technique was hardly appropriate for archaeological excavation. The two women dug a long shallow trench, pausing as often as they had to in deference to sex and age and inexperience. Miss Concher's contribution was a good deal more than token; her zest drove her ruthlessly. Next day they deepened it, leaving a ramp at one end. As their trench descended into the earth they hauled loads of loam, sand and gravel out in a wheeled sample cart never intended for such crude manoeuvrings.

The work was slow, their muscles sore, and both had ugly blisters on their hands despite the heavy gloves. Each day the excavation sank deeper, and their anticipation grew. Down there, perhaps, was tangible evidence of a two-million-year-old culture – a culture to which man probably owed his present eminence. Blisters were beneath consideration, with the solution to such a mystery so near.

At last they struck the rocky outer wall of the cave. The drill-hole penetrated a yard of crumbling stone.

'Either we can keep digging until we come across the natural entrance,' Mrs Rhodes said, touching the aperture with weary fingers, 'or we can break out the sledge-hammer. I'm not at all sure my resources will survive either course.'

'Hammer and chisel will do it,' Miss Concher said, declining to ride with the proferred excuse though she could have done so with grace. Mere stone would not halt her. She demonstrated, flaking off wedges skilfully. 'Variation of a technique used in the Oldowan industry for a million years or so, so it will do for us. The stone age had a lot to recommend it.'

So the old lady knew how to chip stone! The process was slow, but it did promise to get the job done with a minimum of damage to whatever might be in the cave.

They took turns, the sighted women labouring clumsily much of the day, and the blind one continuing far into the night. Miss Concher seemed indefatigable and she needed no illumination. Mrs Rhodes, weary to the marrow, became too dull to marvel further at the resources of her companion. Most women of that age would be crocheting harmlessly in rockers while their grandchildren matured. Purpose animated Miss Concher, provided the motive power – but what would happen once the mission was done? Would there then be a disastrous reckoning?

But she knew the answer to that. Miss Concher would not collapse; she would find another mission, another trail to follow. In fact it was not the trail that gave her purpose, it was her purpose that revealed the trail, where no one else had thought to look. It was, as the saying went, an education merely to know her.

And perhaps within this buried cave lay the answer to the start of that purpose. Not only to this immediate trek, but to the inherent motivation of man. The thing that had given a minor hominid the bug for knowledge, two million years ago, and thrust him mercilessly into greatness. The quality that really made Miss Concher the avid scientist she was, and set her species apart from all others. Intellectual motivation.

Mrs Rhodes felt nervous goose-pimples rise along her arms despite the heat as the breakthrough point approached. The hole was widening, but Miss Concher refused to risk damaging the interior by rushing. Something was down there, though. Broken pieces where the bit had struck? Bones? Pottery? Weapons? Books? Or something more sinister?

She slept at last to the tap-tap of Miss Concher's patient excavation, not attempting to keep up with the woman's nocturnal energy. It would have been useless to urge her to stop, to rest, to sleep, for Miss Concher lived for this discovery. Better to be ready herself, in case the strain brought serious complications.

In indeterminate darkness she woke momentarily, still hearing the tap-tap. Regardless of the outcome of this quest, she knew what she was going to do after it was over. She had already learned enough about the heritage of her species to accept some things she had denied before. She had a better marriage than she had supposed, and it was not too late . . .

In the morning she discovered that Miss Concher had never returned to the truck to sleep. All was silent.

She scrambled up in alarm and ran for the gaping trench. She should have stayed up, kept watch . . . if the grand old lady had hurt herself, or collapsed, or –

She need not have worried. Miss Concher was standing waist-deep in the cave excavation, lifting out objects and using the main trench as a display shelf. Meticulously arranged were a series of irregular objects and portions of an animal skeleton.

'Miss Concher! Have you been up all night?' But the question was gratuitous and rhetorical.

The woman lifted her white head, smiling tiredly. 'Yes, we have found the answer. We know who started man on his way. The artifacts are conclusive.' She caressed the dirt-encrusted object in her hand. 'Mesolithic culture, I would say – shaped tools, but no gardening. They were obviously able to sail on the rivers and oceans, at least with some kind of raft, and to domesticate certain animals – '

'You *know* who trained Australopithecus to – '

'Yes, the hominids were one of their domestics. They recognized in Australopithecus the potential for really effective service, and they took the long view. A few thousand years of selection and training – more than enough to affect the species profoundly – and man was on his way. He even – '

Mrs Rhodes was shocked. 'You mean man started out as – as a pet, like a dog?'

'More like a horse, or an elephant. He was trained to obey simple commands, to carry his master, fetch things, and finally to undertake dinotherium hunts under the direction of a few overseers. You see, mainland Africa was too wild for a gentle, civilized species, then, as it is today for different reasons. Yet they needed certain commodities such as ivory – '

Mrs Rhodes saw a fragment of tusk among the displayed artifacts, and knew that neither elephant nor dinotherium had ever ranged Madagascar. Ivory had to be imported. But how could there have been such a culture on Earth before human civilization arose? 'Who – ' But she was unable to frame the question properly, afraid of the answer.

'Why, the Lemuridae, of course. Didn't I tell you about Archaeolemur, with the almost hominid skull? Here in this cave we have an offshoot new to paleontology, with a comparatively enormous braincase and distinctive configuration. 1,000 cc easily, if my wrinkled old fingers do not deceive me. Easily capable of mesolithic technology, in the circumstances.' She hefted the broken skull. 'Look at this marvellous specimen yourself! Plainly derived from Archaeolemur, but the placement of the foramen magnum – '

'Are you saying the – the *lemurs* are civilized? That they – '

'Lemuridae. Not today's lemurs, but their advanced relatives. Yes, they were the ones. They controlled fire, they were artistic.' Miss Concher patted the skull affectionately. 'But they made one fatal mistake in their choice of domestics. Not the first time a tutor has been out-stripped by his pupil, I'm sure, or the last. Australopithecus was almost as intelligent as this lemuridae, even then – and he had more potential, because of his size and fully bipedal stance. All he needed was a good example and some discipline. What took the lemuridae several million years to develop, man covered in a few hundred thousand.'

Mrs Rhodes stopped fighting it. 'Where is Archaeolemur now? With that head start – '

'Extinct, of course. His mouth was too large, his buttocks too small, his skin too hairy, his taste too good. Alas, he has been replaced on Earth by his domestic. Man could hardly have been a docile, loyal pet – not when trained as a hunter.'

Wood You?

I was raised on a farm without electricity; we used kerosene lamps and a wood stove. Today I am raising my children in the forest so they can share the advantage I had. We do have electricity, but also a wood stove that we use to heat our house and water. I cut up fallen wood – I don't like to hurt living trees – and split it, and that stove keeps us comfortable in winter. I sit by it and write the first drafts of my novels, saving the typing for spring when my unheated study warms. Our bill for heating is zero, but that's an illusion. My working time as a writer is worth an amount you probably wouldn't believe, so that wood actually costs more in lost income than electric heat would cost. But the work is good exercise – I am about as fit physically as any figure in the genre – any mundane figure – and I like that feeling of independence and self-reliance. If civilization collapses tomorrow, we will still be warm. So this one time I drew on my wood-splitting background; perhaps I can say that in this case fiction is the splitting image of experience. 'Wood' was published in the Oct-ogre 1970 *F&SF* 'All Star' issue. Say – I had become a star at last! One critic remarked sourly that I had once again left a moral sticking out at an odd angle. True – but how those critics hate any suggestion of meaning in fiction.

Buddy was an only child in a family of eight. Specifically, he had five adult sisters ranging in age from the neighbourhood of ten to the neighbourhood of sixteen, the least of these more bossy than it was possible to be. In the distance beyond these were one or two harried parents, almost always away at work or home asleep, and of these only Dad was male. It was not a bearable situation for a young man, and Buddy kept to himself as much as possible.

When he was two he found a long sharp kitchen knife under the sink, and brought it proudly into sight. There was an extraordinarily unpleasant fuss. So that diversion was a complete washout.

When he was two and a half he uncovered a broken rusty jackknife in the dirt under the back step. Since he was not stupid, he kept it out of sight. When unobserved – and this was much of the time, for the adult sisters had numerous and trivial concerns of their own – he studied it at leisure. The blade did not taste good, but it was fine for digging, and gradually the pitted, brownish surface became more shiny.

Behind the house a fair distance was a tremendous chopping block, where Dad periodically wielded a massive axe in an effort to reduce unruly chunks of wood to fireplace kindling. Chips and bark were all around, and the ground was scuffed intriguingly. It was a fascinating region, and he liked the smell and feel of the wood, and the fat cockroaches that scuttled under the bark. Because he knew from observation that this was Man's work, he took his knife there and commenced his private apprenticeship as a Split.

At first he cut himself, but had the presence of mind to hide the knife before the distaff commotion centred on him. The second time it happened he managed not to scream, and after a while the blood got sticky and hard. Judiciously applied dirt concealed the wound, and it didn't hurt any more. Soon he found out how to avoid such mishaps by bracing the blade away from his hand. He became adept at carving kindling.

When he was three he was able to render a given wood chip into sections hardly thicker than matchsticks. It was a matter of following the grain and being careful.

Then he came across a battered, gap-toothed hatchet in the garage. This was a splendid find, though it was horrendous to swing. Once he mastered this he was able to split larger sections of wood and do it with real dispatch. Here the lie of the grain was even more important, for if he struck a piece incorrectly, the hatchet could bounce back and fly out of his grasping little fingers. He also discovered that some chunks were harder than others, and some sappier, and others twistier. For each type he evolved a special technique.

At three and a half, Buddy discovered that he could split even the largest logs by hammering in a wedgelike scrap of metal until the wood strained and sundered. But his wedge was brittle and bent, and the hammer he used had a loose handle, so he had to be very careful. Not only did he have to study the grain, he had to analyse the general configuration of the segment, discover any natural cracks, and determine the general type of wood. There was quite a difference between soft, straight pine and hard, curved yellow birch! He also had to work around the knots, and sometimes to flake off outside sections along the circular growth-rings. But one way or another he could, in time, split any piece at all.

In fact, he was an expert wood-splitter by the time he achieved the independent age of four. His adult sisters had long since given up and let him play with his tools, for he could put up a respectable battle when balked. They had no comprehension of the intricacies of wood-craft and were forever and unreasonably scornful of what they called his tall stories about grains and types. 'He's out of bounds!' they exclaimed, not knowing that all boys his age were out of bounds, but few were as specialized as Buddy.

One day a free-lance field agent for the Snurptegian Confederation happened by, attracted by the measured tapping of loose-handled hammer on brittle, bent wedge. The creature ascertained that no adults were present (for they tended to be narrow-minded about extraterrestrials), approached the scene of activity, and waited politely while Buddy completed his incision. A final series of blows, a judicious poke with the jackknife, and the piece fell cleanly cloven.

– Bravo! the Snurp agent exclaimed. – A masterful job.

Buddy was taken aback. He hadn't noticed the visitor, and no one had ever complimented him on his talent before. 'Gee,' he said shyly.

– One is truly skilled at the art, the Snurp said. – What might one do with superior equipment?

Buddy looked at it. The Snurp had bug ears and worm eyes and slug feet, but was otherwise rather strange. Buddy did not understand all the words, but he liked the tone.

– How would one like to compete in the regional wood-splitting junior championship tournament?

Buddy didn't know what 'compete' meant, or 'regional', and the last three words were beyond human assimilation, but he certainly grasped the important part: 'wood-splitting'. 'Is that good?' he asked, knowing that it was.

– Very good, the alien said. – All one has to do is split wood fast and well. There are prizes for the best.

'Is that fun?'

– Much fun, especially for the winners.

Buddy knew his sisters would object, so he agreed to go with the Snurp. He was about to take his hatchet and hammer and chisel and penknife along, but the alien said – One must employ standard equipment.

He followed the glistening trail of the Snurp to a structure resembling a giant washing machine. They climbed in. Actually, the Snurp didn't climb so much as slide uphill. The lid settled down, warm bubbly fluid flowed in to surround them, and the thing went into a violent spin cycle.

Buddy was frightened, for he had never been inside a washing machine before when it was running. But the Snurp reassured him: – One must endure transspace only momentarily.

Sure enough, the spinning stopped and he wasn't even dizzy. The wash water drained, leaving him comfortably dry (he'd have to tell Mom about that!), and the lid lifted. They climbed/slid out.

The sunlight was green and the bushes were transparent, but aside from that the scenery was unusual. Buddy ignored it.

– One is just in time, the Snurp said, – Familiarize oneself with the equipment while one's agent attends to the registration.

Buddy paid no attention to the incomprehensible sentence. He went directly to the nearest chopping block. It was a marvel: great and square, with pockets in the sides for wonderful splitting tools. There was an elegant axe, a hatchet, a maul, six graduated wedges – all smooth and new and brightly coloured. The top of the block was sturdy and flat, without even any chop marks or splinters. Of course the axe and maul were too big and heavy for him to manage, but it was nice having them there to look at.

**Contestants! a voice proclaimed, and Buddy looked up to find a metal eyeball poised above his block. **Assume your stance.

The Snurp reappeared. – Here is a smaller maul for one. Will this suffice?

'Can I use your hammer?' Buddy asked eagerly. 'That's just right!'

The Snurp gave him the small maul. – Excellent. Now one must stand by the block, as the others are doing. Commence attack the moment the initial sample appears.

'Can I have some wood to split?'

**First phase, the eyeball said. **Purple Ash, bias facet. Proceed.

A chunk of wood appeared on the block, startling Buddy. But he saw that the same thing had happened on every block, and the birdlike and lizardlike and crablike aliens were hefting their tools. It was time to split!

The chunk was beautiful: deep blue-red with burnished black grain-ridges that angled through it strangely. It was like no wood he had ever seen, and certainly not like Earthly white ash. But it could be split! His feel for the difficult grain assured him of that.

He pondered, then placed the smallest wedge at a critical nexus, and tapped it in three times, just so. He did not dare hit too hard, here, for that would foul the interior cleavage. He didn't know how he knew, but he knew. And of course he had had long experience with difficult wood. Then he placed the next larger wedge against the appropriate stress point and struck it four times, harder.

On the last blow the log fell open, neatly halved.

– Time! the Snurp cried.

The metal eyeball appeared again and winked open. Buddy saw no support for it; it was just hanging in midair. **Approved, it said, and disappeared.

– Excellent! One has superseded Phase One with credit to spare! the Snurp exulted.

The split pieces vanished. Buddy looked around, having

nothing better to do. This was fun, but he was beginning to feel hungry.

Next block down, a rooster with octopus tentacles was pounding at a large wedge. The placement was wrong, and the wood was resisting and cracking the wrong way. Buddy knew it would finally split, but messily and not into halves.

On the other side a beaver with four monkey-arms was using the axe to chop at his chunk. Chips were flying, but the wood refused to split.

**Disqualified! the official voice said, echoing down the line of blocks wherever wood remained unsplit. All those who had failed retired regretfully. There were still a great many funny-looking creatures in the contest, however.

**Second phase. Vinegar Maple, twitch grain.

Another chunk appeared. Buddy saw at once that it was a really nasty piece. The grain went every which way, folding back on itself jaggedly, and the wood was very hard. It smelled like salad dressing, making him want to sneeze. But it could be split. His head spun with the formless calculations involved, but he finally saw the correct procedure. He tapped five wedges into place, carefully considering each location, so that they were sticking out all over. Then he pounded on them in what he felt to be the proper order. The log began to tick, unevenly. He tapped some more, until the ticking was loud and even. At last he took the hatchet and plunged it into the heartwood exposed between the two largest wedges, severing the twitchiest strand of all.

The chunk stopped ticking. It shuddered, fired off a crackling volley of splinters, expired, and fell apart along the tortuous crevice opened by the wedges. Sap dribbled out, its lifeblood, and in that death agony the salad smell wafted aloft strongly.

– Time! the Snurp cried, heedless of the carnage.

**Approved! the inspector eye said. The wood vanished. Buddy was relieved; there was something he didn't like about the split.

He looked about again. The rooster and the beaver were gone, having been eliminated in the first phase. The adjacent blocks were now occupied by a fish with six handlike fins and a monster ladybug. The ladybug had split her chunk; the fish had misplaced one wedge and was unable to reach the heartwood cleanly. An agonized keening emanated from his wood.

**Disqualified! the fish's eye cried. He swam away sadly, but Buddy was glad that chunk of wood had survived.

Now there were only a dozen splitters left, including Buddy. He was enjoying this, though he was more hungry than ever. Time seemed short when he was working on a sample, but he had been here pretty long.

**Third phase. Scorch Punk, medium rare.

A huge, blackened, grainless mass appeared on his block. He didn't have to worry about killing this; it was more than dead already. And he was in trouble, for he knew the wedges would merely sink into the spongy punk without splitting it. And as for his hatchet –

He saw the ladybug swing her axe at her chunk. The blade cut right into the centre – but the wood closed in above it and wouldn't let go, no matter how hard she yanked. It was as though the punk had become stone, anchoring the tool.

Buddy had a bright idea. He struck the wood with his maul, using no wedge. It hardened on contact, and softened again only gradually. He struck it harder, repeatedly, making a pattern of hardness around the top. Then he chopped with the hatchet – and the block cracked along that hard line!

It was cracked but not split. Now he had to place his wedges quickly in the crevice, tapping each to make the hardness form inside, then removing them before they were trapped. Again he chipped, slicing deep into the crack – and it broke open wider.

After the third round, the entire block clove in two – just as the eye appeared and yelled **Disqualified!

– One succeeded in time! the Snurp cried. – Not disqualified!

The eye peered down. **Correction: Approved.

The Snurp relaxed, relieved.

Buddy hoped there would not be much more of this. The splitting was fun in its way, but his stomach was growling.

Only six contestants remained.

**Final phase. Petrified Poplar, veneer grain.

The wood appeared. It was monstrous: a yard wide, and as hard as rock. Buddy found three suitable stress points, but they were impervious to his wedges. It would take far more strength than he possessed to make headway there – and it looked as though three wedges would have to be pounded at once, to unlock this complex boulder.

At the next block a muscular doglike contestant circled the chunk with his front paws, heaved it up, placed three wedges points-up on the block with his prehensile tail, turned over the chunk and dropped it on top of them. It shattered into thirds, spraying pebbles. //Time! his second called jubilantly.

Buddy gazed at his own stump with dismay. He could never do that! The wood was twenty times his own weight.

He tried the little hatchet on it, hoping for the best. The blade rebounded from the surface, leaving only a scratch. He tried to swing the axe, but this was even worse. He had got nowhere, and time was passing.

– One must turn the – the Snurp began.

**Disqualified! the inspector eye said immediately. **No advice permitted from the sideline during the phase.

And the wood vanished, and Buddy had to step back, disappointed and humiliated. He had really wanted to split that ponderous segment – the biggest slice of wood he had ever seen or imagined.

– Why did not one turn the poplar over to reveal the veneer-ravel point? the Snurp demanded furiously. – One was intolerably stupid!

Buddy took this as a rebuke. He bore up in silence, as he had learned to do under the constant abuse of his sisters, but he was miserable inside.

The inspector eye appeared.

**This contestant places sixth, raw score, it said. **Award ratio now being calculated. What is contestant's maturity index?

– One must provide the information, the Snurp told Buddy.

'Can I go home now? I'm hungry.'

– How mature is one? Of what physical/mental duration, relative to the adult of the species?

Buddy looked at the Snurp in perplexity. 'What?'

– How *old*?

'Oh, I'm four.'

– That would be four sidereal revolutions of one's planet about its star, the Snurp said to the eye. – This species is mature at fifteen or twenty revolutions.

The metal eye focused on Buddy. **One quarter or one fifth of maturity? Standard for this tournament is one half. That would place contestant at par times two plus. First on index, despite failure on final phase.

– The winner! the Snurp cried joyously.

**However, contestant is beneath tournament age of consent. Provide evidence of parental permission.

– Conditions were too pressing to obtain –

'Can I go home now? Everybody'll be mad when they find I'm gone.'

**Conditions too pressing? Violation of regulations, Snurptegian agent. Your species has bad recruitment record.

– Unintentional! Oversight! Misunderstanding!

'Can I go home now?' All this talk reminded him too much of the bickering of his sisters.

**Immediately, the eye said grimly. **There will be a full investigation.

And suddenly Buddy was standing beside the chopping block behind his house, alone. That**was certainly prompt!

'There you are, you little brat!' one of his middle sisters exclaimed. 'Oh, are you going to get it! You're late for supper and Mom's beside herself!'

That meant a spanking, gleefully delivered by massed sibling might. Buddy managed to bite two fingers, but otherwise got the worst of it. Afterwards, he received some leftover food.

At bedtime Dad came to see him. 'Whatever mischief did you get into today, Son?' he asked in his pleasant man-to-man way.

'Wood split.' Generally, it was safe to tell things to Dad.

'Would split what, Son?'

'Purple Ash. Scorch Punk. And funny things – but the last one was too big. And hard. And I was hungry.'

'That's very interesting, Son. You have a fine imagination.'

'The Snurp took me. In the washing machine.'

'But if you try to tell a story like that to your mother – '

Buddy understood that he was being gently reprimanded. Dad didn't believe him.

'Keep my wedge, Dad?'

'Certainly, Son.' Dad reached out for the small red section of metal. 'Where did you find that?'

'I stole it from the wood split.'

Dad's face became grave 'You will have to return it, Son. Right now. Stealing is wrong.'

Dad could be just as unreasonable as Buddy's sisters, when he put his mind to it. Reluctantly, Buddy led the way out into the dark and towards the chopping block. 'The Snurp was here, Dad. He took me to the wood split. Where I stole the wedge.'

'You're sure, Son?' The tone was dangerous.

'And the eye sent me back. Here.'

Dad sighed. 'That's not exactly a story I can accept, Son.'

It sounded suspiciously like another spanking. Buddy didn't know what to say.

Then a light appeared above the chopping block. It was the eye! **Regret uninformed decision, it said. **Investigation discloses Snurptegian agent at fault. Immature should not have been disqualified.

Dad's hand was on Buddy's shoulder, and it clenched painfully. 'Is this the owner of the wedge?'

'Yes, Dad.'

'Then give it back.'

Buddy held out the wedge. 'Here. I stole it.'

**Can not alter decision after the fact, the eye said. **Innocent immature was exploited by Snurptegian field agent. Tournament forwards regrets. Herewith, consolation prize: permit to compete in next regional junior championship tournament, and matched set of samples.

In the dim light shining from the house, or perhaps it was the glow around the eye, Buddy saw a pile of wood rise from nothing. Some chunks reflected the light metallically and some glowed on their own. Elegant wood, faerie wood – all he could ever split. Purple Ash, Vinegar Maple, Scorch Punk – and even the monstrous Petrified Poplar. And countless other exotic varieties amounting to at least a cord. The alien tools were there too – axe, maul, hatchet, wedges.

Dad looked, amazed. 'My son was spanked – for telling the truth.'

**The Snurptegian agent was spanked too, the eye said. **Trust consolation is adequate.

'No,' Dad said. 'My boy will not accept goods he has not earned. Take back your shipment.'

**As desired, the eye said. The wood vanished. **Respects.

'Respects,' Dad replied. The eye winked out.

Buddy was left with nothing. He began to cry.

'It was a payoff,' Dad explained gently, as they walked back to the house. 'You'll have many opportunities in life to earn your way properly. You wouldn't want to prejudice it all by accepting something like this now, would you?'

'Wood you?' Buddy repeated, not comprehending.

Not then.

Hard Sell

I was, as I have hinted before, phasing out of short fiction by 1971, because the editors were too picky and too free with diddles in my text, and the pay was inadequate. Editors claim they are chronically desperate for decent stories, but they often don't seem to know such stories when they see them. John Campbell of *Analog* bounced this one because he said it was right on target, therefore not really fiction. But I wrote six stories in this series, to form a novel in the aggregate, as I had done with the eight *Prostho Plus* stories. You guessed it: the magazines showed little interest, but finally *Galaxy* Publications picked up the first three – and rejected the last three. And no book publisher wanted the novel *Hard Sell*. This was a hard sell indeed! Were the stories inferior? Well, you can judge for yourself; they got stronger as they went, so that some of my best efforts were wasted on the market. The titles were: 1. 'Hard Sell' 2. 'Black Baby' 3. 'Hurdle' 4. 'Death' 5. 'Life' 6. 'Libel'. The first and third are published here. Once again I had shown too much oomph for the market – and I was pretty well fed up with that market.

'Interplanetary call for Mr Fisk, Centers,' the cute operator said.

Fisk almost dropped his sandwich. 'There must be some mistake. I don't know anybody offplanet.'

The girl looked at him with polite annoyance, as though nobody should be startled by such an event. 'Are you Mr Fisk Centers?'

'Yes, of course,' he said. 'But . . .'

Her face sifted out, smiling professionally. The screen bleeped, went blank and finally produced a man. He had handsome grey hair and wore the traditional Mars-resident uniform – a cross between a spacesuit and a tuxedo. He was seated behind a large plastifoam desk and a tremendous colour map of classical Mars covered the wall beyond.

'Welcome to Mars, Mr Centers,' the man said, putting on a contagious grin. 'I am Bondman, of Mars, Limited.' Somehow he had managed to pronounce 'Limited' the way it looked on the map on the office wall behind him: 'Ltd.'

Fisk was fifty and had been around, but he had never been treated to an interplanetary call before. The reason was not only the expense, though he knew that was extraordinary. He simply happened to be one of the several billion who had never had occasion to deal offplanet. Probably Mars, Ltd. was economizing by using OVTS – Open Volume Telephone Service – but the call was still impressive.

'Are you sure – '

'Now, Mr Centers, let's not let modesty interfere with business,' Bondman said, frowning briefly. 'You're far too sensible a man for that. That's why you're one of the privileged few to be selected as eligible for this project.'

'Project? I don't – '

The Marsman's brow wrinkled elegantly. 'Naturally it isn't available to the common run. Mars is too fine a planet to ruin by indiscriminate development, don't you agree?'

Fisk found himself nodding to the persuasive tone before the meaning registered. 'Development? I thought Mars was uninhabitable. Not enouth water, air – '

'Most astute, Mr Centers,' Bondman said, bathing him

with a glance of honest admiration. 'Indeed there is not enough water or air. Not for every person who might want to settle. Selectivity is the key – the vital key – for what can be a very good life indeed. Mars, you see, has space – but what is space without air?'

'Right. There's no good life in a spacesuit. I – '

'Of course not, Mr Centers. The ignorant person believes that man must live on Mars in a cumbersome suit and so he has a low regard for Mars realty. How fortunate that you and I know better.' And before Fisk could protest Bondman continued: 'You and I know that the new static domes conserve air, water and heat, utilizing the greenhouse effect to make an otherwise barren land burst into splendour. Within that invisible protective hemisphere it is completely Earthlike. Not Earth as it is today, but as it was a century ago. Think of it, Mr Centers – pure clean air, gentle sunshine, fresh running water. Horses and carriages – automobiles, guns, hallucinogenic drugs and similar evils prohibited. A haven for retirement in absolute security and comfort.'

Something was bothering Fisk, but the smooth sales patter distracted him and compelled his half-reluctant attention. He certainly was not going to Mars. 'But they don't have such domes on Mars. That technique was developed only a few months ago and is still in the testing stage.'

'Brilliant, Mr Centers,' Bondman exclaimed sincerely. 'You certainly keep abreast of the times. Of course there are no domes on Mars now, as you so astutely point out. Why, it will be years before they are set up, perhaps even as long as a decade. This is what makes it such a superlative investment now, before the news gets out. Provided we restrict it to intelligent men such as yourself. I'm sure – '

'Investment? Now hold on,' Fisk protested. 'I'm not in the market for investment. I'm comfortably set up right now and – '

'I quite understand. Naturally you're not interested in a mediocre investment, Mr Centers,' Bondman said, frowning at his own failure in not having made the point clear. 'Do you think I would insult your intelligence by wasting your time? No, you have the discernment to identify the superior value when you encounter it, unlike the common – '

'What investment?' Fisk demanded, annoyed by the too-heavy flattery. The intrigue of the interplanetary call was wearing thin and the objection he couldn't quite formulate still nagged – and he wanted to finish his sandwich before it got stale.

The man leaned forward to whisper confidentially. 'Marsland,' he breathed, as though it were the secret of the ages. His voice was so charged with excitement and rapture that Fisk had to struggle to maintain his emotional equilibrium. Could there be something in it?

After a pregnant pause Bondman resumed. 'I see you understand. I was sure you would. You comprehend the phenomenal potential in Marsland realty, the incredible opportunity – '

'I don't comprehend it,' Fisk snapped, gesturing with his neglected sandwich. 'I have no use for land on Mars and I would consider it an extremely risky investment. That dome technique is still in the prototype stage; it may not even work on Mars. So if that's what you're – '

'Yes, of course you want to see the brochure,' the salesman agreed irrelevantly. 'And you shall have it, Mr Centers. I will put it in the slot for you immediately, first class. I'm sure you will examine it most – '

Suddenly, facilitated by some devious mental process, Fisk's nagging question came into focus.

'You aren't on Mars,' he said angrily. 'Its orbit is fifty million miles outside Earth's. Even when Mars is closest it should take a good ten minutes to get an answer by phone.'

'Congratulations!' Bondman cried jubilantly. 'You have just qualified for our exclusive genius-intellect bonus certificate. Of course I'm not calling from that Mars you see in the sky – I'm here at the Mars, Limited promotion office. Mr Centers, I'm so glad you were sharp enough to solve our little riddle within the time limit. You're the very kind of investor we prefer. I'll insert the certificate right now. And I'll be seeing you again soon. Bye-bye.'

And while Fisk was marvelling at the peculiarly childish 'bye-bye' the image faded.

He lifted his sandwich, a fine torula-steak on soyrye with enriched onion sauce, but found he was no longer hungry. He was sure this was a sales gimmick for something worthless, but Bondman's contagious excitement had got to him. Maybe there was a good investment on Mars.

Well, no harm in looking at the literature. He certainly didn't have to buy.

He didn't have long to wait, either. His mail receiver was already chiming with an arrival.

He picked up the bulky printing and spread it out. It was a first-class presentation, all right, with colour photographs and glossy surfacing that must have cost dearly to transmit. If he had not been present when it arrived he would have suspected a physical delivery rather than the normal mailfax. Mars, Ltd must have oiled the right palms in the post office.

Well, he had to admit it – he was intrigued. He probably would not buy, but he would enjoy looking.

First there was the bonus certificate, entitling him to a twenty per cent reduction. Fair enough – but hardly sufficient to induce him to buy without his knowing the actual price. Then a spread on Mars – its discovery in prehistoric times, its variable distance from Earth (35–235 million miles), its long year (687 days – Earth days or Mars days, he wondered – or were they the same?), low surface gravity (one-third Earth's), pretty moons (ten-mile diameter Phobos, six-mile Deimos), scenic craters – all familiar material, but calculated to whet the appetite for investment and retirement.

Then down to paydirt. The proposed colony, Elysium Acres, was located on a map dramatically coloured and named. An electrostatic dome a hundred miles in diameter, almost fifty miles high, enclosed a greenhouse atmosphere at Earth-normal pressure and temperature. The development was suitable for homesites, with carefully laid out horse trails and a delightful crater lake. Guaranteed weather, pollution-free atmosphere.

Fisk was middle-aged and cynical, but this gripped him. Earth was such a sweatbox now. He hated having to take weekly shots to protect his system against environmental contamination, and the constantly increasing restrictions invoked in the name of the growing pressure on worldly resources made him rage at times like a prisoned tiger. (What other kind of tiger was there today?) Perhaps if he had married, found someone to share his – but that was another entire dimension of frustration, hardly relevant now.

This Marsdome pitch catered to these very frustrations, he realized. There must be millions like himself, men well enough to do, intelligent and sick of their own lack of purpose. What a beacon it was, an escape to an unspoiled planet – in comfort.

But of course he was old enough to control his foolish fancies. He knew, intellectually, that no such development existed on Mars and probably never would exist.

The sheer expense would be prohibitive. All that technology, all that shipment from Earth – why, passenger fare for one person one way would amount to twenty or thirty thousand dollars, assuming emigration could even be arranged. And for him it was out of the question.

Yet he could not help studying the brochure. Elysium Acres – such a suggestion of bliss! Could it possibly come true by the time he turned sixty? Why not, if they were able to finance it?

There was the real rub. Money. How much to establish the dome, stock it with good atmosphere, import vegetation, calculate and maintain a closed-system ecological balance, construct access highways, lakes, houses, service facilities? There would have to be hospitals, libraries, administrative buildings, emergency staffs – all the accoutrements of civilization, in short. It would cost billions of dollars to maintain – perhaps trillions to construct. Naturally the brochure did not provide the price list.

But if it were affordable and if it were possible for him to go – what a temptation!

He punched his personal info number for his net worth, just checking. The totals flashed on the screen after he had provided his identification code: liquid assets just over fifty thousand dollars; investments at current quotations just under two hundred thousand; miscellaneous properties and options sixty to eighty thousand, pending urgency of sale. Grand total – a generous three hundred thousand.

Enough, with proper management, to tide him through the twenty-five years until his retirement annuities matured. He was hardly fool enough to jeopardize any of it by investing in pie-on-Mars. Still, it had been fun dreaming.

The dream lingered next morning, a welcome guest staying beyond courteous hours. Fisk showered in the sonic booth, depilitated and dressed. As he arranged and set his greying locks he wondered irrelevantly whether he and the salesman, Bondman, used the same brand of hair tint. He studied his face in the mirror, picturing himself as a hard-sell agent, lifting his brow artfully to augment a pregnant pause. Yes, he did look the part – perhaps he would be good at it.

But then, subjectively, he saw the signs of what he knew was there – the circulatory malady that bound him to Earth for life. His quarterly medication kept it under control – but a trip to Mars, with the necessary accelerations and drugstates, was out of the question. That was why Mars would never be more than a dream for Fisk Centers, no matter how alluring the sales pitch. He would always be a portly, subdued Earthman.

So it was time to end it. He filed the Mars, Ltd literature in the recycle bin and watched it disintegrate. Then he punched breakfast. He felt lonely.

The phone lighted. 'Yes?' he said automatically.

'Interplanetary call for Mr Fisk Centers,' the cute operator said. She had changed her hairdo, but she was the same one who had placed the call yesterday.

'Come off it, girl,' he snapped, aware that there was nothing more useless than taking out a personal peeve on an impersonal employee. 'It is not interplanetary.'

Bondman of Mars phased into view. 'Of course it is, Mr Centers,' he said genially. 'The Mars, Limited office is legally Mars soil, you know. An enclave. We have to undergo quarantine before reporting for work, ha-ha! I trust you have studied our brochure – '

'Yes. I'm not buying.'

Bondman looked hurt. 'But you haven't even heard

our price, Mr Centers. I know a man as fair-minded as
you – '

'I'll never go to Mars.'

'Remember, you get a special bonus price because of
your intelligence and judgement. I'm sure you'll
recognize – '

'I have a circulatory disorder. Inoperable. Sorry.'

Bondman laughed with a finely crafted lack of affec-
tation. 'You don't have to go to Mars, Mr Centers. We're
talking about investment.'

'I told you I wasn't looking for – '

'You've studied the plans for Elysium Acres? The
phenomenal hundred-mile dome, the luxurious facilities,
the nineteenth-century atmosphere – literally – the scenic
lots? Of course you have. Mr Centers, you know values.
What do you figure it will cost? I mean the entire setup
on Mars, gross?'

'A trillion dollars,' Fisk said, believing it. 'Plus upkeep
of billions per year.'

'Would you believe three trillion? But you're remarkably close, Mr Centers. You certainly understand investment. You merely underestimated the importance of this
development to us – and to the world. We're putting
everything into it, Mr Centers. Another developer might
do it for one trillion, but we put quality first. Three
trillion – but we know we'll make a profit in the end and
of course we have to consider profit, Mr Centers. We're
businessmen, like you – and believe me, sir, there is a
demand. In ten years Earth will be a veritable nightmare
and Elysium Acres will be an incredible bargain at any
price.' Bondman held up a hand to forestall Fisk's possible
objection. 'I'm not forgetting that you can't go, Mr
Centers. I'm merely pointing out what an attractive
investment this is going to be. Some will have the incalcu-
lable privilege of retiring to Elysium Acres – others will

merely make a fortune from it. I' – here the voice
dropped to its supercharged confidential tone – 'hope to
do both.' Bondman paused long enough for that affirm-
ation of faith to penetrate, but not long enough for Fisk
to generate an interjection. 'Now, we're subdividing EA
into lots of one hundred feet square, give or take a foot –
enough for a comfortable cottage and garden. Twenty
million of them – yes, that's correct, Mr Centers. That
dome is a hundred miles across and there will be eight
thousand square miles inside and two and a half thousand
lots per mile – but I don't need to do elementary math-
ematics for you, Mr Centers. Twenty million lots for
three trillion dollars. That comes to a hundred and fifty
thousand dollars per lot. A bit high for Earth, considering
they're undeveloped – but this is Mars! Those lots are
priceless, Mr Centers, priceless – yet they will be put on
the market at a price any successful man can afford.' He
held up his hand again, though Fisk had made no motion
to interrupt. 'But Mars, Limited needs operating capital,
Mr Centers, and we need it now. So we are offering for a
limited time only a very, very special investment opportunity. You can buy these lots as investment real estate
today for a tiny fraction of their actual value. Later – any
time you wish – you may sell for a handsome profit. So
although you may never have the privilege of going to
Mars yourself – and please accept my heartfelt condol-
ences, Mr Centers, for I know how much you would have
liked to retire to Elysium Acres – you can still benefit
materially while advancing a noble cause through your
investment.'

Fisk was more impressed by the emotive delivery than by
the content. Salesmanship really was an art.

'How much?'

'Mr Centers, we are offering these lots at – now listen

carefully because this is hard to believe – at one-quarter price. Thir-ty sev-en thou-sand five hun-dred dollars for a property worth one hun-dred and fif-ty thou-sand dollars.' Bondman spaced out the syllables to make the figures absolutely clear and emphatic.

'That's my bonus for nabbing your "interplanetary call" gimmick?'

Bondman rolled his eyes expressively but did not take exception to Fisk's choice of words. 'Of course not, Mr Centers. That's our one-time special-offer bargain price. For you alone we provide the bonus price. Don't tell anyone else, because if word got out that anyone beat the bargain price there would be resentment. Even – ' and a great rippling shrug bespoke consequences so vast that to invoke them by name would be foolhardy.

Bondman did not speak that mind-shattering figure. Instead he fed it into his mailfax. The full contract emerged from Fisk's slot. He paged through it while Bondman waited expectantly, anticipating the client's amazed pleasure.

Thirty thousand dollars. In other words, the straight twenty per cent reduction the certificate had promised.

Yes, it did seem like a good buy. Still, Fisk had had some experience in such matters. He skimmed through until he found the small print – actually regular type buried in an otherwise innocuous paragraph.

Ownership remained with Mars, Ltd until the stipulated amount had been paid in full. In the event of default, the property reverted to Mars, Ltd without refund. The risk of capital was all with the purchaser, unless he bought outright for cash. Very interesting.

'Now you see the bargain we are offering you, Mr Centers,' Bondman said gravely. 'Frankly, you are one of the very last to receive the thirty-seven fifty figure, let alone the bonus deal. Demand has been even greater than we anticipated, with many people buying multiple lots. Blocks of four – or even more. There will have to be a price increase. After all, the company needs capital – it is ridiculous for us to sell so low when our own clients are turning around and selling their lots for more. Why only last week a man sold five for two hundred thousand flat – and he'd only bought them last month. He made a twelve thousand profit on a three-week investment – and that's only the one we know about. Others – ' here his shoulders rose in another eloquent shrug. 'Where, Mr Centers, is the limit?'

'Why didn't the second buyer come to you first?' Fisk inquired. Actually the described profit was only about six per cent and normal fluctuation of the market could readily account for it. But it did seem to auger well for the growth prospects. Fisk could buy five lots for $150,000 not $187,500, and make that much more.

'Apparently he didn't realize our price was as low as it was,' Bondman said sadly. 'He thought he had infor-mation. The biggest sucker is the one who thinks he knows it all – right, Mr Centers? If he had only checked with us – but of course our price *won't* be lower after this week. So he has a good investment anyway – though not as good as it could have been. If our lots are going for forty thousand – well, we do need capital,' he finished almost apologetically. 'You understand.'

Yes, Fisk was certainly interested now. Buy for thirty, sell for forty – but he knew better than to appear eager. 'I might take a lot or two,' he said. 'But it's a lot of money. I'd have to liquidate some other investments and that would take time.'

'I understand perfectly,' Bondman agreed instantly. 'I had to do the same when I invested in my own first Mars lot. It was well worth it, of course. Fortunately we have a time payment plan exactly suited to your situation. Ten-year term, so that it will be paid up when Elysium Acres opens and the real gold rush begins. Irrevocable six per cent interest. Just three hundred and twenty-five dollars a month covers all, Mr Centers – we absorb the cover charge. How does that suit you?'

Fisk checked the figures quickly in his head. They were fair – six per cent on a decreasing principal. No funny business there, no usury. And he would be able to liquidate his investments profitably within a year and pay off the rest, saving the interest. Some contracts had penalty clauses for early payment, but this one fortunately did not.

'Sounds good,' he admitted.

'Good? Good?' Bondman demanded rhetorically. 'Mr Centers, how would you like to buy a cyclotron at the sheet metal price? That's how good it is! But that isn't all. What we are talking about is three-twenty-five a month – less than eleven dollars a day to control a genuine Marsland property now selling for – ' He broke off, nodding significantly towards the contract with a secret figure. 'And with values quadrupling – or more – in the period of agreement. Mr Centers, you are actually investing a paltry three-twenty-five a month for a return of at least a hundred and fifty thousand in a mere decade.'

Fisk knew. Thirty thousand dollars, plus nine thousand dollars accumulated interest for the ten-year span. For $150,000 value. A net profit of $111,000, or over eleven thousand per year – per lot. With just three lots he could triple his fortune.

'Still, it's a sizable amount. Are you sure it's safe? I mean, suppose something happens and the dome doesn't get built. The lots would become almost worthless.'

'Mr Centers, it certainly is a pleasure to do business with you,' Bondman exclaimed. 'You don't miss a trick. Of course there is a nominal element of risk. Life itself is the biggest risk of all. But by buying on time you can eliminate even that one-in-a-thousand chance. Just consider. If something should happen to abort Elysium Acres tomorrow – and I assure nothing short of World War Four could squelch our plans – and you had bought today and paid your deposit premium, what would you have lost? Three hundred and twenty-five dollars. Why, Mr Centers – you must blow more than that on one good suit.'

Extremely sharp observation. Fisk *had* paid more than that for his dress suit.

Bondman followed up his advantage, knowing he had scored. 'Considering the hundred and fifty thousand value – just what are you risking? One suit.'

'But suppose something happens in two years. Or nine. I can't afford to lose a suit every month.'

'Mr Centers,' Bondman said sternly. 'I'm a busy man and this call is expensive. Don't waste my time and yours with inconsequentials. If you don't trust the stability of a fine new developer like Mars, Limited, don't invest. Or if you believe it will fail in two years, sell in one year. Your property will have increased in value at least ten per cent – in fact, considering the coming price rise, twenty per cent may be a more accurate estimate. But just keep it simple, let's call it ten per cent. That's between three and four thousand dollars, right? And how much are you paying per year?'

'Between three and four thousand dollars,' Fisk said.

'So if you sell then, your return on your actual investment will be just about one hundred per cent. This is leverage, Mr Centers – using a small amount of money to control a large among of money. And the profit is yours even if, as you say, Mars, Limited fails in two years. Or nine. Ha-ha.' He leaned forward again, speaking intensely. 'The dome may fail, Mr Centers – but you won't.'

Fisk laughed. 'Very well, Mr Bondman. You've sold me. Just give me a little time to check around – ' This was a key ploy. If the salesman were out to take him he would do anything to prevent a fair investigation of the facts. And of course Fisk wouldn't buy without checking. That was the big advantage in being an experienced fifty. He couldn't be stampeded.

'Certainly, Mr Centers. In fact I insist on it. If we were looking for foolish investors we never would have called you. I'll be happy to provide the government property report – '

'Thanks, no. I just want a few days to make some calls.' He was hardly going to use Mars, Ltd data to check out Mars, Ltd.

'By all means. I wouldn't have it otherwise.' Bondman paused as though remembering something. 'Of course, I can't guarantee your price, Mr Centers. That increase is going to come through any day now – perhaps tomorrow. They never let us salesmen know in advance, of course, because some might – uh – profiteer at the expense of the customer. But I know it's soon. Your bonus will still apply, naturally, but five or six thousand per lot is a pretty hefty penalty for a day's time. Uh – do you think you could make it by this afternoon? Say, four o'clock? I don't want to rush you – and of course it might be as late as next week before the rise – but I would feel terrible if – '

Bondman would feel terrible if he lost his commission because an irate customer balked at the higher price. Fisk thought. 'I think I can make it by four.' That would give him six hours – time enough.

'Excellent. I'll see you then. Bye-bye.' And the screen faded.

Fisk had not been bluffing. The Marslot investment seemed attractive indeed, but he never made snap decisions about money. It wasn't just a matter of checking – he wanted to appraise his own motives and inclinations. The best buy in the world – or Mars – was pointless if it failed to relate to his basic preferences and needs.

He punched an early lunch and ate it slowly. Then he began his calls.

First the library informational service for a summary of Mars, Ltd operations. While that was being processed for faxing to him he read the sample contract carefully and completely. It was tight – he would not actually own the lot until it was completely paid for and he couldn't sell it until he owned it. Leverage? Ha!

But apart from that trap, it was straight. He could defang it by purchasing outright. Not to mention the interest he would save.

The rundown on Mars, Ltd arrived. He settled down to his real homework.

Interesting – there was a cautionary note about that 'Ltd.' 'Limited' meant that the developer's liability was limited to its investments on Earthsoil – of which it had none. Its only Earthly enclave was, as Bondman had claimed, legally Mars soil. A nice device for impressive 'interplanetary' calls to clients – but perhaps even nicer as a defence against lawsuit. An irate party might obtain a judgement for a million dollars – but unless he sued on Mars there was nothing for him to collect. What a beautiful foil against crackpots and opportunists.

The company was legitimate. In fact it was the largest of its kind, having sold billions of dollars worth of

Marsland to speculators in the past few years. The Elysium Acres project was listed, too. A note read: SEE GOVERNMENT PROPERTY REPORT. Fisk sighed and punched for it – it had not been attached to the main commentary. He had a lot of dull reading to do.

The phone lighted. The hour was already four. He had meant to make some other checks – well, they hardly mattered, He had verified that Mars, Ltd was no fly-by-night outfit.

'Did you come to a decision, Mr Centers?' Bondman inquired, sounding like an old friend.

Fisk had decided – but a certain innate and cussed caution still restrained him. The deal seemed too good to be true and that was a suspicious sign. But aside from the 'leverage' hoax he could find no fault in it. He decided not to query the salesman about the time payment trap – to do so would only bring a glib explanation and more superfluous compliments on his intelligence. Better to let Bondman think he was fooling the client.

'I might be interested in more than one lot,' Fisk said.

'Absolutely no problem, Mr Centers.' Fisk was sure the salesman's warmth was genuine this time. 'Simply enter the number of lots you are buying on the line on page three where it says "quantity", write your name on the line below, and make out a cheque to Mars, Limited for your first payment. That's all there is to it, since I have already countersigned. Fax a copy back to us and – '

Fisk's mail chime sounded. 'Oh – the property report,' he said. 'Do you mind if I just glance at it first? A formality, of course.'

'Oh, I thought you'd already read that. Didn't I send you one? By all means – '

A buzzer on Bondman's desk interrupted him. 'I'm in conference,' he snapped into his other phone. 'Can't it wait?' Then his expression changed. 'Oh, very well.' he

turned to Fisk. 'I beg your pardon – a priori call ha
just signalled on my other line and – well, it's om my
superior. Can't say no to him, ha-ha, even if is bad
form to interrupt a sales conference. If you do mind
waiting a moment – '

'Not at all. I'll read the property report.'

'Excellent. I'll wrap this up in a moment, I'r e,
Bondman faded, to be replaced by a dramatic
conception of Elysium Acres, buttressed by sweet s
The connection remained. This was merely Mars
privacy shunt.

There was a *snap* as of a shifting connection and B
man's voice was superimposed on the music. '. . .
you I'm closing a sale for several lots. I can't just pull
rug out – he's signing the contract right now . . .
pause, as he listened to a response that Fisk coul
hear. Then: 'To fifty thousand? As of this morning? W
didn't you call me before?'

Fisk realized that Bondman's privacy switch hadn'
locked properly. It wouldn't be ethical to listen and h
did want to skim that property report. But the voic
wrested his attention away from the printed material.

'Look, boss – I just can't do it. I quoted him the thirty
grand bonus . . . no, I can't withdraw it. He's sharp –
and he's got the contract! He'd make a good Mars,
Limited exec . . . terms, I think . . . yes, if we could get
him to default on the payments, so the reversion clause
. . . hate to bilk him like that – I like him . . . no, I'm
sure he wouldn't go for the new price. Not with the
cancellation of the bonus and all. That's a twenty-grand
jump just when he's about to sign . . . okay, okay, I'll try
it – but listen, boss, you torpedo me in midsale again like
this and I'm signing with Venus, Limited before you
finish the call . . . I know they're a gyp outfit. But I

this client the bonus price and now you're makir liar out of me and cheating him out of the finest inve   nt of the century on a time-payment technicality. If I e to operate that way I might as well go whole hog – '

V re was a long pause. Fisk smiled, thinking of the e-lashing Bondman must be getting for putting grity ahead of business.

isk knew it was unfair of him to take advantage of a ped switch and private information – but he had been omised the bonus price and now someone was trying to ipe it out. If Mars, Ltd were trying to con him out of his ivestment, he had a right to con himself back in.

'. . . all right.' Bondman's voice came again. 'That's best. I'll try to talk him out of it so nobody loses. But get those new quotations in the slot right away. Couple of other clients I have to call – they're going to be furious about that increase, but at least they were warned about delaying . . . yes . . . yes . . . okay. Sorry I blew up. Bye-bye.'

The music faded. The picture vanished and Bondman reappeared, looking unsettled. 'Sorry to keep you waiting so long, Mr Centers,' he said. 'Bad news. The offer I was describing to you – well, I'm afraid we'll have to call it off.'

'But I just signed the contract,' Fisk protested innocently. 'Are you telling me to tear it up already?'

Bondman's eyelids hardly flickered. 'What I meant to say is that the conditions have changed. New government restrictions have forced up construction costs and the whole Elysium Acres project is in jeopardy. In fact, Mr Centers, we now have no guarantee that there will even be a dome on Mars. Under the circumstances I don't see how I can recommend – '

So that was the pitch. 'We all have to take chances, as

you pointed out,' Fisk said briefly. 'I should think that if your expenses go up your prices would follow – to compensate. So I should buy now.'

'Er – yes,' Bondman admitted. 'Still, it looks bad. I wouldn't want you to be left holding a title to a worthless lot, Mr Centers. Until this thing settles down – '

'One lot?' Fisk interjected with mock dismay. 'Lots. I signed up for ten.'

For a moment even the supersalesman was at a loss for words. 'T-ten?'

'Why not, for such a good investment? Leverage, you know.'

'Leverage! Let me tell you something – ' Bondman caught himself. He sighed. He put on a smile of rueful admiration. 'You certainly know your business, Mr Centers. I only hope you aren't taking a terrible chance with a great deal of money. Are you sure?' But, observing Fisk's expression, he capitulated. 'Well, then, just make out your first monthly payment for three thousand two hundred and fifty dollars and we'll – '

'Thanks, no. I'm paying cash.'

Bondman looked so woebegone that Fisk felt sorry for him, though he knew the salesman would still receive a handsome commission along with his reprimand for letting so many underpriced lots go. 'Cash? The entire amount?'

'Yes. Here is my check for three hundred thousand dollars, certified against the escrow liquidation of my total holdings. That saves you the annoyance of time payments and gives you a good chunk of the working capital you need. Your boss should be well pleased, considering your rising expenses.'

'Uh, yes.' Bondman agreed faintly as Fisk faxed check and contract back to him. The originals remained with him for his records, but the faxes were legal, too. The deal was closed. He owned the lots outright and could not lose them by payments default. If he needed working capital himself, he could sell one at the fifty-thousand-dollar price tomorrow.

Bondsman stared bleakly at the documents, then pulled himself together. 'It has been a real pleasure doing business with you, Mr Centers,' he said with a brave smile. 'I'm sure you'll never regret your purchase. Uh, bye-bye.'

'Bye-bye!' Fisk returned cheerily as the connection broke.

But something about the salesman's expression just as the picture faded bothered him. It reminded him of what Bondman had said during the morning call: *The biggest sucker is the one who thinks he knows it all . . .*

The library information on Mars, Ltd was general and, of course, bland. Any negative remarks would have made it vulnerable for a libel suit regardless of the truth. It had provided him with essentially the Mars, Ltd publicity release, but added the cautionary note: SEE GOVERNMENT PROPERTY REPORT.

Fisk had been about to look at that report when Bondman's boss had interrupted and the privacy switch had coincidentally malfunctioned. Interesting timing.

After the price-increase call Bondman had been nervous and stuttery, hardly a supersalesman. His facade had disintegrated – yet he had known the word was coming. And a salesman of that calibre should have been able to cover better than that. Unless the whole thing had been an act to puff up the confidence of a sucker who thought he knew it all.

Fisk's hand shook as he lifted the property report, for now he knew what he would find.

Plainly printed in red ink:

This property is not adaptable for terraforming purposes. The lots are unimproved, unsurveyed and without roads, landing facilities or other improvements. Access is extremely poor. Site is subject to frequent ground tremors prohibiting construction of permanent buildings or erection of static-dome generators. Approximate value per lot is $300.00 . . .

Hurdle

I've already commented, but will add this note: I've always been intrigued by alternate sources of power, and it shows here. Perhaps I would have come up with some additional notions, had I written this story a decade later; science keeps advancing, but stories remain fixed in their firmament the moment they see print.

'Up, Fisk,' Yola said. 'Earn your daily bonus and commission or else.'

Fisk Centers rolled over groggily. 'Else what?'

'This.' An avalanche of icy foam descended on his head. He struggled up, gasping for breath, suddenly wide awake. 'What was that for?'

'Well, I did warn you,' she said contritely. 'You look like a walrus surfacing.'

'Nonsense. I don't have tusks.'

'A toothless walrus, then. Fat, wet, stupid – '

'You're about to look like a spanked brat.'

'No time,' she said. 'Bolt your food, Fisky. Today you go to work for your living.'

'What makes you so sure I'll have any better luck today than I've had all week?'

'Because you handled this week. I set up today. While you snored.'

'I should have stayed single,' Fisk muttered as he stumbled to the suiter and let it dry and dress him. 'Or at least got married. The last thing any man would do is become an adoptive father to a pre-teen hellion.'

'Right,' she agreed. 'Especially when he has to live off her money.'

'That's my money! Twenty per cent commission just for – '

'For selling an innocent child on the black mar – '

'Shut up.' He stepped out of the suiter, resplendent in blue jeans, checkered shirt and goggles. 'What did you do to the setting?' he roared.

'You look just right for your job,' she said. 'Hurry up.'

He tore off the goggles. 'My job – doing what?'

'Selling cars, of course.'

'Cars? I'm no mechanic – '

'That's all you know, Dad. Salesmen don't have to know anything about the workings. Just believe in your product and sell, sell, sell!'

Fisk punched a soyomelet. 'Believe in my product? I haven't even *driven* a car for five years,' He took a bite, but paused before masticating it. 'What car am I supposed to sell?'

'Fusion. They've got a real nice commission deal – '

The mouthful of omelet sprayed over the table. 'The atomic racer? The radioactive juggernaut that makes the obituary headlines every other week? The – '

'The same. They're making a play for the middle-class market and they need middle-class salesmen. Hot chance for you.'

'Hot? Listen, Yola – do you realize that my annuities don't mature for another twenty-five years and are voided in the event of deliberate suicide? If I die tomorrow in a Fusion you inherit nothing.'

'Term life insurance,' she answered. 'That's their bonus. Life and commissions. You live off the commissions, of course. But if you die – '

'Enough, child. The longer I listen to you the worse I feel. I'm not going near any – '

'Suit yourself,' she said. 'We'll run out of money tomorrow.'

'Tomorrow? There's enough for at least another week.'

'You forget you have a family to support. Two don't live as cheaply as one, you know.' She paused, serious and for the moment rather pretty in her brown-faced way. 'Fisk, it's a good chance for you. I thought you'd really go for a decent income – '

Fisk sighed. 'I'll talk to the man. But it had better be strictly salesroom. If I have to go near a living Fusion I'll resign on the spot.'

'Sure,' she said. 'Come on – you're due to report in twenty minutes.'

'Fisk Centers? Right,' the executive at Fusion Motors said briskly as Fisk introduced himself. 'Your daughter here set it up. Glad to have a man of your experience with us.'

'Experience? I haven't – '

Yola tromped his toe and Fisk realized that she had invented suitable qualifications for him. Time to set that straight right now. He took a breath.

'You're in the weekly Hurdle, starting at ten today,' the man said.

Fisk's breath wooshed out. 'I beg your – '

The man guided him out through a service exit, led him into a massive garage filled with menacing machinery. 'Bill, he's here.'

Fisk tried again. 'Look, I don't know what she told you, but I'm not – '

'Here's your co-pilot, Bill. Bill, this is Fisk. Used to be with Ferrari before the antipolluters closed down their commercial branch. Drove in the antarctic cross-country a couple times, maybe twenty years ago. Going to sell for us. I want him to get a real feel for the Fusion, but you'll have to carry the burden this time.'

'Great,' Bill said, shaking Fisk's hand with a grip of steel and rubber. 'Come on, Fisk. We've got just thirty-five minutes to blastoff and you'll need briefing.'

'But I – '

'Don't get me wrong,' Bill said, hustling him along while Yola trotted excitedly behind. 'I'm not putting down your experience. But there's been a lot of development in the past two decades and most of it has been led by the Fusion. And the Hurdle is a real workout. If anything happens to me you'll have to take over – because the finish line's the only safe exit. Ever drive over five hundred before?'

'Well, I – ' Then it occurred to Fisk that Bill wasn't talking about distance and certainly not about regular highway travel. Stunned, he fumbled for a suitable way to set things straight immediately.

Yola caught up. She smiled sweetly at Bill. 'Can I come, too? I love racing – '

Bill looked at her with leathery compassion. 'Sorry, kid. No juniors allowed. This is a rough course and it changes every week. You'll have to watch it on the customer screen. Mine's the purple Eight.'

'Oh.' She looked dangerously sullen, but fell back.

'Bill, there's been a misunderstanding,' Fisk said, already out of breath because of the pace Bill was setting through the monstrous garage. 'I can't – I never – '

'Here she is,' Bill said proudly, pulling up at a tremendous sculptured vehicle with eight massive wheels. 'Hop in. We'll get strapped while the tug takes her there. I'll brief you while we're moving.' He gave Fisk a powerful boost into the open cockpit.

The moment the two men landed in the firm moulded

seats, the tug started hauling the car out of its niche and down a ramp. Bill saw to Fisk's complex protective harness before attending to his own.

'But I'm only supposed to be a salesman,' Fisk protested. 'I can't get involved in a race. I have absolutely no – '

'No problem. Boss always breaks in the new men like this. Idea is you don't need to know every detail about the car – you just have to believe in it absolutely, and the details will take care of themselves. So we don't load you down with statistics and all that junk – we just show you. Once you've raced the Fusion Special you're a believer.'

'But I'm trying to tell you that I don't know the first thing about – '

'Sure. The boss explained. You've never touched the Fusion before. And twenty years is a long, long time in racing. We'd have let you sit it out this week, but my regular co-pilot isn't out of the hospital yet. But I know you've got the stuff. I used to watch that antarctic cross-country when I was a kid. Those glaciers, those ice crevasses – ' He shook his head. 'Hell, the Hurdle isn't rougher than that. But it is different – and you've got to ride it several times before you get the feel. So I'll drive and you just handle the map – okay? Nobody tackles a new race in a new car cold.'

Appalled, Fisk could only nod. At this point it almost seemed better to take the horrible ride and keep his mouth shut. At least the driver was competent and it would be a one-time experience.

'Actually, that map is important,' Bill said consolingly. 'I can't take my eyes off the track when I'm at speed. They do it that way to make sure the race stays fair. New track for each run – nobody knows the specific layout until the race starts and then he has to figure his strategy from the map. Yours is a necessary job and don't you doubt it for a moment. One misreading and we're dead.'

Fisk came to an abrupt decision – he would blurt out the truth and get released from this race right now. 'Bill, I – '

'I wouldn't drive without a mapman. My co-pilot tried that a couple weeks ago, when I was out at the last minute with intestinal grippe. You know – bathroom every ten minutes, ready or not. Didn't dare drive. So he took it alone, because you can't get a replacement at the last moment and we didn't want our entry scratched. That's why he cracked up – trying to read the map before he got out of the tunnel – ' Bill shook his head. 'Fifteen hours in surgery and he'll have to drive next time with a prosthetic hand and a plate in his skull. Ran over his insurance and he's got a family to support. That's why I have to run a good race this time. Got to help him out.'

Fisk realized that if he spoke out now Bill would have no co-pilot. Then he would have either to take it alone, risking the same fate that had wiped out his partner, or drop out of the race entirely. Then his friend's medical bills would ruin his family.

Fisk well understood the problems of financial ruin. He had been a moderately wealthy man not so long ago. Being broke was not a fate he would wish on anyone.

'. . . true dual-purpose car,' Bill was saying. He evidently liked to talk. 'Motor's always at full power, of course, so the clutch guides it. Not the kind of clutch you knew, eh? No gearing. Just engage for the percentage of power you want. Depress gently and you've got a gentle touring car. Goose it and you've got a real racer. I use a model just like this for city traffic – '

What could Fisk do but stick with it? Racing terrified him and not just because of his health – but more was riding on this race than his preferences.

'. . . duplicate controls, but yours will be inactive. Except for the indicators – you need to watch them in case of emergency. Regular steering wheel, you see; nothing complicated. Fusion's designed for the simple-minded – that's why I like it. And over here – '

The tug was manoeuvring the car into the starting stall. A giant chronometer above was ticking off the last seconds before the start. Fisk squirmed in his harness, feeling cold sweat on his palms, face and underarms. He hoped that the term insurance was for a large amount.

'The map will fall into the fax hopper there as the gun goes off,' Bill said. 'Grab it and – '

A faint pop came through the armoured hull. Paper dropped. And the car ground forward with such authority that it was all Fisk could do to breathe. There was very little noise. Pollution-control had really clamped down on loud sports jobs; both the hydrogen/helium fusion engine and the mercury vapour working fluid were almost silent. Also, it seemed, the cockpit was soundproof.

Fisk had to admit it – this *was* a nice piece of machinery.

Competing cars shot out of their stalls. Blue, white, green, red, yellow – internal combustion, steam, electric, jet, atomic and assorted hybrids. The car industry had claimed that stiff antipollution standards would ruin it, but in fact they had led to a marvellous flowering of superior new types. The money that had once been wasted on planned obsolescence of style now went into improvement of mechanics. Drivers still had to buy a new car every three years, but now they obtained a superior product in each new model. And this was where that superiority was demonstrated – in professional competition, using the cars sold in the showrooms. It was a drag race start: thirty bright vehicles straining forward on a ten-mile straight-away. No noise or fumes.

Fisk sneaked a look at the speedometer. His duplicate was functioning, but it took him a moment to find the mph scale among the massed dials and digits. The main readings were feet per second and kilometres per hour, but he was pedestrian enough to orient on old-fashioned miles per hour. They were already doing 150, and accelerating rapidly. And the other cars were keeping pace or pulling ahead, so that the group velocity was deceptive.

'Look at the map,' Bill shouted. 'What's the first hurdle?'

Fisk opened the map hastily and scanned it. He had been daydreaming while his very life was at stake in an obstacle race at hundreds of miles per hour.

'The Narrows,' he said.

'The Narrows? That's a stiff location, but good for us. Hang on – we'll have to push it.'

And, astonishingly, the acceleration increased. The Fusion began gaining on other cars.

'I thought you were all-out before,' Fisk gasped.

'Hardly. This is the finest car ever made, overall. The Fusion's got more actual muscle than any car on the market – and unlimited range. It has a little piece of the sun inside, you know – that's the heat of the conversion, four hydrogen atoms transforming into one helium atom in controlled fusion. Fuel's no problem – it's loaded when we make it and it runs on just a little bit of hydrogen until the car is junked. We have no top speed, really – car would shake apart before we ever reached maximum. Only limiting factor – oh, don't worry, we won't shake apart – in a race like this is the frictive surface: the tyres. That's why we've got eight – and they're broad ones, too. But too much acceleration makes them skid a bit and that's bad for control and worse for wear. Got to save the rubber or we'll have trouble finishing, even though the tyres are solid. Guess you were still on pneumatics in the antarctic, huh?'

'I guess.' Fisk realized that he had just received lesson one in Fusion salesmanship. The car was so powerful that even solid composition tyres could wear out of round in the course of an hour.

And Bill was taking that risk now. The Fusion was overhauling car after car. The speedometer read – Fisk looked again, astonished – 390 mph . . . 395 . . . 400 and still rising. Air whistled past the little winglike vanes on the sides that were necessary for control at such velocity – even the sound-proofing could not eliminate every vestige of that hurricane keening. 410 mph . . .

Bill was right. Telling a prospective salesman about the Fusion could not have been nearly as efficient as showing him, regardless of his presumed experience. When he got into the showroom and a customer asked him about power and speed Fisk would not need any artifice to describe the car. He had seen it in action, seen the other racers falling behind at 430 . . .

II

'You haven't raced before,' Bill observed mildly.

And it was out at last – too late. 'I tried to tell you, but – '

Bill smiled. 'But you're a sucker for a sob story.'

'Oh-oh. You mean to say your co-pilot didn't – '

'No, he did, all right. I do need this money for him. But nine men out of ten would not risk their own necks in a grind like this to help someone they'd never seen. You're too soft-hearted. I'll bet you've been stepped on more than once or you wouldn't be looking for a job at your age.'

'Close enough.'

'Don't worry about it, Fisk. Lots of people sneer because they haven't got the guts to be decent when the heat is on. I knew you weren't a racer the moment I saw you. You don't have racer's ways. But I wasn't going to embarrass the boss right before a race – and I did need a mapman.'

'And you're a bit soft yourself,' Fisk said. 'Helping your friend, sparing your boss, giving me a chance at a job – '

Bill laughed easily. 'Takes one to know one, doesn't it? Little girl set it up, right? Wanted her daddy to be a big man? Well, you are one – and not because of any fancy race. Got a child like that myself – wouldn't trade her. No, I'll cover for you, Fisk. They can't hear us here. Only contact is the radio and that's one-way – in. On the public band. So no driver can sneak in tactical info during the race. You're an honest man and I like that, so I stopped you from making an ass of yourself, or seeming to. Man quits a race at the start, the word spreads that he's chicken, no matter what the facts. After this you'll be a racer officially – and nobody has to know the difference.'

Fisk was beginning to find the man's solicitude a bit confining. 'But it isn't honest to – '

'It isn't right to make a scene right before a race, embarrassing the company and hurting the little girl's feelings. Got to choose your course in a hurry – even when the best one is ragged. That's racing. I figured more people would be better off this way, so this is how I played it. Okay?'

What was there to say?

'Okay,' Fisk agreed reluctantly.

Then he saw the end of the track: slanting walls of concrete foam narrowed the thirty-car highway into twenty, ten, five lanes. Bill manoeuvered the vehicle around the few remaining leaders with minute but expert turns of his steering wheel that nevertheless brought anguished squeals from the massive tyres. At 500 mph he passed his last competitor and slammed into the Narrows.

'New leader and winner of the first heat, Fusion!' a voice announced. Fisk jumped, then realized that it was the car radio. The race was being broadcast to the sports fans of the world.

'Sales: Fusion twenty-four, Steamco nineteen, Duperjet seventeen – '

'Hear that?' Bill cried happily. 'The sales follow the performance, roughly. Usually the winner of a Hurdle is good for a hundred and fifty contracts or more right during the race. Much more if something spectacular happens. We're ahead where it counts.'

Fisk was amazed. 'You mean people are buying cars while they watch?'

'They sure are. When a car makes a good move, the saleslines light up. Impulse buyers. Want to own a car with class. We're selling Fusions right now, Fisk – one per cent commission on the gross goes to the driver. Five hundred dollars per unit, if they take the Special – less for the tamer models, though no Fusion is really tame. If I run well this time and sell a hundred cars – that's twenty-five grand. Pretty good for a week's pay. Of course I don't always finish – then I get nothing. And most races I make less than ten grand when I do place. And I'd have to finish at least second or third just to cover my friend's medical expenses if I wanted to do it in one race. But it's living. I figure to retire after I make one really big killing – if it isn't myself I'm killing.'

* * *

'I see,' Fisk said, chilled by the concept and by the rapidly closing walls of the Narrows. Five hundred miles per hour was an outrageous speed for a car and now that there was something to measure it against outside . . .

'Oh, sorry – I didn't mean to rub it in, pal. You aren't a regular driver, so that commission doesn't apply to you. But I'll tell them you helped a lot and if we do well the company'll give you a nice starting bonus. Your commissions will come mostly from your showroom sales.'

Fisk's concern had been about the danger, not the money, but he didn't push the matter.

Bill braked, using small parachutes that blossomed and dragged behind the car. They provided a steady reduction of speed without slewing. Fisk was glad they did. The Narrows, according to the map, was a one-lane chute with thick twelve-foot-high barricades on either side. No vehicle could pass another here and some of the curves could be disastrous at peak velocity.

Studying the map at this point was foolish – Fisk raised his eyes to his surroundings. The crisscrossed timbers were invisible at this range, merely a greying of the view, but he knew they were timbers of steel. Speed here was less essential than control. Any accident would block the Narrows. Bill had ensured his own passage and placement by entering first.

A faint rattle sounded in the car. Bill cocked an ear alertly. 'Check your gauges,' he snapped at Fisk. 'Probably that was an irregularity in the track – felt like it. But just in case – '

Fisk scanned the dials and lights. 'All green and in normal range.'

'Right. Some of these buggies are more manoeuvrable at speed,' Bill explained as he sweated the Fusion down and through. 'They could leave us behind on a track like this – if they could pass us. We're heavy and prone to chassis stresses. Not the fault of the car – it's inherent in the mass and much of that mass is shielding that we simply have to have. If any of those other cars carried our weight penalty they wouldn't have a chance in this race. But here in the Narrows we lose no ground. If anything's wrong we can slow down and check it out. Next straightaway we'll show 'em dust! What's next on the map?'

'Hairpin.'

'Say, we're really in luck! That's our worst time loser and now we've got first crack at it. The big ugly god of Hurdle racers must be smiling on us. We might even win this one, baby!'

Bill continued to slow, but even at 150 the huge racer skewed and tilted on the gentle curves, alarming Fisk.

They shot out of the Narrows and into Hairpin at a comparative crawl of 120 mph. Bill slewed into the approach, deliberately skidding the rear wheels and braking. The car behind the Fusion was a jet. Fisk watched it in the rear-view screen so as not to have to watch the nightmare ahead. He knew the jet's wheels were merely for support. The only thing that stopped it from being a flyaway winner on the straightaway was the pollution damping – its flaming exhaust had to meet almost prohibitive standards of emission contol. It was, of course, chemically fueled and could not travel as far as the Fusion.

Bill whipped around another killer bend of the Hairpin at 90 while metal groaned and dirt flew wide. Fisk thought he heard another rattling, but decided that it was caused by the spray of pebbles thrown up against the bottom of the vehicle. Outside each curve was a six-foot drop-off on to an escape lane – the turn had to be made tightly for there was no second chance.

'Fusion still leads,' the radio announced. 'Excellent

tactics in a slow second heat. Sales: Fusion twenty-six, Duperjet twenty-one . . .'

'Not much pickup on the Narrows,' Bill explained in fragmentary fashion between the body-smashing manoeuvres. He was heel-and-toeing it now, working accelerator clutch and wheelbrake almost simultaneously with his right foot while his left controlled the movable windvanes for additional control. The parachute brakes had been jettisoned – they could not be turned on and off like this. Fisk was amazed Bill still had concentration for chatter while performing such heroic feats. 'I held up the line. Crowd likes action. But we're in good field position. Watch us go once we pass Hairpin.'

He braked down to 60 for the sharpest bend. Fisk thought the turn impossible – it looked like the point of a knife.

And someone ran out into the track.

Fisk became faint with horror, but Bill's reaction time was like an old-fashioned mousetrap. He swerved to miss the figure, throwing the car into a four-wheel tilt, and careened off the bank to drop into the escape lane. The two men bounced like yoyos in their harnesses as the great-car landed, but they and it took the fall without physical damage.

The jet following did likewise, landing more gently because it had only half the Fusion's mass. It pulled up even.

The lane had no passing room. The cars jostled together and spun. The side vane of the jet cut through the Fusion's bubble top, opening a neat incision in the shatterproof material. Then the lighter car shot ahead, reorienting in a fine display of equilibrium and blasting back down the intercept lane to rejoin the race. Missing a turn did not, it seemed, disqualify a car but merely delayed it.

Already three other cars had navigated this fold of the Hairpin and more were coming. The dust was rising higher as the road eroded. The remaining entries would be taking the curve virtually blind – another disadvantage of trailing the leaders.

Bill guided the car to a safe slowdown, then slapped a hand to his head. 'Get her moving,' he said thickly. 'The – '

Fisk saw blood.

'My controls don't – ' he began, but paused as he saw Bill slump. How badly had the man been injured? The harness prevented him from looking more closely.

'New leader,' the radio announced. 'Fusion and Duperjet spun out on Hairpin. Steamco is now first. Sales: Steamco thirty-two, Fusion – one moment, the cancellations are still coming in – Fusion twenty-one, Duperjet fifteen . . .'

The car was blocking the sole escape lane. Any car that missed the turn would shoot right this way at sixty or better, probably out of control. The ballooning dust guaranteed that the on-rushing vehicle would not see the Fusion in time to stop, even if it were in condition to do so.

Something knocked on the bubble and for a heartbeat Fisk thought a collision had already occurred. But the figure who had started this disaster by materializing in the forbidden territory of the Hurdle Hairpin had rematerialized and was dancing outside. This time Fisk recognized her.

'Yola!' he cried in dismay. He should have known.

She yelled something, he couldn't make out in the confusion. Then she pointed at Bill.

'Duperjet clipped him, thanks to you – ' Fisk shouted.

'Fisk, let me in!' Her voice came through the unnatural vent.

He found the canopy switch on Bill's side and jerked it. The bubbletop yanked itself up, its ripped portion catching, then springing loose. Yola jumped about inside.

'Close up and get rolling,' she ordered, setting into Bill's inert lap. 'First car that misses that pretzel – pow!'

An apt summation. 'But I can't – my controls don't – '

'Don't give me that. You'll kill us all – ' She looked back. 'Here comes one now!'

Fisk's hand found the changeover switch and his foot came down on the accelerator clutch. The car lunged aimlessly, all eight wheels spinning in the dirt. He grabbed at the steering wheel, easing up enough on the clutch to let the wheels catch.

'But there's nowhere to go – ' he protested belatedly.

'Back on the main track, stupid! We've got to get this guy to a doctor. He's bleeding – '

And Fisk was somehow guiding the behemoth down the track at rapidly accelerating velocity. His lightest pressure on the pedal elicited a surge of brute animation that was frightening in its strength. No car was behind – that had been a false alarm. But he knew they could not have remained in the escape lane – and Yola was right about Bill. The man was hurt and every minute that kept him from medical attention might reduce his chances of survival. The only way out was straight ahead.

Then a car did appear in the escape lane, nosing out of the dust cloud as though from a brown tunnel, – and Fisk involuntarily goosed the Fusion back on to the main track, his tyres screaming as he turned. Fortunately for him there were no further hairpin loops.

'What are we in for next?' he asked her, his hands sweating. He was moving the monster – but how long could he control it? Every time he pushed down on the pedal the wheels destroyed themselves a little in their effort to accelerate the vehicle instantly. But it was either ride this tiger or be smashed flat by the one following.

Yola scrabbled for the map, which had strewn itself across Fisk's feet. 'The Elevated,' she said. 'Better get up speed.'

'No, thank you. I'm doing eighty now – and I know my limits. We're just going to limp out the safest way we can find and – what were you doing on the track, anyway?'

'Have it your way,' she said with affected nonchalance. 'But I'm a race fan from way back and I think you'd better get it up. Ever see the El on the newscreen?'

'Brilliant recovery by Duperjet,' the radio blared. Fusion is not out of the race, but trails the pack and is moving erratically. Sales: Duperjet fifty-five, Steamco forty-nine, Gasturb thirty . . .'

'Never watched sports.' He looked around nervously. 'Look, Yola – Bill's a nice guy and it's your fault he's hurt. See if you can bandage him up – or something.'

'What do I know about first aid?' she demanded as rebelliously as always when told to do something. But she began looking in the car pockets for the medical supplies that had to be there.

'. . . and Fusion twelve – no, ten.'

Fisk saw what lay ahead of them. 'That?'

'What do you think? Watch those cars behind you.'

Fisk saw them come up on him at an alarming clip as they navigated the last of Hairpin and accelerated. The track was widening here, but one slow vehicle could be disaster. He speeded up.

Yola found a rolled bandage and began stretching it out. Fisk knew her hands were dirty – they always were – but kept his peace. Infection was the least of his present concerns. 'We're taking a beating at the box office,' she said. 'But we're still in the race and we're not last either. Yet.'

Still the cars came, showing no inclination to avoid a possible crash. Fisk's adrenaline squirted. He stamped down hard and the car surged forward as though its speed of a hundred miles per hour had been mere idling. It was a fine piece of machinery and it could hardly perform like this if it had suffered mechanical damage in the accident. There was, indeed, a certain exhilaration in managing a brute like this, Fisk discovered.

They were booming up the steep approach ramp of the Elevated. The combination of acceleration and angle shoved the riders back into their seats, hard. Yola balanced precariously and Fisk felt the first twinge of nausea. He had a circulatory disorder that could be aggravated by sustained physical stress. Ordinarily it didn't bother him – token medication kept the symptoms suppressed – but ordinarily he didn't tackle obstacle races in 500-mph juggernauts.

Yola complained, 'His neck is all icky with hair and gore – I can't make the bandage stay.'

'Then hold it in place with your hand,' Fisk rasped, resenting the need to split his concentration and expend his breath in a situation like this. 'We've got to keep him from bleeding too much. If Bill hadn't swerved to avoid you – '

She uttered a monosyllable Fisk didn't recognize – fortunately. He was pretty sure it would have earned her another week solitary back at the orphanage from whence she sprang. But somehow she fixed the bandage in place.

Then they were up, other cars ahead and behind. Ahead also stretched mind-numbing miles of twisted ribbon, five hundred feet about the ground, tapering into a thread in the distance, though it was four lanes wide.

Two following cars charged past, the whine of their

tyres momentarily loud. The odour of oil and hot rubberoid swirled in through the rent in the bubble.

Yola sneezed. 'There can't be many more behind us,'
she muttered, torn between hope and regret. She clung
to the straps of Bill's harness as the incoming gusts swept
black hair across her brown face. 'But don't stop now –
you have to take the El at speed or you fall off.'

She was speaking literally. The paving contorted like a
living tapeworm, given animation by his speed of 170
mph. In addition, the hole in the bubble interfered with
the streamline contour and created a dangerous drag that
Fisk seemed to feel all the way down to the sliding tyres.
But their forward momentum was not enough. The road
tilted now into a forty-five degree embankment – he
would indeed fall off unless he maintained speed sufficient
to match the needs of the curve.

'Yeah,' Yola said, licking her lips. At eleven, with her
deprived background, she was more enthusiastic than
afraid. He hadn't really needed to ask why she had
sneaked into the racegrounds. She had done so because it
was forbidden. She had wanted a ride and now she had
it. Quite possibly her last.

More wind blasted in as he accelerated. 'Close up that
hole,' Fisk snapped as another warning wave of dizziness
came over him. The blood circulation to his brain was
being inhibited – but to stop was to die. Already they
were sliding towards the nether perimeter and the drag
was making matters worse. He had to keep turning the
wheel and bearing down on the pedal to counter the
drift. But if he accelerated too strongly and broke the
wheels free of the surface . . .

'Don't tell me what to do!' Yola flared.

Fisk twitched the wheel the other way. The Fusion
jerked towards the rail. The bright water of a scenic lake

spread below – a natural safety net. But they could drown, for the massive car would plummet to the bottom.

'Okay! Okay!' she exclaimed with bad grace. 'You're the driver – ' She dug out some harness strap and additional bandage and wedged the mass into the gap. It helped.

Now Fisk was able to gain the speed he needed: 200 . . . 250 . . . 280 – finally the drift abated and they were cruising in a kind of stasis. It was, actually, rather pleasant in its way – the velocity anaesthetized his sense of proportion and the balancing forces lulled his circulatory incapacity. What remained was a growing sense of well-being and power. He was no longer Fisk the hard-sell sucker – he was Fisk the Supreme! The Secret Life of Fisk Centers . . .

Then the curvature and banking reversed.

Fisk was driving for his life and there was suddenly no joy in it. He slewed across the strip at 300 mph without any exact knowledge where he was going or how long he could last. His brain tried to black out. He tilted his head back as far as he could, trying to let the blood in his system flow level to the grey region that needed it.

'Slow up! Speed down!' Yola screamed. 'Watch the sky below!' Which was just about the way Fisk saw it.

'Duperjet is still the leader,' the radio announced. 'Sales: Duperjet seventy-eight, Steamco sixty, Electro forty-four . . .'

The tilt decreased and the car was rolling down the steep exit slope at 350 mph. Fisk knew there had been many miles of elevated ribbon and that he had covered every twist at daredevil speed, but his memory had a short-term blank on the subject. That was fortunate for his equanimity, unfortunate for his security, since memory lapse was another signal of his functional impairment.

Nothing but blind reflex had carried him through, but before long his reflexes would cut out, too.

Yola sat silent and staring. The ride must have been good to faze her like that, Fisk thought.

'. . . Fusion thirteen . . .'

At the foot of the ramp was an impenetrable bank of fog. The road led directly into it.

Fisk sighed. No way to avoid it. This was obviously part of the course. Another hurdle. He turned on lights, searing beams of brilliance that might well have been windowed from the solar activity of the engine, but the best they could do here was about two hundred feet. The car was moving at more than five hundred feet per second, according to the relevant scale of the speedometer. . .360 mph. How many seconds would it take him to come to a stop?

He applied the brakes. The car slowed with neck-wrenching suddenness. Bill groaned. Good – the sound proved he was alive. The smell of burning rubberoid infiltrated from somewhere.

'Keep moving!' Yola screamed. 'Fogbank always has stuff in it – '

A gap opened in the road. By the time Fisk reacted, it was too late to react. The car hurtled the twenty foot void with no more than a nasty jolt.

'Try that at half the speed,' Yola muttered faintly.

Fisk had to agree with her. Undervelocity was just as dangerous here as overvelocity. His conservative course was to maintain middle-range speed – say 300 mph.

A wall appeared, made of stone and steel by its look.

Fisk swerved left barely in time. The wall was oblique, cutting across the lane only gradually, right to left. His instinct had been accurate and he had dodged the hurdle.

'Try *that* at half speed,' he mimicked.

'Luck,' Yola said disparageingly, as though her own life were not part of the stakes.

Not all of the fog was outside. Fisk's arms were becoming leaden on the wheel and his eyelids felt heavy. His system had taken just about all it was going to. He was out of adrenaline. Wisps of cloud passed between his face and the instrument panel – or perhaps between his eyes and brain.

'Wake up!' Yola screamed.

Fisk snapped alert, laughing – and momentarily felt refreshed, ready to continue another couple of minutes. He was giving Yola all the thrills she had asked for – and more.

'Duperjet is out of the race,' the radio announced. 'Crackup in the Slalom – '

Fisk bounced over a washboard trap and emerged from the fog. Fogbank hadn't actually been so bad. It would have been another matter in the press of the pack, however.

They were out of the fog and into a forest. Green concrete pseudotrees or pilings rose from the highway in a seemingly solid mass. They were cold – ice had formed on them and snow coated the ground.

'The Slalom,' Yola said despairingly. 'Doom!'

But the pilings were less impenetrable than they seemed from a distance. In the seconds it took to reach the first, Fisk saw that they were spaced well apart. There was room to skid around them if forward progress were not excessive. The tracks of many wheels showed the routes other cars had taken.

But across the main trail were wheels themselves, and jagged pieces of metal – the debris of a recent accident strewed across the course. Duperjet, surely. This was dangerous territory.

'. . . Fusion nineteen . . . Duperjet nine . . .'

The buyers certainly had little sympathy for a loser. Yet Duperjet was a fine car. It had led the pack after that spinout. Fusion was recovering sales – but what a grisly way to succeed.

Fisk was falling under the sway of stress fatigue again. He willed his remaining strength into his hands and aimed the vehicle at the widest aperture between groups of pilings, following the common trail. Here and there the refrigerative grid showed, scraped temporarily bare by the passage of the pack, giving him slightly improved footing. He was still doing over 300 mph and he knew better than to attempt to change speed here.

Yola covered her eyes. 'You drive like a zombie,' she said.

The trail split. A piling lay dead ahead. Fisk forced a message down along the resistive nerve tissue of his right arm and the arm convulsed a bit, pulling the wheel around just that necessary fraction. The car slewed, scraping against the piling on the left and almost dislodging Yola's hole-stuffing. At this point Fisk hardly cared – it was as though car and racetrack were far away. Even his own extremities were almost beyond reach. His heart was labouring to the point of collapse, but the life-sustaining blood was not getting through. He was numb and terribly tired.

Yet he would not let go entirely. He hung on. A thin rivulet of animation trickled along the buried conduits of his pallid flesh. As the pilings loomed his muscles twitched and the car shaved by, never quite hitting, never quite sacrificing the traction so necessary to keep it from following the Duperjet into destruction. But Fusion's huge mass gave it traction where a lighter car might have skated. The impact of their passage howled about the myriad death traps of the Slalom – if he had been the lyrical type he might have immortalized the experience in poetry – and then they were out of it.

'We're alive,' Yola whispered, amazed. 'At least I am. For a while I almost wished I was back at the orphanage.' She looked at Fisk. 'You can stop here. We're out of the woods and nobody's behind us any more.'

Fisk ignored her. Now he faced a straightaway, long and level and dry. Far ahead he could see several other cars. The Fusion had actually gained on them during this last hurdle. The race wasn't over yet – and as long as he was in it, why not win it?

III

It was madness, he knew – the futile delusion of grandeur of an oxygen-starved brain, its frontal lobes anaesthetized. He didn't care. Bill needed the large sales tally for his friend's medical bills – and perhaps for his own. Fisk was indirectly responsible for the Fusion's fall from first to last place in the Hurdle and for Bill's injury. There was power under his foot if not in his body or brain. Why not invoke it, double or nothing?

'Daddy, what are you doing?' Yola whispered as the car accelerated.

'You wilful little brat – you got me into this,' he snapped. 'Now you're going to see it through.'

He was mad – insane, not angry. His brain had gone berserk and was running faster than the car. He had never suffered this effect of his malady before. It was as though another personality had fought to the surface – a completely un-Fisk monster. No, not true. This was his true personality. Shackled by decades of civilized restraint, it had emerged at last.

'So it's like that, Centers,' Yola muttered. 'Well, want to know what's next? The Mountain.'

Fisk-normal quailed, but the demon aspect who had usurped control of his body said in fine detergent-opera fashion, 'Yeah? So watch this.' And his right foot crunched down harder.

The speedometer read 400 mph. It climbed rapidly as the tireless machine obeyed the imperious command of a lunatic.

'Steamco eighty-six, Electro fifty-nine, Gasturb forty-nine . . .' the radio said and continued on through the entire list of twenty-six cars remaining in the race. Fusion was back up to twenty-four.

The car was doing 500 now and Fisk's foot was a marvel of unremitting ponderosity. This was a fair-sized straightaway – the kind where power counted. Fusion's favourite track. The gap between him and the pack was closing. How much would this buggy do?

'This is suicide,' a small voice whimpered. At first Fisk thought it was that of his civilized-self conscience, but it turned out to be Yola's.

Fisk's eyeballs seemed to be locked in their sockets, able to move only marginally to cover the contours of the road. He himself was a machine, his arms levering more or less together, sharing his drastically limited muscular power as though connected by an old-fashioned limited-slip differential.

600 mph . . .

Suddenly the straightaway was ending and he was overhauling the pack at a phenomenal clip. The demon in him exulted.

'You fool – it's the Mountain!' Yola screamed, afraid. But Fisk saw only his beautiful passing of competitors on the fast track. So they had written off Fusion, had they?

Then his foot came up involuntarily. Yola was down

beside the pedal, prying it loose. And the pack moved ahead again and crammed like so much floating refuse in the drainlike access to the next hurdle.

'Fusion has merged with the pack.' The radio sounded surprised. 'Looked for a moment there as if – but the driver was too smart to risk a pass on Mountain. We thought Fusion had mechanical trouble, but obviously not! Sales: Steamco a hundred and one . . . Electro seventy-five, Gasturb fifty-five, Vaporlock forty-four, Fusion thirty-eight . . .'

'Wow!' Yola cried, forgetting her apprehension of the moment before. 'You may be crazy, but we're back in the sales money! What's your cut of the gross, Fisk?'

He didn't answer, knowing how little money meant, compared to the lives depending on it. She had climbed back into Bill's lap and Fisk's foot was free, but now the ascent was too steep to permit high velocity. He trailed the pack at a poor 380 mph.

The course wedged into a two-lane thread, along which cars were spaced like travelling ants. A cliff developed on the right, the drop-off becoming tall and sheer. A car ahead tried to pass another precipitously. The banking of the road reversed, throwing it too far out and the vehicle sailed into space to torpedo into the water trap below.

'Coaldust slipped,' the radio cried. 'Twenty-four cars remain in the race at the two-thirds point . . .'

The demon that now governed Fisk's ailing body took note. A lot of cars would not finish because their drivers were too eager. He had better bide his time until he hit another straightaway.

Meanwhile, Mountain was a terror. Visibility declined as the blind curves became sharper. A small thunderstorm was anchored at the crest, pelting the entries with rain and hailstones. He had to slow to 280 and pace himself by the car ahead through the blasting rain. Then came the descent and Fisk accelerated down the glassy slope.

'Steamco one-twenty-nine ... Electro one-fourteen ... Vaporlock sixty-eight ... Fusion fifty-nine ...'

Fusion and Fisk were moving up on sales faster than on the pack, perhaps because the spectators knew what would happen on the next level heat, but not fast enough. The demon would settle for nothing less than total victory.

'Oh-oh,' Yola said. 'Loop's coming next. Cool it, leadfoot.'

Bill groaned again. He was showing signs of recovery.

Fisk's eyes were on the desertlike sandflat beyond. Gently rolling dunes were artfully placed to alleviate the monotony and impede progress – a straight-line route would necessarily take in several of them. The alternative was to waste time going around them. He had no idea of what it was like to drive on sand. But if the other cars could handle it, so could Fusion – and this might be its last chance to pass the pack before the finish.

'Steamco still leads going into the Loop,' the radio said. 'Pack's pretty close and tight, though. There's likely to be some action ...'

Indeed there was. Fisk observed the Loop, nestled in the angle between the Mountain terminus and the Dunes plain. It seemed to be about three lanes wide – but the pack contained about fifteen cars and few of them were giving way to let the procession become orderly. The Fusion was gaining, but would strike the Loop just after the pack did.

It didn't look as though there were any inherent limit on speed here – the faster he went, the less likely he would be to fall off at the upsidedown apex, provided he had the car under control. And as long as nothing got in

his way. But could his defective body take the strain?
The Fusion was willing – the flesh was weak.

The first car hit the Loop. Up and over it went at some
five hundred miles per hour, like a toy. Only car lengths
behind it came the second, closing. Then, squeezing in
two and three abreast, the pack, vying for position even
as they encountered the vertical ascent. And the Fusion
was bearing down at 550 mph, still accelerating, still
gaining.

Steamco shot from the corkscrew exit and landed on
the fringe of the sandflat. Dust billowed up momentarily.
Electro smacked into this and swerved, stirring up a
greater cloud. Then the pack was tearing through like so
many piranhas.

Fisk was entering the Loop at 600 mph.

'Hang on!' he yelled, though Yola needed no warning.
They smashed into the vertical curve and Fisk's breath
left him. This was in effect a ten- or fifteen-G takeoff, he
was sure. He clutched at a painful grey awareness.

'. . . spectacular crash!' the radio blared avidly and
Fisk realized he had failed and could expect nothing but
agony before he died. 'Pileup just beyond the Loop . . .'

Not me – someone else . . .

He was headed up at 650 mph. The reality that kept
him fighting was the climbing needle, signifying conquest.

Yola screamed thinly. They were upside down, plummeting headfirst, levelling, taking off, upside down, proceeding along the awful corkscrew of the Loop. Fisk
shoved the pedal all the way to the floor, connecting
engine to wheels without any bleeding of power. He rode
the descent lane into ever increasing velocity.

670 . . . 685 . . . magic pictures on his retina . . . 700
. . . 715 . . . 730 . . . and they were sailing off the skirt of
the Loop. 740 . . . the wheels seemed hardly to touch the
sand and only the little vanes kept the car level. 742 . . .

744 . . . acceleration was slower now. The great machine shuddered as though its stress limit had finally been met and all that was left for Yola was a shaken moan. 745 . . . and the needle quivered, seemed to strain. This was ultimate glory!

'. . . fire prevents recovery of the bodies . . . total loss . . . worst disaster of the year . . . look at Fusion!'

Dead ahead, half concealed by a low dune and a sinking dust cloud, was the roadblock. Licks of flame shot up and smoke was piling into the sky. No chance to turn. A thousand feet away – and in less than one second they were upon it, travelling at 750 mph, Fisk's foot still savagely mashing the pedal. The Fusion was tearing itself apart and eradiction was a microsecond away, but he would not even attempt to ease up. Already he was touching the vane-angle switch.

The low dune shoved the rubberoid and metal aloft in a single mighty convulsion. The great wheels barely touched the flaming corpse of the nearest car.

And they were airborne as the shaking became almost intolerable. Fumes siphoned in through the stuffed hole as the car was bathed in fire. The speedometer stood at 760. 'Great God,' Yola screamed in a whisper. 'We've cracked the speed of sound!'

'Fusion is past!' the radio gasped. 'Fusion hurdled pileup . . .'

The car landed, and sand swirled up behind it in little tornadoes spawned by the vacuum of their passage, but the mighty machine crunched on. The flames were far behind. Fisk's hands and arms were senseless and stiff in a kind of living rigor mortis, but straight ahead was all the car needed in the way of a directive. Now at last his foot began to creep up from the pedal.

'What – What?' a voice mumbled.

'Hey, he's coming to,' Yola cried as Bill stirred.

'Keep him quiet,' Fisk's voice rasped. 'We're still doing six-ninety on sand – '

'Sales,' the radio said. 'Steamco one-fifty-two . . . Fusion – one moment, it's still changing – that feat of piloting really stirred up the – never saw anything like it. Fusion takes the lead in sales! Fusion one-seventy-three . . . And Steamco – one moment – '

Bill lifted his head. 'God, man, that's near my best. What – '

'I had to take over,' Fisk said tersely. He was still fighting the rising tide of grey behind his eyes.

'Yeah – but – '

'Revised sales,' the radio said. 'Fusion two hundred and eight – folks, it's still changing. We can't get a fixed reading. The race isn't even finished . . . Fusion two-forty-nine . . . two-sixty-one – ' There was an unexplained pause, then: 'Folks, to recap: there has been a fifteen-car collision on the Dunes just beyond the Loop, but the remaining cars are still running. Here's the replay – ' Another pause as the screen viewers saw the film. 'Steamco retains the lead on the track, but that's all – and Fusion is coming up fast. The others – seven cars, I believe – are picking their way around the wreckage, avoiding the flames. None of them will finish in the money. It's a two-car race! Fusion, not known for its manoeuvrability, pulled such an extraordinary feat of – Fusion three hundred and nineteen! Those orders are pouring in! Here's the replay on that hurdle of death. That's Fusion firing out of the Loop – look at that! It cracked mach one! We thought the car was out of the running, then this! The buyers are really impressed. Hell, I'm impressed, and I've been in this business for – Most racers would have been smashed to pieces, busting sound

like that, let alone doing it through flame! Fusion three-
seventy . . . four hundred . . . Folks we can't keep up.
Unprecedented sales for an unfinished race. Looks like a
record in the making, even if Fusion doesn't win the
Hurdle. Four-fifty-two . . . I gotta buy one myself . . .'
The announcer panted into silence.

'That tells it,' Bill exclaimed. 'Sweetest music I ever
heard. And I thought you couldn't drive – '

'I can't,' Fisk said. 'I'm sicker than you are.'

Bill looked at him. 'You're white as bones – you have
a heart condition? I've lost some blood, but I've taken
lumps before – better let me take over. Kid, get down on
the floor or somewhere.'

Yola scrambled down, finding a place to squat between
the bucket seats. Bill threw the switch and Fisk's controls
were dead. Now he could relax. These regular racing
drivers were almost as tough as their cars.

'What's next?' Bill demanded, angling the car gently
around another dune.

'Tunnel,' Yola said, wrestling with the map.

'Fusion six hundred and seven . . .'

Fisk lay back and let himself slide into whatever oblivion
awaited. The demon had left him, but Fisk-normal still
needed his medicine. The race's end could not be far off
and it did look as though he were planning to survive.

'Fusion seven-twenty-six . . .'

Bill shook his head. 'Fisk, I don't know exactly how
you did it – but you've just made us rich. Those sales are
going to hit a thousand. It's a bandwagon now – everybody in the world will want a Fusion. We'll get a quarter
million dollars in commissions – '

'They'll come to their senses and begin cancelling after
the excitement passes,' Fisk pointed out. Now that he

could afford to faint, he seemed perversely to be recovering strength.

'Sure – but the cancellations will be made up by other buyers reading about this in the fax. That always happens. Don't worry – we've got record winnings and the credit's yours. So you took her through mach, did you? I never had the nerve.'

'Terrific!' Yola cried, liking the idea of fame.

'Uh – better not,' Fisk said, eyeing the tiny mouth of the approaching tunnel. Bill sounded normal, but Fisk didn't trust the man's condition. He had been unconscious for a fair period and must have lost a significant quantity of blood – and an error in judgement of so much as six inches could be fatal, in that tight passage ahead.

'No, no, Fisk – you did it and you'll get the commission. When I tell the boss how you pulled it out – '

'We'll be rich!' Yola exclaimed with childish avarice.

Fisk hadn't been talking about money. His concern had been to see them through the tunnel alive. Steamco had just entered and at the rate the Fusion was going there would be contact between them inside that darkness. Was Bill intending to vie for position even now?

But it seemed money was a factor, because of the tremendous sales spurred by his mad exploit of moments ago. Yola's greed and Bill's misunderstanding sent a negative ripple through the weary convolutions of his brain. 'When you tell your boss that he'll fire you for allowing an unqualified driver to take over and play roulette with machinery and people's lives in the Hurdle. Because you knew about me and he didn't. It was blind luck that got us through – as the tapes of the race will show.'

Bill slid the car into the Tunnel as though he had done it all his life – as perhaps he had. 'Maybe so,' he said soberly. 'But luck doesn't usually operate that way – not

on the El or the Mountain – and especially not in getting
up speed to hurdle wreckage. There was driving genius in
your hands and feet, like it or not. But you're right – it's
bad business and my boss would rather not know. Okay –
we'll split the take, half and half. It's right to share,
because I got hurt and you – '

As the Tunnel closed about them the rag-and-strap plug
popped out of the hole in the bubble, urged by the
suddenly compressing air within the confined space. An
almost solid blast of atmosphere rammed in, striking Bill
in the face and making a stormlike turbulence within the
bubble. The car swerved, partly because Bill could barely
see in the gale, but mostly, Fisk knew, because of
the drag of the aperture itself. There was no room to
compensate here. The stony walls were inches away.

But Yola knew what to do and since no one had *told*
her to do it, she did it. She crawled across Bill's lap,
probably kneeing him painfully in the process, fetched in
the tattered wad and jammed it back into the hole. The
storm subsided.

Fisk was able to speak again. 'You were hurt because
my daughter ran out in front of us while you were going
through Hairpin. She almost killed us all.'

'Take the money – take the money!' Yola cried.

'You sure are one for making objections,' Bill said
ruefully. 'What *do* you want?'

'I think we'd better just walk out of your life when the
race is over. A good – '

He had to pause, for they had caught up with Steamco.
The Tunnel was lighted, but irregularly – the width varied
from one to three lanes with curves thrown in. Passing
could be tricky – and Steamco had no intention of being
passed.

'A good sales day is the least we can do to repay – '

But Fisk had to stop again as Bill swerved to pass on a subterranean straightaway and was quickly blocked off. Steamco had to know that there was no car to beat but Fusion – all the drivers would have been hearing the radio reports. The only way Steamco could recoup was by finishing ahead – or by putting Fusion out of the race entirely.

The passage narrowed, halting the manoeuvring for the moment.

' – the trouble we have caused you,' Fisk continued. 'I'll find another job.'

'Fisk, shut up,' Yola said. 'You're throwing away a quarter million dollars.'

'Fusion nine hundred and eighty-one sales . . .'

'Look, Fisk,' Bill said earnestly as the dark walls rushed past and trickles of wind whined in through the stuffed hole. 'I told you I'd cover for you about your lack of experience, laughable as that seems now. You've had experience somewhere – somehow – even if you don't remember it. You're covering for me, really. And I'd never make trouble for your little girl. You don't have to sign over the money for that. I want you to have your share because you earned it. I wouldn't feel right letting you go away with nothing after the way you – '

'I wouldn't feel right taking it,' Fisk said firmly. 'You were right – any idiot can drive this car and one just did – '

'Fisk,' Yola said, 'if you don't take that money, I'm going to – '

The dark track opened into a dual lane, then into a broad cavern spiked with stalagmites casting multiple and deceptive shadows. Many trails seemed to be opened. Bill goosed the Fusion and angled for the far right opening. The Steamco moved over to block him, staying just ahead so that passing was impossible.

'I'll take the commission myself and make out a check for you,' Bill said, as though nothing special were going on. 'I'll take all the credit for the race, if that's the way you want it – but you've got to have your share of the commission. I can't take all the money for a race I didn't drive.'

'I don't want it,' Fisk said.

Bill tried to pass again. The manoeuvre was impossible at 400 mph in the partially lighted cavern. But Steamco was ready and stayed ahead.

'Fusion one thousand and thirty-eight . . .'

'I'll give it to your daughter, then,' Bill said. 'An irrevocable trust for her education, so she doesn't have to run on to any more racetracks.'

'Yeah, yeah!' Yola agreed, but with less enthusiasm.

Fisk shook his head. 'That money should go to your injured partner.'

Another dangerous dodge that nearly put both cars into a post. 'Twenty-five per cent to your little girl, then.' Bill looked grim. 'A hundred grand will cover my friend's bill. You're making me settle for twice that. I don't like profiteering on something like this. I'm hurting in my conscience worse than on my head and I can't dicker with you any more. That's my final offer.'

'Flip for it,' Yola said. 'You go left next split – last moment. If Steamco goes right, you pass and Fisk takes the share.'

'Okay.'

Fisk was about to demur again, when the radio interrupted: 'Folks, you'll be glad to know the drivers survived Duperjet's crash. They blame themselves for misjudgment – too much speed in the Slalom . . .'

Fisk felt a tremendous relief.

Bill accelerated again, almost touching Steamco's persistent tail. As the post zoomed in on them, the first of a line of them, he nudged right, then cut sharply left. Steamco was caught on the right side, too late to compensate without cracking into the pylon.

'What's the matter with you?' Yola demanded as she and Fisk stepped out of the tube at his apartment building. 'We need money and you know it. Why wouldn't you take your share?'

Fisk himself hardly understood his reasons. 'What I did wasn't real. Some demon in me wanted the glory of winning the Hurdle, no matter what the cost. I was too sick to control it – '

'That's right. You looked like a corpse, I thought sure you meant to kill us.'

'But once the pressure was off I regained control. By then it was too late to undo the damage – '

'But you're the one who brought off the win.'

'The demon brought it off. But at least I didn't have to give that demon the satisfaction of making a profit from the episode. With no credit and no money – '

'Except that trust Bill's setting up for me that nobody can touch,' she said. 'Fisk, that money would have bought a lot of fun for both of us and now all it's good for is education. Ugh!'

'Precisely. Education abolishes demons.'

'I just don't get it,' she said crossly.

'Neither do I,' Fisk admitted. 'I just knew that neither the racing credit nor the money was rightfully mine. I will earn my fortune in my own way or not at all. That's my particular hurdle. Maybe it's a question of whether Dr Jekyll or Mr Hyde will govern.'

'Who?'

He sighed. 'Never mind. It's a devious point of characterization – and perhaps illusory. But disaster strikes every time I compromise my principles. I tried to make an illicit profit in Marsland speculation and lost everything. I got involved in black market adoption and almost landed in jail. This time I very nearly killed us all. The demon offers material riches, but his real goal is misery.'

She uttered the expletive he still didn't understand. 'The first time you got a new, exciting life. The second time you got me. This time you could have had – '

'At any rate – I'll never go near another racing car as long as I – '

'Hey, what's this?' she cried, lifting something out of the package slot of the apartment door.

Fisk looked at what she had found. It was a small square item with a gift tag.

Yola read it aloud. '"You're a great sport. Sink Bill."'

'That's "sinc", not "sink",' Fisk said. 'For "sincerely".'

But she was already tearing open the wrapping with juvenile impatience.

Inside was the personalized ID ownership key for a new Fusion Special.

Gone to the Dogs

In 1969 we were getting ready for the arrival of our second daughter, Cheryl. Our first, Penny, then two years old, was a charming blonde, blue-eyed, hyperactive child – but we feared she would be jealous of the baby. We had lost three babies before getting one we could keep, and we wanted everything to be as right as we could make it. There may be parents who take their children for granted; not so with us. So we decided to get a pet to take Penny's attention. The rule of thumb is, the smaller the child, the larger the dog should be. We don't tolerate animal abuse, but you can't watch children and pets all the time; a big dog that liked children should be best. We saw an ad for a grown female Weimaraner who loved children; we went to see her at the kennel, liked her, phoned the owner – and discovered we were too late; she had just been sold. We didn't want to disappoint our child, so next day we bought the most similar dog we could find: a Dalmation. Similar in size and shape, that is; in colour the Dalmation stands out from all others. We named his Canute, for this was the breed of Kings, and he merged instantly with the family. I wrote him into a juvenile science fiction novel, *Race Against Time*, and all was well.

But we had made a fatal miscalculation. When the baby arrived, Penny took it in stride. It was the dog who was jealous. In retrospect it becomes obvious, but then it was a mystery. We had not owned a dog before, and did not understand dog psychology. Had we realized, we might have worked things out. Human misunderstandings can be that way too; who among us would not do some things differently if we could carry our present knowledge back to relive the event? There are few things in my adult life that I really regret, and this is perhaps the one: that I did not understand. Canute came down with kidney stones, evidently the result of emotional stress. He had surgery five times to alleviate them, but in the end it was too much and we had to put him away. He had lost the joy of living, and while I will not kill an animal for food or clothing or sport, I will do so to alleviate pain and hopelessness. We got another dog who remains with us today, and we are far more conscious of animal psychology than we were. I still miss Canute; he would have loved it here in the forest. But if we had got that Weimaraner, who already understood about children, we might have avoided the tragedy entirely.

One day some years later a strange dog wandered on to our property. He was emaciated. Penny went out to pet him, but I warned her away, as he was a big dog and an unknown quality. Suddenly I recognized the breed: 'That's a Weimaraner!' I exclaimed. No mongrel, but a valuable purebreed animal. I am not snobbish about pedigrees; our present dogs are mongrels. But I realized that a Weimaraner probably had a home, and would have been well cared for before getting lost. So I let my daughter pet him, cautiously – and he was friendly. We fed him, and he was ravenous. We couldn't take him into the fenced portion of our yard because we had another dog, a purebreed Basenji foundling who hated all other animals except our half-Basenji female; it would be death for the weakened Weimaraner. Fortunately we had neighbours who cared about animals even more than we did; they put the Weimaraner in their yard while we tried to locate the owner. They couldn't keep the visitor long either, because they had a dog who weighed 101 pounds and tended to overwhelm the Weimaraner, so this arrangement was strictly temporary. They called the visitor Waldo.

But Waldo was lonely. He couldn't stand to be by himself. He had to remain outside, and he howled. So Penny stayed with him for hours each day. She was then six or seven years old, and this was a considerable chore for her, but she has always had strong sympathy for those with problems, and she stayed the course. I was proud of her effort; it saved us much trouble and that dog much grief. We never located the owner, so finally we placed an ad in the paper and gave Waldo away. He was fortunate; the new owners had loved a former Weimaraner pet, and were very good to this one. We visited once, and saw that Waldo, now renamed Schatze, was happy. It was enough; we were satisfied that we had done the right thing.

The experience moved me to write a story, 'Gone to the Dogs', about the possible origin of Waldo Weimaraner, the dog who had come to us too late for us to keep. It is one way I react to the ironies of life. Once I have written about a thing or an experience, it is mine forever. So I did it, and marketed this story – and no publisher was interested. It was about the last straw; I departed the story field, never really to return. So perhaps it is fitting that this formerly unpublished story concludes this volume; now you understand why I left this particular arena. I can sell my science fiction or fantasy novels for ten times the word-rate I would get for a story – if I could even place the story. I can prevent arbitrary editorial interference in my novels. It's a better situation, all around.

I have been criticized for inadequate characterization in my fiction. Now characterization is the essence of fiction, and I feel strongly about it. It is my contention that the typical critic does not comprehend the kind of characterization that I do, just as he doesn't grasp my position on style. I do not stop the story to pontificate on the psychology of the protagonist: I prefer to show it in his reactions. This story serves as an example. The human character is a blank; he is Anyman, behaving as anyone in that situation would. But the dog – watch how Waldo behaves, and you will see what *I* mean by characterization.

The pain came suddenly to my chest. For a moment I couldn't breathe. I fell back on the couch, gasping, pressing my palms futilely to my rib-cage.

Waldo came up to nuzzle my hand, his yellow-grey eyes looking up at me with concern, his clipped tail wagging. He was a beautiful mouse-grey Weimaraner with silky ears. We had found him as a stray, gaunt and lonely – and by the time we had given up trying to locate his original home, he was ours. He had put on twenty pounds, and was now a sleek, powerful, and affectionate dog.

But this agony in my chest – I was too young to have a heart attack! So it couldn't be that. If only my wife were here! But she and the children were away with her folks for the weekend. I was on my own.

I had to get to a doctor. I started for the phone, hunched over as the pain gripped my chest again, and finally got there. I dropped the phone book before I had the number, scrambled for it on hands and knees – and of course Waldo gave me a good slurp on the face.

Where had the dog come from, originally? I had often wondered. He had such perfect manners, but had never been trained to come when called. It was as though he had been brought up as master, not pet. But he accepted equality in our household with singular grace, and even condescended to use the leash for walks.

When I dialled the number, I got the answering service. This was Sunday afternoon – the worse time to catch a doctor! I could die before he came off the golf links and called back to advise me to take two aspirin and come in Monday morning.

One thing this experience was doing for me: it made me appreciate the position of an animal. A sick stray had no resources, and was dependent for his very life upon the dubious largess of strangers – even as I was now. Where was pride, at such a time?

I tried other doctors, but already I knew it was useless. I needed attention *now*, not during business hours! I wasn't even sure I could drive safely; if I had a seizure on the highway –

Waldo had been pacing the floor somewhat nervously. Now he caught my sleeve with his teeth. 'Not now, doggie,' I said. 'I'm sick – I need a doctor. *Any* doctor! I can't play with you.'

Still he tugged. I lacked the gumption to resist. 'All right – I'll let you out,' I said. I hobbled to the door.

But Waldo, always a sociable dog, didn't want to go out alone. He took the end of the leash in his mouth, tugging it from its hook on the wall.

There was a faint, odd barking in the distance. Arf – arf – arf!

'I can't take you for a walk!' I cried. 'My chest – '

I went back to the living room and collapsed on the couch. I could breathe a little better now, but only in shallow gasps; whatever was wrong was still wrong. If I didn't have it attended to soon –

Waldo tugged at my sleeve again, looking at me beseechingly. He whined. One of his floppy ears was inside out.

What was the use? I couldn't get a doctor. If I was going to conk out from some mysterious malady I might as well do it while making my dog happy.

I snapped the leash to his collar and stumbled out the door, almost slipping on the back steps. The pain eased as I walked, fortunately. The fresh air was helping, and maybe the adrenaline. I let Waldo take the lead, not paying attention to the route. He took me through a devious pattern, sniffing out some trail that only he could perceive – and he seemed oddly nervous. Perhaps that strange barking bothered him. It was louder now. ARF – ARF – ARF! Was it an Arfgan hound?

I was getting lightheaded. If this lurking pain wasn't a heart attack, could it be a collapsed lung? What would my obituary say: died of a frazzled gizzard while the hound went ARF?

Something jogged my attention, and I looked up. I didn't recognize the neighbourhood – yet we had been walking only five minutes or so. Waldo was striding forward now as if he knew what he was doing and where he was going. Still, I could tell he remained on edge. What was there to disturb his canine mind? I was the one who had the pain!

The houses here were not only unfamiliar, they were strange. They looked like huge, fancy dog houses. A man was in the front yard of the house we were passing – and I saw to my horror that he was chained. He had a heavy collar around his neck, and the chain was fastened securely to a tree.

I stopped. 'What on earth – ?' I demanded, facing him.

Waldo tugged at the leash, urging me on. But I held back, waiting for the man's response. It was prompt: he charged up to the end of his tether and jerked hard at the chain. 'Stay off my territory, stranger!' he snarled. He was big and hairy and muscular and dirty and, I realized, stark naked.

'Uh, sure,' I said, taken aback by the whole thing. I was hardly looking for trouble. Even without a hurting chest, I would have hesitated to tangle with an ugly customer like this. Also, I saw the door of the house open to disgorge a grossly fat Soxer, evidently attracted by the commotion. That corpulent canine acted just as if he owned the premises! I let Waldo pull me on down the street, while the chained man sat down and scratched at a flea.

A lady was coming towards us, walking her dog. She too was naked – and there was a brightly embossed collar about *her* neck. She was pulling forward, while the pretty little Sulky dog had the handle of the leash between her dainty teeth.

I stepped towards them, heedless of Waldo's attempted warning. Something was awfully funny here! 'Lady, what – ?' I began.

She wiggled her butt. 'Well, now!' she said, eyeing me in an embarrassingly frank manner.

The Sulky gave a short 'Woof!' The friendly woman veered away from me as if I had suddenly turned to poison. Amazed, I just stood there.

Waldo went up to the Sulky and made a series of barks and yips, and she answered in kind. Somehow it was as if they were conversing: he apologizing, she affronted but gracious. Then the female couple – canine and human – moved on.

I shook my head in perplexity. Something very strange was going on here!

Waldo tugged me on just as I had another chest seizure, so I followed him more or less blindly.

A few minutes later a trio of dogs came down the street. There were no human beings with them, and the animals walked as though they had complete right of way. Obviously the leash law was not enforced in this section of town! The first was a black and white spotted Damnation about the size and build of my Weimaraner. The second was a longhaired Sleepdog, with only his black nose sticking out from his face. The third was a beautiful Colleen, evidently being escorted by the two males.

Waldo barked at them in apologetic fashion, and the Damnation paused. The two exchanged woofs, and the Damnation turned his head and pointed briefly to the south. Waldo made a final bark that sounded like 'Thanks' and led the way – south.

I began to have a phenomenal suspicion – but it was ludicrous, and besides, I wasn't well. I put it out of my mind.

In due course we came to a kennel. A small spotted Bugle bayed at the entrance, until Waldo explained with a few more woofs. We entered the compound.

Inside were branches on which assorted dogs sat. Each had a leash, and each leash led to the collar of a human being. Squatting naked on the floor.

Waldo took the last empty seat and woofed at me in peremptory fashion. Never before had he addressed me in that manner! My chest gave another twinge, so I just squatted down amongst the nudes and tried to look inconspicuous despite my clothing and lack of collar. What else could I do?

I looked about. A pretty female Scooty sat up at a desk as though she were a receptionist, and a squatnosed Plug stood by like an orderly. But the canines and people here in the waiting room were a strange collection.

An elegant Puddle held the leash to a fluffy-haired blonde that in other circumstances I would have liked to know better. But the girl had a bad rash on her skin. A short-legged Baskethound had a short-legged man – who had a broken arm. A whiskery Schneezer had a little boy with a bad cold. A furry little Chomp-Chomp had another long-haired woman who looked as if she'd been chewed on. And a Pox Terror had a man who seemed to be ill with the plague.

In fact, all the dogs were well-groomed and healthy, while all the people were sick. Waldo and I were no exceptions.

Every so often the Plug would bark authoritatively, and one of the canines would take his human into another room. Sometimes there were awful screams – *human* screams – and all the people would cower in fear. I was cowering with the best of them! How had I got into this?

A Growling Shepherd entered, dragging a shaggy man. There didn't seem to be anything wrong with the man, so I assumed he was merely being brought in for his rabies shot.

Then is was my turn. Waldo led me to the other room. There was something vaguely awful about it, and my whole body was shaking with apprehension. There was a high table there, and I had to climb up on it and perch uncomfortably on the clammy surface. Until the Vet arrived.

The Doctor Dog entered – and I almost wet my pants. He was a huge Massive with jowls like those of a senator, and he must have weighed two hundred pounds. But it was his aspect more than his size that terrified me. I wanted to leap off that table and run, but the Massive showed his teeth and I was petrified. My chest hurt worse than ever as I laboured to breathe.

The Massive took my shirt in his teeth and ripped it from my quaking body. I huddled there, unable to move. He sniffed me thoroughly, then gave a short, sharp, ominous bark. A little Peek&See trotted in with a huge horse pill in her teeth. She dropped it on the table next to me and fluffed out again. As the door swung open for her I saw through it to a black Lab-Raider making tests in the lab. This place was well staffed!

The Massive nudged the pill towards me. The thing must have been an inch in diameter! 'Oh, no!' I cried, my voice coming out in falsetto so that it sounded like a yipe. 'I'd choke to death on that monster!'

Waldo tried to calm me, but I was already on edge because of the screams I had heard coming from this room before I entered. I scrambled off the table and broke for the door. Undismayed, the Doctor woofed – and a giant shape loomed before me.

It was a Great Damn – I mean, a Great Dame – the biggest bitch I'd ever seen. She didn't even bother to growl. She just advanced ponderously, smiling with all her teeth, and I retreated, step by step. When I backed into the table I snatched up that horse pill and gulped it right down. The Great Dame woofed approvingly and turned her bulk about, going her matronly way.

They certainly knew how to keep errant humans in line! I was glad Waldo was there to watch out for my interests. I only hoped he wouldn't leave me in the kennel.

At last Waldo took me out. At the entrance we met a beautiful red Settler towing an Irishman. 'Sure, an' I've never been here before,' the man cried to me. 'Is it bad?'

'Nothing to it,' I replied, sticking out my chest – and you know, it didn't hurt any more! That pill had somehow fixed it, and I felt just fine.

Then Waldo urged me on, leaving Irish and Settler to their fate. Almost frisking, I trotted towards home, ignoring the mean human animals that guarded their canine masters' lots. But Waldo remained strangely nervous.

What was he afraid of? This was his world, wasn't it? Where the dogs ran things?

Two Police Dogs came towards us. Waldo whined – and abruptly I understood. This was his world – but he was in some kind of trouble with the canine law! So he had had to flee, going hungry in an alien world, until I had taken him in. To help me, he had ventured once more into this realm, taking me to a qualified vet. But some dirty dog must have checked his registry, and now the police had sniffed him out.

I am not a large man, but I'm a sight bigger than the average dog. My shirt was in tatters and I knew I looked fierce. I took a menacing step towards those Police Dogs, and saw them draw up short, seeing me unleashed. 'Get your tails out of here!' I bawled fiercely.

It was too much for them. They were trained to handle unruly creatures, but there was a psychological horror to a wild man. They retreated.

We ran down an alley, the Police Dogs following at a fair distance and baying out an all-points bulletin. Soon we would be surrounded and overwhelmed!

Suddenly there was a nondescript cat in front of us. This, too, was strange; my Weimaraner had never before chased cats.

Then I saw that the cat was not fleeing, but leading. She dodged around a Painter mutt working on a house, hissed off a slender Dayhound, and leapt right over a sleeping Balldog. She was showing us an escape route!

Could that have been Waldo's crime, here? Helping a cat? Now she or one of her friends was repaying the favour!

Abruptly we were at my door, and the cat was gone. I stopped to look back – and the neighbourhood was familiar. No big dog houses or cat houses in sight, no chained, naked men. Just the conventional human suburban sprawl.

I knew it would do no good to backtrack; I would never find the realm of the canine masters. Waldo would not dare show his muzzle there again, either; they would be on watch for him. But now the favours were all even, and I comprehended at last the scheme from which my dog had come.

I reached down and rubbed his floppy grey ear. 'Come on, pal,' I said, taking a deep painless breath. 'I'll split a steak with you.'